The Migrant Report

Mohanalakshmi Rajakumar

dear Nneka,
enjoy!
Mohana Rajkumar
Nov 2017

The Migrant Report
Copyright © 2015 **Mohanalakshmi Rajakumar**

This is a work of fiction. Any similarity between the characters and situations within its pages and places or persons, living or dead, is unintentional and co-incidental.

Cover photography by Alexander Cheek
Cover design by Marsya Affrin

ISBN-13: 978-1514646922
ISBN-10: 1514646927

For those who built (and are building) malls, houses, and
universities in the Arabian Gulf

Chapter One

Thursday morning began like every other, the desert sun rising in the sky, as yellow as a yolk in a pan.

"Get out of the way! Doesn't anyone know how to drive in this country," Ali snarled, his temper rising with the temperature. Heat shimmered on the windshields of the undulating column of sedans and SUVs between him and the office. "Yes, let's all take the same road and turn the highway into the parking lot." He scanned radio channels. Only morning Arabic talk shows full of complaining callers.

"Why are so many foreigners working at the national university?" A speaker said in rapid Khaleeji dialect. "And why do I have to take the TOFEL to study at a university in an Arab country?"

"Uh huh, uh huh," the host agreed.

Ali switched to the national broadcaster, blaring English pop music at barely eight a.m. *We found love in a hopeless place. We found love in a hopeless place. We found love in a hopeless place,* the woman sang.

He snapped the radio off. *Were there no other words to the song?* There was a tape deck, an anachronism the Sandhurst cadets would have guffawed at. Cassettes were still popular in the Middle East and one of his sisters, Aisha, had left behind a Nancy Ajram tape. Those were his options: whiners who couldn't get the standards low enough, unapologetic westerners, or his teenager sister's view of cool.

Persistent sand rolled across the asphalt. A lone *sidra* tree reached green branches into the otherwise beige landscape. Concrete everywhere. A winding highway curved away into other parts of the city, taking traffic into the business district, glass-fronted skyscrapers glittering in the distance. He pressed the accelerator as the congestion cleared after the West Bay exit.

The heat, the dust, the boredom—they were all familiar and yet, since his return from England, like grains of sand, they were lingering irritants that couldn't be swept away.

He skidded to a stop. Another clump of cars clogged the three lanes of the exit on his right. Traffic on the other side of the road sped by. *My luck.* Ali wished for the red Internal Security vehicle he used while on patrol. In this unmarked car, he would add to the problem if he jumped the curb. His fingers drummed the wheel. Two men in the car next to him flung open the passenger doors and began running towards a knot of people a few meters up the road. A man in the SUV in front of him hopped out, leaving the engine running.

"What's going on?" Ali opened the door. He stood on his running board, his height giving him a vantage point. Ahead, a corner of the concrete building was like a splayed honeycomb, the metal of the scaffold twisting into the sky instead of hugging the concrete structure.

More men ran by. Every passenger in a thirty-car radius streamed toward some event on the ground. He pulled on his beret and joined the crowd, heading towards the center of the traffic jam.

When he crested the group, many moved aside at the sight of his dark blue uniform. Ali pushed the gawkers aside. That couldn't be good for whoever was at the center of all the attention. He pressed on, past the elbows and jangle of Indian languages that rang like sing-song jabber, their collared shirts a meld of pastels.

"*Bismillah,*" he blurted. *In the name of God.* The sun beat on them even as gooseflesh rose on Ali's arms.

Blue overalls, spattered with the gore of the owner's smashed head, brain matter spread like polka dots on the black asphalt.

"Back!"

The crowd stood mesmerized, as if frozen in the moment.

"I said move, now!" Ali rested a hand on his pistol.

The audience of men scuttled back.

Ali dialed the emergency number, 999, and spat out a description of the scene, focused on the task at hand and not what the heat was doing to the remains on the ground. "Now," he urged into the phone, swallowing against the bile in his throat.

"*Inna lillahi wa inna ilayhi raji'un.*" An older man, dressed in the same worker overalls, lost his breakfast. Sweat poured off his forehead.

Ali guided the man to sit on the curb. *Surely we belong to Allah and to Him we shall return*, the man had said, meaning he was probably a Muslim, unusual from what Ali knew of Indians.

A few other men from the work crew, he surmised from the look-alike blue uniforms, were standing around, their faces tight with fear, eyes skidding away from Ali like the horses on branding day on the family farm. On this side street, they could have been in a corner of Delhi, but for the Arabic lettering on the strip mall shops, transliterating the sounds of unlikely titles of small eateries like Hot Chicken.

"Water," Ali called to the standersby. "Mai?"

The murmur continued.

"Pani!" he shouted in his passing Hindi. "Pani." He pointed a finger at a young boy who swayed to his feet. The boy trotted over, drawn by Ali's gaze as though it were a tractor beam. "Pani," he shoved a fifty riyal note into the boy's hand and gave him a push towards the shop a few meters on the opposite side of the door. More men were hanging out of the window, chattering like pigeons.

"Right," Ali said. He surveyed the remaining crowd. Most had dispersed after seeing the body, slinking back to their cars with an image that would haunt them for days, if not the rest of their lives. He took the biggest guy from the crew by the elbow. "Help me," Ali said.

The man, who felt like solid muscle, obliged. Ali took the hands, indicating with his head the man should take the feet. *Don't move a body, you don't know where it might be broken inside* the first aid trainer had said to them. *I know where this one is broken.* The bigger man shuddered, reaching for the feet with closed eyes. Ali backed up, taking the body into the shade of the shops across the street. They were squat, one-story structures, no air conditioning, and glass storefronts dingy with dust. Traffic began to flow again, the tires taking the man's blood with him to mark other parts of the city. Ali focused on his steps, training his eyes on his partner, willing the man to maintain eye contact so that they could avoid the pulpy mass dangling at the top of their charge.

In front of a tailor shop with a greyish curtain pulled to one side to indicate they were open, a short, bushy-haired man spread out a bolt of black cotton. If the deceased was Muslim, he would have to be buried by sundown. Ali's thoughts went to the family, somewhere in India or Sri Lanka, to be notified by phone call days, weeks, or months from today, depending on how long the company took to notify them.

A scrawny shopkeeper was hanging nets with various goods from his awning. On seeing Ali, he paused with a large orange one full of balls of different sizes.

Ali ignored him. He folded the fabric over the body from the head to the feet. The boy came stumbling out of the mini mart, arms overflowing with bottles of water. Ali took one, taking off his beret and taking a big gulp. He indicated the boy should distribute the rest to the work crew who looked like forgotten chess pieces, scattered on both sides of the street.

"Who saw what?" He began with the tailor.

"Mafi." The man stammered, backing into the shop's doorway.

Ali sighed. He wished the local police would hurry up and take over. No one would talk to him, not in his uniform, and not when his white SUV announced he was a local. With the body wrapped up, the shock was fading, the uniqueness of the life taken, the sadness of his loved ones receding. Another worker death, chalked up to negligence.

A short woman, dark skinned, her hair wrapped in a blue and white scarf, hurried down the narrow sidewalk, peering into shops and speaking in rapid Hindi.

For a second he thought she might be the wife of one of the workers, but these guys made far too little to be allowed to host their family members inside the country, as required by law. She exited one shop and came towards the tailor, whose eyes bugged out of his head. The man scurried back inside his shop to avoid her.

"No reporters." Ali put himself between the woman and the boy. *And this is no place for a woman.* The work crew eyed her as if she were an advertisement for ice cream, the stupor of the tragedy lifting.

"I only have a few questions," she protested in a rush of English.

"No." Ali's gruffness was due to a lack of vocabulary, not aggression. "*Mamnuoa.*" He growled. *Forbidden.*

He should have paid more attention in the Language and Academic Culture classes. No media was the government line. Another worker death was all they needed in the international headlines. She took the warning in either case and backtracked to a black car waiting at the curb. She disappeared behind tinted windows. The flashing blue lights of the regular police and sirens announced Ali's relief on the way.

~~~

8

He reported to the office, swinging past the iron gate at the perimeter. He parked in the shade of castle façade, newly constructed in the image of past glory. The adobe structure rose above him, the wide towers on the four corners stretching several stories into the sky. Ali switched his white Nissan SUV with the red Internal Security vehicle he would use to patrol the assigned area for the day. He pocketed the keys and went inside to receive his assignment. Here, there were marble floors and wooden doors to offices as you'd see in any government ministry in the country, although theirs was newer.

"Let's hope we get someone with indoor meetings." Ali adjusted the two stars on either side of his shoulder. The lingering fall heat made the city a cauldron of moisture and sweat. A new face greeted him in place of the regular security detail for the ministers. "Where's Hamad?"

"The captain wants to see you." The young man's beard filled his cheeks, putting the rest of his features in competition with the curly hair.

"Okay." Ali shrugged. He flicked dust from the thigh of his uniform.

If his boss had already heard about the morning's incident, he would have to write a report to provide details to the police. Writing a report could mean endless hours in the courts, waiting to hear the verdict against a company, the representatives of which had three chances to show for the charges to be read.

Ali groaned inwardly. His boots clomped on the marble floor down the hall to his superior's office. Surely someone else could take over. Ali had been in the Internal Security service as long as Khalifa, though the other man had been promoted from the regular police force. "*Al salaam alaikum,*" he said in greeting.

Khalifa waved him in from behind a desk the size of an SUV hood. He was on the phone, the cord stretching to the other side of the desk across several open folders. In one of the wealthiest countries in the world, they still had desk phones. These were the sort of contradictions he couldn't overlook as he had before. Or maybe he hadn't seen them. Ali inspected the framed calligraphy on the wall behind his supervisor's desk. There was a massive piece that had likely taken several men to hang, intertwining the ninety-nine names of God.

"Fine, I'll tell him. But this is ridiculous. He's a good officer." Khalifa threw the phone in the cradle, causing several pieces of paper to drift to the floor.

"Don't tell me they want to fire Hamad because of one day," Ali said. "Where is he anyway?"

"Sit down." Khalifa leaned back in his chair, his hands folding over a thickening waistline.

Ali did as instructed, removing his beret from where it was tucked in the loop at his waist.

Khalifa cleared his throat. "There's no easy way to say this," he said, switching from the dialect of the Arabian Gulf into English. Ali frowned. English was not his strong suit, and he expected to speak Arabic in government offices. "You shouldn't apply for the Internal Service. You'll be declined."

Ali stared at the white hairs in Khalifa's beard. "Is this because of this morning? I did everything according to the book. I even bought the guys water."

"What?"

"On my way, I saw a crowd in the middle of the road. Turned out a worker died. Faulty structure, suicide maybe or someone pushed him." Ali smacked one hand into the other. "Nothing working. I called it in, stayed at the scene, turned everything over. Told a reporter to leave."

Khalifa waved a shaking hand. He was trying to give up smoking, since the government was getting more serious about enforcing the no smoking indoors.

"Nothing to do with this morning. I'm sure someone is looking into it."
Which means no one is. Too many of them.

"You are being reassigned. You can ask questions. You won't like the answer."

Ali edged forward, his hands dangling between his knees. His mind raced through the last few cases, turning them over, looking for an angle he had missed in how he had dealt with things.

"If it's about that Ethiopian maid." He switched back to the *Khaleeji* dialect. "The one harassing that family. I looked up the phone right away. Maybe I shouldn't have shown the sponsor everything we can see on people's machines, but she was so upset. I thought it would make her feel better. Has that woman been calling? Still making threats?"

Khalifa pushed a folder toward him. Ali took it, his fingers pulling out the sheaf of paper, full of scrawled handwriting in Arabic.

"The results from my physical."

"Second page."

Ali flipped to the next insert. There was a drawing of a man's private area: the shaft, two branches, and only one pouch where there should have been two. The drawing swam before his eyes. Ali felt lightheaded, his collar too tight around his throat. He let the folder fall closed on his lap.

"You shouldn't apply."

Ali struggled to breathe, the mortification of his secret revealed constricting his lungs. He needed to get out of here. "I completed the overseas cadet training."

The weeks in the rain, eating the repetitive meat and potatoes, listening to jokes he didn't understand. That he had done for this job.

"You did well." Khalifa's words had the effect of a buzzing insect. "From today, you'll be with the general patrol. At the New Salata station. They need good men there. Crime is on the rise, so close to the Industrial Area. The workers are starting to wander into the neighborhoods. Your training will suit you well."

~~~

Ali rose, taking the folder with him, clenching it in his fist. "Who else knows?"

"The doctor. No one else."

Ali glanced down at the report. The Arabic was slanted, running along below the hand drawn diagram at the bottom of his physical. *Unfit for official service because of lack of manhood.* "Someone else surely, or how else am I marked unfit for service?" Men in a police office were like a group of gossipy girls. Sitting around all day, they shared stories like teenagers.

"You have my word," Khalifa said.

"So you—you're kicking me out?"

"Reassigned," Khalifa emphasized. "You pursue entering the academy, and do another exam, another doctor finds out, and tells others. Everyone." Khalifa pressed his fingers together over his stomach, leaning back in his chair. "You can appeal to the Minister of Interior, but that will mean explaining the nature of your dismissal, which means..." Khalifa cleared his throat. "Your condition will be discussed by others."

There it was: that word again that summed up life in their small country. Others. The threat of ruining one's reputation mattered only to the individual.

"Think of your future." Khalifa switched to softer tones. He leaned across the desk. "Work is important. Think of your future family also, *enshallah.*

11

Your sisters. People are not as understanding as they should be about these things. Not your fault, of course."

Ali turned on his heel, away from the look of pity creasing Khalifa's brow. He bumped into the arm of the chair, knocking it over. All these future marriages rested on his shoulders, as the oldest son.

"Leave your uniform in the bathroom." Khalifa indicated Ali should use the private one inside the office. "There's a set of blues for you. Get changed and report for duty so no one suspects you've changed your mind."

"I haven't changed my mind," Ali said.

"You'll keep your stars," Khalifa said. "See, I am thinking of you."

The five-pointed uniform epaulets were what every officer hoped to amass, until the next stage, which was a brass crown. Ali struggled into the en suite bathroom, pulling a roll of toilet tissue to mop his forehead. The gilt faucets and rim of the sink reflected his shell-shocked features. He pulled off the ISF uniform, pausing to retch, then left it in a pile on the counter, slamming the keys down on the speckled marble countertop. Khalifa had left him the dark blue of his police officer uniform. Ali shrugged into the top, which strained at his shoulders and hung at his belly button instead of his waist. He would have to custom order several sets, as he had done with the IS blue and gray fatigues. His frame was not built for the one-size-fits-all male Arab model. He left the shirttail out, then pulled up the zipper with shaking fingers.

"This is for the best," Khalifa said. "Your only other option is surgery, and that you can be sure no one will keep quiet."

"*Enshallah*," Ali mumbled. As if the same God who had allowed this to happen was concerned about a half-man's future.

In the hallway, he sped past the open office doors, dodging eye contact with the other officers drinking milky *karak* from glass cups and reading the newspaper. They eyed him, the dark blue uniform of the regular police force. He climbed into his nondescript private vehicle, a white Nissan SUV. His vision swam as he drove toward the New Salata police station on the fringes of the city. *This was inevitable*, he repeated to himself. *No one else knows*.

Ali's cell phone rang, filling the vehicle's speakers with its metallic ring. He raised a hand to the man directing traffic at a roundabout, the regular police wearing dark blue trousers and a lighter blue shirt, belted at the waist with a thick black strip of cloth. His arm pumped, his hand waved as if he could will the cars through. *There's always someone worse off than you,* Ali reminded himself, gripping the wheel grimly. The other man didn't pause in his frantic urging of the morning traffic, as if by his wave he could solve the city's congestion problem.

"*Salaam alaikum,*" the dispatcher said.

"*Alakium a salam.*" Ali managed to hide the gravelly tone of his voice with a cough. He felt anything but peaceful.

"You the new guy, right? Get down to the mall bridge. There's an accident."

"Send a recruit," he snapped. "I'm an officer."

There was a muffled discussion on the other end of the line before the voice came back, high and insistent. "Captain says it must be you, the new guy."

Ali groaned and hung up. This was to be his life now, mundane tasks that had nothing to do with Internal Security, or much else other than dealing with idiots who didn't know to keep a safe following distance with the next vehicle. He made a sharp U-turn at the next roundabout, cursing his location, mere minutes from the busiest cross-city artery. He would now be the first call for this area. There was an accident on or near the bridge every weekend.

When he arrived, traffic was already crawling up the bridge like burdened ants. "Send a tow truck," he texted to dispatch.

Ali drummed his fingers on the dash, inching forward. If he had the red of the ISF vehicle, the other cars would make way, edging apart like the waters of the Red Sea for Musa. A regular traffic police vehicle might do as well; a rooftop siren would come in handy at times like this, though he despised the way others abused the blue, white, and gray SUVs, putting on their flashers to get past slow drivers, or turning on the siren to careen through crowded streets. He inched forward in his white Nissan like hundreds of others on the roads.

After twenty minutes of bumper to bumper, he pulled over in front of a white Land Cruiser with gold racing stripes that had rammed into the back of a pick-up truck. The force of the impact from the much larger Land Cruiser had flattened the truck bed like a piece of pita bread. Ali strode to the first vehicle; on the other side of the vehicle, squeezed between the passenger door and the bridge's railing, were two skinny cinnamon colored men.

"You okay?"

They looked up, wide-eyed, stunned like camels that had fallen off their transport, taking in his full height, crisp blue and black uniform. "Fine?" The men looked at each other, then turned to him, doing the side to side head movement that always confused him. Did it mean yes? Or no? From the way they used it, apparently the head lilt could be both at once. Horns started to sound from the other drivers who wanted to get onto the bridge. Ali reassured himself he saw no blood or bones. He kept walking to check on the other driver.

The other driver was talking animatedly on the phone, his head visible behind the airbag, which had deflated like a child's party balloon. Ali rapped on the window, expecting to hear a litany about how Indians didn't know how to drive. Instead, the boy, for that's how he revealed himself, hung out of the driver side window, his hands shaking.

"This is a new car," he said in the dialect of the Arabian Gulf, the sun glinting on his braces. "My father is going to kill me."

"Are you hurt?"

The boy shook his head. Ali could see the purple knot forming on his forehead, pushing to the surface. That was going to hurt. Ali nodded, indicating the boy should stay in the car. There was no sign of facial hair on the boy's angled cheekbones or curved lip. Ali didn't bother asking for a license.

"No one has been hurt." Ali reported to the dispatcher, who grunted a blessing. "This is going to be a bigger mess in ten minutes."

He hung up, trying in vain with the Indians to get the pickup to start. The engine protested, failing to turn over, the belts screeching like a cat being stretched between two poles. They were on the tail end of the bridge, slightly past the ascending slope on this side, so that ruled out pushing the vehicle two hundred meters to the other end. Going backward made more sense as they could find room to stash the vehicle under the overpass, but that would mean heading into oncoming traffic. Ali's Nissan could tow the truck, but the captain would frown on him getting personally involved. They watched traffic halt on either side for two kilometers, the drivers of oncoming traffic braking to see what had happened. When the tow truck arrived, sunlight scorched the city, the call to prayer rose from the mosques in the area. Ali turned over management of the accident to the officer who had arrived with the tow truck driver.

"Don't tell my dad," the teenager pleaded. His cousins, around the same age judging by their narrow shoulders, had shown up, taking photos of both vehicles with their shiny smart phones.

~~~

Sweating for the two hours they had waited for the tow truck further soured Ali's mood, as well as his uniform. The aircon blasting on the drive to the station was ineffectual against the sweat stains around his collar and under the arms. An Indian man eyed Ali. His cream shirt and brown pants said he was an office assistant, someone who made photocopies and helped the officers fill out paperwork.

"See captain." The man's bony finger pointed down a hallway to the right of the counter. Ali proceeded, unsure of what else to do.

"Ah, yes." The portly captain swiveled in a black leather office chair, eyeing Ali. He fidgeted with his hands behind his back, fighting the urge to not bring them around to the front. Was the captain eyeing him or was his groin in the line of sight? "Ali, right?"

"Sir," Ali said. A gold plated desk blotter said OMAR.

"Good to have someone of your experience with us." The captain stroked his full, wiry. Was he smirking? Ali said nothing. "You take first station. Aqeel will show you the way."

The Indian man who had pointed out the captain's office materialized in the doorway. He must have been listening out of sight. Ali was dismissed without another word. The captain's attention returned to the various Arabic newspapers spread out in front of him.

"Here," Aqeel said with a chicken-like head bob.

Ali sat at his desk, which was one of many workstations punctuating the slab of plastic counter. His eyes angled downward toward his phone, like so many of the other policemen he had seen in stations growing up. Well, when there were others. This being the middle of the afternoon, as the desert heat rippled the air outside like a shimmering wave, he was the only one around during the shift change. Anyone entering the office would think he was watching a YouTube video or reading the Qur'an and maybe take a seat, waiting for someone else to show up.

The sliding glass doors whooshed open. He bent his neck further, his nose pointing at his sternum. Ali resolved any other accidents would have to come back on Saturday, the next working day, to be reported. He had done his bit for road safety. Ali anticipated the weekend, which in the Arabian

Gulf began with Friday as the day of prayer.

"We need someone at the Sheraton," said a man, whose starched white *thobe* ended at mid-calf. He stood in the middle of the empty foyer. During the week, the chairs would be full with people reporting traffic accidents, paying fines, or renewing their vehicle registrations. "Immorality," he bellowed in Arabic.

The force of the man's rage, or more likely the volume, caused the captain's door at the end of the hallway to open. Aqeel scuttled forward with a tray dangling to one side. "Sir? *Fee* problem?" Aqeel peppered English with Khaleeji slang, creating a hybrid of En-bric. The wheedling, deferential tone of the moment grated on Ali's nerves.

"Officer!" boomed the guy. "I need an officer. No one working today?"

Aqeel sent Ali a pleading look. "Thursday afternoon," Aqeel said. "Holiday."

"No one cares about the country on the weekend?"

Ali pressed his palms on the desk and rose. His full height made even Aqeel take a step back. Ali was tall, especially for an Arab man, towering over most police officers. At six foot four, he loomed over the desk, the phone, and everyone in the radius.

"Yes," he said. "What's the problem?"

The man swallowed, his eyes darting around the empty seats on either side of Ali. "Problem," he said.

"Tell me more," Ali said. He leaned a hip on the counter.

"At the Sheraton," the man mumbled, glancing down at his hands. "There's immorality, indecency at the Sheraton." His voice rose to full volume, as if he had only then remembered his reason for coming in.

Ali raised an eyebrow. Like his beard, the rest of the hair on his face was curly, including the eyelashes his mother had bemoaned throughout his childhood as wasted on a man. She stopped saying that when they discovered his injury.

"The cakes!" The man rushed forward and thumped the counter.

Aqeel hovered nearby, as much for gossip, Ali suspected, as to offer any kind of hospitality through tea or coffee.

"They are in the shape of"—the man leaned forward, his jowls shaking with the force of his indignation—"you know." He gestured to Ali's crotch, several feet from his hand.

Ali shrank. *He can't possibly know*, he reminded himself. His parents had kept it secret, lest it affect his marriage prospects. They hadn't taken into consideration his employability.

"They made these cakes and they gave them to unmarried women," the man hissed.

Aqeel leaned in, his gaze reflecting Ali's confusion. "Who?"

Ali shot him a look of warning, but their complainant was in full lather and didn't notice.

He lifted his arms, raising the hem of his *thobe*. "They made these cakes for a ladies' party." He crossed his arms as if the full weight of the crime should be evident. "I catch them in the security line."

"I see." Ali cleared his throat. Aqeel tilted his head toward the hallway, asking Ali silently if he should call the captain. Ali shook his head.

"Okay, let's file a report," Ali said. He pulled out a piece of paper and placed it on the desk. "They will investigate on Saturday."

"The party is going on now!" The man thumped a meaty fist on the lip of the counter. "Saturday will be too late."

Aqeel moved aside as the captain strode into the reception area.

"That voice can only be Abu Issa," the captain said. He embraced the man warmly, greeting him with three nose-to-nose touches, the traditional greeting between close male friends or relatives.

Ali's right eye twitched as the visitor explained for a second time the immoral scene at the Sheraton.

"Ali," the captain said without turning, "go and investigate."

"Sir," Ali said, "there's no one else here."

"Aqeel can take over." He waved his hand at Ali as if he were a fly. "Go, go."

Ali put on his blue hat, fidgeting to delay the inevitable.

"If Abu Issa saw this in the security line at the Sheraton, we must investigate." The captain slapped his friend on the back. The two men exchanged another series of pleasantries, asking about each other's health and children, avoiding the taboo subject of their wives.

Ali strode out of the station into the tepid night air even as the captain and the hotel security informant continued asking about the health of their various shared family members. Aqeel would be serving them round after round of coffee. Ali hoped they'd both be gone before he came back.

He slung his body behind the wheel of his SUV, considering for a moment whether he should spend his time driving around town instead of going to the hotel. He wheeled out of the parking lot, checking that none of the teenage neighborhood boys were zipping around on their four-by-fours before revving the engine through the stop sign.

He slid the vehicle through the growing gloom, angry with himself, angry that fate had brought him to this moment—to investigating penis cakes at bachelorette parties in five star hotels. The engine hummed as he shot under the flashing yellow light. Well, if he was going to be relegated to city cop, he might as well enjoy some of the perks. He kept speeding through the winding roads until he came to the Corniche. Making a sharp right, he entered the Sheraton's parking lot and pulled up to the valet station.

"Police," he murmured to the Indian guys waiting to take his car. "Park it in front."

He didn't have to go very far into the hotel before he found the scene. He mentally catalogued everyone: a thin male in a black striped suit, probably the catering manager from the event company, two blond expat women, their thigh skimming dresses and sprayed hair marking them as partygoers, and three hotel security guards crowded around a scanner. Others entering the hotel lobby were waved to one side and scanned by the shortest of the guards with a handheld wand.

"But I ordered this," the blond with frosted pink nails that matched her five inch heels was saying. "It was a private party, an outside vendor," she counted the excuses on her manicured fingers. "Not one of the public saw it. And no one from the party would be offended, so who was being hurt?"

"Then maybe you too go to jail," the shortest security guard said, coming back to the conveyor belt. He didn't look at either one of the women while he spoke to them.

The blond chewed her lip in frustration. "I asked him to make this for my friend."

"Alright," Ali said. "Let's see it."

The four of them turned to Ali. No one spoke, taking in his height. He counted to five before he repeated his request. No one made a move toward the brightly colored square box on the end of the screening belt.

He took a step and opened it. There, nestled in the pink interior, was a cake shaped like an erect penis. Ali contemplated it, even as the woman began again, stuttering this time, eyes averted, about how this was her friend's last night before she got married, and didn't they know that this was a tradition, they hadn't done anything illegal, there weren't any strippers after all. The other security guard didn't bat an eye. Ali wasn't sure if this was because of his limited command of English or because he thought looking at non-*mehram* women, non-relatives, would send him to hell.

Ali let the glittery pink lid close, reminding himself again that no one else knew the irony of his being called to this particular scene.

"Who made this?"

"The chef," the caterer said.

"Is he here?"

The thin man, whom Ali guessed was Lebanese by the snug fit of his trousers, shook his head.

"Come with me," Ali said. He took the man by the elbow. The security guard sat down on his chair behind the screening station.

"Where are you taking him?" the woman protested. Her friend, who wore a white half veil attached to a headband that read BRIDE in pink lettering, burst into tears.

"The station." Ali didn't break his stride. He kept his grip on the man's elbow, propelling him forward. Without any religious police like Saudi Arabia, the city police force was all the population had to protect their virtue. Ali snapped for the Nissan when they reached the front of the hotel. The youngish valet ran to get it from where he had parked in front of the ATM.

"Am I going to jail, brother?"

Ali released the man, watching as the valet carefully reversed the car so as to avoid any of the planters. He strode to the front and indicated the catering manger should climb into the back. One valet opened the door for Ali, another opened the one in the back for the manager.

Ali clicked his seatbelt, and grunted that his passenger should do the same. He slipped a ten-riyal note to the valet. "I don't know," he said. His eyes met those of the caterer in the back. "The judge will decide." He took in the sprayed bouffant and the wide-lapelled jacket, the pink striped shirt. *This was not a guy who could spend a lot of time without his products*, he thought.

"I didn't know she ordered that cake," he said, looking out the window.

Ali steered them through the line waiting to exit the hotel parking lot. "Who did?"

"The chef. He did it as a favor to her."

"Tell the judge," Ali said as they pulled out into traffic.

Chapter Two

Maryam felt as though fifty dirham coins weighed down her eyelids. "Sorry to see I'm boring you, Mohammed," Professor Paul said. He pressed a button on the wall to lower the screens over the bank of windows on the east side of the room, shrouding them in shadow. "I won't put down the blackout shades or you'll all fall asleep."

The guy next to Maryam sat up, stammering apologies. Maryam blinked herself awake; the professor had moved on and was fiddling with the lectern, the top of his thinning strawberry-blond hairline visible.

"Why do we have this technology if no one knows how to use it?" Professor Paul muttered to no one in particular.

"Can I try, Professor?" Amal asked from her perch close to his desk.

Maryam averted her eyes. They had once been very friendly, more bookish than the rest of the local girls at the international school. The small classes at university had been like a greenhouse for the studious duo, the proximity of other designer-loving peers, turning Amal into a brand wearing, professor appeasing hothouse flower.

Paul stepped aside with a flourish, as if to say by all means. "Coax the beast if you can."

Amal rose from her seat at the top of the rectangle of chairs. She glided to the lectern as if she were at the mall on the weekend, not in class. Her *abaya* rippled, revealing cobalt blue satin shoes. Most girls in the university wore the same ones, many a teardrop pearl dangling across the front. Even Maryam's mother wore them for special occasions. The western designer Manolo Blanik was a Gulf favorite.

Under the table, Maryam shook her leg in agitation. The simpering walk, the voice, all of it was wrong, and disoriented her. Dislodged from both her high school best friends, Maryam was trying to stay afloat in university life.

"The rest of you, see if you can get the website to load on your machines. I'm writing it here." In neat script that any elementary teacher would be proud of, Paul wrote the letters for the web address on the dry erase board. "Ethics in journalism," he intoned. "Very important, as some of us learned the hard way with this assignment."

Maryam squirmed, her leg shaking harder, threatening to jostle the table with the rapid movement.

"No laptop?"

"I forgot it," she said. She tried a small smile, but Paul was shaking his head. "But professor, I was on time today."

"Bare minimum is to be on time and be prepared," Paul said, pinching the bridge of his nose. "Not a great start to a new semester."

Someone a few seats over snickered. Maryam flushed.

"What can we learn from the sports academy's request to take down the report?" Paul continued.

"Sometimes people are going to be upset with what we have to say," Amal offered.

Paul added that to the growing list of concerns on the whiteboard.

Like she would ever write anything objectionable, Maryam thought. The report in question, hers, had been about the attitudes toward sports in the country, and whether or not locals wanted to host the 2024 Olympics.

"Clear your permissions first," Mohammed added, trying to make up for his earlier drowsiness.

"I did have permission," Maryam said. "They changed their minds after it was printed. We don't have to retract if they agreed, right?" This much trouble over the first assignment did not bode well. Dread grew in her stomach over the thought of five more months like this.

Paul crossed his arms, the monogramed pocket of his button-down shirt stretching across his chest. "An interesting question with no clear answer."

Maryam tapped the screen of her phone to see what time it was. Unlike high school, the university did not have clocks in the room. Nor did Maryam sport a Rolex like many of her classmates.

"First warning, everyone," Paul intoned. "Maryam is on her phone. Next one, and I'm taking them all. Haven't done that yet this week."

The class groaned.

Maryam blushed, this time all the way down her neck and across her shoulders, but no one could see the prickling heat spreading under her *abaya*. "I was going to the website," she said.

"Stop testing me."

"Professor, I—"

The sound of an audience clapping filled the classroom through the speakers mounted in the corners. Images of young Arab men doing stan-dup comedy filled the four plasma screens stationed around the room, two on the west wall, one at the front, and one at the back. This was a state of the art classroom, one of dozens at the purpose-built American university. Maryam loved having a reason to come to the three-story marble building, the water in the fountains of the entryway masking the reality beyond these walls.

"The beast is tamed," Amal said, stepping back from the lectern with a small flourish, then glided back to her seat.

"You're a magician," Paul said. "This is how to get an inside story. Embed yourself with your subjects. Study them until they forget you're there. This is how sociology can inform your journalism."

Maryam wheeled around in her chair, watching the screen on the back wall so she wouldn't have to see Amal's self-satisfied grin. She tuned them all out. Mohammed twitched nervously lest he break out in another yawn, and the foreign students twirled their hair. She leaned against the high back of the office style chair, one of dozens in the classroom.

The room was divided, a self-selected seating pattern: the sea of hair closer to the front, including Amal, her *shayla* on her shoulders. Like the good girls they were, the locals sat at the back, a wave of black headscarves. They watched the documentary the professor had worked on about stan-dup comedy in the GCC region, showing a clip of his comedic performance about being a white man entering the mall on Family Friday while his Paki-stani colleagues were turned away.

"Professor, weren't you scared? What if no one laughed?" Noor, the girl on the other side of Maryam, asked. The smell of nail polish, Noor's fa-vorite pre-class activity, lingered in the air. Maryam had come to associate the formaldehyde-like scent with the girl.

"Well, standup is not that different from teaching." Paul chortled and the rest of the students couldn't help but chuckle too.

"Alright, that's enough from me. Go out there and find some social com-mentary. And I don't want fifteen articles about how the *abaya* design has changed."

A few girls giggled. They loved Paul's reddish hair and blue eyes; his muscular frame was another plus, making him a favorite for students at the journalism school, even though he was a professor of their electives rather than core classes.

"Professor, I'm sorry." Maryam approached the lectern as the other students shuffled out. "I wasn't trying to be rude. I'm really interested in this project."

Paul was gathering his folders, pens, and dry erase markers into his leather carryall, avoiding eye contact. "Really? Because it doesn't seem like it."

"Professor!" The panic caused her voice to spike. "I need to do well in this class, or—"

"Or your life is ruined." Paul fastened his bag and tossed the strap over his shoulder. I know, Maryam. I had you last semester also, remember?"

"I'll be kicked out of uni!"

He blinked at her. "Whose problem is that?"

"Mine," she mumbled, eyes downcast as if she were being dressed down by her father. "But I really can't leave uni." The thought of her father, another one of his disappointed looks, caused a gnawing hole in her stomach.

Paul sighed. He propped his hip on the table and folded his arms, revealing the brown patches on his jacket elbows.

"I mean it," she said. "My family, you know, they all graduated from top universities. You know, like you're always saying, I'm an outlier," she amended. "Only not the good kind." She had the full force of those blue eyes on her.

"Oh, sorry," said a lanky boy in tight jeans and a black T-shirt from the doorway.

"No, you can come in, Faisal," Paul said as the students streamed in for the next class. "We're finished," he added to Samantha, the English professor using the room next.

"I'd like to help you." Paul indicated Maryam should follow him out. She ducked, avoiding eye contact with Faisal, the son of her mother's best friend. The mothers, also cousins by marriage, were plotting and hoping their husbands would see the advisability of a union between their offspring. They could plan the wedding of their dreams. Maryam had given Faisal a wide berth since Orientation, when she overhead him declaring Communication was his chosen major because it was easier than the engineering degree his father wanted.

Maryam grabbed her purse and caught up with Paul. "You would?"

"Yes, of course."

They walked down the marble hallway. Paul nodded hello to other faculties and students they passed. Maryam focused on keeping pace with him. Swerving to avoid the printer in the corner, she scuttled closer, but not so close as to bump into him or any of the other students. She was like a pinball that didn't know its trajectory. Paul swung around the corner, pushing open the door to his office. He flung his briefcase on the circular table before throwing himself into a chair like a discarded folder.

"I'll do anything," Maryam said. "Anything."

Paul was gazing at her, those blue eyes glassy like an undisturbed lake. "I do need some help," he said.

She wondered if this was the moment Paul would show his true colors. Would he ask for a Rolex, or help getting a job for a friend like some of her cousins in Kuwait had provided to their faculty for grades they had not earned?

"Find me a new story," Paul said.

"Sorry?"

Paul rolled his eyes at her. "Find me a unique story about Khaleeji life," he said, "and you'll pass the class. Write an original story."

"But about what?" Maryam asked, wailing. "I have nothing to say about *abayas*."

Paul shook his head. "There are three English dailies and three Arabic," he said. "Find them. Read them. Get some ideas. Come back to me with something original."

"And if I can't?"

He spread his hands, palms up, in a shrug. "This is not *our* assignment, Maryam, to do together. Whose assignment is it to complete?"

"Mine," she mumbled.

"And who should be your first point of contact?"

"You?"

He threw back his head and laughed. The blush scalded her again.

"Wrong," he said. "Your colleagues. Don't you have friends in class?" His eyes narrowed, taking her in more closely.

"Yes, right." She nodded. "Of course."

"Professor, should I come back?" Amal appeared in the doorway next to

Maryam.

"No, no, let's have our research group meeting." Paul waved her in. "But Maryam may want to talk to you about something later on." Amal slid into a chair opposite Paul, her back to Maryam.

Maryam smiled, a gesture that didn't reach the corners of her lips. "I'll let you get to work," she said. She beat a hasty retreat.

"Babu, come quickly to college," she said into her phone before the driver could hear the sob rising in her chest. Maryam sped down the hallway, headed for the elevator at the opposite end. Her ballet slippers slid across the marble. She swerved away when she saw the knot of students in the lounge area waiting and made for the building's central stairway. She was thankful for sensible shoes that allowed her to reach the lobby before anyone else.

Too late, she noticed a yellow cleaner's cart at the top of the stairway. She slid right into it. "Oh! Sorry."

The young woman in a cream top with brown uniform pants shied from her.

Maryam gathered the transparent bottles of cleaner she had sent flying in the collision. "Where are you from?" She tried to fill the awkward silence as the other woman, about half her size, worked without raising her eyes.

"Nepal, madam."

Maryam leaned in to hear the words. She paused in replacing a stack of paper towels. "Do you like it here?" The kneejerk question was one her mother put to the foreigner doctors Nasser brought home for dinner parties.

"Yes, very safe." The woman gripped her cart and nodded. She wheeled it around and walked away, not turning to look at Maryam.

Paul's face floated in her mind's eye. *Get me a new angle on life in the Gulf*, he had said.

"Wait!"

The cleaner didn't stop. Maryam quickened her step. The woman was also picking up speed, the gap between them widening. "I only want to ask you a few questions."

"Is there a problem?" A dark-skinned woman in grey trousers and pink button down blouse put a hand out to halt the cart, bringing the cleaner up short.

The timid girl's hands dropped from the edge of the cart and hung at her sides. Her head remained bent.

"What did you do?" The darker woman leaned into the young Nepali's face, raising her voice.

The cleaner's lip trembled.

"Nothing," Maryam said. She regretted the scene she had caused, seeing now the other students and staff, having coffees and late lunches in the open-air cafeteria, eyeing their trio with growing interest. "I wanted to thank her," Maryam improvised.

The darker woman straightened, a clipboard clutched in her right hand.

"These bathrooms are so clean," Maryam rushed on. "It's so nice to see someone do their work well."

The other woman harrumphed, her hand lifting from the cart. The cleaner scuttled away, making a beeline for the back of the building.

"Have a nice afternoon ma'am," the boss said, strolling away.

"You too," Maryam murmured. Her phone buzzed. Babu was waiting outside to take her home. *Interview attempt one: failed*.

~ ~ ~

Maryam threw down another paper on top of the first two. The black Arabic script blended into the red, black, and white striped traditional *sadu* fabric of the men's sitting area, the *majlis*. That's where she'd had to go to find the newspapers in the house, but there were no English versions. She scrolled through those on the Internet. The past few hours had been a lesson in futility. The Arabic and English newspapers were tied like sister companies.

Your dad's a … there was no emoticon to substitute for the word she wanted but wouldn't use. Maryam tossed the phone aside. Her friend Daniel would find it hilarious that she couldn't complete the sentence, chalk up her recalcitrance to the takeover of her local identity.

"You're a woman now," he said when she stumbled through yet another excuse why they couldn't have lunch at the mall or go to the movies or visit each other at home. "My mom says this was bound to happen."

Hope you get someone like your dad at uni.

They'll all be like my dad, came the swift reply. *That's what professors are like*.

Maryam groaned. She smacked the palm of her hand against her head several times. *Focus.*

In the English papers, she scanned the same press releases about the welcoming of dignitaries by the country's rulers, or the events held by various social organizations like the American Women's Association, in Arabic or

English. The only difference was the opinion section. The Arabic newspaper complained about the way English was replacing Arabic, and the English papers reviewed the latest films in the cinemas, already several months on from their international release dates.

"Hey, what are you doing in here?" Her brother, Nasser, came up short in the doorway. He buttoned the top of his *thobe*.

Maryam started. "Reading," she said, wondering how much Nasser knew about her grades. Her eyes narrowed, taking in her brother's angular features, older, male versions of her own.

"Not in here," he said. "*Yuba*'s friends are on their way over."

Maryam stood, scooping up the newspapers, some of the leaves spilling from her grasp.

"What are you going to do with those, turn them into wallpaper?"

"I'm writing a paper, I'll have you know. A report."

"Sounds riveting." Nasser snorted.

"It would be if I could find something worth writing about," Maryam grumbled. "Do you think anyone is embezzling? What about *Yuba*'s financial sheets?"

"I certainly hope not." Nasser collected the scattered pencils. "You can't share those numbers with anyone, anyway."

Maryam groaned.

"You're not in trouble again, are you?"

"No, why?"

"The records are in the study." Nasser folded the stack and handed it to her. He eyed her stained T-shirt and worn jeans.

"I won't be able figure them out," she said. "All tiny numbers with letters on paper. It's like algebra or something."

"Those are timesheets, silly. They store them here for a few months and then destroy them. The important stuff is online." He scanned a page of her notes before she snatched them away. "Don't let **Yema** see you wandering the house like this, your hair all out where someone could see you."

"I'm not staying in the *majlis*. I needed somewhere quiet to think." She grabbed the newspapers, knowing he was right about their mother.

She would spout off into a lecture about femininity and the importance of Maryam not becoming too studious, lest it get out that Maryam was not interested in marriage. "I need some stories," she said, switching tack. "Maybe medical malpractice? Please, this is really important."

He sighed. "Why not an inside story on workers?"

"Really? What exactly? How they got here?"

Nasser was tapping away on one of the new iPhones, the screen a few inches smaller than a tablet.

"Where did you get that?"

"Duty free," he mumbled. "Sent." He tapped her on the shoulder. "Ideas on what they do in their free time, their health, most frequent injuries. We see guys in emergency all the time for broken arms from parking lot cricket."

The ding of her cell phone indicated a new email. Maryam set down everything she had picked up. A few clicks later, the white spreadsheet of a pdf was on her screen, the columns neatly labeled, the charts showing the numbers of injuries in the last month. "The hospital lets you share this?"

"I made that spreadsheet." He reached to tousle her hair in amusement. "No one really cares what happens to those guys."

"Uff." She ducked out of his reach. "Don't you have lives to save or set bones or something?

"I don't have clinical this week." Nasser gave her a mock bow. As he rose, he passed her laptop.

She took it, tucking the thin machine under her arm.

"Poking your nose into things is going to get you into trouble, you know." His brows knitted.

She wanted to blurt out everything as he pressed her shoulder. "I know."

Nasser had always been her guiding light in the family of six. He was the closest to her in age, and at his urging she had joined the newspaper in high school, becoming the editor in her senior year. Then he had disappeared into the bowels of the house while studying for his medical boards.

"I have this assignment. The professor wants a story no one else knows. And we can't write about *abayas*."

Nasser laughed. "Smart guy."

"He wants 'an original' look at *Khaleeji* life." She made air quotes that Paul was so fond of using about the Arabian Gulf. "*Madri*, I don't know what to write about."

"The fact we own a business that makes money is not news," Nasser said.

"But the how." Maryam's vision swam with the memory of the ramshackle worker housing, juxtaposed with the glamor of her father's *majlis* "The how might be."

28

"The coffee is ready?" Jaber, their father, strode into the room, rolling down the sleeves of his *thobe*.

"I'll check, *Yuba*," Nasser said.

"Everything fine?" Jaber asked Maryam.

"Yes, *Yuba*," she said.

"I'm on the board for your university," her father intoned. "I'll find out eventually what's happening."

"Yes, *Yuba*," Maryam said. Her father was in good mood, humoring her, but like lightening, he could switch.

"*Masalama*." She backed out of the room.

Nasser caught up with her.

"God help me," Maryam moaned.

"Write about the workers," Nasser said, parting with her in the court-yard. The house loomed above them, rising three stories, the blue tile roof the only one in the entire country.

"What?"

"You know, the blue jumpsuit guys. Foreigners love that kind of thing. But everyone here is tired of hearing about it."

The sweep of headlights shimmered across the windows on the front of the house like a beacon. Maryam scurried inside before anyone else could remind her not to linger as her father's friends and male relatives arrived. As an unmarried female, the youngest girl, she was, as her mother was so fond of saying, the jewel of the house.

"You are a girl from a very good family," her mother, Fatma, would often say, usually when she was forcing Maryam into some designer creation or other for a distant cousin's wedding. "Who knows whose eye you will catch? Maybe even..." her mother would giggle. *Maybe even*, everyone in the house knew, was Fatma's aspiration to royalty. Her family was close to the ruling tribe; their men were known to choose from among Maryam's family's women to strengthen their alliance.

She trudged through the yawning foyer to the central staircase. Other parts of her university life were littered around the flowers at the entryway: textbooks she hadn't opened since they had been assigned, a t-shirt from freshman orientation, a water bottle from a fundraiser for Gaza. One of the maids would tidy it away, or come knocking, asking her if she was finished with them. This report, however, these materials, she had to safeguard.

She pushed at the brass door handle with her elbow. Her room, white, and safe from her mother's decorative ministrations, had the heavy oak furniture typical of local homes. The upholstered headboard was cream and green with gold brocade, same for the drapes at the window that were drawn against prying eyes. She didn't ask for a new set because her mother would take the opportunity to redo the entire space in her version of young femininity. She wouldn't put pink past her.

Maryam dumped the research materials on her queen size bed. Nasser would be with the visiting men for several hours, not able to get her any materials. She needed to see the place again, this time without letting others know she was observing them. Take some exterior photos and maybe create a video of the living conditions as an accompanying piece. Paul loved those extra touches, but she would need help. Maryam raced back down the stairs and through the semi-dark hallway, past sitting rooms scattered throughout the bottom floor of the house, towards the back.

"Yes, madam?"

Maryam waved aside Maria, the newest housemaid, who jumped up from where she was watching television in the annex to the kitchen. The cream and white striped uniform highlighted the girl's youth.

On second thought, better to not get her involved. Who knew if she'd be compelled to tell Maryam's mother everything she knew. "Nothing."

"Babu." Maryam knocked on the kitchen door, interrupting the driver's dinner. "You know where the camp is?"

"Farm, madam?" Babu paused in eating, dropping the chicken bone he had been gnashing with relish. He was alone at the dark wood table. They were in between cooks, her mother having fallen out with the last one over the addition of cumin to salad that had not called for any.

"*La*, Babu, no, not our farm. The camp. You know, where the workers are." She drew closer to him, seeing the dark circles under his eyes.

The lines around his mouth and eyes were more pronounced, like frames for his lips, dragging down the mustache that had tickled her when she was a child. Maryam saw white flecks in the broad carpet of hair covering his upper lip. White strands were scattered like grains of sand in his hair. When had Babu aged? Between driving her mother on errands and Maryam graduating from high school?

She wondered if she could do a piece on him, the family driver who had been with them as long as she had been alive. But Paul's sonorous tones echoed in her mind. No, she needed something really unique, maybe even something undercover.

"Can you take me to the MBJ camp?"

Babu put down his coffee cup. "Madam, Sir knowing about this?"

"Yes, yes." Maryam waved in dismissal. "My father knows. Let's go now."

"Now?" Babu looked out the open back door into the milky blackness of night, then glanced at his half-empty plate.

"I'll meet you in the GMC," Maryam called over her shoulder.

Most local families had at least one SUV for the driver to cart their women around the country. Theirs was a black, extended cab SUV, made by the General Motor Corporation.

She headed to the clothing rack in the anteroom, picking up the simplest *abaya,* free of any adornment, without the popular cinched waist. Maryam slung on the outer robe, masking her tank top and leggings. She wound the gauzy black fabric over the crown of her head in layers until her hair, neck, and ears were covered. Still no sign of Babu. Maryam called him from her phone, the backlit screen throwing a glow onto her features.

"Babu, where are you?"

"Sir call me to make delivery. I no come. Sorry."

Maryam stared at the dead line in her hand. Was Babu lying? She had no way of getting out to the worker housing without his help. Her mother didn't think it was a good idea for Maryam to drive, in case it discouraged suitors.

Chapter Three

Manu knelt, bowing his head to his mother's feet for what might be the last time, the bluish-green veins on the back of her hand trembling under his lips as if the pulse of life inside her were buoyed by his. *If this were a Bollywood movie,* he forced himself to think of the scene in less personal terms, *the music would be slow and reedy, the camera panning out to a doe-eyed girl, crying about the devoted son.* He clutched the fine bones of her hand until his mother turned in her sleep, the slope of her nose pressing into the pillow, her restless limbs tossing on the woven mat on the dirt floor.

Her sari rode up to reveal her calves, the ant bites scattered like the moon's craters across her muscles. This wasn't a Bollywood movie. He was no hero who could strengthen his mother's aging body. The veins around her ankles were the twisted roots of an ailing tree. His sister, Meena, wrung a stained handkerchief and dabbed the frail forehead.

The driver of the microbus beeped, this time long, the high-pitched bleat of a wounded animal.

"I'll send something as soon as I can," Manu said. The sight of his mother's feverish petite frame filled his vision, dominating the small cement structure that was home to five of his siblings and their mother.

Turning so his younger siblings would not see the tears slipping out the corner of his eye, he made for the low-ceilinged entrance. The youngest ones, Raju and Ram, the unlikely fruit of his mother's dwindling years, clutched at each of his knees and whimpered. They were six years old.

Outside, the horn sounded again, causing their cow to give a low bleating answer. Their family, like most in their village, had fresh milk, and a garden fertilized by homemade manure. His siblings could grow up the way he had, on a plentiful vegetable garden, playing in the long grass, and doing household chores, living from their eldest sister's wage, a replacement for their deceased father's business.

His mother's long illness had drained their resources. The shadow of the Maoists lingered, the tendrils of fear reaching all men of Manu's age.

"Soon." Meena repeated the word, her lips pressed tight. She nodded as if this were a guaranteed date. "We used *Didi's* salary for the medicine."

Meena had been a child when her older sister had gone off to work. She was still too young to manage a household, but there was no one else. She followed him to the front wheel of the microbus with his bag. He didn't have much to take for his job as an office worker, but that was good, because more would not have fit in the passenger area.

"Say hello to *Didi* for us." Meena handed off the bag and attempted a half-smile.

"I'll tell her first thing." He ducked into the cab's once-cream interior. The driver hacked a cough, opening his door to spit.

"Bus station?"

"How long?" Manu asked, though he knew the answer. "How many stops?" His mother would have chided him for his incessant questions.

"Two hours," the man grunted, picking his teeth with a splintered toothpick.

The tears flowed unchecked. Manu turned to the side, the hot breeze little comfort as the microbus bumped the unpaved road from his village to the bigger one next door. To the bus station that would take him to Kathmandu. To the airplane that would take him to his new life. A life that would allow him to revive his mother from subsisting on the meager vegetables of their garden.

He dozed off, despite their halting progress over uneven dirt roads.

"Make room," the driver said. The microbus slowed to a stop.

A man in a button-down shirt, hair slicked with oil, eyes wide with promise, boarded the auto. Manu slid behind the driver, putting his feet on either side of the bag.

"Great day for a journey!" His companion bounced on the seat like one of the twins. Manu offered a smile that didn't raise the corners of his lips. The auto began again. The driver coaxed the vehicle ever faster, which was more difficult to do now with the added weight.

"I am Hitesh."

"Manu."

Hitesh shared a continuous stream of thoughts. This was the furthest he had ever gone from his village. How, he contemplated, did airplanes manage to stay in the sky? He wondered if he could learn to cook quickly enough to avoid starving.

These preoccupations had occurred to Manu as well in the months preparing for his new job as an office worker in the Gulf state, but he had an ace card that Hitesh lacked. Manu's eldest sister, Sanjana, had been working abroad for years. Her salary had kept the family afloat, at least until their father had been killed.

Manu could have joined the army or started a shop with the leftovers of his father's trading connections and risked the Maoists' wrath. These had been Manu's choices once the Maoists had gotten hold of his businessman father trading in a village west of Butwal. As he had contemplated the options, Nepal's civil war ripped away any sense of security.

"You know my family, they pay everything for me to have this job." Hitesh bounced on the seat with the jolts from the potholes. May as well have been with excitement, Manu thought wryly.

"I have to borrow money to get my ticket, and to pay for finding the job, and even this bus ride." Hitesh ticked these off on his fingers. His calculations were staggering.

"How will you pay this?" Manu asked, despite himself, drawn into the conversation.

Hitesh shrugged. "The man from the agency say they will take it from my salary, until debt is finished."

Manu looked out the window. He hoped his relief didn't show. Sanjana had been saving money for him for several years. Well, for him to go to university in the capital, to study, become educated, like their father would have wanted. The money had gone to pay for all these fees that Hitesh was outlining, using up most of their savings. There were worse things than not attending university, Manu thought. Like being in debt to a company you didn't know.

~~~

Life in the middle hills was not what it had been when he was Raju and Ram's age. Now it was his turn to contribute. He was joining Sanjana in the country she now called home. Any fears he felt were assuaged, knowing Sanjana would be nearby.

The microbus trundled along past several villages, until it arrived at the regional bus station. A maroon poster announced the interview dates for an international airline. Manu turned to look out the other window. The airline job had been out of his reach, even with his SLC grade-10 certificate.

Hitesh fell silent at the sight of so many people, four times the amount in their village. They swarmed the bus area like ants, shoulders and heads loaded with their possessions. From villagers with cousins abroad, they had heard of people making good with companies, working in glass offices, coming home every two years. For these jobs, Manu would have needed to go to university, a luxury he could not afford.

"Wow," Hitesh said.

The driver took pity on them and got down, indicating they should do the same. He weaved in and out of the crowd with surprising agility for someone with stooped shoulders and spindly legs. Manu kept him in sight as sweat beaded on his forehead. Hitesh was panting behind him. After several minutes, during which Manu's grip on the vinyl bag grew more slippery, the driver stopped abruptly in front of a bus with a long queue. The men were of various heights and ages, as if this queue were an assembly representing the diversity of Nepalese masculinity.

At the very top of the line was a clump of men, pushing to get onto the bus. Other buses were pulling away from the station with six or so men on the steps, their arms and legs hanging into the air. Forlorn faces were pushed against the glass, the headless hips, legs, and waists of other passengers in the aisle behind them.

"Here," the driver said simply.

Manu paid him from the precious few rupees he had. Hitesh slid a few folded notes over as well. The driver strode away without a backward glance.

Manu's stomach grumbled at the sight of bags of chips hanging from the kiosks facing the adjacent street. Women sat in front of pyramid piles of yellow and green mangoes. Biscuits and sweets littered counters in multicolor wrappers. Raju and Ram would have clamored for a taste. Meena would have scolded them. If she had been on her bi-annual visit home, Sanjana would have indulged them all. Manu smiled at the idea of coming back through with his older sister, preparing to lavish presents on their siblings. Sanjana's hard work had sustained him through his youth. Through her help he would work in an office, not at a menial job, like a housemaid. Now it was his turn to do the same for the younger ones.

A bus creaked into the dirt lot, sending up a cloud of dust. Bare arms dangled out of the windows, the heads of others visible as they stood in the middle aisle. The vehicle groaned under the weight of the passengers. Another cloud of dust rose as the wheels churned, pulling rectangular blue bulk out of the parking lot that served as the transport hub.

Men selling bottles of water and phone cards squeezed into the tangle of arms and legs as others disembarked, emerging like wilted clothing, damp from sweat and humidity. They hawked their goods at full volume, sounding like the rooster at home, working from the top to the end of the bus as quickly as possible. Manu marveled at how a stooped older man weaved among the bags of rice, hands of reaching children, and an occasional goat, all while taking change and distributing homemade fried snacks.

"We'll take the next one," Hitesh said, as if in answer to a question.

"We can get on this one," Manu said. "Can you run?"

Hitesh bit his lip.

"I'm running." Manu hitched his bag onto his shoulder and ran to catch up with the bus, which was slowly crawling through the street like an over-burdened ant groaning under a hefty crumb. Men hanging from the step cheered him on. He broke into a sprint, the bag banging against his head and neck. In the next few seconds, he realized he would have to take one of their outstretched hands and pull himself up onto the step in order to get onto the bus. A man with two missing front teeth grinned, extending the flat of his palm. Manu would need both hands to grab it; he would have to drop his bag—the one that contained his new office clothes and the photo of himself with his six siblings that a tourist with an instant camera had taken of them, grinning at the ice cream stall, vanilla ice cream dripping down the front of Sanjana's shirt. He would have to let it go, or get the next bus.

"Are you coming or not?" someone jeered from the window.

Manu released the bag and the weight rolled down his back. Better to miss the bag than his flight, which his company would not pay for twice. He leapt for the bottom step of the bus, now moving fairly quickly without the lumbering burden of the bag. He grasped the toothless man's hand and pulled himself forward, the jungle of limbs ensnaring him, their owners bracing so as not to fall. The bus swallowed him whole. He couldn't see past the arms and legs to make out what happened to his bag, but he was the last addition. There was no sign of Hitesh.

When the bus stopped a few hundred yards from the entrance to the regional airport, Manu and the other men poured out like spilled water, dispersing in all directions. A gaggle of passengers trouped into the restaurants on the side of the street, preceded by the bus driver, whose shirt was as limp as a damp towel. Rows of tables and chairs gave the appearance of a banquet. The men set ladles of rice, curry and lentils from enormous pots straight onto stainless steel plates.

He wished to join them, but he had no time. A smaller group headed toward the airport. They smelled like the pickled vegetables that always accompanied meals, spicy and full of onion. Manu shuffled along, swept up in the stream. The hours on his feet numbed his hips, knees, and brain. His ears rang from the blaring Bollywood tunes the driver played on a loop. He was thankful to make the next stage of the journey seated, again due to Sanjana's provisions. Most others would catch another bus to the capital.

The peaks of mountains rose in the distance like fingers clawing for the sky, their white tips blending in with the clouds. He saw jets, hovering above the earth, gliding ever downward, closer than those that flew thousands of meters above his head in his village. Their animalistic rumble reverberated in his stomach. As if cued, the group's shuffling picked up the pace and they surged forward. Manu's heartbeat quickened as they seethed into the airport's metallic interior. The security guards parted them, all the while rapping out orders to present papers. Many others were confused by this, but Sanjana had prepared Manu. He had the printed copy of his contract and plane ticket, which she had insisted he ask the agency to provide, folded into his back pocket. A guard, his paunch dipping between his legs, waved Manu through. Manu went inside, the air hot against his sweaty skin. There was minimal circulation inside the airport. The dim overhead lighting had little effect against the encroaching twilight.

He scanned the area, wondering how to decide which booth to approach. Three men, wheeling metal carts laden with bright red rectangular cases, were winding their way against the flow of foot traffic entering the airport. As Manu passed the column of men, the middle one slowed, battling a contrary wheel, casting the cart into a passer-by. Manu hoped he would one day be able to afford to return to Nepal with many things to replace the belongings he had left by the wayside. As the first cart swept by him, he could read the letters inscribed on the outside. They were names. Ah, people so rich they could afford for their possessions to be delivered to them. Sanjana had told him of the strange ordering processes of her mistress, who sent away for packages of creams, costumes, and books, all of which arrived within a matter of weeks.

"Which company?" A man with a thick lock of hair hanging down his forehead was shouting at Manu, while dozens of other men scattered around the mouth of the entrance like ants. The men he pulled aside were given white hats with Arabic calligraphy on the front in black.

"MBJ? MBJ!" Another man, with a pristine white shirt and sunglasses pushed back on his head, was waving a yellow flag. "MBJ here." Others, shorter than Manu, were jostling to get in line in front of the man with a pink and purple paisley shirt, the white stone on his pinky ring winking. The men were a hodgepodge of Nepali features, heads full of dark hair, skinny to the point of waifishness, having grown up largely on the produce from organic family gardens. They were handing over signed documents.

"Me, me," Manu said. MBJ Holding was his new employer, a company with vast projects whose employees were so busy they could pay for people to make photocopies and drive their documents around the one-city country.

"Where are your papers? You have to pay for transport and ticket and employment fee."

"I paid directly." Manu produced the printed flight ticket his sister sent him.

The man eyed him, taking in Manu's clean, but rumpled, shirt and cuffed pants.

A cart with the stray wheel skidded, sending the box into Manu's path.

"Oops," the sweating man said. "Sorry."

"No worry," Manu replied politely, though the crowd behind him was impatient with the delay. The man braced his sinewy arms to swing the cart around as the crowd behind Manu surged forward, pressing him into the box. He cried out from sharp pain when the corner of the container poked his knee. The top of the box gave way, splintering like an oft-used dinner plate. Men behind him kept pushing, unable to see the obstruction. A brush of fingers on his leg made him wonder if someone had fallen. The first cart-wheeling man, his angular features pinched in annoyance, left his cart by the side and came to sort out his companion. He pushed everyone back, clearing the space for his shorter comrade, and also Manu.

"*Chuup!*" the sharp-featured one shouted. His comrade scuttled toward Manu. He lifted the lid to scoop back whatever had fallen out.

Was that a hand? Manu blinked as the two men weaved the cart out of the way and the crowd surged forward again. They carried him like the tide to the line in front of the MBJ person. Manu craned his neck, hoping to catch a glimpse of the cart pushers to deny what he had seen. A human hand, attached to arm, had disappeared under the red lid of the container. And inside, attached to what? *Or whom?* Manu thought.

"MBJ only. MBJ."

This company would bring Manu over as an office worker and pay him three times what he could ever hope to make at home, even if he could find a scarce job.

"You there." The company rep's teeth gleamed white against bronze skin. His features were like those of anyone around: dark eyes, dark hair, square shoulders, except this man's hands did not look used. They were plump, the insides pink, the nail beds free of dirt.

His proprietary eyes flicked over Manu and the dozen or so men behind him in one swoop. He motioned for them to line up against the far wall, snapping his fingers to hurry and gesturing for their passports. Again, even in this smaller group, the others surged forward. When it was his turn, Manu held his passport back for a fraction of a second, causing the other man to look up.

"But we give passport only at big airport." Manu wiped the sweat from his palms on his dusty pant legs. "Inside country we no need passport."

The company rep passed a hand over his slicked back hair. "I checking identity." He looked from the photo to Manu's face and back, palming the passport under his arm with a stack of others.

"When will you give it back?" Manu asked, switching to Nepali.

"On the other side." The rep shooed Manu as if he were one of the stray cats lurking on the airport's perimeter.

Manu took his place on the wall, not letting the agent out of his sight. He was the second person in the family to get a passport, the only one other than Sanjana, and he couldn't help feel this loss was bigger than his vinyl bag of possessions, likely picked through thirty seconds after he had dropped it. He wondered if Hitesh had taken a look. When he cast around again for the cart pushers, they were nowhere in sight.

Chapter Four

Laxmi rifled through the stack of agreements, the rustle of the paper akin to the sound of riyal notes in her ears. She was in charge of these papers. She leaned back in her chair, swirling around, letting the wheels take her in a circle behind the desk like a dance. There was no boss in the backroom to whom she must report.

The papers represented three years worth of salary as a school receptionist. Salary she couldn't have dreamed of earning without the agency's contract to supply office assistants to the companies overseeing the building of the Olympic stadium. Such important people did not have time to make copies or their tea and coffee.

They needed someone to run the papers, stamps, and folders between floors in the glass fronted skyscrapers of West Bay. Someone who would be happy to wash the left over lunch dishes and return them to their proper owners, dried, ready to use for the next day.

She paused to run her fingers through her hair, humming. Setting up the new office had been an adventure for her, someone who had taken orders for so long.

"You have so much potential." The consular officer sighed. "I don't blame you for moving on."

Her own countryman, who had rarely smiled or made eye contact with Laxmi in the five years they had worked together brought in a store-bought cake topped with strawberries on Laxmi's last day of work. All the years of scrimping and saving had resulted in the pair of dark cherry desks, swivel office chairs, and a black computer monitor and a fax, printer, copy machine.

Here they were, at last, on the second floor of an adobe-colored building jammed into the capital's original commercial district. If you ignored the store signs in Arabic, you could be in India. If you squinted, this could be the Nepal of the future. Their new business shared a floor with an Indian printing company and Lebanese design firm. No long lines of laborers waiting for stamps to apply for their work permits. Gone were the tired faces that had comprised her daily view.

No, in her new life she teetered over the jammed city streets below. The office was the first upgrade of many, though her husband was more cautious. Laxmi had plans, money tucked away from offering contracts to those who came into the embassy, looking for work for their family members aspiring to get ahead in the Arabian Gulf. She said nothing about the years of toil, the race to stay ahead of the rising price of food, the pressure to cut corners to splurge for her child's birthday.

Laxmi smiled, promised a good job in their new company, and kept her cut. First a nursery for Sajita, like all the expat children she saw dropped off while she was on her way to work. Next, a standalone villa, not a cramped apartment with the paint peeling from the ceiling.

The phone rang but she ignored it. Her job was to see that the supply of workers went straight to the site everyday, made legible photocopies, served hot tea and cold water. She was excellent at her job, perfecting in a few weeks the key points of the transition. She coordinated the van to transport the new crop of workers to the glass fronted offices, showing them how to work a copy machine and fax.

No one needed to know about the few choice jobs she arranged on the side, the family members paying directly into her pocket, not the agency. They would finish the house in Kathmandu, enjoy the summer holiday, and then come back to train another crop of assistants. So it had been for five years. So it would be, her nest egg for her daughter's wedding growing and growing, until one day, she would make a brilliant match. Maybe to an agency owner or other businessman. Her husband would object. He would want a teacher or some such honorable job at low pay.

The phone jangled again. Laxmi checked her eyeliner. Since they had set up the agency, every Nepali they had ever met during their five years in the country had been calling. They offered all kinds of stories. This one had a sick mother, the other had a father who died. They all wanted to move up higher on their list.

Sajish had insisted they pay at least fifty percent of what the workers made directly to them, easily done, since there was still enough to split between the finder in Kathmandu, the local sponsor, and themselves. Every small amount added up when you were dealing in the volume of labor that the country required. With the games seven years away, a historic moment for an Arab country to host the world, she envisioned her own car and driver in the near future.

A new crop of men was due to arrive this week. They were so shy, these new arrivals, afraid to ask her to repeat herself, intimidated by her crisp English vowels. She never translated for them. They were going to work in English, with English-speaking foreigners, and the sooner they learned, the better.

Sajish burst into her station, his hair standing on end. "Why aren't you answering the phone?"

"I was getting ready to go see Sajita." She laid her hands on the table. "What's wrong? Stay calm. You know your heart."

He was the intemperate one, unsure of how to deal with the Americans' demand for fair salaries or the Brits who wanted service, even after hours. His fragile health had been one reason her mother had objected to the match when Sajish came to propose after seeing Laxmi in the corner shop. Once she heard he had plans to leave Kathmandu, she had said yes, heart murmur and possible early widowhood and all.

"Who wants what now?"

Sajish flopped into the chair opposite her, his growing belly bouncing with the effort. She had started serving soda at dinner, a specialty they used to save for birthdays.

"It's who doesn't want." He slapped a letter of Arabic script on the desk.

"They don't want soda again in the offices." She smoothed hand cream across her knuckles. "Another healthy campaign."

"They don't want us." Sajish jabbed a finger at the letter.

She paused in zipping up her purse.

"The price of petrol is low." He switched from English to Nepali. "Prices are sinking. Everyone is cutting back. Our contracts are cancelled."

She sat bolt upright. "They can't do that."

Sajish pulled at his hair. "They can. We are within the probationary thirty-day period."

"They signed for three years!" She waved the faxed contracts at him.

Sajish scanned the pieces of paper. He began laughing, his belly shaking with the effort, a low guttural sound, and then threw his head back into loud guffaws.

She took the documents back, eyeing the Arabic lettering and stamps for any signs of incongruity.

"These are our contracts, now sold to a construction company."

She stared at him blankly.

"They want our guys to work construction." He rested his elbows on the table. "The group arriving this week. They want those guys to build a stadium."

Laxmi slumped in her chair as if a heavy weight were pressing against her chest. The image of Sajita in their box of an apartment, the disinterested Sri Lankan nanny scrolling through her mobile in the background while Laxmi returned to sifting through the unending queues at the embassy.

"They want them to work construction for half the price of the contract." Sajish glanced at the documents again, and then dropped the stack on her desk. He tilted his head on the back of the chair, staring at the ceiling.

"Our fee was cut?" She dragged the documents back to her, cursing her lackadaisicalness at languages. Most people went from Hindi into Arabic without much effort but she hadn't bothered.

Her husband began laughing again.

"This isn't funny."

"Oh, but it is," he said. "Our fee is the same."

Her heartbeat steadied. "Then it's not so bad."

"To find twice the number of workers."

"Fine," she said.

"Fine?"

"Fine, we take it out of their first year salary. Use that to bring over other guys. Rise in agency fee. All our calculations are based on that standard fee."

Sajish gaped at her. "We'll be changing their jobs. After they're already here."

She shrugged. "They're still making money." she said. "They come to the big city, have an adventure, and then go home and brag to their families."

They contemplated each other, neither one blinking.

"You're ready to go home." She rapped her fingers on the desk, one of two they had used their savings to purchase. "That's the other option. We turn these guys back around on the first flight and go with them. Because that's what it would cost."

"Sleep on it." She used a soothing tone, knowing the idea of returning to Nepal without the ability to buy a house to share with his entire family would keep Sajish awake, tossing and turning, same as when they were newlyweds in Nepal. "I'll see you at home."

She took the elevator down to the ground floor, stepping out as two men got in wearing snug black suits with slicked back hair and the top two buttons of their shirts. Laxmi hoisted her purse higher as she entered the street. There was the woosh of cars clearing the streetlight. Someone honked at unexpected taillights.

Sweat beaded on her forehead. She was five streets away from their apart-ment, but with few options for sidewalks, Laxmi weaved through the side streets, stopping and starting as cars disregarded her trying to make her way through the latticework of neighborhood lanes. Many drivers sped up to avoid having to wait for her to cross.

There was no direct way to get to their apartment because of the con-struction. The shoulders of men in blue overalls were visible from a trench that had been open for several weeks. What should have been a ten-minute walk took her thirty. She arrived drenched, clambering up to the fifth floor rather than wait for the unreliable elevator, anxious to see Sajita.

"Where's the baby?" She asked panting, after unlocking the door.

"Sleeping."The sixty-year-old nanny drooped at the kitchen table that also served as their eating space.

"How long?"

"Since morning." She shrugged.

Laxmi poured a glass of water, mopping at her brow with a handkerchief. She gulped big mouthfuls to avoid a tart putdown. They couldn't afford a younger woman who would also balk at sleeping on the sofa in the living room instead of the privacy of her own space. She went into the apart-ment's bedroom.

"Time to wake up," she whispered to Sajita's sleeping form, tangled in the sheets of their single bed.

Chapter Five

The metal steps leading into the belly of the plane were like a mountain ascent into the unknown. Manu climbed a step at a time, waiting for the others in front of him while those behind pressed into his back.

Based on the others climbing the staircase with him, Manu felt as though he were looking into a fractured mirror. Most of the other men were of his height and slight build. They wore pressed shirts, frayed at the cuffs and collars, the colors drained from them as though they had been rolled in dust, and black thick-soled shoes.

The man directly in front of him a few stairs up looked around with an air of the same panic Manu felt. He had a close-cropped haircut, one that revealed oversize ears. His head swiveled right and left, right and left, taking in the basin that was Kathmandu Airport. Manu peeked over his shoulder. A line of passengers snaked from the bus to the foot of the staircase.

To his left was another metal staircase like the one they were crowding, only this one was empty. Instead of a hundred men of medium height and slight build, there was a tall, bald white man at the top of the stairs greeting a woman in a maroon uniform. He extended a hand to her, she reached out for a small piece of paper. She read it, taking the time to smile back at him revealing dimples, and gestured for the man to follow her. He disappeared into the plane's dim interior.

"Move." Someone jabbed Manu in the back.

He stumbled up the next step. When he crested, the small platform made pushing possible. Elbows and shoulders jostled him. The doorway narrowed again, pressing the men back into a single column like a human funnel.

Here the woman in uniform offered no smile. She glanced at their tickets without touching Manu and flicked a hand toward the right side, near the back. He did as he was told, passing three rows of chairs in a middle cabin as large as his entire home.

A man in a maroon uniform shuffled him to the seat by the window with an impatient harrumph. Manu collapsed into the seat. He had no packages to ferret into the holding areas above their heads or squeeze underneath the seat.

In two years he would be on another one of these planes, wearing a maroon suit, something with those small diamonds like the latest film hero, striding between these chairs, arms stuffed with packages for the kids, the other passengers stepping aside as he made his way back to his family.

Right now, however, he fumbled with the clasps of the metal seatbelt, raised and lowered the window shade, pressed the buttons on the small television in front of him, discovering films in Hindi, Tamil, and Malayalam. He leaned forward, nose a few inches from the screen, wishing he could fly around in this plane until he had watched all of them.

How to hear the sound? His seatmate fished out a small plastic pouch from the seatback, unwinding wires for headphones, inserting the pointy end into his armrest. Free headphones? Manu broke into a grin. Things were looking up already, on his way to his new life. He did the same, turning up the volume, laughing and singing along with the movie's best moments.

His seatmate bumped his arm from the armrest. Manu quieted, aware of the others for the first time. He slipped off the earphones, rubbing his eyes, fatigue coming over him like a blanket.

Lulled by the plane's mechanical drone, he fell into a waking sleep. His head bumped against the Plexiglas window. He leaned against it, wishing for the support of his siblings' shared bed instead of the sharp elbow of the stranger next to him. He slept, even as the sounds of others around him filtered through—the cough of someone a few rows behind, the tinkle of the food cart as the stewards began serving dinner. He shrugged off the hand on his shoulder, though his stomach rumbled at the smell of cooked meat.

Manu burrowed into himself, wishing he could take back the last few months. If he were going to start there, he might as well go back further, to the moment his father began limping, unable to load trucks. Or maybe it would be more useful to go back to the first time Sanjana had left, setting the stage for the longing of his parents for their firstborn, their cheerful extroverted daughter who could work as hard as three women, while looking after all of them.

He would keep his sister there at home, and no one would know how nice it was to have fresh milk or factory-made blankets. She wouldn't be sending money every month that allowed them to buy a goat or start planting new crops. She wouldn't be working in some other house far away. She would be there, with them, and she would know how to nurse Mother back to health, how to put the spring in her step.

"Window shades up." The male steward rapped his knuckles on Manu's shoulder.

Manu started awake as the man's long fingers reached past him to snap the shade up. Below twinkled the exterior lights of buildings, dim in the growing darkness and dust. A purplish plume of smoke extended in a column, like fingers reaching for the plane as it sped over a set of linked industrial-sized drums. An open flame shot out from another part of this complex. Oil, Manu realized as he gazed at the orange flame. They were burning oil.

The plane decreased speed, running parallel with a well-lit road. Neon signs of storefronts flickered past as they descended. Manu gripped the arms of his chair, frightened that the bottom of the plane would scrape on the light poles speeding by underneath. Like a brick tossed from a great height, they slammed onto the tarmac, the wheels screeching with the effort of stopping. Manu pressed back against his seat to avoid being smashed into the seat in front of him. A few of the other passengers clapped. He swallowed convulsively, wishing he had taken some water from the cart when it passed.

The plane swung wide. A metallic voice spoke to them while the attendants urged everyone to keep sitting. Men were in the aisles, pulling at their parcels wrapped in paper bags.

Manu filed out with the others, exiting down another set of stairs into an airport that had four times the number of planes he'd seen in Kathmandu, most of them marked with a maroon Oryx and gray stripes. They marched down the stairs, clanging the metal steps. This time to his right, Manu saw the bald man exiting, the same woman smiling in farewell. A white car with shiny spokes on rotating on the wheels waited for the man at the end of the steps.

At the bottom of Manu's staircase stood a shiny bus that hissed as the doors opened. Manu surged forward with the rest of the crowd onto the bus. The doors groaned closed again as the others from the plane waited on the steps. They pulled away. Someone grabbed Manu's arm. He braced his legs to avoid falling over. The bus wound around the airport. Driving past so many planes, Manu wondered if the world had more countries than he knew of. When they stopped again, a man with a gleaming fluorescent vest was shouting for transfers. Half the bus exited.

"The city?" He pointed at Manu and the dozen or so other men waiting.

They nodded. The doors shut with a whoosh, and they traveled a few hundred yards to another entrance. Manu blinked in the fluorescent light. The marble interior was white, unrelentingly clean like the robes worn by the airport officials.

"Workers, workers." A man in a robe called out, waving a handheld radio at Manu's group of men. They were herded away from the roped-off lines in front of the visa counters.

"Passport, passport." The man came back, calling toward them.

"We don't have." Manu used what little English he had picked up from Sanjana during her diligent lessons on the phone. "He took."

The man in the robe looked back toward the entrance, calling out phrases in Arabic. The MBJ representative strode in, his hands full of green documents with oversize papers peeking out of the tops. He handed them over and the airport official thumbed through them, indicating Manu's group should follow to the visa counter.

Manu walked forward.

"No, no, wait." The MBJ man motioned them to stay. "I return with visa."

Manu glanced at the men around him. The one next to him shuffled from foot to foot, demonstrating their collective uncertainty. A few of them tried to ask questions.

"One minute." The rep crossed to the visa counter alone.

One minute turned into many as they waited for him to reappear. Manu's view of the rep was obstructed by dozens of men, some wearing black suits, their sleeves worn at the elbows, their hands full of the documents of others, who also went forward. On the indigo covers of a set of passports, he saw the three-headed lion, the symbol of India. Groups of men similar to his were sitting against a wall. Manu realized he had not moved at all on the five and a half hour flight, not even to use the toilet.

He looked around, wondering where one would be found. Several men were entering and leaving a doorway, wiping their hands. He was moving toward the doorway when he saw another door opposite where women were taking babies in diapers.

"You! Where you go?" The man in the robe was back, making a straight line for Manu.

"Toilet," Manu said. He didn't stop walking, lest he embarrass himself in front of all the eyes, now watching. The man in the robe grumbled, but matched Manu's pace. He entered the bathroom, amazed at how clean it was compared to the latrines he used in Nepal.

When he re-emerged, the man in the robe was waiting for him. The man looked up from his phone and indicated with the radio antennae Manu was to rejoin the group. Manu walked as slowly as he could, taking in the glittery countertops on the other side of the visa line. There were perfumes, chocolates, and toys.

"Okay, now." The MBJ representative shooed them all like schoolboys toward a roped column in front of the visa desk. "One by one."

They stepped forward. Manu looked at the young man who stamped their documents. He took each passport from the ledge above his desk, flicking through the pages, his eyes passing over the face in front of him in an instant before the heavy stamp descended.

The MBJ rep scuttled them to the baggage area where the men waded through a heap of plaid, vinyl bags and taped boxes, trying to identify their own.

"Mafi?"

Manu turned, not understanding.

"Your bag?" The rep eyed Manu with suspicion.

"I lost it."

The rep shook his head, but handed Manu a piece of paper. "Sign."

Manu looked at it, wishing he had stayed in school longer as Sanjana had insisted. He couldn't have made out much anyway, since the contract was in Arabic. But there, above the signature, he could make out numbers, since they often used the same ones in Nepal for license plates.

"Sign." The man put an arm across Manu's chest, pressing the contract and the pen at him.

"This says one thousand," Manu said. "What's this? The salary? They promised me fifteen hundred."

The rep clicked his tongue, peering at Manu as if seeing him for the first time. "You don't want this job? You can go back."

The other men were signing their contracts, passing the one pen among them.

"I want to work," Manu protested, "but for the amount they said."

The rep walked away, the column of men following him, coming to a stop in front of two conveyor belt stations with blue-shirted police men leaning back in their chairs. The men in front of Manu hauled their bags to be scanned again, the giant mouths swallowing the parcels, spitting them out at the other end.

To their left, another column of passengers shuffled along. The officer at the top of that column stood up, straightening his hat. He tapped the screen, calling over the man at the top of the station Manu was passing. They leaned together, eyeing an object on the screen.

A tall man in a wilted suit tapped his foot. "Is there a problem?" Manu struggled to make sense of the words in that pinched, pronounced way of speaking.

The policeman flicked his hand, indicating the bag should be hoisted onto the table and opened.

The white man moved to unzip his bag.

The officer rummaged around, tossing aside dress shirts and loafers. "This is forbidden." The officer dangled a bottle in front of the white man.

Manu felt a rush of relief that his bag was missing. Who knew what could have gotten him into trouble.

He exited the brightly lit airport into the warm night. Their column walked the length of the parking lot to a dark corner, where another bus waited for them, lumbering in the dark. Palm trees waved their hellos in the humid breeze.

They trailed the rep around a large domed structure that Manu realized was a mosque from the spired tower next to it. Adjacent to the terracotta mosque was a green oval of grass. A few men were sprawled on the ground, several with their arms shading their eyes. Otherwise, asphalt, sand, and rocks bordered the road leaving the airport. *The desert,* he said to himself with a thrill.

Manu signed, promising himself he would speak to the rep later. He climbed the steps. His legs quivered after so much standing. He collapsed into a seat, his shirt sticking to him. Unlike the airplane or the airport, the bus had no air conditioning. Humidity rolled through the open window and up and down the aisle like a beast with moist breath.

They rushed over a lake that in Nepal many people would have crowded around the outskirts to wash dishes, their clothing, or to draw water. Here were ceramic jars in the middle that water streamed back into the lake. This was man made, Manu realized, that's how rich these people were. They could make their own lake in the middle of all this dry land.

They creaked their way through the city, which was mostly asleep and largely in the dark. The bus followed roads that snaked away from the bright lights of the perimeter, until they entered a neighborhood with dusty streets and gray bricks made of concrete. Laundry hung on drooping lines and smashed vehicles waited outside of garages. Men walked around in collared shirts and *dhotis*, the cotton long kilt-like garments of the Indian subcontinent. Some wore the printed fabric to their ankles. Others draped the solid or plaid cloth around bony hips, doubling back through the legs in a drape that allowed for a longer stride.

When they shuddered to a stop outside a group of squat brown buildings, spotlights illuminated the guard station at the front gate. The pit of dread in Manu's stomach grew. He had traded the cleanliness of his stone and thatch house for this dingy set of structures, life with strangers, and constant surveillance.

The company rep from the airport stood at the front of the bus, indicating they should all get down. Manu shuffled forward, stepping onto the packed sand. Blue plastic bags rolled in the twilight, the dirt punctuated by other debris, discarded cards, and scraps of paper.

"Uniform." The agent pushed a blue bundle into Manu's arms. "We deduct from your first salary, 100 riyals."

Manu felt the broadcloth between his fingers. The material was thin, a one-piece outfit pulled up over pant legs and arms, covering the trunk of his body. No other garments were included, like shoes or undershirts. A hundred riyals was over 2000 Nepalese rupees. He wouldn't have paid 100 rupees for fabric this cheap. The one size fits all had none of the movie star stylishness of Bollywood story lines when the rural hero comes to the big city.

"You, you, and you." The pinky ring gleamed in the bare bulb of the courtyard. Manu came forward and followed the representative to a room beside a smoky grease-stained kitchen. Seven men with worn faces tracked Manu's entry into the shared sleeping quarters. No Hollywood posters here, like he used to paste up in the corner of the sleeping area shared with his brothers, only eyes rimmed by deep purple circles that watched his every move.

"There's no bed." Manu stepped back into the outdoor hallway and called after the rep, who now led other new arrivals down the corridor. "Where do I sleep?"

"Floor," the man called back over his shoulder. "If there are no beds, the new guy sleeps on the floor."

This could not have been the job Sanjana arranged for him. The concrete walls that rose around him bore no resemblance to the office job making photocopies and bringing tea to western men she had described. His protests were dismissed by the agent.

"If you want, I take you back to the airport." The man mopped his brow. "But you have to pay for the return ticket."

Manu could say nothing. They had spent all their money getting him here. "I want to call my sister." He had the man's full attention.

"Your sister? Where she working?" Manu noted the gleam in the other man's eye, so familiar to the way men, both army and Maoist, had been sizing up Sanjana's curves before she left for the Gulf.

"She's probably asleep by now." Manu shuffled away from the man and his leer. He would have to somehow contact her later.

Manu returned to the cinderblock box of a room where the other men were turning in for the night. Metal frame bunk beds lined the perimeter, topped by off-white mattresses.

They would wake up before sunrise in order to be on the bus. He knew this from the stream of directions the company rep had given them on the way from the airport. There was a thin mattress under the bunk on the far side of the room. Manu moved toward it, pulling it out from the frame. No one said anything as the men with blankets spread them out.

He sat on the floor to take off his shoes. He used the removed shoe to stamp on the cockroach near his knee. The bare overhead blub snapped off. Manu was grateful to escape the dreariness. He could imagine he was somewhere, anywhere else.

"New guys, listen," someone hissed into the night. "Don't trust anyone here unless he's from your country. My friend, he became close with a Chinaman. The guy was so nice, shared his water at the site, split the cost of dinner. He said he would make a dinner with all the specialties from his country."

Manu drew closer, as the others sat up in their bunks. His eyes adjusted to the darkness of the room and he could make out the speaker's profile in the south corner.

"My friend went to the dinner." The man's voice lowered, deepening, expanding in silence. "He ate and ate and ate. They drank. He left."

Manu released his pent up breath. Okay, so the guy didn't die.

"But the next morning, he was sick. He couldn't go to work. We took him to the doctor. You know what the doctor said?"

There was the sound of scuttling, fingernails on the cement. Rats? Manu coughed. The sound receded.

"Where have you been eating? These are human fingernails! They arrested him and he was deported."

Manu throat convulsed.

Someone on the other side of the room guffawed. "As if you ever had a friend."

"It's true, every word of it!"

"Go to sleep new guys. You'll need it."

Heist movie, Manu thought, anything to replace the image of his fingernails floating around in around in someone else's intestines. The one with the dance competition for diamonds, the one set in Dubai, the one where life in the desert was full of crystal, not a rat-infested room full of strangers.

Chapter Six

Humidity so thick Cindy could cut it with her spade wilted her hair like cabbage. Her friends at home thought desert heat was a high, dry temperature. A few days in the Arabian Gulf would singe pink the flesh on their faces. Though October, the cooler breezes of a desert fall were yet to arrive. Dig, dig, dig. The pointed edge of the spade tunneled inside the earth as the lost babies had once burrowed in her womb. She pushed the earth away, holding tears at bay. *Decades* her husband's voice echoed in the therapist's minimalist office. *She thinks about these pregnancies and it's been decades.*

Paul, who had seen women enslaved through conflict in the Congo and young boys toting weapons as long as they were tall in Sudan. He'd abandoned his disappointments in order to write about the sorrows of others.

Cindy, sounds like you will move on from this or this will be the end of the road. The greying hair at the therapist's temples had made him seem paternal, comforting when they had started the sessions. Alone with him in her individual session, however, his age made him Pauls' ally.

Canon in D rang out from the phone in her back pocket. *Going to the worker camps to pass out water and toiletries. Want to come?* Being with those undernourished men wouldn't make her feel better. Their worn faces and penetrating eyes would trivialize her pain. Another group of men telling her to move on. *You could a piece about migrants. Start your blog.* Cindy deleted the message.

She pushed the last of the basil plants into their row, wishing she could impose order into mind. The compound maintenance men had come last year, pulled up the entire fifty-foot yard brick by brick, and piled it in the corner. Another group of workers had rolled out grass. Each year Cindy tried to foster these commemorative plants, before the blistering desert heat obliterated everything outdoors.

These anniversaries were the hardest because there were so many of them, scattered throughout the spring. Not birthdays but death days. The days the doctors told her the hearts had stopped beating and her womb had failed her. Again.

And each year, these plants shriveled and died like each of her three babies, the plants making it no longer than those fragile embryos, giving up in the first few weeks of summer. She welcomed the ache in her arms and continued to dig her twelfth hole, making a bed for the herbs that she determined to grow this season.

"Daniel." She sat back on her heels and looked up as her son sauntered through the yard's side gate. The one who had made it, slid from between her legs after six months of bed rest, hurtling into life with the lusty yell of unconsidered privilege.

"Oh, hey, Mom." Those blue eyes, so like his father's, trained on her. "You need help?"

"Yes, to stand," she said with a forced laugh. He came over and gave her a hand. She pulled herself up, more to feel his palm in hers, let those ropy muscles take her weight, have the full force of his attention, than any real need for help.

They walked arm in arm into the university-provided villa. The adobe colored exterior was the same for all the units in the compound, or gated community they had lived in since moving to the country. Inside, however, Cindy had her way, picking colors for each of the living spaces, and swapping the management provided furniture for her own pieces, chosen for their overstuffed comfort.

Daniel stopped in the living room that extended through much of the bottom floor of the villa. He fished out a game cartridge from the corner or the sofa and pocketed a set of headphones, stuffing the wire down. Sunlight streamed in from the window, bouncing off the umber walls.

"Homework? Dinner?"

"Relax, Mom," he said. "I already got early acceptance into Georgetown, remember? Sharif's mom said I could eat with them."

"I hope Sharif is feeling better," she said. "No more trouble at school."

"They took those ADD pills away," Daniel mumbled. "His focus is better."

Because Sharif won't be getting into college doesn't mean you shouldn't. Earlier that year, Sharif had been caught reselling his ADD medication to local students at their international high school, triggering a police raid of the school and threats of deportation for the kids involved. Daniel hadn't bought any of the pills, but she wished he would put some distance between himself and Sharif.

"Getting caught selling them to others couldn't have helped," Cindy said. She bit her lip the minute it was out. Daniel's non-committal sound, between a grunt of agreement and squeak of protest, was her punishment. "Any other friends?" she said brightly, hoping to move past her least favorite of Daniel's choices. "Still in touch with Maryam?"

"Her family forbade her from seeing me."

"Seeing? I thought you two weren't dating."

"We weren't." Daniel's eyes flashed. "Her local parents don't get that a guy and girl can be friends."

"Probably for the best," Cindy had blundered twice. "She's in your father's university now and that could cause complications."

He had gone silent and she decided to leave it for now. She retreated to the kitchen, the area of the house that remained immune to her efforts. There were three sets of cabinets. The original had come with the villa, a non-descript brown with black trim, hanging over the counters and beside stove.

When the residents had complained there wasn't enough storage space, the university rushed to install a new set above the opposite wall, a lighter brown with yellowish handles. And Cindy had resorted to putting her own set next to the sink, needing even more space for an ambitious spurt of cooking. Someone in her writers' group had said cooking was another form of creativity and might jumpstart her writing.

The sound of the water muffled the closing of the front door.

Everyone at home bemoaned how difficult it was to raise teenagers. There were books for them. Not so many on how to bring up an American boy in the Middle East.

Cindy dried her hands, first the right then the left, staring at her reflection in the kitchen window. Her once-blond hair was shot through with silver. There were rings of skin on her neck, as if she were an aging tree, the elasticity drooping. She stretched this way and that. Yes, she looked good for a woman with a senior in high school. Her breasts were still firm, rising high. Her waist was small, her butt round, not sagging. The front door creaked on its hinges. She peered around the corner, in case Daniel had changed his mind and become chatty.

"I'm sorry I'm late." Paul plunked his briefcase on the floor inside the doorway. His curls were standing on end, meaning he had been running his fingers through his hair on the ride home—likely to avoid flipping a finger to anyone.

"Ten percent of your grade is based on attendance, Professor." Cindy crossed her arms.

He avoided her on one of these anniversaries, unable to take the tears, what he viewed as moping. Everything was a statistic to him, a newspaper story waiting to be written. Twenty five percent of women had miscarriages. She was filed under Unfortunate Outlier. He discouraged her from talking about the others with Daniel. He was an only child. He couldn't be much more special. Except that he was.

"Give me a chance for extra credit, Professor," he said, coming into the kitchen to peck her cheek.

She leaned into him.

"What's for dinner?"

"I don't know," she said, drawing away. "I haven't seen Sanjana all day."

He palmed a green apple from the bowl on the counter. "You're both home and you haven't seen her?" He shook his head.

"Hey," she said, wagging her finger at him. "Don't start. I was not at lunch or the salon. I was planting herbs." She gestured outside.

"I didn't say anything." He took a big bite of the apple, raising his hands. "Going to wash up."

"In the study, please!" Cindy motioned toward the briefcase.

"Sanjana will move it." He started up the stairs.

Cindy rapped her knuckles on the marble counter. She couldn't talk about the maid problem with anyone else either. Her friends at home already thought she was spoiled, going on safari in Africa for her wedding anniversary and having a full-time live-in employee. Her expat friends had nanny complaints, but they were of the 'she's-so-lazy' variety. No one was concerned about the way the nanny absolved everyone else in the house of responsibility. Everyone, Cindy knew, including herself.

"Sanjana," she said more sharply than she had intended when the maid answered her phone, "Where are you? Paul is home and there's no dinner."

"Sorry, Madam," Sanjana said in the singsong that could drive you crazy. "I come now."

Cindy hung up. She looked in the oven. Nothing. She looked in the fridge. Empty. Had Sanjana not gone to the grocery store either? The screen door clattered. Sanjana shuffled into view, her face worn.

"Sanjana, he's hungry." Cindy said. "What is going on?"

"I make it quickly," Sanjana said. She moved toward the fridge at glacial speed.

"What are you going to make?" Cindy asked. She opened the freezer in exasperation. "The boys ate everything over the weekend. Even the undated freezer meals."

Sanjana raised her eyebrows, giving Cindy a frightened rather than surprised look. "I didn't know, Madam," she stammered. "But you know, I am fast. I make fried rice."

"Paul wants to eat healthy," Cindy said. "He won't eat rice or bread or potatoes."

Sanjana's lip trembled. "Okay, but Sir likes pancakes. I make pancake."

"That's for breakfast," Cindy said. She drummed the marble countertop.

A tear raced down Sanjana's cheek, hovering on her mouth until she swallowed it. "Sorry, Madam," she said, wincing as if Cindy had slapped her.

"I count on you, Sanjana," Cindy said. "You were supposed to tell me where Daniel has been all afternoon. He'll notice if I'm snooping around. He's back at Sharif's house."

"Sorry, sorry," Sanjana said. "I know Daniel good boy, his heart too big. That Sharif make trouble." She was sobbing now, the tears coming so fast they were dropping onto the Peter Pan collar of her shirt, one of Cindy's discards.

"What's for—whoa, everything okay?" Paul skidded to a stop in the doorway to the kitchen, his arms bracing himself on the frame. He glanced from Cindy to Sanjana and back, raising his shoulders as if to say "What on earth?"

"Sir, there's no dinner, and Madam says you won't eat pancakes because is for breakfast not dinner, and I am sorry," Sanjana managed to get out between shuddering sobs.

"I'll eat breakfast at dinner," Paul said as if soothing a skittish horse. He fanned his hands out, coming into the kitchen where Sanjana and Cindy stood near the marble-topped island. "Pancakes are fine. Like you make when Daniel and Cindy are traveling. Completely fine. Pancakes, bacon, eggs. I'm happy." He gave her a smile. "Right?" His gaze locked with Cindy's.

"Fine," she said. "Let's pretend like we're on holiday in the middle of the week. But that doesn't explain what you've been doing all day, Sanjana."

"Are you not feeling well?"

Cindy gritted her teeth against the patronizing tone in Paul's voice. He was treating this like one of his students' meltdowns. Only Sanjana was an employee, not someone questing for knowledge.

Sanjana's sob rattled through her chest. Paul passed her some tissues. Cindy crossed her arms, leaning a hip against the island.

"I..." Sanjana's voice broke. She cleared her throat.

"Whatever it is," Paul said, as if he were talking to a younger version of Daniel, "you can tell us."

"If you broke something," Cindy said, seeing the shudders taking over the woman's slight frame, "tell me. I won't take it out of your salary." Her friends would have groaned at that, saying she shouldn't make such promises without hearing what the item was first.

"My brother," Sanjana said. Her voice was steady for the first time in several minutes. "He missing, same when my father died."

Cindy shook her head when Paul's glance asked if she knew anything about a brother. There were younger siblings, she knew, but she had never delved further into the maid's family history. The story of Sanjana's trader father dying at the hands of Maoist militants had tumbled out in the interview when Cindy had spoken to several potential housemaids at the hiring agency.

Sanjana's tears had shimmered along the black eyelashes like a screen of sorrow. If she had been a woman to worry about her husband's fidelity, like Amira, Cindy would have walked away from the young woman in that moment. She'd grown accustomed to the long absences of a conflict correspondent, the intermittent visits home, almost like a military wife. She had traded physical absence for mental preoccupation. Paul's academic obligations rendered him into an asexual workaholic, except during university holidays.

When she had recounted the story to Paul, testing it for veracity, he had said Sanjana was the one they should hire. "The population was torn between the Army and rebels." He had taken on the posture of the lecturing professor. "One day they were forced to give food and shelter to the Maoists. The next day the Army would come and punish them for supporting the rebels. She's almost a political refugee, when you think about it."

"Well, her father was traveling in the west of Nepal selling electronics or something. Wrong place at the wrong time," Cindy had said. "Hardly a political activist."

"We're looking for a way to do good. This is it. And maybe, if the back-story—"

"I'll hire her." Cindy tapped his cheek. "But you cannot write about her. This is not a case study. This is our employee."

Paul wrote about anything and everything that came across his path. His study was littered with awards for features, profiles, and piles of journals that had published his academic work. She let him know the minute Daniel was born that their family life was off limits. "We need boundaries."

Paul agreed and left management of the maid to her, as he did the rest of the household.

"Maybe we should sit down." Cindy went to the breakfast table in the glassed-in alcove and sat down.

Paul slid in next to her. He linked his fingers with hers under the table, giving her a squeeze.

Cindy heard the stories at ladies' coffee mornings about maids going home on annual leave and not returning. Or they'd borrow money to help ailing relatives and then post photos of husbands on new scooters on Facebook.

Sanjana sat across from them gingerly, as if she didn't want to indent the sea foam cushion—not that she would have, even if she'd pressed with all her weight. She fidgeted with her hands under the table.

"Your brother," Paul prompted. "He's missing from your village? I thought the Maoists had given up years ago."

"No, no, not Maoists." Sanjana shook her head. "No, Sir. He's here."

"Here?" Cindy started.

"I mean, in the country. He has job." Sanjana swallowed hard. "I find job through same agency that bring me here. Laxmi Pande, the wife of owner, she say she know someone in embassy who give office job. Good job. I give passport copy, money, and they bring him."

"You bribed someone for a job?" Paul's brow contracted.

"Bribe? No, fee. Only way to get good job. Remember you pay my agency fee?" She met both of their gazes with a shimmer in her eyes. "You pay agency to find me." Fresh tears streamed from her eyes. "Then you pay me salary. You very good, Madam and Sir. I not find another one like you."

Cindy gripped Paul's hand, thankful for his solid bulk, his shoulder pressing against hers. "Okay. You want him to live here, with us?"

Sanjana shook her head. "I cannot find him, Madam."

"What?" For the second or third time that night, Cindy felt her mind spinning. The first had been the haunted look in Sanjana's eyes at the sight of her displeasure. Now the worry Cindy had missed was etched in her drooping lips, written in the hunch of her shoulders, outlined in the waxy skin underneath her eyes. "He hasn't called you?"

The sobbing began again. Paul stood to gather more tissues.

"Seven days. He left Nepal a week ago. Nothing."

Paul passed the tissues to Sanjana before sitting down again. She clutched them in her right hand.

"A week isn't that long." Paul splayed his fingers on the glass-topped table. "He's probably settling in."

"You call Madam from the airport," Sanjana wailed. "You sending text the seconds before plane take off."

Cindy and Paul exchanged a glance.

"Single men are a bit different," Cindy said. "You know I have to train him to communicate. He didn't always."

"My brother calling me when he come." Sanjana's voice took on a new, determined tone. "We so happy to be in the same city again. So many years."

Paul cleared his throat. "Should we call the agency? Ask to speak to this Pande person?"

"I call every day. They tell me she not there, on holiday. And the manager say they not give visas for men." Sanjana shuddered.

Cindy felt a frisson of worry for the boy. The Gulf's labor practices for lower-skilled workers made international headlines every week. Headlines Paul followed with the excitement only a journalist could have.

"Right, we can get to the bottom of this. Get me his passport number." Paul indicated Sanjana, just like one of his students.

She dashed off to her room, showing the most energy she had all evening.

Paul sank against the cushion of the breakfast nook. "What a mess."

Cindy rubbed her hands over her face. "God only knows who he's working for and where. How is the passport going to help?"

"I'll put the guys in HR on it. You know Ibrahim is ex-royal guard. He can ask someone who can ask someone else to look in the system." He kissed the top of her head. "You're too hard on her."

"Don't start." She drew away.

"Here." Sanjana slid the black and white photocopy across the table to them. A wide-eyed young man with a shock of dark hair falling over his forehead stared at the camera. In the slope of his nose and width of his forehead there were echoes of Sanjana's petite features, but on the male canvas they were broader, less delicate.

"Manu. Probably he's been busy and had jetlag. You know how men are, like Daniel. They always forget about others." Cindy's voice was tinny as she maintained a sense of calm.

"Hey," Paul protested in his lecture volume. "Men do need more time to adapt than women." He turned to Sanjana. "Your brother is probably adjusting to his new office."

They collectively contemplated the photo, each lost in their own thoughts.

"Pancakes are happy." Sanjana broke the silence. "I make supply of happiness. And joke, yes?"

Paul squeezed out a laugh, the sound booming from his throat instead of his stomach.

"Sort of," Cindy said. Paul pinched the side of her hip when Sanjana's smile drooped. "Yes," she said. "Pancakes will make him happy."

The maid busied herself pulling ingredients from the cabinets. *And if I were so easy to please,* Cindy thought, *maybe happiness would be much closer.*

Chapter Seven

The teenager's room was untidy, but not filthy like the ones maids talked about in the clubhouse. Sanjana swung open the door to assess how much of her afternoon would be spent picking through dirty laundry and leftover dinner plates.

Maybe two hours, Sanjana thought, since there were no dishes. She wheeled in the bucket, guiding it by the mop handle. A simple sweep and mop of the bathroom, and then straighten the linens. She would have time to review the notes her friend had passed her about how to prepare to apply for nursery assistant position. If she hurried, maybe she could practice a few of the English sentences Analyn had taught her.

Her phone buzzed with the announcement of a text message. Sanjana pulled it out of her pocket with trembling fingers.

Please make an apple cake. Ma'am has a party.

Yet another false alarm. Not Manu. And not the agency. Sanjana erased the text from Madam Amira's latest maid. The woman hadn't been able to keep anyone in employment in the years since Maya had left. She returned the phone to the pocket of her sweat pants, her preferred attire for cleaning.

Analyn was nicer to her than most of the Filipinas on the compound. She would talk to her while walking the dog and ask Sanjana if she wanted anything from the store. She told Sanjana she was too smart to spend her life working as a housemaid. She could make twice as much money as an assistant in a nursery class.

"Madam and Sir are very nice to me," she said automatically. "They are good family. I not finding another."

Analyn tutted at these disclaimers.

Sanjana couldn't stop herself from listening to the younger woman's schemes for what she would do when she left here. The other maid's ramblings nourished hope, a luxury Sanjana had not indulged in. Her advice came at the price of Sanjana doing small favors.

Daniel was out at one of his numerous practices. She wasn't sure if it was a sports one like swimming, which he complained about despite being very fast in the water, or something he enjoyed, like chess.

Teach me how to make it. Please. Ma'am will be angry if nothing made at home.

The boy's bedroom was bigger than Sanjana's bedroom and bathroom, which housed the family's laundry machines. Late afternoon sun streamed in past the blue curtains Madam had specially-made. The bed was dark wood, with a curved headboard as long as Sanjana's but twice as wide. Nautical sheets, striped with anchors and sails, lay piled in a knot at the foot of the bed. Sanjana stripped them off.

You want me to lose my job?

Sorry Daniel in trouble with my Madam. Have to stay home to watch him. Sanjana replied or the deluge of messages would persist. She lied because the care of the boys was one thing neither she nor Analyn could ignore. And the other maid's job was much worse with that boy Sharif who never listened to no one.

If she were at home, she'd be doing this for her siblings. Her heart clenched at the thought of the younger ones at home without either Manu or her. The girls were older, but they were still girls. She shuddered at the idea they would one day be in a room, looking after someone else's brother like this. She sent them all the money she could, so they could go to university.

That had been the plan for Manu, but her adventure-loving brother had not complained when it was sidelined. Sanjana could not put the idea of studying out of her mind. If she worked in a nursery, maybe she could save more, and she could go to classes at night. There was a program that helped teach English to guards and cleaners at Sir Paul's university. Maybe she could find something like that.

As she rolled up the rug in the center of the room, a spasm in her back brought her to her knees. She paused to catch her breath. Her reflection in the mirror on the opposite wall gave her pause. When had she gotten so old that rolling up a rug could knock the breath out of her? Sanjana closed her eyes for a moment, and tried to sort out the lingering confusion over Manu's disappearance.

They said it was a good job, she thought, as if Manu were standing in front of her and she could give an account for her actions. *They said office work.* There had been nothing from the embassy. No news yet, though Sir Paul promised to call every week. How many more weeks could she go without losing her mind?

Sanjana knelt, rolling the rug away. How many more weeks could her family do without the money? She shouldered the mop, brushing it across the blondish tiles in an even rhythm. Sanjana loved to clean, though after this many years her body was starting to protest.

She enjoyed the methodical way she could work through every room, re-moving the signs of chaos and restoring order. *First mop the middle, then work the perimeter when it dried,* she thought, crossing to the built-in cedar closets. Madam preferred her clothes to be hung by sleeve length, both dresses and shirts. Skirts were in a separate area, and Sir's clothes were in a different bedroom altogether. They didn't share bathrooms.

Daniel, however, had no rhyme or reason besides that which Sanjana im-posed. She clucked at the dozens of empty hangers swinging on the pole. The shelves below were mostly empty as well.

I will take care of the boy first when Sir is traveling, Sanjana resolved when she saw the knot of clothes next to the hamper. At this rate it would be a wonder if he had anything to wear to school tomorrow. She bent, stuffing everything into the hamper.

"No, I didn't tell anyone." Daniel slammed into the room, talking on his phone.

"Oh!" Sanjana started, banging her head on the door of the wardrobe.

"Sanjana!" Daniel hung up the phone, dropping it on the stripped bed. "What are you doing in here?" He threw a backpack down on top of the phone, with several books and the edge of a laptop pressing against the black teeth of the partially closed zipper.

"Don't step there!" She raised a pleading hand as he made his way toward her.

He paused, eyeing the glass-like surface of the mopped floor. "My room's fine." He ran his hands through the reddish hair so many of the maids gig-gled about. "I'd like some privacy."

"I am almost done." Her arms tightened around the wicker hamper. "Why you straight home from school?" She gave him an up-down glance. Same wrinkled T-shirt, and shorts with many side pockets, all of them empty. Nothing different. And yet his hands were fidgeting as if playing a song against his thigh. "You sick?"

His face drained of color. "Yes, yes, I need some rest."

Sanjana dropped the basket. "I get some sheets so you sleep," she said. She made to walk across the same floor she had dissuaded him from disturbing.

"I'll do it." He put his arms out. "I'll get them." He disappeared into the hallway.

She didn't realize he knew where the extra sheets and towels were kept, but he was back in a flash, purple sheets dangling from his arms. "Those are your mother's." Sanjana picked up the basket again, making her way around the room. "I get you some more." She indicated with her chin that he should put the too large set on the top of the hamper.

"You sure?" His blue eyes showed distraction and discomfort, like his father when making any kind of request.

"I strong." She boosted the basket. "You put."

"I know you are." Daniel flashed that familiar smile. "You used to haul me around, remember?"

"Heavy boy, you were," she grumbled. "Stubborn, too."

"No one carries an eight-year-old," Daniel protested. "Maybe in Nepal they are smaller."

Sanjana turned away before he could see her smile. She had come to the house when Daniel was eight, and ten years later she counted him as one of her brothers. She set the hamper at the foot of the stairs. The laundry and her room were at the top of the landing. She would haul it all up later. Sanjana grabbed a set of plain white sheets, more appropriate for the boy— more like a man, judging from the signs of the small reddish hairs scattered on the discarded striped pair.

When she returned to the room, Daniel pawed through the few items left in his closet. There was an array of athletic shoes in various shades scattered around the open door, and the shorts he wore as underwear in a variety of colored stripe combinations. She blushed.

"Need help?" She began dressing the bed. He started, turning toward her.

"I'm looking for something," he said. "Have you seen it?"

She squinted at him. His voice broke in the telltale sign she knew meant a lie. "What it is?"

"What is it," he corrected her absentmindedly.

"What is it you look for?" When he didn't reply, she went on, pulling the fitted sheet onto the four corners. "You tell me now or I tell your parents."

"Don't be a snitch!"

"I not this word!" Sanjana surprised them both with her shout. "What it mean? You explain right now."

"Sanjana?" The sound of Sir Paul's voice made them both freeze. Paul poked his head around the door. He glanced from one to the other. "Everything okay in here?"

"Yes," Sanjana snapped the flat sheet open and pressed it under the corners.

"Daniel." Paul came into the room. "You're home early. What about..." Paul snapped his fingers "...swimming?"

"Pool cleaning." Daniel averted his eyes. "They'll reschedule."

Sir moved aside for Sanjana to exit the room. "I moved my talk in Copenhagen around to watch that meet. Is it still on? Even without practice?"

"Yes, Sir," Daniel mumbled.

Sanjana went downstairs, the sound of Sir's steps behind her spurring her to pick up her pace.

"Any chance there's something I could eat?" Paul asked.

She made straight for the fridge, pulling out the curry and rice she had eaten for dinner the night before. Sir sat on a barstool instead of at the table in the corner like when Madam was home. He rubbed the bridge of his nose, reading messages on his phone. The smell of fish curry filled the air.

"Ah, you know how to welcome a guy home," he said as Sanjana brought over a tray with bowls of rice and curry, steam rising from them both.

They only ate curry when Madam was out. The smell turned her stomach, she said. Sir began eating, the fork clanging against his teeth with the force of his hunger. "You think Daniel is doing okay? If he's giving you a hard time, you tell me."

Sanjana leaned against the sink, willing her heartbeat to steady itself instead of roaring through her head like a herd of goats. "He's tired. Too many activities, and that homework. You know how boys are behaving." She shrugged like she had seen Madam do, hoping it gave the same casual effect.

He chewed thoughtfully. "Any news from your brother?"

She shook her head, biting her lip to keep the ever-ready tears from starting.

"My guys said he did come in a month ago." Paul put down his spoon, pulling out a piece of folded paper. He smoothed it out on the bar, indicating she should come closer.

Sanjana approached, seeing typed Arabic and the seal of the Ministry of Interior.

"See, this is his name, and this is the date he came in." Paul tapped the paper. "At least that's what our ministry liaison says. I can't read Arabic." He gave a laugh, fading as Sanjana stared at the piece of paper without blinking. "I'll take this to the embassy and make them speed up their search."

She nodded, taking the tray with the empty containers back to sink as a way to distract herself from asking the rush of questions running through her mind.

"Don't bother them with this," the embassy man had warned her on the phone the last time she had called in order to open a case. "They don't like to get involved in these matters. You lose your job too, then where your family will be?"

"Okay." Paul rapped his knuckles on the bar. "Back to work for me." He left, as quietly as he had appeared, to go upstairs.

The first few times Sir had had one of these chats with her, Sanjana had been sure he was looking for reasons to fire her. Years ago she had quaked in fear whenever he appeared in the same room, catching her alone. Either he would set his hands on her, a prospect that made her so queasy she had walked around with a pair of scissors the first six months she lived here, or he would inspect every task she undertook and find something to criticize.

But Sir Paul took neither of the approaches the other maids most often complained about at the compound playground while their charges raced around, unaware of the bile their nannies were spilling about their parents. He talked to her about Nepal, asked her if she missed her village, what she liked to eat, if she had made any friends. They were never long conversations, and he rarely said much, listening, his eyes watching her. Usually they were interrupted by Daniel or Madam, or a phone call.

The buzz of the refrigerator coming back on made her jump. She thought of Daniel's harried appearance earlier, the way he had been almost shouting on the phone. Sanjana resolved to look in his room again for signs of any trouble the boy was mixed up in, if only to save him from his father's quiet disappointment.

Chapter Eight

Maryam wouldn't get any ideas or a listening ear right now. Nasser lay sleeping with his arms gathered at the side like an arrow, his torso turned into the crevice of the cream sofa in his rectangular room. His blue cotton scrubs were wrinkled like the skin under his eyes.

She snapped off the recess lighting shining on the crown of his head like a halo. The saucer shaped lights and egg white wallpaper were two of her mother's projects that had finished according to Fatma's high standards. The small touches masked the concrete walls most of the local houses were made from.

"Ah, for your room, we'll do gold," she said, her eyes gleaming with the success of the new gate installation.

"Yellow," Maryam had retorted.

"The house is going to look like a cupcake," her father grumbled.

Remodeling was latest fashion among local women with the introduction of shops on the decline in the west. How to explain to her mother that Laura Ashley was the favorite of octogenarians in the South of the United States? Or that Ikea was for poor college students? That was according to Mike's latest reply when she had sent a Snapchat of the stacks of catalogs. Nasser's space was the calmest in the house, without any of the floral arrangements or gilt-edged furniture in the rest of the rooms. White walls, white sheets, his cherry wood wardrobe gleaming in the corner. This was like the hospital he spent so many hours in.

On her way to the door, Maryam stumbled on pencil, breaking it half. "Ouch!"

Maryam gathered the pieces, knocking over a pile of books.

"I'm coming!" Nasser bolted up.

"Everything's fine, doctor." She giggled at the hair standing up all over the crown of his head.

"Oh." Nasser fell back onto the sofa, his hands clasping his chest. "I thought I was late for rounds."

Maryam righted the books, trying to keep the glossy-coated journals from slipping out of the stack.

"Were you looking for me?"

"Get some sleep," she said. Like a rising tide, she felt sadness well in her when she imagined the look on her hardworking brother's face if she failed out school.

"What's Amal writing about?"

Maryam paused in re-stacking. "Huh?"

"You know, your bestie from high school, the girl with the Ghandi glasses. Didn't she go to uni with you, next Arab Oprah or something." He was on his side, head on the armrest, tracking her movements. "I assume you came here looking for the magic beans to grow an assignment."

"She doesn't wear those anymore," Maryam barked. "She got lenses."

He ducked, putting his hands around his head. "Sore spot, I see, sorry, sorry."

"Anyway, these days she's all about writing positive stories about how great the country is and the problems aren't the government's fault but problems the enforcement of the rule of law."

"Trouble in bestie paradise?"

"Something like that."

"Have you made any new friends?"

"Leave me alone."

He opened his mouth to say more.

"I'm not a kid anymore."

"Interviews," Nasser said, his eyes fluttering closed. "Always start by interviewing the patient."

She left, giving up on the stack of books that toppled, despite her best efforts. "No patients will talk to me." Maryam retorted, but only after she shut the door.

She ambled through the east wing of the house, avoiding the study and ladies' living room, in case either of her parents were home. Her feet, slippered in house shoes, slid from area rugs her father had collected on business trips to India over marble. Groupings of armchairs in the smaller living room were placed around framed photos of her grandfather and father as young men. Maryam skirted the heart of the house, the foyer, a completely open space where you could see anyone entering, leaving, or lingering on the upstairs landing. If Nasser was a dead end, there were other options.

~~~

She made her way around the perimeter of the house. A green strip of grass ran alongside the exterior, marking the house off the grey brick courtyard. She came up short at Babu's room, a purpose-built cement structure at the back of the property, hidden by the three floors of the main house. The maroon trim running the top of the room had been her mother's idea.

There were plants growing along in the shaded space between the room and the exterior boundary wall. Some type of fruit. *Mangoes*? Maryam touched the plant that was bent with the weight of the lump of fruit, the thin stalk straining to keep it a few inches above the ground.

She picked at something with short leaves and a sharp aroma filled her nostrils. Babu's patch of grass said more about him than the few words about his persona life they had exchanged in as many years. She retreated to sit on the cement step in front of the room.

Maryam hadn't been in the car with Babu for weeks. He was out whenever she left for university, which meant she had to wake up Nasser, recovering from the nightshift, to get a ride to university.

Maryam sprang up as the older man ambled around the corner from the main house. "You will take me to the camps."

Babu stopped, his eyes looking right and left.

"I have to go." She stomped her foot as she had when a child, asking for candy at the neighborhood convenience shop. "Now."

"Madam called me, I—"

Maryam followed him into his room. Babu whirled around but she was taller and already in the doorway. Her eyes adjusted to the yellowish light from the ceiling. There was a bed in the corner with plaid sheets, her mother's doing. On the wall by the bed was a sheet of photos, made into a collage with pieces of tape.

They were alternating images of Maryam when she was younger with another girl, darker in skin, same big eyes, growing up alongside her, at least photographically. In garang'o costume, the children's festival for Ramadan, Maryam smiled next to the little girl who was wearing a hot pink party dress. Interspersed between snapshots of Maryam in the garden at the nursery were photos of the girl's twin braids hanging over a blue pinafore. The last one of her high school graduation, before Maryam began wearing *hijab* and the other girl was festooned in flowers, eyes rimmed with kohl, sitting demurely next to a man as family crowded around them.

"Is that your daughter?" Maryam drew closer, recognizing Babu's nose, reinterpreted as more petite and less bulbous on the younger woman's face.

"We go now," Babu stammered. He had his hands out at his sides as if holding the photos back on the wall. "We go now, we no tell anyone." His voice shook.

Maryam hovered in the doorway. Part of her wanted to sit down and flip through those photos again and ask Babu what he had been doing when each of them were taken. Had he been driving her around the day of his daughter's wedding?

"You no tell Sir or Madam about this. And I take you. Now." He jiggled the key in front of her, eyes wide.

"Okay," Maryam said. She backed away from the wall of photos. If her mother knew, she would send Babu on the next flight to India. "We go now."

~~~

The engines of dump trucks growled like hungry beasts. A line of potbellied cement trucks waited their turn, shuddering on the side of the road. Her GMC bumped along the road, knocking Maryam's head on the ceiling. Sand kicked up by their movement swirled in tendrils between the vehicles.

"Sorry, Madam," Babu mumbled.

"Slow down." Maryam slid on her seatbelt. At the next pothole, she gripped the handle above her head.

"Sorry."

Out here, on the perimeter of the city, there were hardly any streetlights. The larger car shops had floodlights, illuminating Honda or Volvo, but that had been several blocks ago. Now the streets were narrow, the buildings made of crumbling graying concrete. Through the tinted windows of the SUV, she could make out wire antennas on squat roofs like the ones she had seen on houses in the mountains of Lebanon. There were blue street signs on the corners of whatever building happened to be on the end of each street.

Every two hundred meters or so, they came into anarchy, a four-way intersection without a signal or stop light. The biggest vehicle won, and that put them at a major disadvantage. Cement mixers, dump trucks, and eighteen-wheelers filled the major arteries, trying to get to their docking stations. Their drivers were engaged in a machinery version of chicken fighting, each careening into the empty intersection without applying their breaks. The oncoming traffic gave way.

Babu muttered under his breath, Maryam assumed swearing in Hindi, as the higher lights of an oncoming vehicle flashed across their cabin, temporarily blinding them both.

Maryam blocked the glare with one hand and squinted. "We need to stop outside Street 45."

"We're almost there."

How he knew, she had no idea. Each street more or less resembled another, as though they were engaged in a competition to see which could be more derelict. Everywhere she could see, men were walking, either in blue overalls, the top halves folded around their waists to expose dingy T-shirts, or long cotton skirts marked in faded plaid, with undershirts overtop their rotund bellies. Eyeing the shadows of the passing men, Maryam pressed against the doorframe, checking to make sure the doors were locked.

Professor Paul will be impressed I made it all the way out here, Maryam thought. Then she remembered that he really wanted a story. Paul was not like her female relatives, who would be shocked she had ventured this far from the highway without her stand-in chaperone, the housemaid. No, he wanted an un-gettable get.

She fingered her phone, which would double as her voice recorder. There were no bars for signal. The vehicle rocked to a stop.

"Here?" Babu asked.

They had stopped across the street from the entrance to the worker accommodation for her father's company. What Maryam could see in glimpses, as buses kept rolling by, looked like an anthill. There were men streaming from the buses outside the gates, blocking the guard station, backlit by lights mounted on the top of the building facing the street. They were dressed alike, and of such similar build and height that they blended, one into the other, like an endless column. The bus driver hunched over a wheel the size of the GMC's tires, his eyes closed as if the effort to get everyone offsite had been his only animation.

Maryam took a deep breath. *I'm fine,* she reminded herself. *This is the safest country in the world, and I can get home any time I want.*

At the sound of the door opening, Babu turned to her, his eyes wide in alarm. "Madam, where are you going?"

"Inside." Maryam exuded more confidence than she felt. The SUV's mechanized running board hummed into place. She hovered on it for a second before stepping on the dirt beneath.

"No, no, no, no." Babu climbed down. "This not allowed."

Maryam shut the door and walked toward the guard station, knowing that Babu would not touch her. Most of the men had filed inside the compound. A few stragglers lumbered toward the accommodation. With the edges of her *abaya* swirling in the dust, she strode across the street, thankful she had worn her Converse. The guard took a step back in surprise when she rapped on the window of the office.

"Yes?" There were three of them.

"I'm Sheikha Maryam." She swallowed, clenching and unclenching her hands behind her back. "And I want to see our facility."

The men looked at each other. One had a handlebar mustache that he smoothed on either side before speaking. "No one is—"

"I own this camp! My family does and I will see it now."

Babu arrived, out of breath, next to her. He exchanged words with the guards, and both men becoming grew more and more animated. She knew their dilemma. It was the dilemma of servants all over the country. If they let her in, they could be in trouble later, but if they didn't let her in, there would be trouble with her right now.

The back door to the office was cracked. Another guard came in, taking a step back when he saw Maryam.

"I call supervisor." the first reached for his phone.

"No, it's fine. I'll be very quick." She darted through the exit before anyone else could say a word. Babu called out for her, but she kept going, stepping down the concrete blocks assembled as a dismount from the portable building.

A distinct splash sent fetid water shin high on her *abaya*. Maryam saw smaller pools, glinting green in the intermittent light, scattered around the ground in front of a squat two-story structure that looked more like a forgotten motel at the bottom of an aquarium than a place anyone would want to live.

Her heart sank at the sight of so many blue uniforms hanging up on the guardrail out front. This was how they dried their clothes?

She moved quickly to the nearest staircase lest Babu lead a charge of people after her. There was a door open on the main floor. Without a glance to the left or right, she entered. She put her hand to her mouth to obscure the odor, like wet socks and overripe onions.

The room was concrete, with light blue gas tanks on the floor plugged into hot plates on the counter. Nearly all the surfaces were tinged black, as if there had been a fire. And, she realized, there *had* been dozens of little ones, likely on a daily basis. She saw discarded skillets, and a large, two-handled pot that had once been red. A flashlight, the protective cover of which had broken or long been discarded, hung from a socket on the wall and offered the only light. Hot oil and spices had spattered the wall a few meters high. Blue tape held together the top of the pipe descending from the ceiling.

Maryam breathed lightly, not wanting to take in any more air than necessary. This was a kitchen, where the men cooked. She took a series of photos on her phone, without the flash or pausing to focus. Maryam heard voices outside passing by and swept from the room. She took a left, away from the front entrance, toward the back staircase. Her long legs allowed her to descend two steps at a time, moving soundlessly through the unlit stairwell. She shivered at the sound of insects scuttling alongside her.

At the back of the building, no light from the street or the office filtered in. The doors were shut under a low roof that looked like a sulking lip. She tripped on a knot of discarded plastic bags, catching herself before she fell, scraping her hand on the unfinished concrete.

I should go home, she thought. *Yuba would kill me if he knew I was here.* She turned to go, sucking the knuckle of her forefinger where spots of blood were appearing.

"Where is she? Find her!" Footsteps sounded from the other side of the stairwell.

A door to the right was open. Maryam ducked into the room, slipping against the wall. There were bunk beds pressed up against the wall, and eight or so men—it was hard to tell as they were mostly the same size—clustered in the middle.

The black metal frames of the beds reminded her of the maids' quarters at home, only mattresses on these had no cushioned pads or linens from Zara Home. In fact, she saw as she leaned closer, there were no linens at all. And there was a mattress underneath each of the beds, bringing the count up to ten men in total, she realized. Someone slept on the floor, the bulk of the man above pressing into his face. Her stomach turned. She shouldn't have come, but here she was.

Maryam fished out her phone and snapped a photo. The white glare of the flash froze the intense discussion in the middle of the room. She swore inwardly.

"Sorry!" she said brightly, hoping her English would scare them off. "Accident."

Three men turned toward her, their pupils dilated from the phone's flashlight. She must have bumped it on when she pulled it out.

As she went to turn it off, the other men jostled to cover up whatever lay on the ground.

"What is that?" She moved forward.

"You go." Someone stepped in her way. "No place for woman."

Maryam towered over him. "I know." From her position, she could see a worker's sprawled body, his limbs splayed as if he had fallen from one of the desert bikes her brothers rode on the weekend. "Is he hurt?" Her grip tightened on her phone. "We should call an ambulance."

The man attempting to block her view moved toward her. "Not hurt. You go now."

Maryam stepped back, the intensity of his eyes reminding her that although she was the tallest in the room, she was the only woman. He advanced, and she had no choice but to retreat until the handle of the door bumped her in the back.

"Madam." Babu's desperate voice echoed down the hall.

"Here," she whispered. She gripped the door handle, flinging it open.

There was Babu, the collar of his orange short-sleeve shirt askew, his hair standing on end. She had never been so happy to see his jowls in her life, not even when she was a child and he had stopped by the local hypermarket so she could select her favorite candy in secret.

"Something's going on in here," Maryam said. "One of the guys is hurt."

Babu's gaze flicked beyond her to the man standing in the doorway. "You come now."

She stepped into the exterior hallway. "But ask them. Please."

Babu exchanged a terse greeting with the man while Maryam adjusted her *shayla,* which had slipped to the back of her head.

"Let's go," Babu said.

"But what happened to that man?"

Babu took her by the arm, surprising her with the force of his grip as much as the contact. He propelled her toward the stairwell.

"Babu? Should we call an ambulance?"

He shook his head, lips tight.

"Babu!" She shook off his arm on the second step of the stairs. "What is going on?"

In the semi-dark she couldn't see his eyes, though they were almost nose-to-nose.

"He's hurt."

"What?" Maryam pounded down the stairs after her driver, who had picked up his pace.

"Maybe dead."

"Did they kill him? How did he die? What happened?"

"I don't know. These men, fighting always. We go now."

They were brought up short by the sight of the police car outside the office.

"Tonight I lose my job twice." Babu groaned. "And then I lose my head."

"If the police are here, then there's —"

"Ah, Madam, you need to hide." He pushed Maryam into the kitchen at the foot of the stairs.

Chapter Nine

Ali's phone vibrated across the dashboard, alerting him to dozens of unanswered messages. The SUV inched along the main artery of the business district. Steel and glass skyscrapers towered forty or fifty floors above him, the floor to ceiling windows glinting.

An elevated metal tunnel, a few feet wide, ran parallel to the road. This was a mini version of the train that would take the hundreds of office workers home and off the streets. For now though, the tunnel was a system to move the dirt dredged up to make space for the underground transit.

And Ali was stuck in the middle of rush hour. He idled at a red light, gazing at a building shaped like the helmet of ancient warriors, dropped over an entirely glass structure. The chain-link covering provided a screen against the unrelenting sun. He smirked at the blunt, curved top. Maybe you needed a dirty mind to see these things. Or maybe he had body parts on the mind. He looked away.

The building next to it was shaped like the funnel of a tornado, blue windows crisscrossed with metal girders. Ali squinted at ropes dangling from the top of the building. A man, no—several men—dangled in harnesses, their blue overalls pricks of color, swaying back and forth against the glass. *So there are worse places to be than stuck behind people who don't know how to drive.*

Ali turned the air conditioning vent so he felt the blast brush his stubble. He could grow it out and fit in with many of the other traffic officers, hairs curling on their cheeks. The phone persisted with an insistent buzz like the sound of trapped bee. His cousin Hassan wanted to know where Ali was, what he had eaten for lunch, and when he was coming to the *majlis*. If Ali declined another invitation, what he was doing instead.

The fatigue of the day pulled at his eyelids. Since his new assignment, he felt as though he had been dodging rubber bullets in training, not seeing to actual police work. He squinted as an orange-ish fog blanketed the road. Exactly what he needed—a *shamal*, an unseasonal dust storm, that would turn congested roads to gridlock.

He drummed his fingers on the wheel. White SUVs were swerving to the right, into the emergency lane, and overtaking the smaller sedans. *You're not fifteen anymore,* he thought, the memory of the boy on the bridge floating before him. Technically, he had the right to fine these drivers. That was the result of his military training.

The phone continued to dance, dropping into the console between the seats. He glanced at it. The station.

Ali groaned. He looked up at the SUV's ceiling. If only there were a vial of patience hanging there. He could no longer make out the men dangling in their moronic task. Yet, he knew, they were still there. If they were lucky. He grit his teeth. Ah for a knife with which he could stab out his eye and thereby avoid answering.

"*Salam alkieum.*"

"*Alkieum a salam.*" The captain rushed through the greeting. "You've got to get to Street 45 now."

"I'm on the other side of town." Ali resented the way his voice rose like a boy in a fight with his father. "Plus, my duty is finished." *Call someone else to do the prostitute patrol.*

The Industrial Area housed most of the laborers brought in to work on the country's infrastructure. For years this had meant widening streets, erecting skyscrapers, and building malls. Now it meant hundreds of men arrived every day to assemble the Olympic stadiums.

With them came low-level crime, contained among their countrymen, on the fringes of the city. Bootleg alcohol made from cleaning supplies and housemaids making extra riyals on desperate men. These were the two most frequent worker related incidents.

"It's a death."

Green lights turned to yellow flashing ones, signaling the red was next. The driver two cars in front of Ali halted, reluctant to risk a two thousand dollar ticket for running the signal.

"It was yellow!" He slammed on his brakes. The red Sunny immediately in front skidded to a stop but not before his fender kissed the bumper of a black Mercedes with a smack.

"Where?"

"Street 45." The captain's voice carried a tinge of impatience. "Get over there to the MBJ workers, and phone in after your interviews." The call ended without any further information.

The drivers were out of their vehicles. A man in the white robes of a local gesticulated at the young woman in a skimpy tank top and black leggings.

Ali decided not to stop. He had done his duty by fender benders for the week.

Ali angled the nose of the SUV into the emergency lane. After a few minutes, he pulled the entire vehicle in, incrementally increasing the pressure on the gas until the odometer read 120km. Neither of them had said it, but Ali knew the reason the captain had called him and not the Criminal Investigation Department was because all their files were checked and reviewed on a monthly basis by human rights organizations.

"You coming?"

Ali started when the sound of his cousin's voice filled the SUV. Hassan's number was up on the Bluetooth screen. He must have accidentally hit a button on the phone while talking to the captain, routing all future calls to the car's speakers.

"*La*," Ali said, using the curt Arabic no. Next to him, a blond in a Range Rover was shaking her head as he sped past. "Police!" he yelled, though his windows were closed.

She flinched, turning away her frosted pink lips and massive sunglasses.

"What?"

"Police business," Ali said to Hassan in a normal tone.

"Oh. What's going on? Accident?"

"I can't talk about it. I have to go outside the city," he added, in case Hassan persisted. Heading to the scene of an accident could be a popular pastime for people with little else to do but drink endless cups of coffee at Starbucks and harass women in lingerie shops.

"Fine, but tomorrow—"

"I'll call you back." Ali punched the disconnect button on the steering wheel. The highway curved under him, one branch extending right, the other left. He increased his speed on the straightaway, past the dozens of furniture shops, situated next to each other in the old style of a *souq* or market, where similar items were grouped together.

Ornate living room arrangements with brocade upholstery and gilt edges littered the storefronts. He kept speeding away from the center of the city, the skyscrapers of downtown disappearing from his rearview mirror. Swirling purple graffiti flashed by in the underpass, created by an artist flown in especially for the purpose. The Arabic scripted calligraphy was acceptable public art. No human forms to offend Islamic sensibilities.

Expect Amazing! He swept by an outdated Olympic bid campaign billboard as the SUV crested the highway exit. Four empty lanes ushered him toward the Industrial Area, a place of garages and worker camps. Most of the heavy duty trucks were sheltered for the night already, their drivers having lined them up on the empty dirt lots scattered throughout the area where workers lived and garages fixed crashed cars.

His phone buzzed. "MBJ camp" flashed on the screen. Ali narrowed his eyes in the encroaching darkness. He pulled off the highway, into the rabbit warren of neighborhood streets, cursing as he hit a pothole. The pavement here was broken in places, bumpy in others, worn away by the unending volume of cement trucks, dump trucks, and other heavy machinery.

Here you could see the scale of a country under construction. Rows of diggers of various sizes, their yellow dulled by dust, were lined up next to bulldozers and eighteen-wheelers. This was like an encampment of sleeping building materials.

"Pay attention," he said as the SUV bounced into another crevice.

Out here there were few streetlights, so he switched to high beams, blinding some guys who had been sitting on a dilapidated sofa propped against a low unfinished wall. They scattered like baby camels, frightened by the purr of his engine. The pristine white Nissan meant someone with money.

Ali pulled up to the camp's gate, thankful to be in uniform. "Police."

The MBJ holding was bigger than most of the worker housing, which was usually a few buildings grouped together and shared by dozens of men. Gated entry was unusual, but if the company was big enough, maybe they wanted to keep them separate from the thousands of other workers housed in the area.

Fights were known to break out between those of different nationalities. Theft was rampant and rarely reported. Many of the men outside the makeshift holding area may have overstayed their residency permits, having fallen out with their sponsors. A scan of the doors told Ali there were hundreds of men housed here.

"Sir," the guard stammered.

"Let me in," Ali growled.

The chain-link gate creaked open. He pulled behind the improvised guard building, a clay-colored porta-cabin raised on a concrete platform with two double windows facing opposite directions, one onto the road, the other the interior of the housing.

The guard was hovering at the driver side door, so Ali had to open the door carefully to avoid hitting him. He towered over him, a slight man of indeterminable age, head full of black hair, eyes lifting up at the sides, like the ends of an almond. Ali placed him as Nepalese. He wore the standard white shirt and black trousers, his belt cinched around a waist his sisters would have envied.

"Where is it?"

The guard's wide eyes darted to Ali's face, the whites expanding.

"The body, where is it?" Ali said more slowly. Usually the Group Four guys, the ones in uniform all over the city, had better English than most. But, as Ali knew all too well, there were always duds.

"We didn't know she was here."

"It's a woman?" Ali swore mentally. Now he would have to solve a homicide and prostitution.

"No," the man stammered. He cowered, somehow making himself even smaller.

"Out with it." Ali's voice rose. "Where is the body, and what was a woman doing out here?"

"There!" Someone shouted from the second story of the building across from them. "That way."

Ali ran. He didn't have a gun—who needed one in the police station? The sand burned the lining of his throat. Concrete bit into his shoes. He dodged gaping holes here and there. A few other guards were pointing to the building to his right. Ali curved like an arrow toward the stairwell.

He ran smack into a dark figure, slight—maybe a boy, judging by the cry with which he fell away from Ali. There was an older man, an Indian with black slacks and a button-down shirt, who threw himself in front of Ali.

"You!" Ali shoved the man against the wall, hearing a sharp crack as the man's body hit the rough surface. "Don't move." His stomach flip-flopped at the thought of the boy with this man.

All the stories he had heard about the Industrial Area came flashing back.

They were child's fables, ones told to keep you close to you mother's embrace, about someone, a woman or man, who wanted to steal children. When you were a child, you never asked why. Your eyes would be round with fear as your grandmother or auntie told you about these stolen children, chubby and misbehaved, never seen again. Ali assumed they were always eaten. As an adult, he knew differently.

"Come here." He lowered his voice. "I won't hurt you."

The boy crouched, scooting backward, the black and white sneakers visible in the light from the courtyard.

"I won't hurt you," Ali repeated. "Come."

Behind him, the man bent over, groaning. The boy clutched the wall, the delicate wrist pushing until he could stand.

Ali noted with mounting horror that the "boy," whom he had originally assumed to be around thirteen or fourteen, was in fact a very tall woman, whose angular face showed her equal dismay. She gathered the folds of her *abaya* around her, avoiding eye contact.

"What—"

"We were leaving." She swept past him.

Ali stepped aside, at the same time catching the arm of the man who was moving away from the wall. "Can't you find somewhere closer to home to have your fun?"

The woman's dark eyes, with eyelashes as spindly as a spider's legs, flashed at him. "Don't be disgusting. He's as old as my father."

"Disgusting? Do you know where you are?" Ali spread his arms, dropping the trembling limb of the Indian, who he now realized was the woman's driver.

He swiveled around to reassure himself she was the crazy one, and saw they had an audience. The other guards were a few feet away. Men had come to the railing across from them, dozens of eyes watching like they were animals in a zoo.

Prostitution was the second most frequent crime among the laborers, though it was usually Filipina women. There were stories, Ali knew. Rumors circulated about a Land Cruiser full of local women who prowled the Industrial Area looking for men they could experiment on, paying for the pleasure. This one was alone.

"There's a body." Her shoulders slumped. The defiance seemed to drain from her. Ali saw again the signs of youth that had first caused him to think she was a teenage boy. She may not have been thirteen, but she wasn't much older. Seventeen, he guessed by the sound of her voice, then he glanced away, embarrassed when his eyes instinctively sought out curves beneath her *abaya* for confirmation.

"Where?" He dragged the driver with him into the nearest open door, figuring she couldn't leave without him.

This caused another flurry of activity from the guards behind him. Ali entered the room to find seven men crouched on filthy mattresses. He steeled himself against the stench of so many unwashed bodies.

"There," she said. "When I came in here to hide, he was like that."

The man was in the standard blue jumpsuit. But for the angle of his head, you might think he was sleeping, not fortunate enough to have a bed. Ali stomped on a cockroach heading toward the body. He opened his mouth to apologize. His sisters would have screamed in horror at the spattered remains.

The girl ignored the cockroach. She was transfixed with sympathy for the other men in the room. Ali had seen such gazes of pity from children for the Eid goat before slaughter.

Ali's phone rang. "Probably heart attack, or exhaustion from heat." He scanned the worn faces of the men around them. His uniform was already sticking to his underarms. "I'll get him to the morgue."

"Maybe one of them did it." Her voice was husky, like she'd been crying. The smell of *oud*, flowery, hung in the air. Ali remembered he had two problems.

"What were you doing here?" He switched to Arabic. He resisted the urge to empty the room. Where would these men go? This dingy room was all they had.

"I came to interview someone. Maybe we will volunteer here. These men need help."

Ali snorted. "Local girls don't volunteer."

Her eyes flashed. "I do. We don't all want to make cupcakes or *abayas*."

In her reply, he heard the hint of an accent, someone unfamiliar with the inflections of vowels in the local dialect. "Your mother's American?" This would also explain the do-gooding non-frivolous tendencies.

"No," she retorted, the full force of her attention washing over him like a breeze.

"Ah, American educated." He was finally fitting the puzzle pieces toge-

84

ther. "You wanted to talk to someone for your blog?"

"My class assignment."

The door cracked open. The Group Four guys peered in.

"You need to get out of here." Ali motioned her to the doorway. "Before the foreman comes."

That seemed to get her attention. Her hands swept the crown of her head, drawing her headscarf under her chin. There was a long black strand of hair across her forehead. He resisted the urge to tell her to cover it. He was nothing to her, after all, not her father or brother or husband. "Out," he repeated, wondering where that last association had come from. His cousins had been married by her age, of course, many of them with their first child a year later.

"Won't you ask them what happened?" She moved toward the door, her driver trailing her, clutching his rib. "They should send a doctor."

"I know what to do," he said. "I'll take care of this."

"I thought it was all lies." She stared at the men leaning against the railing, who turned away when her eyes landed on them. "All those articles. But now..." She caught a sob in her throat. "This is our camp."

In the courtyard, he leaned in to catch the last whispered confession and peered more closely.

"You're Jaber's daughter?"

She drew away, as if he had slapped her. "You know my father."

"You know mine." He laughed. "You're probably too young to have met him, *Allahyerhamah*." He sobered up when realizing her age. "We're cousins. Our grandmothers are sisters."

Her stricken look said she wasn't amused at the coincidence.

"Take him to the doctor." Ali gestured to the driver and covered the tail end of his smile with a cough. "His rib is probably broken. Tell them—"

"He fell." She swept him with the kind of look he reserved for petty criminals.

For the first time, Ali realized she wasn't craning her neck to look at him, but meeting his gaze. She nodded, turning, taking the driver's arm in hers. He protested, but she supported the older man, matching her gait to his shorter one as they shuffled toward the entrance.

"Get him up." Ali shouted above the voices rising behind him. "We have to take him to the morgue." *May God grant him peace,* Ali prayed as they turned the prone figure over. The boyish face couldn't have been much older than the girl who had left.

Glass clinked as a man stuffed an object behind a pillowcase on the lower bunk. "Show me," Ali said sharply.

The slight man, several heads shorter than Ali, shuffled forward as the other occupants shrank away. He produced a squat bottle of cologne that read *Luma* in cursive script. Ali exhaled. The man's eyes were red rimmed, his pupils unfocused.

"Don't drink this." Ali took the bottle from the man's limp hand, which gave it up without protest. "This bad." Ali turned in a circle, holding the cologne above his head like a trophy. "Bad for eyes, bad for remembering." Ali pointed at his eyes and head.

The men looked at their shoes.

"If you get really bad bottle, you die." He thumped his heart to indicate it would stop beating.

The men's eyes were wide, like the sheep stacked in the back of a pick-up truck, driven through the city from the farm to the butcher.

The ring of Ali's cell phone burst through his dark thoughts, which were wavering between pity and disgust. "Captain Ali." The pause on the other end reminded Ali this was not a title he could use. "Yes," he said, to cover his dismay.

"This is Khalifa."

"Sir." Ali kicked at a stone on the lip of the sidewalk.

"Have you reported to MBJ camp?"

"Yes." Ali gazed at the laundry hanging on the string draped in front of the doors. "One body, appears to be poor health. No signs of distress."

"This is an Internal Security matter," Khalifa intoned. "I asked them to send you rather than a regular officer. Keep me informed."

Ali's heart thudded. Was the captain saying this was his way to prove he was worthy of the ISF?

"I need eyes and ears in the Industrial Area," Khalifa continued. "The human rights agencies keep harping about these double contracts and upholding the law. You're trained. You keep me informed when there's something new."

The call ended. Hope fluttered in Ali's chest like a caged butterfly.

Chapter Ten

Sanjana handed the driver of the aquamarine taxi a fifty-*riyal* note, holding it at one edge so as not brush his fingers. He took it, flicking her a glance in the rearview mirror. The red numbers on the meter showed fifteen. She cracked the window, hoping fresh air, however humid, would ease the smell of stale cigarettes and unwashed man. Someone had scratched F^&* into the back of the headrest in front of her.

"No change." His mustache was thick, curving down toward his chin. "Sorry." He ran his fingers across the ends of the mustache while turning to give her a direct glance.

"I need change," she replied in Hindi, shrinking away from him. "To go home."

The driver fingered the flat bill, wider than a dollar or Nepali currency. "I wait for you, sister." His milky skin made it difficult to place his origins, but she would have guessed from his accented Hindi a South Indian state, maybe Kerala.

Sanjana preferred African drivers who couldn't tell the difference between Indians and Nepalese, and therefore thought she was a beautiful descendant of Bollywood actresses, serenading her with old film songs. Those from the sub-continent considered her beneath them, but used the sister card to try to build a sense of solidarity.

She bit her lip. "Too much money, you running the meter."

He turned off the engine. "I not charge." The red digits were frozen at fifteen.

The gates in front of the villa that served as the Nepali Embassy opened.

Have you seen Sharif? The school call and left message. He not go today.

Not now, she shouted at Analyn in her mind. *I can't take care of everyone. I'm already failing at mine.*

"Fine," she said, "but no meter for waiting."

No, sorry. She managed to reply. Analyn was going to be angry but Sanjana had to keep her mind on finding Manu. Her plan to apply for other jobs would have to wait. She jumped out of the taxi, rushing across the street. She had to be back and ready with lunch before Madam Cindy's exercise class finished.

Men milled around the entrance, their skin as dark as hers. Their eyes traveled over Sanjana's red blouse and black skirt. She didn't have to wear a uniform like the other Nepalese or Indonesian maids she saw in the malls and grocery stores. Sanjana thanked her horoscope every time she passed them, laden with bags and carrying the drinks of their employers who sashayed a few steps ahead.

She entered the embassy compound, past the beige cement boundary wall and the black metal gate. Entering the government facility made her more nervous than the men eyeing her like a piece of meat. There was no way anyone would know what had happened to her family, Sir had reassured her over and over again. Her father's name had not been on a list, like those of the teachers and shop owners in the village. What had happened to him was an accident. Bad luck. Ill-fated stars.

Once over the threshold, Sanjana crossed a tiled courtyard in front of a two-story house. She could make out the word "Visas" on a tattered vinyl sign above a side entrance on the right in Arabic, English, and Nepalese lettering. The wooden front door to the main part of the house was closed, shapes flickering behind a glass mosaic. For the moment, she was alone in the courtyard, but the sounds of car doors opening and closing filtered in from the street. She rushed toward the visa entrance.

The bigger countries had purpose-built properties. She had been stunned the first time Madam Cindy had driven by the American Embassy, casually pointing out the bending palm trees and arched windows rising above a walled property the size of their entire neighborhood. The Nepali Embassy, a converted local house with grounds minus vegetation like palm trees or bougainvillea, was much more modest, like an auntie who had fallen asleep after her meal. The visa area was in the smaller part of the house. The ambassador saved the main part to greet guests and hold official gatherings— though what kind of guests the Nepali ambassador could have, Sanjana was not sure.

She went to the Plexiglas window around the reception desk, leaning forward, waiting for the man who was writing in Nepalese to look up. He kept writing, his thin fingers moving a black pen across a stack of papers.

The men who had been lounging in the shade outside moved into the room behind her. They skipped the reception area, sitting on the curved plastic chairs, clutching various papers.

A bank of desks on the far wall faced the room at large, more Plexiglas sectioning between the visitors and the embassy employees with semi-circular cutouts at the bottom to pass documents back and forth. Each station had a handwritten sign with labels like "Contracts" or "Visas." Everyone in this part of the embassy was a man. She was the only woman, perhaps in the entire embassy.

Sanjana cleared her throat. Surely he could feel her gaze since she hadn't moved for several minutes.

"We'll be waiting all day." A man's voice boomed behind her in clipped British tones.

Sanjana and the clerk flinched. She could see how young the clerk was in the unlined thinness of his face. He couldn't be much older than Manu. Her heart clenched at the thought, wishing her brother could be as easy to find as this embassy clerk.

The clerk's eyes shot past her to the white man and his wife. Sanjana could see their outlines in her periphery. "Yes?" he said, his voice filled with impatience, his eyes on the couple.

"She was here first."

Sanjana took another step forward, grateful he hadn't pushed past her like so many other Europeans did when given half the chance.

"I look for my brother." She pushed the passport copy of Manu and his approved work visa under the opening.

"You housemaid?" the clerk asked, his hands unmoving.

"I'm looking for Laxmi Pande." Sanjana switched to Nepalese.

The man's narrowed gaze was why she had hoped Madam Cindy would take her to the embassy. Her whiteness would have shamed him into being helpful.

"She not here," he replied in English. "She not working for embassy. Only her husband."

"My brother missing. He here for three weeks. I no see him," Sanjana managed in the English he was forcing her to speak. She pressed the paper

Sir had left on his desk, the one with Manu's entry date and government seal.

"That's terrible," the woman murmured behind her.

"Miss Laxmi, she arrange contract for him."

The clerk picked up Manu's documents from the steel tray under the opening. There was no nametag for her to record a name, like Sir Paul had asked her to do before he left on his trip. He would have come with her, but he had to go to a conference in Paris. Busy. Everyone was busy.

"Contracts." The clerk tossed the paper back at her.

"This not contract?" The woman had supplied this document when Sanjana visited the embassy, looking for a job for Manu. The woman had promised an office job as a kitchen service man—boy as they were called here—where he would bring water, tea, coffee, or juice to those having meetings.

The man turned in his chair and tapped the window in the direction of one of the stations in the main room. "Contracts, there. Go see contracts."

Sanjana picked up the copies of the visa and passport, the only tangible proof she had that her brother had made plans to join her in the Arabian Gulf. She moved through the rows of chairs to the counter the receptionist had indicated. There were two men here, one seated, the other standing and pointing out something in a stack of papers. Similar stacks rose like towers on every surface of the room, some in chairs as well. The men stopped talking when she approached.

"My brother." She pressed the papers forward again. "I no hear from my brother." The two men shared a glance. The seated one, about the receptionist's age if she had to guess, picked the papers up one by one, reading and then passing them to his colleague, an older man whose shirt was beginning to strain at his stomach.

"Where is he?" the older man asked in Nepali. Sanjana let the entire story tumble out in the comfort of her mother tongue.

"We spoke a month ago, before he was to come. He came to work for MBJ in an office. Like you." She ventured a small smile.

The seated clerk took the papers from the older man. "Where's the contract?"

Sanjana shook her head. "He has it. They asked me for the passport copy only and gave me the visa to send to him."

"Who?" The older man leaned his hands on the desk, jutting his chin forward.

"Ms. Pande's agency," she said. "One day, they said come if you are looking for work."

The younger clerk folded the papers in half. Sanjana stifled a small cry of protest as he pressed a crease right across Manu's face.

"Come." The older man stepped around the corner of the counter. Sanjana followed him into the back hallway. Here were a series of offices—smaller bedrooms converted into working spaces, with tables and chairs, phones, and a fax machine. "She's looking for family," he said to two women seated at desks facing each other. "Open a file."

A woman in a red sari took out a legal size blue ledger. "Name?"

"Manu." Sanjana pressed the paperwork onto the desk.

Red nail polish matched the woman's sari. Gold bangles jangled as her hand moved across the page. Name. Passport number. Expiration date. The other woman pushed a set of glasses back up her nose and kept stamping a large stack of papers.

"We'll call you." The older man handed Sanjana's papers back.

She smiled. "Thank you."

Neither woman looked up. Sanjana left the embassy, her steps lighter than when she had entered.

Her phone buzzed with a text from her pocket. *You sure your boy go to school today? Maybe they together.*

Someone else knew that Manu was here, somewhere in the city, and would help her find him. She squinted in the glare of the morning desert sun, painting everything below in flashes of brilliant light.

Will check when I home. Sanjana groaned at her mistake. Sure enough, Analyn had spotted the opening.

You where? Not at home?

The taxi was nowhere to be seen.

Chapter Eleven

Sunlight streamed past the gauzy white curtains. Cindy was under a purple satin blanket, cozy and warm, but someone wrapped a metallic sheet around her, the foil creasing.

"The baby," she said to the unseen person who tucked the foil around her feet as though she were a burrito on a warming plate. "Please, is the baby okay?"

The fans buzzed on, the hum resonating with the shivers racking her body, shooting out hot air at incremental inches around her limbs. At the hissing sound, she gave a convulsive shudder. Cindy had been here before. She had lost a baby last year. Tears streamed down her face. She ached for her husband, who was embedded with troops in Afghanistan. *Paul!*

Cindy started awake. Friday. She reclined against the eggplant-colored pillows, waiting for her pulse to return to normal. Paul was traveling to Europe for a steering group negotiating another ten-year contract for the university. And Daniel was…She pulled herself out of bed. She hadn't seen him since he left for the basketball game last night. The screen on her phone was blank. Whatever time he had returned, he had not checked in.

"Daniel?" She stood at the top of the stairs.

He had turned the room downstairs into his bedroom, the same one he had used as a playroom when they moved to the country. Back then he was a toddler and still needed such things. Nowadays everything that entertained him had become electronic with flashing lights.

The room was also closest to the front door for a quick getaway.

She showered, dressing for the morning, skipping heels, but choosing a floral print dress, a moderate ensemble if she had been home in Texas on a Sunday. But she wasn't.

Gone were those rules and codes of feminine behavior. In the desert, she could wear linen almost any month of the year, or white past Labor Day. She went downstairs to Daniel's room. His bed was a tangle of nautical blue sheets, but the boy himself was nowhere to be found. She checked the adjoining bathroom, wrinkling her nose at the discarded toothbrush and toothpaste oozing out of the tube.

She scrolled through her phone to see if he had left any messages. Maybe he had fallen asleep in front of the television. She padded through the house. The living room was shrouded in semi-dark, the curtains drawn against the main street. She pulled them back, securing the cream brocade with the sash, Sanjana's task every other day of the week.

"There you are," Cindy said to the top of his head, bent over a bowl of cereal in the kitchen. "I was calling for you."

He made a noise of apology, which disappeared into the granola and milk.

"Coming to church with me?" She ran water into the kettle.

He shrugged. Cindy resisted the urge to brush the hair out of his eyes.

"I'll take that as a yes." She put the kettle on the stove, leaning against the counter to watch him. "Get much sleep?" Cindy eyed the worn T-shirt and pillow lines still crisscrossing his face.

"You should go back to work." He pushed back from the counter.

"Excuse me?"

He loped to the sink opposite her and ran water in his bowl. "I mean, weren't you this big feminist or something?"

Cindy crossed her arms, though all the articles said this was a defensive posture. "I was a writer, yes."

"Well, you should write something." He flipped his hair out of his eyes, tucking the strawberry blond curls that would spring out from behind his ears at each step.

"In this place?" Cindy knew all the parenting books cautioned against the tone in her voice, but she couldn't keep her back from tensing up. "What would I write—some chick lit drama?"

"Dad finds it inspiring," he said. "You could write something political about censorship."

"And get us all kicked out? You need to finish high school first."

"Seems like a waste." He gestured vaguely around the kitchen.

"Well, I stepped off the track to have you, and I haven't regretted it." She smoothed her hands over his shoulders with a smile. "I had several miscarriages before you."

"I know."

"You do?"

"Uncle Steve told me one day, when I was a kid and saw you crying. On one of the days they died."

Cindy had to tilt her head back slightly to meet his gaze. Relief coursed through her veins and a prick of irritation at her brother. *When had that conversation happened?*

"You shouldn't have." He drew away from her. "There's more to life than me. Look at Dad. He's always up to something."

Her mouth flopped open and closed. *Was it a burden, not a blessing, being the only one who had survived?*

He left the kitchen. Cindy trailed after him, as if someone had punched her in the stomach.

"What? Where is this coming from?"

He paused on the stairs. "That article Uncle Steve sent. About helicopter parenting. I got one of each, one who ignores me totally and another who can't leave me alone."

"He sent that to you too?" Cindy hated the parroting quality of her voice, but she couldn't hide her incredulity.

"He sent it BCC. Thinks I should read everything you do." Daniel shrugged. "I'm going to get ready."

Cindy picked up a copy of *O* magazine, resisting the urge to call Paul and scream at him that this was all his fault. Paul, the scholar whose star had been rising, who had found her young adult series playful, entertaining, and irrelevant.

His had been the main mission, his program at the American university abroad. He was the real breadwinner with a free house, tickets home, and educational allowance for their child. They had moved here ten years ago.

She had always intended to go back to writing. In the beginning she had told herself she was getting her feet under her. She had a young child, after all. But the arid landscape and heat of this new country had enfolded her, squeezing out her convoluted plotlines of fantastical worlds. So had PTA meetings, ladies' lunches, and Bible studies.

Daniel bounced down the stairs. "Ready?"

"Hmm." She nodded. They went out the side door to the garage.

"Can I drive?"

She racked her brain for a reason to say no, but the empty roads on a Friday morning gave no excuse.

"Sure," she said. She passed the key of the Range Rover over. Cindy sat in the passenger seat, wondering what Paul would say about the exchange in the kitchen.

"So, I loved being home with you," Cindy said, as Daniel reversed out of the garage. *I had to make sure you would survive.* The first three months of his life she hadn't let the baby out of her sight, forcing Paul to sleep in another room in case he rolled over during nightly feedings.

"Did I hurt your feelings?" He fixed his eyes on the reverse camera in the dash.

"Not at all," she lied, looking in the rearview mirror. "I'm wondering where you got those ideas. You know, about feminism and stuff." She wondered if she sounded like the off-hand teenager she was going for. The leather seat creaked as she reached for her purse.

"Well, you know, in language arts we're studying *A Doll's House*." He pulled through the compound guard station, waiting for the barrier to lower, waving hello the guard.

"Right, Mrs....what's her name again?"

"Ms. Mason" he said.

"She's not married?"

"That's the point. We don't know."

"Right." Cindy clutched the side handle of the SUV as he sped through a yellow light.

"No traffic camera there." He winked.

"That's not the only reason we stop at red lights."

He weaved the vehicle into the turn lane, taking them through the quiet streets toward the country's religious complex that housed the Catholic Church and an atrium for their own non-denominational congregation.

"Anyway, Ms. Mason says women have been sacrificing for humanity since the species began. That if you charged us for all the things you do, you'd be rich. That men would have found a way, if they were the child bearers."

Cindy watched his hands, large and sturdy, hinting at the man he would become. *Is becoming*, she thought with a start, as she took in how he filled the driver's seat, his head at the top of the seatback.

"Yes," she said. "She's probably right."

They slowed. Daniel waited for someone to vacate a street spot so he could reverse into it.

"Take your time," she said. "Line up the wheels."

He got it on the second try, his brow furrowing as his gaze swiveled between the rear camera and side mirrors like a distracted puppy. He pushed the car into park, and then ran a hand through his hair.

"It wasn't a sacrifice." She said put her hand on his arm. He didn't blink. "I mean, yes, I gave up some things, but it was worth it. To be there for you." She held her breath, hoping he wouldn't say the words she had unintentionally set up for: *I don't need you anymore.*

"I know." Daniel's long fingers lay on top of hers, squeezing them. "That's the whole point, right? Jesus and the Father, parents and children, and all that."

Tears welled in her eyes. She nodded, chin trembling, afraid to say a word that would break this spell.

"I love you, Mom." He kissed her cheek.

She closed her eyes, imagining the kiss was a coin, like her therapist had taught her. The grooved edges turned end over end as the token that was the kiss plunked into the chasm of hurt. *Now keep doing this until it fills up,* had been the instructions.

"I need your love," she whispered, as they had done when he was a child. The years of bringing Daniel to church, even as Paul's commitment wandered, shifting to professional advancement as the events and activities became a way to fill her empty hours, had paid off in this five-minute conversation. You couldn't fill a chasm with teenage love. The coin rung against the hollow walls, bouncing and spinning to land on a dozen or so others.

"I need your love," he said back, switching to her other cheek.

"I have an idea for a project," Cindy said.

"Hm? What about?" Daniel smoothed his hair in the rear view mirror.

"Well, a couple of things actually. Love, loss, some of the things you were talking about. The pain of motherhood—"

"Hey! Service is starting." Sharif rapped on the window, snapping Daniel away from her.

"Coming." Daniel unbuckled his seatbelt, slid open and then jumped out the door.

Cindy drew a deep breath. *He doesn't need proof of how special he is.* She repeated the litany. She stuffed the notes she carried with her, the outline for a book on grieving mothers, scratched at stoplights or waiting in line at the bank. She buried it back into the side pocket of the car and murmured her hello when Sharif threw her a greeting. His mother, Amira, came up after her, clasping her shoulder.

"Can you believe these kids? They're so big now, I can't keep up with how quickly Sharif needs new clothes."

"You think school is going well?"

"They'll be fine." Amira flicked her hair. The area under her eyes was translucent, patched up with a concealer in a skin tone that didn't quite match.

"The boys are getting quite close." Cindy gave Amira a sidelong glance. "Does Sharif have plans for August?"

"I wouldn't mind him staying with me a little while longer," Amira said. Since her split with a cheating husband, Amira had thrown herself into religion as if the material world didn't matter, transforming from a discarded pilot's wife into a church lady, complete with patent leather pumps. Her husband John had taken their younger child, Ahmed, back to America.

"Won't he go to college?"

"Eventually, when he's ready." Amira linked her arm with Cindy's, forcing her to fall in step.

Cindy clutched her Bible with her free arm, reassuring herself there was no chance of Daniel missing college. She wanted him away, safe from this place they had been forced to make their home.

"You going to sign up to go to the camps?"

"Sorry, what?" Cindy slid next to Amira on the pew, glancing at the multicolored abstract canvas hanging at the front of the chapel in the place of a cross. Apparently the cross would have been a step too far for the Muslims.

"They're doing an outreach this week. Going to the camp, getting ready for winter. Giving out blankets and canned food."

"I'll see." Cindy reached for the bulletin offered by the usher from Nigeria, who'd been coming to the chapel as long as she had. . "Good morning, Mr. Atoo,"

He gave a wink in reply.

"Room for two more?"

Curled Southern vowels raised a wave of nostalgia in Cindy. "Ah, yes." She moved over next to Amira. Two men with identical haircuts, biceps straining at their T-shirts, slid onto the bench. Military, Paul would have said with the same relish he had in spotting servicemen while walking around the mall.

"Morning." Amira leaned over with a flash of white teeth. Ah, were they the reason for Amira's newfound piety? She let them exchange greetings across her, training her eyes on the bulletin.

Cindy tugged the hem of her dress past her knee. The announcements swam in front of her as the arm of the one closest to her brushed Cindy's elbow.

"Sorry," he said.

She turned the bulletin over, murmuring a never mind. The contact sent the hairs on her arms standing up. *So desperate for affection, the random guy at the pew turns her on.* Cindy was grateful Protestantism didn't require priest-moderated confessions.

"What else are you doing? Come on." Amira cajoled as the praise team took their place at the front. "We'll be handing out water and blankets."

The strains of the first song rose from the guitar and drummer.

"The church wants to do that?" Cindy was itching to ask who the twenty-something men were.

"Spreading the gospel," Amira said, standing a few seconds before everyone else.

"That's illegal." Cindy stood with the rest of the congregation.

"Proselytizing is illegal," Amira corrected. They leaned back to let a family of late arrivals into their pew. "If they choose to convert, that's their own decision."

They began singing "It Is Well With My Soul" before Cindy could reply.

Chapter Twelve

Manu wiped sweat from the back of his neck and rolled onto his other side. The cinderblock walls trapped heat, turning the interior into a pressure cooker, singing his body and mind.

Droplets formed on all parts of Manu's body. He had nothing to use besides his hand to wipe away the moisture. The effort felt like he was slinging the perspiration around his collar rather than removing it, like a baby sloshing water in a bucket.

The chatter among the men as the police collected the body had been unending speculation about how much money the company had paid out to the deceased's family. There was overcrowding in the camp, but no one had come to take the vacated bed, superstition keeping men away from the promise of a more comfortable night's sleep.

Manu was tempted to climb into the bunk from his position in the middle of the floor, from where he could hear the sounds of scuttling insects, and worse. The stares of his new roommates, directed at the empty mattress, kept him away. As the new guy, he couldn't afford to make anyone upset.

Two men in the corner continued discussing the compensation to the dead man's family. "Not like the others," one man whispered. "You know." He indicated with his hands a belt around the neck.

"If not suicide, they pay."

Suicide? The word sent a chill through Manu, despite the lack of circulation in the room.

"Very least, they send the body home," the first speaker said.

"Shut up," a deep voice said from the top bunk. "Go to sleep."

During the cursory questioning from the police, Manu had been sipping from a used water bottle, filled with tap water. He pushed himself up to head for the bathroom. Others protested when the door creaked open, letting in the courtyard floodlight.

He was thankful for the discarded black flip-flops he had found under the bunk. Probably the dead man's, but the filth on the toilet floor made them necessary. He held his breath, adding to the pooled waste. They may not have had a western toilet at home, but what they had the girls kept clean. With so many using the same facility, cleanliness was impossible in the camp.

Manu pushed away thoughts of his family. The images of Raju and Ram made tears prick his eyes, tears he could ill afford.

He needed to find a way to call his sister.

He walked back to the room, wondering how long before he could save enough to buy a phone from one of the shops in the crumbling buildings facing their housing area. A group of three men were squatting on their haunches outside the room door, their voices carrying. The floodlight was out, turning the night into liquid blackness, masking Manu's approach.

"If they no pay, we strike," the biggest guy said.

"We strike, they beat us." The skinny man's voice was high pitched, like a girl's.

Manu slowed his step.

The big guy leaned forward. "They no pay for men who die. They no pay for men who work. What else can we do?"

"They beat us." The skinny one was much younger, his collarbones protruding at the base of his neck, his overalls hanging on the slight frame.

Manu stood over them now, wishing he had hung back to hear more of what they were saying. His father would have joined this group in a second. He had believed the idea that a man could raise his station with honest work. He had paid for that belief with his life,

"You." The big guy stood, towering over Manu. "What are you doing out?"

"Toilet," Manu said. He whisked himself into the room before anyone else could object. His heartbeat raced as he waited for someone to drag him out into the courtyard and question him further. There were low murmurs. The big guy entered the room.

A hand clenched over Manu's mouth. "Tell no one." His breath was hot on Manu's face. "Or you won't live to say another word." As suddenly as the pressure was applied, it lifted.

Manu took a deep breath, shaking. *I'm on your side.* He had been too young

100

to know the ins and outs of his father's dealings with the Maoists. Judging by his untimely demise, their tactics couldn't have been much different.

He lost track of how many hours he plotted getting a reassignment to another room. Manu jerked awake after what seemed like minutes. His roommates were a blur of arms and legs preparing for their day, footsteps falling close to his head.

Manu rose, his bones creaking. He went through the motions quickly, splashing water on his face, wiping under his arms, and pulling on his company-issue blue jumpsuit and black work boots. He kept his head down, not wanting to make eye contact with the men he overhead last night, and rushed into the line waiting for a good seat on the bus.

"I need doctor," a reedy guy said to the foreman, pausing at the first step of the bus. Everyone behind Manu protested at the hold up. "My hand, see?" A gash, about an inch wide, split the skin between the man's thumb and forefinger.

"You have health card?" The foreman's bleary eyes fixed on the line behind them.

"Expired. I waiting for my residency renewal also."

The foreman spat to one side. "No health card, you pay for doctor."

"We get treatment." The man waved his hand closer to the foreman's face.

"Let's go!" Hands shoved Manu in the back, sending him into the man in front of him. He stumbled onto the first step of the bus. The foreman waved the rest of them on. The man clutched his hand and sat down on a green upholstered seat, next to the window.

Manu had nothing to pass to him, not a bandage or a piece of cloth to substitute as one. He shuffled on, unsure if sympathy would be welcome, and slid into a seat as the other men poured onto the bus like lava.

They bumped through the uniformly beige landscape, above which was a sky tinted by hues of pink and red, as the sun rose over. As they hurtled onto the highway, a mournful cry ascended, first from one mosque and then another, in a cascading crescendo of the call to prayer. The Arabic words tumbled over him along with the humidity.

They headed into the city, with wider lanes, and splinted palm trees in the medians. Manu was breathless at the sight of steel and glass rising out of the flat sand—twenty, thirty, forty stories tall. He craned his head out of the bus's open window, while others rested their foreheads on the seat in front in an attempt to catch another hour of sleep.

This was the glitz he had imagined in the Gulf. He was an office worker for a high-power boss. They stumbled across a case of espionage and he was rewarded with a briefcase full of cash. His eyes searched the never-ending stream of cars, shiny, many of them white, their windows tinted against the sun's punishing rays. He wondered who rode in these vehicles and where they lived.

"Don't look at their women," the person behind him whispered. "They will cut off your head."

Manu turned around with a start.

"If you ever see one of them, look down." The man's earnest face pressed in the space between the seat and the window.

Manu nodded in assent or thanks, he wasn't quite sure which, and turned back around.

The streets were wide, palm trees unfurling green fronds in the medians. Manu marveled at this city, this place of fantasy, wondering if there would be a Bollywood movie made here. They had made a few in Dubai.

They skidded to a stop in front of a crater in the ground, the men stepping out of the bus in a constant stream of blue jumpsuits. The work crew was assembled from men across the camps, from other floors and rooms Manu had not discovered yet. All around them were unfinished buildings, with red reinforcement bars jutting out of cinderblock like pieces of a child's toy.

They were assigned haphazardly to various tasks on the building site, depending on what order they came off the bus. The other two workmen assigned with Manu were Indian, as far as he could tell from their accents and preferences for Hindi.

"Where can we go?" he muttered to the man next to him. This was a new site, a place he had been brought to that morning for the first time. Last month he had poured concrete, holding the cement mixer while the machine ground through the mud, water, and silt, his arms aching from the effort of making sure the tray didn't jar from the shuddering movement of the truck as it spewed out the contents.

Today they were perched on the edge of an unfinished three-story building. An office or a house? Manu had no idea. And he no longer cared. The reddish rusty bars extending several meters above his head had to be capped with tape. That's all he cared about. Well, that and the fact he needed a toilet.

"You know, go." He mimed a rude gesture, the one they used in the camp when someone was taking too long in the bathroom, rapping on the door repeatedly, making the others laugh.

The other man wore dark plastic sunglasses that hid his eyes. A greenish scarf covered the lower part of his face and mouth. Another scarf, once white, covered his forehead. Overall, the effect should have been comic, a man with his face covered like the women who passed them throughout the city in their shiny cars without a sidelong glance. Women whose eyes showed through tiny slits. But this was a man, and the effect of not being able to make eye contact was sinister rather than silly.

"There." The man with encased head and eyes gestured to the opposite edge of the building, where the floor curved downward into a spiral staircase. "Anywhere."

Manu followed the curve of the casual finger toward the other end of the floor they were working on. Behind the support columns there was shade, and also privacy from the others on the roof. He could see others had had the same urge and resorted to the same solution. He did as he had been told, pulling down the sleeves of his jumpsuit quickly before anyone could see him, peeing like a schoolboy inside.

"Bad news about Raju." Another man, one Manu didn't recognize as being from his room, came up next to him, relieving himself in the corner. For a second Manu's heart sped up, until he remembered the name of the figure lying prone on the floor had been the same as that of his youngest brother.

"Terrible," Manu said. He worked his clothing back on as fast as he could. The other man finished, flipping up a cloth that covered most of his mouth, chin, and neck.

"Why do you all wear that?" Manu asked. They fell in step back to the main part of the floor where everyone else was working. This was the first person to give him more than a passing glance since he had arrived into the camp.

"My skin gets dark in the sun," the other man said with a smile, revealing contrasting white teeth. "No one will marry me when I go home. They'll say I was working concrete."

"We *are* working concrete," Manu said dryly as the sound of the cement mixer kicking on ricocheted through the structure.

"Don't tell anyone at home." The man's smile disappeared from his face, replaced by pinched lips. "They know that, they won't like you for leaving them to take such a common job."

The words caused a sharp pain, like a knife twisting in his gut. Manu felt further from his family than ever. He had no money or phone with which to call Sanjana. And now this stranger had given him several reasons not to call home. The sad sounds of a Bollywood soundtrack filled his ears. This was the moment the hero would break into contemplative song, wondering what would become of his life.

"Anyway, the real story is how much they paid Raju's family."

Manu grunted, putting a little distance between himself and the other man. "Vultures."

"They paid nothing," the other man said, as if he hadn't heard Manu's condemnation.

"Hey! You there. Come."

Manu snapped around, his hands dropping from the chest high zipper that would lower the entire one-piece outfit. His underwear was still damp from the previous night's washing in the sink. The sun had no chance to dry it since their bus collected them at 4 a.m. to bring them to the site.

"They say heart attack, not their fault. Raju not healthy," the other man whispered and sidled off.

"Move this." The foreman yelled at Manu and two men with their heads wrapped in oil-stained red-checkered cloth to keep the sun's more determined rays away.

The foreman was pointing to a slab of marble. Marble, Manu surmised, needed to be downstairs, in the entryway with all the other pieces they had unloaded from the truck that morning. Manu and the two men joined another that the foreman waved over. Their foursome trudged toward the edge of the unfinished floor, hoping to load the marble onto the pulley and lower it to the main floor.

"No time," the foreman yelled. "Down the stairs."

The man across from Manu grunted. Manu recognized him from the late night chat outside their bunk, the one telling the others they should agitate for their pay. The fibers of the muscles in Manu's biceps felt as though they were threads unraveling on a spool.

Their eight-legged apparatus inched toward the staircase. Manu's heart raced. He had grown up in rural Nepal, sure, and had carried an occasional injured goat a few meters. But this, his nicked hands clutching at the cream and brown swirls—nothing could prepare you for this. *Unless,* he thought, *you were a builder.*

The earlier conversation buzzed in his ears. Raju had appeared to be a youngish twenty-something, not that far from Manu's age. He had been in robust health, or at least as close to it as one could get on camp food, sleep, and water.

"Wait," came the high-pitched protest next to Manu. He hadn't put the face with the younger man from last night's discussion. There was no mistaking that voice. They paused at the top of the stairs, leaning the piece of marble on the side, careful, despite their fatigue, of toes.

They eyed each other, the unspoken question hovering over them. How could they balance the weight of the marble on the two who would descend the stairs first? The weight of the slab would only increase as they turned down the corkscrew of the staircase.

"I'm heavier," the big man across from Manu said in Hindi. They lowered the slab to the ground, the boy sighed in relief. Everyone wiped perspiring brows on their sleeves. The bigger guy came around, jerking his chin, indicating Manu should go to the other end—the end that would hold the piece, controlling the pace at which they descended.

"Jeldi!" the foreman shouted. This was one of the few Hindi words in the man's meager vocabulary. "Quickly, quickly." He added more variations of hurry up or *yella.*

Manu took a deep breath, wishing he had gloves to get a better grip. He grabbed the corner, hoisting it on his thigh, feeling the flesh give way before he could get his left hand underneath. They began their descent.

"You tell when," Manu said to the men under him on the other side of the slab. They should set the pace. But the young guy next to him, his teeth yellow and eyes shot with red veins, pressed on, taking the steps.

"Slower." The man on the other side's voice was muffled, as if heard through a wall. Manu tried to halt his partner. To do so he would have to let go of his side, which would upset the momentum, potentially catch a foot, or break the piece, which would make the grumpy foreman incendiary.

"Slow down." Manu grunted under the weight.

The boy next to him didn't hear or chose to ignore him. He pressed forward.

"I can't hold it..." A man's voice from the other side carried a tinge of panic.

Manu heard the crack of the man's spine before he felt the slab jerk out of his hands. There was a tumble.

A crash of sounds like a child's plaything rolling down the stairs preceded a flash of blue uniforms. The marble slab fell on top.

First came the crunch of breaking bones, then a crack of marble, a hair-line fracture appearing across the cream surface.

The boy next to him jumped out of the way, hopping on one foot, the other protruding at an awkward angle. Of the man who had exchanged his spot with Manu, however, only hands emerged, splayed at the top of the slab as if they had been pasted on by some child with a wicked imagination.

"Help!" Manu called hoarsely. A few men raced up the stairs, their eyes wide, the buckles of their jumpsuits coming undone with the effort. They tugged and tugged, raising the edge of the marble by a few inches, but not enough to get the man out, much less check on him.

"No, only one guy. No fire." The foreman was talking into his cell phone in uncharacteristically low tones, his back turned away from them.

"Get some wood," Manu shouted. "Something to stick under here."

They all started to scramble, until Manu reminded the remaining men not to drop the slab again. There was no sound, not even a groan or cry of pain, from the man underneath. Sweat prickled on Manu's forehead and under his arms.

Someone produced a metal pipe. They raised the slab again a few precious inches, and slid the pipe in a bit at a time. When they released the slab, for a second it balanced and Manu exhaled. Then the slab crushed the pipe, and the trapped man anew.

"Oh God," Manu said. Tears streamed down his face. If the man had had a chance before, any possibility was gone now.

"Break," the foreman called. "Thirty minutes."

Manu took a swig from the two liter Pepsi bottle the men on his floor of the structure passed around. The carbonation burned his tongue, causing him to cough. Soda was cheaper than water, only two riyals compared to five. And if they split it, cheaper still.

The others melted away, as if they were figments of Manu's imagination. He was left at the top of the stairs, looking at the discarded piece of marble. He wished he could get the image of those reaching hands out of his vision.

Even as he sat against the central column, giving in to the shuddering sobs in the bounty of privacy, he couldn't get those splayed fingers out of his mind's eye. Or the idea that it could have been him, crushed out of existence like a human cigarette. He wiped the backs of his hands across his eyes, and then went to search for the others.

"We need to talk to someone about this," Manu said in a low voice. The man's limbs reminded him of the body on the floor of his shared room—unmoving, still, dead. "This is not right."

No one made eye contact, the men spreading out across the empty lower floor. Some went to the edge, gazing out into the heat of midday. Others slouched against a wall, heads on their knees.

"Not right," Manu repeated.

"This kind of talk not right." The man with the yellow teeth jabbed a finger at Manu. "You need money, no?"

Manu stared at him. "I need money. Maybe I also need to live."

"You keep talking like this, you not have either," the man muttered.

Manu leaned closer, unsure if he had heard correctly. "You making a threat?"

"Come and give statement. What you see in accident, okay?" The foreman was back, herding them downstairs.

Manu stared at the other man, who looked away first, the vein next to his eye pulsing. Manu was the last to leave the floor. The other six men avoided him completely. No one interviewed him about what had happened to the man, who he learned had been called Kahn.

That evening, before they left the construction site, a red box waited on the bottom floor. An oblong container that Manu recalled.

When he saw a few men hauling the remains of the man crushed by the falling marble, wrapped in a plastic trap like so much garbage, his mind reeled with the connection. *Coffins.* Those red boxes he had seen in the regional airport were the remains of men returning to their families. He shivered, despite the humid night air.

The phone call to his sister was now urgent. Manu wouldn't worry about her perceptions of his job as a grunt on construction, but he needed to borrow a phone. The foreman was out, he knew, because the man kept as wide a berth from them as Manu did the stray cats that circled their accommodation. *Maybe the bus driver,* he thought as he waited in the shade for someone to come and ask him what he had seen of the accident. The gangly bus driver, who slept in the bus all day while the crew worked, was often playing Hindi film songs on his phone.

I'll be the first on the bus tonight, he thought, desperate to erase the sight of the red box waiting for its journey back to India. But the line to enter the bus was a pushing match worthy of any boys' secondary school. No guaranteed seat after a hard day's work. They jostled each other, trying to get a seat with a window fan.

Somehow his big sister was going to have to get him out of this mess, the one she had put him in through her assurances that the maid agency could get him a work visa for an office job. He leaned his head on the window, surrendering to exhaustion the way others had done all around him. This way the resentment against his sister would have no room to grow.

Chapter Thirteen

The encroaching darkness filled her father's office, which often Maryam used as studying space since her mother didn't want her spending long hours at university. The rest of the family, including the maids, rarely came into the room that doubled as his library. She was alone with her thoughts.

She pawed through the shelves of the filing cabinets, hoping to find something she could use for her theory that the company was underpaying the employees. There were dozens of ledgers, blue lines filled in with black ink, rows upon rows of numbers. She couldn't make any sense of them; the columns corresponded to numbers on either side: on the left single digits, and on the right double. The third column was full of letters and numbers in a code she couldn't have understood without a guide.

She slammed a drawer shut, drumming her fingers on top of the last gray filing cabinet. She strode to the opposite wall of newspaper clippings, many of them printed from online articles by international outlets.

All of them contained headlines like "The Death Games" or "4000 Bodies by 2023."

On and on the headlines went with images of worn looking men, downcast faces mingling in a sea of overalls that reminded her of the swarm of ants that invaded the house as temperatures rose. The men were indistinguishable to her from one another. *Every man has a mother* Maryam reminded herself. And these men were dying, a few here and there, every month. She couldn't find a pattern.

Some were accidents, so said a local report about a man falling four stories to his death due to faulty scaffolding. Other outlets, though, outside the country, blamed the men themselves for poor health.

"At twenty five years old, in prime health, these men were declared heart attack victims," another report read, the British journalist scoffing at the possibility.

"Companies declare these deaths the result of suicide," said one, "because in such cases they don't have to pay compensation to the families."

She chewed at the end of a pencil, the eraser giving away to her worrying teeth. The numbers from the company balance sheet said these men were paid so little. Could they not spare a month's salary for the family? If Nasser was home she could ask him where to find copies of the contracts they issued.

Maryam propped her head on her hand, staring at the blinking cursor, sinking further into the leather armchair. Her feet dangled off one arm. She slung her head back to stare at the recessed lights in the ceiling. She had all night to work on the assignment for Paul's class, a piece of original reporting, based on a local issue, with quotes from an interviewee.

He considered these the basics of journalism. The cursor taunted her like a winking electronic beast. She wrestled with the knots inside her, hoping the one around her heart would loosen so she could put into words what she had seen in the worker housing.

Pieces of paper lay around the machine and on the floor. She had tried to begin with pen and paper. Paul's favorite recommendation was to kick-start creativity by activating the mind-hand connection, but all that thirty minutes had achieved was a waste of paper. She chewed on a pencil, turning it over between her teeth.

"You'll ruin your eyes." Jaber snapped on the hanging lights. The sleeves of his *thobe* were rolled up to reveal wiry arms. The yellowish glow illuminated the books lining the walls, his leather-bound collectors' editions of classic American novels. They were as useful to her as an oil well would have been in the courtyard. "How can you see anything in this dark?"

"I didn't notice," Maryam put the pencil on the table before he started in on her missing glasses next.

"When is it due?" The leather armchair hissed as he sat down. Though he was speaking to her, his attention was on the Arabic newspapers on the low table next to her laptop. Jaber picked up the nearest one. His long fingers resembled her own. The sharp features of his profile, including the slope of his nose, reminded her that she was a female version of her father.

"Tomorrow." She blew at a strand of hair that had crossed into her line of sight.

Her father turned a page, glancing at his watch. "Ten hours."

"I know." She chewed the edge of her pencil again.

Jaber cleared his throat. "Maryam, if you aren't going to take university seriously, then—"

"I am! I'm trying to find words to write." She shot him a venomous look.

"There are other options," Jaber said.

She turned from the blinking cursor. "Options to make words appear on the page?"

"No, other ways to spend your time." Jaber fidgeted with the cuffs of his *thobe*. "You know your mother says there are people interested in you."

The injustice of the familiar speech at this particular moment was her undoing. "They might be less interested once they find out what our company is doing."

Jaber turned another page. "As long as you aren't wasting time or money." He peered at her over the newspaper. "You know that university is very expensive. You're not a ministry student like the others who are sponsored. You chose journalism."

"Like we can't afford it," she said. "The money we make off the backs of those men." The idea made her queasy.

"We?"

"I'm writing about the workers." She continued with her chin raised. "I know what we do to them." She had his full attention.

His gaze narrowed on her like one of the falcons her brothers trained.

"Yes, even us." She thumped her fist on the arm of the chair, the memory of the prone figure on the floor flashing before her eyes. Her hand stung from where she had hit one of the brass tack accents. "In our camp, we are as bad as the media says we are."

Jaber rose. His full height caused her to tilt her head back, reminding her of the police officer she had seen in the labor housing. Few local men were this tall. She stood, leaning on the table for support.

"Maryam, you can't be hasty," he said. "The foreign media has many reasons for the stories they print. I'm surprised they haven't taught you this in your classes."

"Here," she said. "See? As terrible as the Amnesty report says." She scrolled through the photos she had managed to take on her phone before Babu fished her out of the overcrowded room. He snatched it from her, his fingers trembling as they closing around the device. The force of her father's gaze bore down on her, his pupils contracting.

"You went there?" Her phone trembled in Jaber's hand as now the full force of his attention was directed to the photos.

"I…"Too late, Maryam saw her error. She was always one to lose her temper in an argument, especially with her father who was equally hotheaded. "Someone died! A man was on the ground, dead—at least Babu said he was—and no one was doing anything!"

"Babu took you there?" Jaber dropped the phone into the front pocket of his *thobe*.

Maryam opened her mouth to protest.

"I'll cancel his visa."

"What? No!" Maryam eyed the pocket where he'd placed her phone. "I made him do it. He didn't want to. Believe me, he told me all the reasons it was a bad idea." Her fingers worried at her father's sleeve, itching to reach for the phone, but knowing that would send him over the edge.

"You should have listened to him." Jaber slapped at her prying hand. "You honestly don't have any sense, Maryam."

"Me? *Yuba*, did you receive any calls that someone was hurt? You didn't, did you?" She noted the blank look on his face. "See? There's things happening out there, and you don't even know. That's what I'm going to put in my paper."

"You will not write about this," her father thundered. He moved away from her, pacing a rug with an enormous tree at the center of its design. The rug was as old as Maryam, maybe older.

"This is for university. So I can get an A."

"This is the kind of thing they are teaching you there?" He paused, jabbing a finger at her. "Then no, I'm taking you out. I'm taking you out immediately."

"You can't do that!"

He rounded the room, taking out her phone again to look at the photos. She came from behind the table, her hands fisting.

"What will I do at home, alone? You're traveling half the time, and all the others are gone." A lump rose in her throat at the thought of her older siblings, five of them, the boys studying, her sisters married, settled in homes of their own.

"If you can't take studying seriously, then you'll have to get married." Her father's thundering voice filled her ears with a ringing sound.

"Married!" Her knees were about to give way. She wanted to grab the table or sit down, but that would be admitting weakness. With *Yuba,* if he was standing, you had to stand too if you wanted a prayer of getting your way.

"A husband will cure you of these impulses."

"In this day and age that's still the solution?" This time Maryam did sit down, her elbow clanking on the table. "But, this was for school. I was doing this to get an A in my journalism class."

"Abu Nasser, can we eat before you go to the *majlis?* Some men have already arrived," Fatma called from the doorway. They kept odd hours in the house, based on her father's meeting schedule.

Fatma stopped short at the sight of them, the edges of her *jalabiya* quivering. "Ya, Maryam, Babu is looking for you. He said he was ready to take you."

"She's not going anywhere," Jaber said. "And I'm going to talk to that driver."

Her mother looked from one to the other. "Now what's she done?"

"Nothing," Maryam said. "*Yuba* is showing his Bedouin side."

"That's enough," Jaber thundered.

She gave her father a pleading look. How angry he must be with her. He usually stood against her traditional mother's schemes to get Maryam settled. "Working on a class project."

"A group project?" Fatma hovered in hope. His name was unspoken, but ran like a current through the air from her mother. Maryam knew what she was wondering. Was her ideal groom, Faisal, somehow involved?

"No, an individual paper."

"*Ya rub,* when will we get this girl married so someone else will watch over her?"

"I can watch over myself, *Yema,*" Maryam protested.

Her mother was quick to jump into whatever tide her father was creating. Jaber waved a hand. "I'll take care of this. Call the driver."

"Please, Abu Nasser, don't do anything hasty," Fatma said, using the Arab custom of calling her husband by the name of their first-born son. She shimmered in the doorway, her yellow chiffon *jalabiya* draping her ample curves. "Whatever happened, I'm sure Babu wasn't to blame. Maryam is very convincing. This is the only driver we've managed to keep who she hasn't driven crazy with her demands."

"I'm to blame," Maryam agreed, hoping her mother wouldn't ask for what she was to blame. "Not Babu."

Jaber let out a sigh. "Let's eat. I'll deal with Babu later. You behave yourself."

Fatma gave Maryam a look over her shoulder as she turned to follow Jaber from the room. "Work hard, and you'll be fine. You're a smart girl. Remember your father wants to see you settled."

"How about happy?"

"Happily settled, of course, silly girl. Who says such things?"

Maryam said nothing. Her burst of confidence passed as quickly as a desert rain. Her mother lingered for a few seconds, raising her eyebrows, wanting to know what they had discussed.

"Are we eating or no?" Jaber called.

Fatma passed in a swish of chiffon, patting her lacquered hair. "Stay out of trouble," she whispered to Maryam. "You think your father is bad." *Your uncles are worse*—the unspoken words hung in the air after her parents had left.

She threw herself sideways into the armchair, knocking the pencil and a sheaf of newspaper to the floor. If her father had been serious about his plan, that marriage was his last option with her, he would have told her mother.

Plenty of women asked about her, she knew from hushed conversations her mother had with her sisters during the family lunches on Fridays. They didn't tell a girl when someone had the intent to propose lest she become fixated on him, and the relationship turn into a scandal if the proposal didn't proceed.

Until now, her father had insisted she be allowed to finish her education. This was the excuse for everyone who came to ask about her—*not now, she's still studying*—but her mother's more traditional family protested, complaining that Maryam's consistent refusals were preventing their daughters from receiving offers.

"People are saying we don't give our girls," her aunt huffed the past Friday, with Maryam at the table. "Why is your daughter so picky? Who does she want, a sheikh?"

The rest of the women had been looking at fashion magazines in the living room. Maryam had held her breath, the kebab sticking in her throat.

"Maryam is very interested in her studies." Her mother passed a basket of flatbread. Fatma was loyal in front of others, relatives included, though Maryam got an earful about this embarrassment later.

Maryam slid the laptop closer. The cursor was going to have to do its best to keep up and produce the words flying from her fingertips.

Chapter Fourteen

Ali pulled under one of the tan awnings that extended over the white boundary wall of the house. The vehicle umbrella was a sign of a social family, so that guests could park out of the continuous sun. *There were enough Land Cruisers for a Toyota showroom*, he thought, glancing down the row of a dozen or so cars.

The seven-seat SUV was a practical choice in a country where average family size was eight. A definite sign he was in the right place. This family had money, judging by the neighborhood. There were several estates on this street, with walls twice the height of the one at his house that ran for several meters before a sharp turn towards the back of the properties.

Vegetation reached tendrils over the privacy barriers, blooming pink and red bougainvillea beckoning the curious, even as the walls kept the prying eyes out. Hassan pestered Ali to come socialize, not to turn into the old man Hassan swore he was on the verge of becoming. Here he was, in the nexus of local homes. A group of drivers hanging out on wooden benches next to the entryway a few meters down.

Ali checked his *gutra* in the rearview mirror. Yes, there was the peak, like a cobra, that said he was a young unmarried local male. He turned off the car. The *thobe* felt stiff, like in high school when he used to wear it on Fridays to the family gatherings.

These days he spent more time in the dark blue pants and lighter blue short-sleeved shirt of the police uniform than in any other clothing. He walked in steps truncated by the width of the *thobe's* hem. *Like a geisha*, he thought dryly, a smile twisting his lips. *We are so proud of our masculinity, but in fact we are all walking around in long white dresses.* He laughed, straightening his collar.

"Finally in a good mood." Hassan greeted him with three nose kisses, his cousin's mustache tickling Ali's lip.

"You need a trim."

If Hassan knew the sardonic bend of Ali's thoughts, he would be more concerned than he already was.

"*Yella*, come." Hassan took him by the arm, leading him down a staircase to a lower level of the house. The male gathering area was set apart from the house so men could enter and leave without seeing anyone inside, the system created to shield the women from strangers. Hassan swept him inside sliding glass doors.

Ali gave a low whistle, despite himself. A modern living room spanned the entire bottom of the house. The entryway had a floor-to-ceiling piece of calligraphy displaying the ninety-nine names of God, designed both to impress the visitor and bless the space.

"They're missing a water fountain," Ali said.

Hassan shook his head, his step quickening.

The *majlis* inside gleamed white and gold. The oily smell of recent paint probably meant a wedding in the works. Ali glanced around, regretting the impulse that had made him listen to Hassan's pleas to join them tonight.

"These guys are cool, young, like us. You won't be sorry."

Ali shook free of Hassan's hovering presence and moved to the corner. There were a few younger guys, teenagers by the look of their bony shoulders, playing an Xbox a few feet away. He would have to wait before he could leave without his hosts remembering him as an ass. Twenty minutes and at least three cups of coffee.

He sat, making sure his *thobe* didn't rise above his ankles. Not that his grandfather was there to yell at the boys for being disrespectful. Still, some habits were ingrained from boyhood.

"*Salam Aikelium*."

Everyone stood, even the teenagers, as the man of the house entered. Ali recognized the broad features of his grandmother, remixed and redistributed on Jaber's face. The sight of the man brought back another face, this one more delicate with a nose sloped like a scimitar—the ornamental swords all the poets praised.

"This is Ali," Hassan said.

"You're Yusuf's son, is that right?" Jaber approached Ali, taking his shoulder in one hand and his opposite elbow in the other.

"Yes." Ali resisted the urge to fidget. He wondered if the man knew what his daughter was up to at night. Ali flushed as Jaber leaned in for the nose kiss.

"*Allah yerhamho*," Jaber said, the greeting to bless the dead.

The stab of longing caught Ali between the ribs. In situations like this, he missed his father the most. Yusuf would have regaled all of them with his stories about days in the royal guard, the smugglers he had busted trying to get alcohol across the Saudi border.

Jaber's deep voice rumbled, asking after the rest of his family, Ali's own health.

Ali mumbled the appropriate responses. "Well, thank you, God be praised."

"You were in the royal forces," Jaber lingered, while Ali wished someone else would call him to be introduced to the next guest.

"I was, for a few years. After military school."

"Yes." Jaber tapped his finger on his lips. "Yusuf told me you had a special commendation for the espionage case? What was it, you found someone smuggling drugs?"

"A long time ago," Ali said. "I got a tip from someone in the circle who wanted to get out, but they wouldn't let him."

"Why did you leave Internal Security?"

"Illness." No matter how many times Ali prepared this lie, it still stung. A kernel of truth to mask the greater ill. He was missing a part of his manhood. An admission of being lesser than the men they all were.

The attention passed like the sun disappearing behind a cloud, a faint smile as the other man inclined his head, indicating the conversation was over. Jaber moved on through the room, a ring of amber prayer beads clicking through his fingers. Ali let out a pent-up breath.

Jaber's son replaced him.

"Nasser, this is Ali," Hassan said.

They greeted each other politely, not leaning in for the kiss but settling for the more informal clasped palms.

"A working man," Nasser said. "Like myself."

"He's going to be a doctor," Hassan said.

"That must be hard work." Ali was impressed, despite himself. Most men Nasser's age cruised the streets or gathered in Starbucks around the country on their fathers' largesse.

"Well, a good way to put off getting married, anyway." Nasser laughed. "Don't tell anyone I said that."

Ali smiled. There was infectious energy about the man that buoyed anyone he was talking to, a calmer, steadier presence than his sister. Ali saw the familiar features of her cheekbones and eyebrows in this masculine face. Their sharp features were younger versions of the father, who sat on a gilt-edged sofa sipping *gahwa,* the sweet Arab coffee, from a small cup, his gaze taking in the scene.

"You must have some great stories, the police and all."

"Hmm," Ali said with a modest shake of his head. He couldn't betray the girl, not in front of so many men. But, he realized with a start, he should tell her brother that her recklessness could get her in trouble. There was no way to begin that conversation. Men did not speak about women in the majlis—not their sisters or daughters, anyway.

"So modest." Nasser slapped his arm. "I know the country is getting more dangerous. We see the people in the emergency room."

Ali handed back his empty *finjal,* shaking it to show the boy serving the coffee he was finished. These were the relatives a man who married into this family would spend most of his time with. No way a family like this would take him, half a man. The thought, constant ever since his mother had raised it when he was forced to share news of his demotion, cast a pall on him.

"Look at this! This one is a lion in a teacup." One of the boys called to Nasser and Hassan, waving an iPad mini. Ali eyed Nasser, laughing easily with two others who were admiring the photos.

"He took him out for a walk, on a leash!" Hassan exclaimed.

The group chortled.

In his mind, Ali pictured snatching the phone out of their hands and arresting the friend they were admiring in the photos. Exotic pets were another taboo on the long list of official no-nos that many officers turned a blind eye towards.

"I've got a call." Ali raised his arms in defense as Hassan protested his leaving. "I'll come again," he lied. He slipped his sandals back on, waiting until the car pulled around before he could take off his *gutra* and *agal.*

He whistled in annoyance at the dark SUV blocking his exit. Ali went to the passenger window and knocked, startling the sleeping driver. The man lowered the tinted window, the whites of his eyes showing when he recognized Ali.

"Move, yeah." Ali shooed him as if he were one of the hundreds of cars waiting for the sign to go on the congested roadways. "I take my car." He jerked his thumb at the blocked Nissan.

"Okay, okay," the driver said, his head nodding in that to-fro tilt Ali couldn't understand.

"Babu, wait!" A moving force, all arms and legs, shot out of the smaller door in the boundary wall surrounding the house. Ali was caught in the wide-eyed stare of the girl he had met at camp. Nasser's sister.

"You." Maryam fell backward a step. "Did you tell them anything?"

"This is what they teach you in that university?" Ali took a step back from the glare spitting from her eyes. "To talk like this?"

Maryam sighed. Her lip trembled. "You too. All of you are living in another century."

"I didn't." He kept his tone low. The signs of female vulnerability were all too familiar to him from his sisters. Ali realized with a start he preferred her spitting nails.

"Then why are you here?" Her shoulders relaxed a bit. She clutched at her *abaya*, one of the newer designs that didn't have buttons, but gaped open like a man's *bisht*.

"Your brother invited me to the *majlis*. I'm leaving."

"Then go." She shooed him like a goat.

"I'm trying." He raised his hand toward Babu, who had moved their SUV down a few feet. "Your hospitality is hard to refuse."

She turned away, opening the door and stepping onto the running board to get inside. "Did you find anything out about that man?"

Ali climbed into his own vehicle to distract himself. He lowered his window so he could hear her. "Who?"

"The worker. The one on the floor."

Ali shook his head, and then adjusted a side mirror that needed no attention. Jaber would kill him if he knew Ali had exchanged words with his youngest daughter, Ali was sure. "Surely it was the lack of air-conditioning, all those men. Heat stroke. Very common."

"So common, it's like swatting a fly? God have mercy on him," she said. "And on us for being so careless. A perfectly healthy twenty-something drops dead, and no one asks any questions." Her door slammed shut. "Maybe it'll be you next," she called out from the open window. "Maybe me."

120

Before he could answer, the SUV pulled off. Sand rose in a fine cloud of dust. Ali sat clutching the steering wheel.

Chapter Fifteen

They had come right after Friday service, Amira leading the way, away from the towering skyscrapers across the flat plain of the city, until the glittering glass structures were pinpricks in her rearview mirror.

Cindy had never been out this far. She and Paul used a service. A smiling Filipino man came out, picked up their vehicles, and took them to a place everyone else called the Industrial Area. He returned them, smelling of air freshener, with the gas tanks full.

Cindy squinted as sand filled the windshield. She couldn't remember how much they paid him, but she vowed to give that man—was his name Miguel?—a raise. No, no, Miguel had been their gardener at home. This man's name was—she braked, swerving around a cement mixer.

"Watch your turns!" she shouted, as if giving instructions to Daniel. The driver was so high up in the other vehicle, she doubted he could even see her. Cindy sped past, not wanting to lose sight of Amira's gray BMW.

They pulled to a stop next to a gas station full of eighteen-wheelers, lined up waiting for fuel. She smiled at Amira, who wore her windbreaker and wraparound Ray-Bans, and slid from the driver's side of the Range Rover. The dust was whipping up fast, sticking to Cindy's lip-gloss, creating a dusty patina, which she made worse by rubbing her lips together.

There were two men with Amira, people from church whose names Cindy could not remember, who set up a foldout table. They pinned down the cherry tablecloth with scattered rocks from the lot. In this piece of barren desert, your eye could roam for miles and only see squat two-story housing, grouped like old ladies who had fallen asleep while at a knitting circle.

"Jonah. Nice to see you again, ma'am," the younger one said in her direction.

The country boy. "You too." Cindy remembered the chiseled lips in profile. "You from Raleigh?"

"Highpoint." When he smiled, his dimples showed like brackets on a perfect set of teeth. "That's Robert."

"Right," Cindy said. "Hello again."

Robert lifted his chin. Across the short distance, she noted the snug gray T-shirt and pectoral muscles. She looked away as she had to when Daniel's swim coach was talking to them about how her son could improve his strokes.

"Hello," Amira handed out water bottles to a few men who had shuffled over while their vehicles were being filled. "Hi." She had a smile for each of them, though they could not see her eyes.

"He's quite the looker," Cindy whispered to Amira, lining up more bottles of water. "He's really into Bibles?"

"I swore off men. I told you," Amira's white teeth flashed in contrast to her olive skin.

"Well, this was certainly the place to come."

There was an assembly line of sorts. Robert handed out paper bags filled with toiletries that the teenagers had assembled during their Sunday school class: toothpaste, toothbrushes, and mouthwash. Cindy moved further down the line and became the last stop in front of a pile of blankets.

In the late afternoon glare, it was difficult to imagine a time when these would be in need, but she had been caught unaware by her first desert winter. The houses were not designed to retain heat, and marble made for a decidedly un-cozy surface when the sun disappeared, dropping the temperature into the sixties. These men, Cindy realized as their hands reached for anything she gave them, would have taken blankets in the dead of summer, they were in such need.

She smiled, wishing she had brought sunglasses, not only for the sand that was whipping around, but also to shield the shock, which surely showed in her eyes.

These men were thin and tiny. She towered over them, though she only came to Paul's shoulder. As a nondescript line of humanity, they passed in front of her wearing dark pants, tattered T-shirts, mismatched socks, and shoes with soles that flapped when they walked.

Her feet ached from standing, but when the stack of blankets ran out, Robert replenished her pile.

"Thanks," Cindy murmured.

He nodded, returning to hover at Amira's elbow. Cindy wanted to ask if anything was going on between them, but the hard shell of silence around her friend since John's betrayal was not easily breached.

Cindy turned her attention back to the line of men. Rather than it diminishing, more men were coming as word spread of the little station. Friday was the bright spot in their six-day workweek.

Several hundred meters to their right, a shopping complex teemed with dozens of men, with more approaching by foot. This was like a colony, and the growing number of men a swarm of ants in search of a picnic. Those near her table pressed forward, their dark eyes searching the boxes for signs of the freebies being handed out.

The tallest were shoulder height to her, with full heads of hair that would have been the envy of most middle-aged American men. Groups from the strip mall eyed the men assembled in the lot next to them. Cindy's breath caught in her throat. She could see how outnumbered they were.

"Make a line, please," she called out when their reaching hands became more than she could keep up with.

"I take two." A man smiled at her. He had teeth missing from the side and top like a fence that needed mending. "Please. Cold."

"One per person," she said.

He was too quick, his hands whisking the blankets to his chest. Others began reaching for the stack of giveaways. Like bailing water from a sinking ship, she couldn't get blankets into the outstretched palms quickly enough. *They're not dangerous, they're desperate,* she said to herself as several men bumped the table in their haste to get blankets before they ran out.

"A line." Her voice was thin and reedy, inaudible above their steady chatter. The words fell on deaf ears. Either they didn't speak English or they chose not to answer.

A few men swiped blankets from the corner of the table. She took a step back, stumbling against one of the boxes. Jonah steadied her under the elbow to keep her from falling. Out here, without the safety of the glass malls or the cement compound boundary walls, she could see how many more workers there were in this country than people like her.

"Form a line, gentleman." Jonah's baritone rumbled. "Three lines." He indicated with his meaty hands for the men to wait in order. "One behind another."

Lines formed, snaking back from the front of the table. *Free Tibet!* one man's T-shirt read. A few men pushed each other, attempting to get to the front.

"One at a time." Jonah raised his voice. This quelled the pushing. He joined Cindy in passing out blankets.

A young man who wasn't much older than Daniel stood in front of her. She was grateful for Jonah, an anchor beside her. Realizing with a start she could have seen Sanjana's missing brother, she stood straighter, bending her knees to give her more energy.

She had no idea how she would identify him. Racking her brain for the name Sanjana had mentioned, she came up with nothing, wondering how that was possible. Surely the woman had said his name—hadn't she?

Cindy could do little but smile and nod, pressing another blanket into waiting hands as the sense of frustration inside her mounted. She could call Sanjana, sure, and then what? Raise the woman's hopes based on no concrete evidence, as Paul would say.

Cindy ducked as Amira snapped photos with her smart phone. Jonah and Robert posed with a few men in line. She hadn't told Paul she was coming. He would have either warned her away, saying these men wanted nothing to do with Jesus, or asked her to take notes about the whole experience, neither of which Cindy was willing to do. Daniel's rebuke still rang in her ears.

"That's it," Amira called. "We're out. Time to pack up." She put her red lacquered nails on the small of her back to stretch.

Jonah took down the table as a dozen or so late arrivals milled around. Cindy's stomach twisted at the sight of their worn faces. One man's hands were cut in several places, the white pulp of dry skin showing in the cracks.

"I have a first aid kit." Cindy raced to her car, thankful to be able to offer aid in whatever small way possible. She came back, elbowing her way to him, reaching out for his hands.

He jumped back. The other men around them looked nonplussed.

"Hurt?" She waved the box. He didn't seem to recognize the universal sign for first aid, the cross on the cover. *Not universal*, Cindy thought to herself, not to Buddhists, or whatever Nepalis were. She flushed, opening the kit to dispel the thought she had never asked Sanjana about her faith. Cindy set the box on the floor, pulling out a tube of ointment.

"Cindy," Amira called. "It's time to go."

"One minute." Cindy opened the tube, inserting the reverse end of the top to pierce the silver foil. Cindy squeezed a thin line of ointment onto her hand, showing the men around her the clear substance like it was a magic trick. They drew closer.

She reached for the man's hand again. This time he let her take it. She worked quickly, as she had with Daniel's cuts dozens of times, applying the ointment and then smoothing it with her fingers. He had been working with something unfinished, Cindy could tell from the new calluses on his hands.

"Here." She wrapped a bandage around the worst of the cuts. "Wait, does that hurt?"

He had drawn his palm back, cradling it with the other one.

"If that hurts, you should get it looked at," she said.

"Cindy! Let's go." Amira pushed her way to stand next to Cindy. "This isn't safe." Amira whispered the warning so only Cindy could hear.

Cindy looked around, for the first time noticing the amount of attention they had drawn. There were twice as many men as had filed through their makeshift line.

"Okay," Cindy said. She had never been afraid of these men. She outweighed them, and was confident she could take them if needed when they roamed the compound doing their maintenance work in twos and threes. But a crowd this size? This was ripe for zombies in the apocalypse, as Daniel would say.

"For you." Cindy handed the first aid box to the man with the injured hands, aware that dozens of eyes watched her every move. *What made him special?*

Are you here? Cindy asked a question of her own as Amira took her by the elbow, steering her back to their vehicles. *Sanjana's brother, I don't even know your name to yell it. Are you here?*

Amira waited for her to dig out the key from her pocket and clamber up behind the wheel before turning, with Jonah and Robert flanking her like a presidential detail, back to the BMW. They revved their engines. Cindy checked her makeup by force of habit, aware she still had an audience.

The sight of those raw, chapped hands would not leave her. She cast around, wishing she had more to give them. She could have raided Paul's closet for his discarded shirts and shoes, though a pair of Kenneth Cole loafers would be as out of place here as she had been today.

"You!" She lowered her window, ignoring Amira flickering her lights in the rearview mirror. "For you!" She motioned to the man with the raw hands, whose friends elbowed him because he was walking away. He turned around. Cindy drove to where he stood, nosing others out of the way. "Wear these," she said, passing a pair of gardening gloves through the window. She had distractedly gotten into the car with them on the way to the grocery store earlier in the week. Without Daniel there to remind her, she could be so absentminded.

He took the gloves. She had to lower her window all the way in order for him to reach them.

"Thank you."

His coal-black eyes stared into hers.

"You bet," Cindy chirped. She raised the window as Amira gave a short honk. Cindy wiggled her fingers in farewell and pulled out of the lot, picking up speed as she merged onto the paved road. Like a mirage, the dilapidated barracks receded into the twilight, the swirls of sand covering their tracks as the sun skidded across the glass fronted buildings of downtown that loomed on the horizon. If she hadn't been there, she wouldn't even know such places existed.

Chapter Sixteen

Manu hid the gloves the American woman had given him under his mattress, although this meant at least one cockroach was likely to make its bed for the evening inside. The gloves were nicer than anything Manu had seen since arriving in the country—at least inside the camp.

In the gleaming city they drove through on the old school bus, their limbs hanging out the windows like animals being led to the slaughter, everything and everyone looked new. The other residents, black, white, and brown, cruised by in their crisp clothes and shiny gadgets. They passed by the laborers as though they were in a parallel universe rather than inhabiting the same space, breathing the same air, sharing the same humanity. In the flashes he had of neighborhoods, people seemed to live as they drove, behind high walls, protecting local women from prying eyes.

Manu stood outside the room, stretching his back. "Brother, can I use your phone?" Manu bit his lip, waiting for an answer from his bunkmate, who was on his way inside the shared sleeping area.

"My name is Adith." The man shook his head. "No credit."

"Here," Manu said. He handed over a phone card the women gave out along with the blankets and Bibles. Adith's eyes lit up at the sight of the fifty-riyal card, his lips breaking into a broad smile, revealing a chipped front tooth. He scratched off the foil, punching the numbers into a palm size Nokia.

He turned his back. "First I make call, then your turn."

Manu couldn't argue. Without the device, the phone card was no good to him. He slipped off the plastic sandals and crossed to the grass of the courtyard where one of the newest men was leading a group in yoga poses. The night air was as damp as an armpit. Manu stretched, breathing deeply as the boy showed them, in through the nose and out through the mouth.

"Your turn," Adith called from the walkway.

Manu shot over to the pavement, taking the phone from Adith's out-stretched hand with trembling fingers. The metallic tone rang in his ear. One ring. Two rings. They kept pinging in his ear and with them the hope of rescue. Adith clucked. "Disconnected?"

"Maybe sleeping." Manu gulped some air to stem the rising bile. If Sanjana hadn't been able to find him, maybe she had gone home.

He dialed the shop next to his family's house. One, two, three rings. Bitter, acrid despair rose in his throat. He cursed his luck—Nepal was a little less than three hours ahead. He had missed the chance of talking to his siblings.

"Namaste," a scratchy voice said on the other end.

"Namaste!" Manu closed his eyes with the sheer joy of hearing someone from his village. "I am Manu Kulse. Please, you finding my sister, Meena." The line crackled like a live thing in his ear before it went dead.

"They disconnect." Manu stared at the device in disbelief. His heart hummed with the thought that his voice had been a few meters from his home. The kids were probably in bed. He allowed himself the image of his mother on her rope bed, Meena pressing a cloth to her forehead.

Adith hovered nearby. "Call again, but not too much. Each connection they take a fee."

Manu dialed again, having to stop in between to halt the shaking of his fingers. "Meena Kulse," he said as soon as he heard a voice on the other end. "I call back in twenty minute."

"*Bhai*," a halting voice said. "Is it you?"

Tears sprang to Manu's eyes at the term of respect for an older brother. He paced only a few meters from Adith lest the man think he was running off with his phone. "Yes. Me."

There was a shout of relief on the other end. He could hear younger voices clamoring. Ram and Raju. "Don't give difficulty." He laughed, though they couldn't hear him. His breath caught at the hesitation in their replies. He had become a distant memory.

"*Bhai*." Meena again. "Where are you?"

His gaze circled the courtyard. Wire hung across the walkway on the upper level, men's garments on the makeshift line to dry. Two cats squabbled in a corner, scratching and caterwauling. Tears filled his eyes again as he looked at the night sky, which was the same night sky he knew Meena gazed at through the window of the small shop.

"Hello? This line cut." Meena called away from the phone.

"No, no, I here," Manu said. "I fine." Silence. His turn to be nervous. "Hello? Is *Didi* there?"

"No, why would she be here? *Bhai*, why you no send money?"

He wasn't prepared for this question, the grown-up tone in Meena's voice. A pit opened up in his stomach. "Sanjana not sending?"

"She send like always," Meena said. "But we needing extra. Mother died. Why neither of you call for one month? We have funeral for mother. Village say not good to wait. Expensive too for ice."

The pit in his stomach swallowed Manu whole. His vision swam. He leaned against a pole holding up the second floor. Sanjana was nowhere he could find. And his mother was gone. "My company not pay me yet."

A yawning hole grew in his heart at the thought his mother was gone. He had assumed, or wished, that Sanjana's salary would keep them afloat as it always had, that she was calling them regularly, as she had done once a week since she came to work for the American family in this country.

He gulped air, laced with the odors of the men's meals, their unwashed bodies, and the overflowing dumpster. The stoicism he had been raised with crumbled. "I have no money." His voice broke at the admission.

"Why you go work for company that no pay?" Meena snapped. "I go. Someone need phone. Send money soon. The boys hungry."

Manu stared at the receiver in his hand, the bleat of the dial tone turning from one continuous note into spasmodic beeps. He had no privacy to weep, to pull his hair at the thought of his mother's body, prone and lifeless.

Seeing he had finished talking, Adith fetched the phone. He pushed a few numbers. "Credit finished. Any time you have phone card, you can use." He squeezed Manu's shoulder.

Manu shrugged off the contact. He slid under the bed on his pallet, his nose centimeters away from the back of the man above him. He slept under the bunk. That was better than out in the open, where someone would stumble into you on their way to the toilet or risk rolling into the new arrivals.

The man above him groaned, pressing his bulk into Manu's face. He had tried sleeping with his head to the south so his face was where the man's feet were, but this meant he often lost feeling in his legs if the pressure of the man's shoulders pinned his ankles and feet to the floor. The best way to handle being crushed was to turn on his side, so his shoulder blade jutted into the thin mattress above. This way the man knew to roll to the side, usually closest to the wall, and his weight could have free rein in the corner of the mattress.

Manu drew breath through his mouth, as a way to relax and save himself the stench of so many men housed together. Someone tossed on an upper bunk, crying out in his sleep. Manu thought again of the mountains of his home, the fresh air, bracing in the winter, languid and as lazy as his youngest brother in the summer. With the fetid smell of unwashed bodies and the filthy squatty potties, the floor-based toilets with a porcelain foothold on either side of the hole the ten men shared, they were difficult to visualize.

Oh, but the American woman's green eyes today. Manu forced himself to remember the way her irises had constricted when she saw his hands, and the way her long, pale fingers fluttered over his skin, the fleshy pads firm in their grip. Her hands had been smooth as she had applied the ointment. He didn't tell her that her ministrations would slide off the second he picked up a piece of concrete, marble, a tool—but the gloves. Ah, the gloves. Now those he could use.

Manu turned again onto his other shoulder. Tears leaked, unchecked, from the corners of his eyes. The man above him grunted. Manu couldn't move too much or risk his wrath. He had seen men fight over much less. His gaze fell on the center of the room, his thoughts turning toward the body that had lain there a few weeks ago.

They had never seen him again. Manu hadn't had a chance to learn his name. Heart attack, some had said. Suicide, others whispered. Manu hadn't seen either before. Only old people died in his village. Or they went away to places like this, not to be heard from again. He shuddered, unable to help from turning yet again to get the spot out of his line of sight.

Now he could see the hand, flopping out of the red casket at the airport. It hadn't taken long to realize that while housemaids like his sister were lucky enough to find a nice family. Men like him were as numerous as the grains of sand in the desert. When one was crushed, another ten would come forward.

The thought of Sanjana stung his eyes. *Was her madam like the one who gave me the gloves?* Manu wondered. *Did she drive such an expensive car? And was she so clueless that she would hand out books in Hindi, when what they could use most of all were clothes or food?* He had tossed his book alongside the dozen or so others in the corner. Some men used the pages to roll cigarettes. Others used the tissue-thin insides to help get the kerosene stoves going if the pilot light was out.

Manu turned, eliciting a louder grunt from above. The blanket was soft against his cheek and smelled of something flowery, though he couldn't place the scent among the flowers that grew on the floor of his valley at home. At least the woman and her companions had given them water, and something useful, a cover against the mattresses where untold numbers had lain.

Sleep pulled at Manu's eyes with a kaleidoscope of images. Women with green eyes, his sister laughing in the front seat of a shiny cement truck, a man with stumps for hands wearing his gloves, Meena with the boys clutching her skirts, shouting at him from atop his mother's burning body on the funeral pyre.

~~~

"You'll miss the bus." Adith's gruff voice started Manu awake.

"Coming." He braced his hands on the shelf above and pulled himself out like turtle leaving its shell. Manu splashed water on his face while the others in his room lined up on the pavement, eating leftover bread from last night's meal.

"Do you ever think this is wrong?"

Adith's eyes rounded in question above a mouthful of flatbread.

"This." Manu gestured to the men scarfing down their breakfast, the filthy toilet behind them.

Adith chewed, his jaw working through his makeshift meal. He passed Manu a portion of his bread no bigger than the palm of his hand. Manu tried to decline, but after the fourth insistence, he took it.

"You new here." Adith switched to English. "Better to work, get pay, and go home in two years." He pushed up from the pavement, heading for the bus. "Not looking for trouble, no reason trouble find you."

In that advice, Manu heard the fights between his parents—his father's protestations against the Maoists and his mother's pleas for her husband to think of the family. He ran to catch up with him. "There are so many of us," Manu whispered into the shorter man's ear as they stood in line to enter the bus. "More of us than them. What would they do if we refused to go?"

Men jostled, trying to cut the line to avoid having to stand the hour or so journey into the city.

"Queue!" A few shouted, pushing back in a blur of blue uniforms.

Adith stared straight ahead as if he hadn't heard. Manu soaked in the sight of so many men, three buses idling on the side of the road like tired beasts. The lowered windows in the midst of the drab white gave the appearance of a mouthful of gap teeth.

Chapter Seventeen

The engine hummed as the driver pulled the car into the sand outside the nursery.

"Leave the AC on." Laxmi hoisted herself out of the white sedan. In a silver SUV next to them, a woman in black tights and sleeveless top buckled her child into a car seat. Laxmi's belly jiggled with the force of standing up, having given up keeping her stomach muscles tight after the first pregnancy. They'd already rounded out in the first trimester.

She hadn't been sure they could afford another little one, but the new agreement with the construction company had proved so lucrative. She mollified Sajish with the idea of giving the workers a few free dinners for the Eid holidays, since Hindu ones were not looked upon kindly by the monotheistic government.

"Sorry, baby." Laxmi rubbed knuckles across the growing mound that in the months to come would rival her husband's girth. She stood to one side, smiling at the blonde girl, who was riding high in her father's arms, exiting the nursery. "Good afternoon."

Unlike at the grocery store or in traffic, the man answered her, blue eyes crinkling.

"Bye," chirped the girl, who would have looked past Laxmi in a mall or brought her some trash to throw away in a park.

This rectangular white gate kept unruly children from running headlong into the neighborhood street. Drivers of SUVS treated the road running parallel to the nursery's entryway as a shortcut to bypass the main thoroughfare. It was usually clogged as vehicles waited to enter the highway.

The heavy metal door enclosing the lush outdoor play area creaked behind her. Laxmi nodded to the Ethiopian worker standing at the ready to push the entrance button so that none of the parents would have to wait a second if the gate were closed. The waifish woman with curly hair raised the black lock on yet another small barrier to enter the nursery proper.

Three means to catch your wayward child. Westerners were so cautious. She smiled with the knowledge her daughter was benefitting from all this caution and care.

Laxmi crossed the open courtyard, painted with a small racetrack, past the bikes piled up against the cream wall. She hummed.

This nursery was much better than Sajita spending the whole day at home with the retirement-age nanny. She took the steps slowly, another mother stepping aside when she saw her belly. *And this baby will get an even better nanny.*

She went into the Tiny Tots room where the children were in various stages of sleep. Their limbs sprawled across the multicolored foam squares used for naptime. In the back corner were white cribs for the younger ones. *He will sleep here.*

"So sweet," she whispered at the sight of Sajita bundled in a blanket between two white twins, pacifiers dangling from their lips. The teaching assistant, whose covered hair and brown face suggested a South Asian heritage, offered a shy smile.

The door opened behind them. A small housemaid in matching peach top and pants with white pockets entered, scanning the room for her charge. She moved toward a dark-haired boy, who screamed the second she laid her fingers on him. The South Asian assistant went to hush the child before he woke the others.

"Come, my baby." Laxmi cradled Sajita, taking a second to steady herself on her knees before rising with effort.

She had printed photos of Sajita to send home to her mother, who would take the images of the long haired, sparkling-eyed toddler around to the rest of the family, bragging.

Sajish didn't understand her desire for their child to compete with those of Westerners. He would be happy for her to stay home and take of Sajita. But if something happened to him—if his tricky heart stopped working one hot day—well then, she knew where they would be: on the first flight back to Nepal with her daughter. Then she'd fly right back to the Gulf as a housemaid. No thank you.

The maid bundled her now screaming charge out the door as the remaining sleepers shifted in their sleep, the girl nearest Sajita giving a loud sigh.

Laxmi made her way back to the car. The Ethiopian opened the smaller barrier and then the main gate for her. A man in a black chef's uniform with curly hair falling over sunglasses held open the white outer gate.

"Thank you," she murmured as she heard the other mothers do to one another. She rapped her knuckles on the door, rousing the driver from his stupor. The skinny guy hopped up, and then hoisted up his black pants before coming around to the passenger side.

Laxmi bent to lay Sajita on the backseat. She couldn't quite get the idea of those seats all the westerners used for their children. She slid in next to her, cradling her daughter's feet in her lap. The child was so peaceful, why make her neck hang at an angle like a hung chicken, bobbing around with traffic when she could be settled nicely like this.

"Go slowly," she instructed.

The driver was new, one of the guys who had come from this month's arrivals. Sajish liked him because he spoke some Arabic and could be sent to the Ministry if needed.

"Home." She leaned her head back against the back of the seat, overcome by drowsiness.

The clanging of musical tones woke her. "Turn that down."

"Not radio, madam," the driver said. "Madam's phone."

Laxmi sat up, nudging Sajita further back into the car. Her dark hair fell across cheeks plump with baby fat. The screen flashed with the photo icon of Sajish's face, deadpan, non-smiling, ever awkward in front of a camera.

"Yes." She stifled a yawn. "You feeling well?"

"We have a problem."

"We will be there soon. I want to drop the application for the American school on the way."

She had stayed up last night filling out the form for the American school, buzzing with the idea that her daughter might be the first to go to college.

"No. Come straight home."

"Did you ask cook about lunch?" Laxmi had pulled one of the guys who had been injured from a nail going through his foot. Since he'd be incapacitated for construction work, she hired him to chop vegetables and prepare ingredients for dishes. They paid him, the big-eyed guy, no more than a boy, and allowed him to take food back to the accommodation.

"Company issue," he said tersely.

Laxmi sat up. She turned toward the window, cupping a hand between her cheek and the phone. "What is it now?"

Sajita stirred, a hand flinging out into the space between the seat and the driver's chair. Laxmi's heart clenched.

"The workers are talking. They want more money."

"That's fine," she whispered, as the driver steered the car around the corner. "Protesting is illegal. We find someone in the camp who will keep tabs on the troublemakers and we can have them arrested."

Her husband's breath came through the phone speaker like a storm wind.

"Stay calm," she said.

"I am trying."

"In and out," she said in the voice she used to put Sajita to bed. "In and out, through your nose." Laxmi read as much as she could on the Internet about Sajish's condition, and watched video after video of people breathing into paper bags. She was better at soothing him in person.

"A spy," he said, his voice steady. "Not a bad idea. We need someone we can trust."

"Money," she said. "We offer the guy money."

"I'll go down now and see if I can find someone."

The line went dead in her hand.

Chapter Eighteen

Sanjana closed the lid on the washing machine. The hum drowned out the other sounds, including the thoughts whirring in her head. She had had no answer from the embassy, and Sir Paul was away again for something called a steering committee, Madam said. Sanjana understood that to mean Sir liked being away from them as much as he liked living with them.

A knock on her bedroom door roused her from her reverie. She bustled forward, worried Madam had been calling her.

Analyn stood on the porch, her hands on her hips, black leggings and white t-shirt stained with sweat. "Why you no answer your phone?"

"How you get in here?"

The taller woman stepped forward. "No shouting."

"Sorry," Sanjana put a hand to her head when what she wanted to do was put them around Analyn's neck. "My phone fell in toilet," she improvised. "I not talking to anybody."

Analyn glanced around, as if wanting to see the water source. "The gate was open."

Sanjana saw the side entrance, open from when she watered the plants in the morning. She really was losing it.

"Anyway, I come to see if you have sponge. Washing cars and mine all broken." Analyn dangled a yellow bedraggled piece of foam.

"Ask your Madam to buy."

Analyn bit her lip. "I forget to put it on the grocery list. She get very angry with me."

"Yes, I coming quickly," Sanjana wanted to be rid of the woman and her searching eyes. She entered the kitchen from adjacent door and pulled out a sponge from the stack under the counter. On second thought, she reached for another one. "There." She piled them into Analyn's hands. "Two."

"Thanks."

"Go before it gets too hot."

"I call you later. Or I come by. You without a phone."

"I tell you when I have new phone." Sanjana escorted Analyn to the gate. She closed it behind her, leaning against the warm metal. She didn't have to wash cars like Analyn. She didn't have to keep her eye always out for Daniel. She did have to do laundry.

Sanjana retreated into the house to collect the never-ending pile of laundry from the boy's room. Her nail caught on the thread of a sock. She put down the basket she held with her right arm, and pulled the string out of the hairline crack. The effort ripped the rest of the nail. Sanjana tore off the remaining piece of the fingernail and tossed it in the trash, along with the dryer sheets and lint balls.

She yanked at the stray piece of string, pulling out the hem in one of Daniel's white athletic socks. This followed her nail into the trashcan. In went the other of the pair, the one that wouldn't have a partner with the first gone. He had others. She bent and resumed pulling the fluffy contents from the dryer, the T-shirts and shorts smelling faintly floral.

Sanjana trudged with the full basket to her room. She sat on the edge of the bed, letting gravity pull her body to the mattress. Her undamaged phone slid out of her pocket. The black screen stared at her like an unblinking eye. No phone calls home for six weeks now, lest anyone catch on that she had no idea what had happened to Manu.

And no calls from him, though she checked her phone a hundred times a day, waiting for him to find her or news from the embassy. She still sent money home, knowing it was half of what her family expected since his salary was unlikely to show up.

Sanjana closed her eyes at the thought of the kids having to go without because of her stupid mistake. She was gullible. Her brother had always told her that while chuffing her on the cheek as if she were their goat, in need of guidance and a little affection.

One of the other maids on the compound had recommended Laxmi Pande because her son had gotten a job at a university that way. During the initial meeting, Sanjana had listened as Laxmi spoke in rounded English vowels, so much like an American. She was cowed by the woman's impressive command of the language and pin-straight hair, her black slacks, her ivory silk shirt.

They had met at a coffee shop in a gas station near the embassy. Laxmi had explained about her private company and ability to bring over workers. Sanjana, normally cautious and likely to ask Sir Paul for advice on everything when he was around, had needed to give Laxmi an answer within a few minutes. She handed over the fee and Manu's passport copy, feeling lucky that she had made it ahead of others who were desperate to do the same. The woman worked at the embassy, after all. She knew about all the newest and best jobs.

There were only so many times Sanjana could go to the embassy without falling behind on her work. She needed the taxi money to send home, and if Madam knew she was letting a few tasks slide here and there—the refrigerator not cleaned, the cans expiring in the pantry—she could dock Sanjana's salary.

Sanjana groaned. She sat up, shaking her head from side to side. Manu would turn up. She had to believe he would. The invisible cord tying him to her, the sibling bond, was still there. She would know in some way if it were severed.

She bent to fold the laundry, turning over the well-washed items automatically. Worn T-shirts Daniel insisted on keeping, despite the holes and the rising hems that were unable to keep up with his continued growth. A pouch fell out of a pocket of one of the shorts. She sniffed it. Even wet, there was no mistaking this smell—the one that wafted from houses late in the evenings in the middle of winter in her remote village. *Hashish*, she thought, her fingers curling around the ball. Madam was right. Daniel was up to no good.

"Sanjana?"

She started, as if thinking about Madam had conjured her back in the house.

"Sanjana, I need your help."

She bit her lip, eyes casting around for somewhere to stash the bundle, but Madam's tread was already on the stairs.

"There you are." Cindy propped herself in the doorway, panting slightly. Her blond hair was tied back. She wore a pink T-shirt that fell at mid-thigh over her exercise pants. "Want to go for a drive?"

"Yes." Sanjana attempted what she hoped was a bright smile. She clutched the ball of leaves behind her back. "You wanting to change? I come."

"No, I'm fine." Cindy smiled. "The camps are casual. Those poor men don't have very much."

Sanjana rose obediently, worried that any hesitation would be an alarm bell that something was out of the ordinary.

"I went somewhere last weekend. I think you should have a look." Madam walked beside her as they trooped through the house to the side door, like Sanjana used to do when escorting Daniel to his various afternoon activities. "I may have seen your brother."

"Manu?" Sanjana squeaked in surprise. She almost dropped the ball.

Cindy nodded vigorously. "Yes, that's right. I was in the Industrial Area, and we were passing out water…"

The flare of hope in Sanjana's chest died. This was another of Madam's rescue missions—missions that meant the rest of them had to step in when her far-reaching plans failed. She had met some men and thought of Manu. That was all.

"Madam, we not help everyone." Sanjana laid a hand on Cindy's arm, palming the mesh bag in her other hand. Cindy flinched underneath her touch and moved away. Sanjana pushed the mesh bag inside her waistband while the other woman's back was turned.

"Remembering all those cats? They come, they have their babies here. Too many cats." Sanjana overlooked Cindy's rebuff. This was their dance. Sanjana stepped over the line from trusted servant now and then, and Madam's wordless rebuke reminded Sanjana of her place.

"We help who we can."

Sanjana cringed as Madam fluffed her hair in the reflection of the metal fridge. This type of help would last as long as Madam's attention span, which, judging by the stray cat project, had been until the situation became messy. Sanjana was the one who'd had to distribute those kittens, door to door in the compound, until finally Paul loaded up the remaining ten to take to the animal shelter.

"Anyway, I kept thinking maybe I'd see your brother, so if you come with me, maybe you'll see him."

Madam's idea was crazy. *This would be harder than getting an old chicken to lay an egg*, Sanjana thought. There were thousands of men in the country. The odds of finding her brother were next to none, but a flutter of hope rose in her chest all the same.

The side door slammed. Sanjana narrowed her eyes at Daniel and his friend Sharif, who slunk in after him. The other boy was shorter than Daniel, his dark hair and eyes making the pair a study in contrasts.

"Hi, boys," Madam said.

"Hi, Mrs. Johnson," Sharif replied. Daniel swiped an apple from a tricolored bowl on the counter.

"We're going out to the camps with your mother," Cindy said to Sharif. "Would you like to join us?"

"Homework," Daniel said around a mouthful of apple.

"Alright." Cindy's gaze lingered on the two of them. "We'll be back soon."

Sanjana knew by the way she swung her purse that Madam was forcing herself to leave. She didn't want to take her eyes off Sharif.

"I get some water," Sanjana said.

Cindy nodded, leaving through the garage door to the Range Rover.

"You naughty boy," Sanjana hissed.

"What?" Daniel said. "I cleaned my room."

"You think your mother not angry when she knowing about this?" Sanjana pulled out the clenched bag of hash and waved it at both of them. "Why you bring this?"

The color drained from Daniel's face. Sharif broke into a grin. "Did you try some?"

"No," Sanjana hissed. "I not try."

"Give it to me." Daniel moved toward her, his green eyes intent. "I'll get rid of it."

"You not touching this," Sanjana slapped his hand away. She scuttled in reverse, her back to the door. "I am the one to throw it away."

"Are you insane?" Sharif approached her. He was more her size, his body lacking the muscles that roped through Daniel's swimmer's shoulders. "Do you know how much that cost? Probably your monthly salary."

"You not bring danger to our house and be insulting me," Sanjana snapped. "I telling Madam, that's what."

"It's not mine. I swear." Daniel's eyes pleaded in that way she had never been able to resist. "Don't tell my mother, please."

"Don't tell me what?" Cindy poked her head back into the kitchen.

Sanjana almost dropped the ball of hash.

"Boys, scrounge for your own food, okay? I need Sanjana."

Sanjana squeezed the mesh tight, hoping she had broken all the leaves so it would be no good for smoking. "He not doing his homework, Madam. He playing that computer. Sharif not study either."

Cindy shook her head, snapping her fingers to indicate Daniel should get to the kitchen table. "Sharif, you want to scoot on home, then."

"Mrs. Johnson, I need Daniel's help with calculus."

Daniel said nothing. Cindy let out an exasperated huff. She gave the boys a reluctant nod. This, in Sanjana's opinion, was why Sharif had a hold on Daniel. Childhood friend or not, they did not need to spend time alone together.

"Sanjana, we need to get going or we'll be stuck in the traffic at sunset when all the trucks come in."

"Coming." Sanjana stepped behind Cindy, hands at her sides, ignoring Daniel's coughs and Sharif's broad smile.

Chapter Nineteen

Ali tossed in bed. Even the sound of his own breathing was an irritation. He threw back the covers, pulled on sweatpants, and then stalked downstairs to the kitchen in hotel slippers from the last Eid holiday.

Well, the last one before the family became housebound, waiting for the end. The shuffling sound reminded him of the final days of his father's illness, when Yusuf was so worn out from the chemo that even walking required effort.

Ali moved through the marbled entryway, past the ladies' sitting room, the dark like a comforting blanket. The rest of the house was shrouded in sleep, the lights off, the lateness of the hour sending the most stalwart of insomniacs to their rooms. Or maybe they were awake, like he was, locked in private grief, as they had been in the months since their father's death.

Three sisters, he thought, pulling open the fridge. *Three sisters, and they're left with me as the man.* Well, semi-man. He contemplated the tray of hummus, a dish of *tabouli*, a parcel of ground meat, and a bag of nuts in the fridge. His stomach rumbled in protest at the thought of accepting the cold contents. Ali shut the door. He didn't want something reheated. He wanted something hot.

The microwave clock glowed 3 a.m. There was a twenty-four hour McDonald's not two hundred meters from the house. He could walk there, if one did such a thing anymore in his country. *The fresh air would do some good.* He slipped on his sneakers.

"*Ya Rub!*" he exclaimed as a shadow passed over his reflection in the sliding glass door. Ali snapped the lights on. Maybe he had woken one of the maids, whose rooms were off the kitchen.

His youngest sister stood in front of him with hair tousled, rubbing her eyes.

"God, Aisha, you scared me. What are you doing awake?"

"I could ask you the same thing." She eyed his shoes.

"I'm going to get something to eat."

Aisha's twelve-year-old tummy showed the same curves he had suffered from as a child, before the accident. Ali had tended toward fat. Childhood chubbiness never quite left him as he approached his teenage years, until the fever took hold of him, burning his body, searing his mind, and other pathways of nerves. Some had recovered. Others had not.

"Can I come?"

"*Ayoosh*. You should go back to sleep. You have school tomorrow."

"I'm hungry."

"You should eat dinner."

"I do!" She pounded a fist into her stomach. "It's not enough. They put me on a diet. Mom says I'm fat." Her gaze drifted to her shoes.

"You're awake because you're hungry."

Aisha's face drooped, the lingering pounds of childhood visible in the curve of her cheek.

"You'll grow out of this," he said. "Everyone in our family is tall. You'll be fine."

"So do the girls at school."

Ali took a breath. The stories of bullying in the government schools were legendary. He had gone to a government school with Hassan, the two of them a wall against any of the other boys looking for amusement. His gut twisted at the thought of someone making fun of Aisha.

"Am I fat?"

He had to lean forward to hear her whisper. "No." Ali bristled with indignation. His mother was forever worried that her daughters would never get married because of her son's condition. She fretted day and night, like a character from one of the English novels she had kept from graduate school. As a widow, she was bent on securing good matches for her daughters, since their house had no man.

"Come on, then," he said. "Let's be quick."

The brilliant smile she flashed him gave Ali pause. Maybe things weren't so bad after all. Maybe she wanted out of the house. Like he did. Aisha scampered to get her shoes, her energy reminding him she was so very young. Young enough for him not to remind her to wear an *abaya*, another oversight his mother would disapprove of.

Ali disagreed with his mother's approach, but was in no position to offer his sisters his protection. The closer he got to them, the more they might find out about his condition. He couldn't take another rejection like Khalifa's when the medical results had come back for the National Service review. *Unfit for protective detail*—the evaluation came unbidden to mind. *Demotion necessary*.

"Someone specific bothering you at school?" Ali asked to distract himself from the dark bent of his thoughts.

"No." Aisha kept her eyes downcast.

He edged her chin up with a forefinger. "Tell me the truth."

Aisha glanced to one side and sighed.

"We are not leaving this house until you tell me what is going on." *And I'll put them in jail,* Ali thought fiercely, gazing at the curve of his sister's cheek which showed lingering prepubescent chubbiness.

"The girls, they like things different than me. Like make-up and dresses, going to weddings."

Ali's heart eased. He squeezed her shoulder. "That's fine. You keep your distance and focus on your studies." *You'll join them soon enough, like your sisters,* he didn't add.

His mind wandered to Maryam, the only exception he knew in this sea of femininity who was unconcerned with parties and impressing others. Ali and Aisha left the house through the side entrance, past the closed doors of the servants' quarters. Aisha moved with a stealth that surprised him, her shoes gliding over the concrete courtyard.

"Narena doesn't take you anywhere he shouldn't, does he?" Ali asked as they passed the family SUV, a glistening black GMC with tinted windows.

"Like where?" Aisha gave a high-pitched giggle at the possibility, underscoring her submissive youthfulness. "The mall without the maid?"

"Never mind." There he was, jumpy because some western-educated girl had done something she wasn't supposed to. Not his sisters. They were good girls. Besides, his mother watched them with the eagerness of a peregrine falcon guarding her nest.

They walked in companionable silence through the neighborhood street, two and three story villas casting shadows on their path. Up ahead, a Land Cruiser was parked on the corner with its passenger-side window lowered. Ali couldn't hear the conversation. As they approached, the driver swiveled his head out the window. Seeing Ali and Aisha, he screeched off, revealing the woman in black leggings and pink Ed Hardy T-shirt who had been standing on the other side.

"Go home," Ali told the woman in an even voice.

She scurried away as fast as her wedge sandals allowed. He waited for the string of questions Aisha would volley at him, wondering how he would hide the stories of assignations between housemaids and anyone willing to boost their meager salaries.

Khalifa needs to increase the night patrols, he thought. The growth of the country meant more buildings, and more buildings meant more people, more men, more crime, and more danger.

Within a few minutes, at the curve of the road, the yellowish glow of lights from the McDonald's appeared. Cars snaked around the twenty-four hour drive-thru. The arms of young men, those who had snuck out or were cruising the neighborhood, were visible in the lowered windows. Aisha hummed to herself, occasionally bumping into him due to a lifelong inability to walk in a straight line that their sisters chided her about if they were in airports or sightseeing.

Ali held the door for Aisha, a custom he had seen in American movies, one that other brothers would have laughed at him for. *Did Nasser hold the door for his sister?* There. Another thought about that girl. He distracted himself by trying to remember as many of the digits from the Land Cruiser's license plate as he could. He brushed it off. She was memorable because of her strangeness, wandering into camps, caring for laborers—traits he didn't think local girls growing up with maids to feed, wash, and clothe them would ever have.

Eventually the majority would swallow her memory. The majority, he had to admit, he disliked because they were likely to dislike him if they found out his secret. Ali went to the counter, rattling off requests for cheeseburgers and nuggets for Aisha. The dining area was lit as though it were dinnertime, not closer to *fajer,* the dawn prayer a few hours away.

He could not get the green-eyed girl out of his mind. Probably because she was the only girl he had talked to this month, Hassan would say, if Ali had been one to confide such things. At any one time, Hassan was messaging at least three girls he had met in some chat room or the other.

"Thank you, sir, come again, sir." The Filipina worker flashed her teeth as she handed him a receipt.

Ali mumbled his thanks. They were such cheerful people. He couldn't imagine being happy to stand on his feet in the middle of the night, serving binge eaters. He brought over two drinks, sitting in the booth across from Aisha, pushing a box of milk at her. She pulled a face, and he laughed.

"You couldn't get me Pepsi?" Her p sounded like a b. She wasn't exaggerating the accent like Hassan often did to make fun of Arab speakers who couldn't cope with the English p, a sound that didn't exist in Arabic.

"How many beoble call the bolice today?" Hassan would say, dissolving into a spasm of laughter.

"You're too young for Pepsi."

She stabbed the foil circle with her straw. "I'm too old for this." She sipped at the chocolate-flavored milk and twirled a piece of her hair around her finger until it was completely covered. They sat in the booth, waiting for their food.

"Are you in love?"

"*Shinoo?*" Ali snorted on the soda that went up his nose. "Excuse me?"

"Well, you know, Maha says that when people are in love, they can't sleep, and they can eat lots of food. Like in *The Little Mermaid*."

"They have McDonald's underwater?" Ali joked, stalling, making Aisha snort this time. "That's an old movie, anyway." He chewed. "Aren't you seeing *Frozen* or something?"

"No. Maha watched *The Little Mermaid* for this class, something about women in fairytales. She says the food is a metaphor for rebellion, since a life without love is misery. Like Ariel's love for Eric."

"That's supposed to be a good university," Ali grumbled. "Sounds like Americans watch movies and call it education."

"I'm going there too." Aisha sat up straighter. "I want to be a writer."

"God willing." Ali wanted to shake Maha, the older sister, for putting these ideas into Aisha's head, but maybe it was better that the girls prepare for a life of work in case neither of them could make good unions.

A male Filipino worker arrived and placed the tray of food onto the table. "Thank you, ma'am, sir." His singsong voice carried across the almost-empty restaurant.

Ali gave him a curt nod, and stuffed a handful of French fries into his mouth to avoid answering more questions.

"Good, because it's not mixed like the other ones?" Aisha opened the sweet and sour sauce container, pulling at the foil cover gingerly.

"Well, it's the oldest." If he disagreed too much, then Aisha would know that she was saying something she shouldn't, a common complaint of the older siblings against the younger.

"Doesn't mean it's the best." Aisha dipped a nugget into the sauce and then pointed it at him. "You're not also going to make me go there, are you?"

"What else does Maha say?" He hoped his questions had the casual air of conversation rather than interest, so he could dodge the education question. Aisha sounded like Maryam, and he wondered how much of his sisters' lives he didn't know about.

"Maha is an English major. They think about everything." Aisha emphasized this by biting a nugget in half. If Ali hadn't been so disturbed by her conversation, he would have been amused by the gusto with which Aisha was tackling the rare fast food treat. He made a mental note to speak to his mother about harassing the girls for their weight.

"She says we'll never find love because you're only half a man, so no one will marry us. Even if it isn't in the family, they'll see it as a weakness."

"What?" Ali gripped the plastic table until his hands trembled. "She told you that?"

Aisha nodded, her eyes round, her cheeks wobbling. "Okay, not exactly. I heard her telling AlDana that's why the last guy who proposed didn't come back after the look at the bride. But when they saw I could hear, they stopped talking."

Ali swallowed, forcing the bread of his burger down his now dry throat. "What did she mean?"

A sesame seed was caught in the soft part of his palate, irritating him like the pea had the princess in the fairy tale.

"I was sick when I was your age." Ali realized this had been ten years ago, when Aisha was a toddler. "You wouldn't remember, but it was a fever and it did a lot of damage." He wasn't sure how much she understood and cursed Maha's wagging tongue.

"I was lucky to live." He repeated the line he had heard a dozen times in the hospital in London as the British doctors worked on him, his mother wailing that the surgery would ruin their family forever. The persistent half-space haunted him, the one testicle pressing against his thigh where there should have been two. "There's no reason a non-genetic, childhood condition would affect any of you."

"We won't get it, will we?"

Ali snorted, Pepsi rushing out his nose. This sent Aisha into peals of laughter. He recovered with gasping breaths. "No, you can't get this."

"They're afraid anyway?"

"Something like that." Ali balled up the remainder of his meal, his appetite gone. "Let's head back. Almost time for *fajer*." Dawn prayer was the last thing on his mind, but it would send Aisha off to bed, which is what he needed right then.

So his missing testicle was not only responsible for getting him demoted from the ISF, but may also keep his sisters from settling in good homes. *Conservative homes*, he corrected himself. Would a girl's family mind? A family who sent their daughter to sit in classrooms with men? Ali quickened the pace as if he could outrun the thought. He should have died with that fever and put an end to all this misery.

Chapter Twenty

Maryam stapled the five pages together and then passed her assignment to the right, so Mohammed could put it in with the stack being handed toward Professor Paul's desk. *The Migrant Report*—her title flashed from the top of the pile. She felt a flash of pride at the byline, even if it was only for a class assignment. The lowered blinds shrouded the classroom in semi-dark, though the sun beat cheerful rays on the world outside the university building.

"The final will be ten questions." Paul gathered the essays.

Maryam drew her *abaya* closer, shivering in the air conditioning that made sweaters inside necessary. A few knocks on the window caught her attention.

A man in blue overalls was being lowered in a rectangular box, hanging from the roof by four anchor ropes. He had a power washer in one hand, blasting the windows opposite their classroom. The water gushed forward, hitting the window with the force of a cannon. The laborer braced himself, both hands on the top of the hose, his legs absorbing the recoil.

What a life, she thought. *One snap and that box hits the ground.*

"In this room?" Mohammed asked, taking her attention from morbid thoughts. She turned away from the window, determined to focus on what was being said around her. *I couldn't help that man, anyway, if he did plunge to his death.* She thought of the man who had inspired her report for the class. *I don't know his name.* She drew a prone figure on the blank page in her notebook, where her review notes for the exam should have been.

"The very same," Paul said.

The overhead fluorescent light was like a pinprick in both of her eyeballs. She had stayed up all night, asking Babu to drive her past the camp one more time, his aching ribs and all, in search of inspiration. The squat buildings had been more menacing in the semi-dark. No signs of life that late at night.

And that cop. She frowned in irritation as she drew in others at the scene, including her own shocked face. There were so many nameless men like the one hanging by a few ropes outside the window, the police couldn't be bothered to get involved.

"When will we see our grades?" Maryam ventured.

"As soon as I post them." Paul smiled. Someone—was it Amal?—snickered.

"You won't get an A, not after all that with the Olympic committee." Mohammed sized her up in sympathy. Maryam shied away from him.

"That wasn't my fault," she protested. "They changed their story. Besides, the website guys already took it down."

"You should write about that." Mohammed jabbed his finger at her. "Censorship. In a media school."

"Care to share what's so interesting with the rest of us?" Paul frowned.

Mohammed opened his mouth to reply, but Maryam coughed, shaking her head.

"Lucky for you two we are out of time." Paul dismissed the class.

The rest of the class bolted. Amal left with an arch "Have a good day, Professor."

Mohammed shot Maryam an irritated look. "Coward," he hissed and left.

Faisal hovered in the doorway, his *thobe* immaculate as though straight from the dry cleaners. Phone in hand, he scrolled through social media feeds.

Maryam gathered her laptop and notebook. "I really need a good grade in this class."

Paul paused in gathering and unplugging the computer from the projector on the podium. "You can't expect special treatment. If people find out I've known you since you were eight or nine, and you are my son's friend, they'll say I shouldn't have let you enroll in this class." He wrapped the power cord, winding the cable around on itself. "That whole Olympic committee thing was a mess enough."

"Professor, this has nothing to do with that. My friendship with Daniel is irrelevant." She rounded the desk to stand on his right. "I worked really hard on that assignment. I—"

Paul waved his hand, shoving the stack of assignments into his leather carryall. "I recommended you to the admissions team. You showed so much promise in high school. It's difficult to sustain that intellectual prowess around here. Daniel's going through some difficulties as well."

Maryam stepped back as if he had slapped her. "Wait until you read this one. If you knew what I had to do to get that story."

"You are not being graded on effort, but on your ability to fulfill the assignment." He gave her a wan smile. "I'll do what I can, but you have to do your part as well."

She nodded, the image of her father's irate face flashing next to Paul's concerned one.

"I have to go to a faculty meeting."

Maryam waved, but his back was already turned. He left her in the empty room. She dodged Faisal, who was chatting with students from the next class, entered the security code for her phone, and opened a new WhatsApp chat with Daniel.

How are you? She typed while walking down the hallway, past the streams of people entering other classrooms. Most of the other local girls had formed their packs, either continuing existing relationships from high school or by major.

Maryam didn't have the energy to force herself on anyone, nor the desire to conform to their expectations for dress and speech. Amal's tittering laugh floated back to her. The girls in Amal's clique wore Manolo Blahniks to class and sported the latest in *abaya* fashion—embroidery or lace. This was their everyday dress.

Maryam avoided them all, taking the hallway to the right, a short cut to the elevator. In the middle of the building was a walkway, bifurcating the third floor. Here was the light and air she craved, missing from every other place in the city.

A boy stood on the bridge below, hands on his ears, feet spread, his head thrown back as he gave the call to prayer. The sound was haunting, eerie in the sunlight that glinted off the building's glass entryway. Maryam wanted to take a picture of him giving the *athan,* but even from behind, where she could not disturb his prayer, she felt like a polluting substance, and instead scurried along.

There was one gray check on the app. She stared at the screen for a few more steps, willing it to turn double blue checks, the indication the other person had the program open and had read the message.

She could have gone to a university with fewer locals, like the one offering the medical program, which was how Nasser had ended up there. Her mother had refused, saying medicine was no profession for a woman who also had to balance a household and raise her children. Maryam had begged to be allowed to study overseas, elsewhere in the Arab world if the West was out of the question, but this was even too forward for her father. He wouldn't send her to study alone.

"You know what they say about girls who study abroad," Fatma wailed. "Do you never want a groom to come to this house?"

"What groom?" Maryam had protested. "I'm not even in uni and there's no one in sight."

"And no one is ever likely to come with MD attached to your name!" Her mother's retort had been the final word. Journalism was less objectionable, though Fatma had still sniffed when Maryam brought her the acceptance papers. "Classes with boys." She had huffed and thrust the letter with a university seal back at Maryam.

"Don't you trust me?" Maryam had asked.

There had been many people who had misunderstood her friendship with Daniel in high school, but she had been able to keep it secret from her parents, as though there was something dirty going on. Daniel was younger, like the baby sibling she had never had and always wanted. He was always going from one incident to the next, getting into scrapes with Sharif.

She had often bailed them out by pulling all-nighters to help finish their projects, but she had left those carefree days behind. In exchange for what, she wasn't sure. Her academic performance had been much stronger with those two around.

Her phone buzzed in her hand. *Hey!*

Her footsteps slowed in relief, taking her to the elevator.

Daniel: *Where have you been?*

She entered the elevator, their communication cut off as she descended to the first floor. *Nuts,* she replied. *I thought getting into uni was the hardest part, but staying in will be much harder.*

Daniel sent a row of emoticons: a yellow face laughing, another one laughing while spouting tears, and a third one winking with a tongue extended. *My dad's not giving you a hard time, is he?*

She waited, unsure of how to answer.

Daniel: *Coming to the alumni event tonight?*

The black GMC slid into view. Babu waited for her. Maryam bounded down the steps. In the rush to finish the assignment for Paul's class, she had forgotten tonight was alumni night at her international high school. All the graduates, mature and wise after four months in university, came back to share their wisdom with seniors who were now applying themselves.

I'll try, she replied, triggering another set of emoticons in response, this time showing dismay.

Daniel: *Say no, if that's what you really mean.*

She entered the vehicle, hoisting herself up onto the seat, throwing her bag on the floor. *Okay, okay. I'll be there,* she typed. That had always been their joke, how people used evasive tactics to let others down gently.

Daniel: *I'll believe it when I see you.*

The phone fell onto her lap. Maryam gazed out the window. The beiges of the landscape and grays of the roads whizzed by. Daniel had been a good friend to her when the other local girls found her too tomboyish, not interested in make-up or designer brands, and the expat students were so many she was outnumbered.

He had overcome the obscurity of being another expat in their AP classes. Despite being a year younger, he had kept pace with her in English, Spanish, and European History. She closed her eyes, hoping fatigue would take away the longing clawing at her for high school, when she had still been allowed to have male friends. When her father wasn't threatening her with marriage as a way to wash his hands of her.

Daniel had invited her to his birthday party at the end of summer, dinner at Chili's, one of their favorite afterschool haunts, but her mother had refused.

"What if someone sees you at a table full of expat boys?" Her mother had paused in applying her mascara, on her way to another ladies' party. "They call your father and say you have a boyfriend!" Her mother's voice rose as though reciting the lines from a Ramadan dramatic series.

"His mother isn't so keen on local girls either." Maryam didn't say that Daniel's mother flittered around at school functions like parents' night, which her own parents had been too busy to attend, hovering round her precious charges like a helicopter. Her presence served as a barrier against impropriety as much as any cultural taboo.

"What are you saying?" Fatma had penciled in her lips. "The Americans think they're too good for us?"

"*Yema*, no one goes to eat at Chili's." Maryam took another tack to sideline the question. "Not at six o'clock. He's my friend, not my boyfriend."

Her pleas had fallen on deaf ears. She had been frightened of being found out, or she would have gone anyway. Her mother had too many of the details. She could have shown up and dragged Maryam out by her ear.

Daniel hadn't said anything when she'd called to wish him happy birthday, but she could tell by his silence that he was hurt.

The SUV pulled into the driveway. She would go tonight, despite the knowledge that high school would remind her of all she had lost because she couldn't stop herself from growing up. She needed to talk to someone about all of this, these men, their deaths, and her family. Daniel was her sole connection to the community outside her bubble of locals. He would help her make sense of what this was.

Chapter Twenty-One

Cindy checked her rearview mirror for the third time, making sure Amira was still behind her. She had been following the BMW back to the site to pass out more blankets and Bibles, but her lane had moved more quickly.

Traffic was like a leaky faucet, with construction vehicles clogging the main pipeline out of the city, and every now and then a car or SUV dodged around the dump trucks or between cement mixers to get ahead.

"I don't know if we'll see him," Cindy cautioned. "We have been coming here for weeks and there are hundreds of men."

Sanjana was working her hands nervously backward and forward in her lap in the passenger seat. She didn't answer.

"Almost caused a riot the first time." At the tight lines around the woman's lips, Cindy wondered if she had done the wrong thing asking the housemaid to come with her.

Amira flashed her lights. This was the exit. Cindy indicated, though the stream of eighteen-wheelers did not pause. Out here, as the sun lingered above the horizon for an hour or so longer, they had command of the road. She took a breath and jerked the wheel, taking the SUV into the exit lane, accelerating to avoid being flattened into a pancake against the bumper of the truck in front. Cindy thought again of Paul. If she were in an accident, what would she say she had been doing out here?

The road curved to the right. She pulled onto the shoulder, waiting for Amira. There was the BMW, built to maneuver in tight conditions, shooting past them.

"I know, Madam," Sanjana said.

Cindy snapped out of her reverie. "Since the embassy isn't helping, and I know you want to do something for these men, I thought you might want to come along."

"Yes," Sanjana said. "Daniel is going out to his school."

Cindy looked at her again to see if this was a code for evasion. Sanjana rarely spoke her mind. Her breakdown over Manu's whereabouts was one of the few times she had let them past the polite veneer of servitude.

"Ah, right, it's college night or something. I think Paul was going to go with him."

Nothing. Not even a flinch. Cindy flexed her fingers on the steering wheel as they ground to a stop in a line of vehicles waiting to enter the gas station. "How has Daniel been, do you think?"

Sanjana's full lips flattened into a thin line. "I not liking that friend of his. That boy."

"Sharif?" Cindy watched Amira's BMW swing into the parking lot. *They're almost adults,* she chided herself. *Hardly boys anymore.*

Sanjana seemed shocked by the sight of so many men lounging around the gas station. "They all live here?"

Cindy pulled in next to Amira. "Nearby."

Sanjana followed her as they carried a few boxes of Paul's old clothing over to the table Amira was setting up. She showed Sanjana how to stack the piles of clothing. First shirts, then pants and shoes, lining up the pairs.

The biceps bulged on the new recruits helping her. They were as much the reason for these good deeds, Cindy surmised, as any goodwill Amira had for the laborers.

"Hello," Amira said. "Thanks for coming."

"Of course," Cindy said. She joined them in making bundles of blankets and toiletries, and saw slim leather-bound books at the end of the assembly line. "These are fancy diaries. Do they know how to write? I suppose in their native language," she added, lest she sound imperious.

Amira glanced over her shoulder, accepting a folded blanket and Ziplock bag of toothpaste, soap, and deodorant. "They're New Testaments."

Cindy kept handing over blankets as they were passed to her to hide her objections.

"Madam," a man said in low tones.

"Yes?" Amira flipped back her frosted ends.

"Sorry, this madam." The man shuffled forward toward Cindy. She saw her gardening gloves stuffed in his side pockets like cotton balls. "Thank you,

Madam. My hands better now."

Cindy smiled. "Yes, of course——"

"*Bhai!*" Sanjana was over in a flash, her hands clutching at the startled man, her speech dissolving into an indistinguishable flow of Nepalese.

The man embraced her, to the consternation of the dozens of others crowding the table. "My brother." Sanjana wiped at tears streaming down her face. "Manu! This is my Madam."

Manu bobbed his head like a pleased chicken.

This was the moment they had hoped for. Cindy's smile froze on her lips. The difference between the brother and sister was alarming.

Manu was stooped, his jumpsuit stained at the armpits and around his collar. Dark circles ringed his eyes, and his hands, despite his professions to Cindy, were nicked, many of the marks turning the brown skin black with scabs.

Sanjana stood erect as she continued exclaiming over her brother, her white blouse pristine against a blue skirt. Her hands were clean, her cheeks round, plump even, with her good health.

We can't leave him here, Cindy realized with a sinking feeling. *Now that we have found him, we have to take him with us.* The weekend was approaching. How could she explain to Paul what had happened, where they had found finally found him? As she racked her brain for alternate explanations, several SUVS pulled into the empty lot, their tires kicking sand into her eyes. Cindy raised her hand, blinking vigorously.

Several burly men with long beards and the dark blue uniform of the CID were surrounding them. "What you do here?"

Jonah attempted to reply. "These men need help."

The officers were behind the table, rifling through their boxes.

"Blankets, toothpaste," Amira said. "We are trying to help."

"With this?" One of them fished out a copy of the New Testament. "This not allowed."

"That's a book," Cindy protested. "Surely they can read."

"Excuse me," the youngest one said confidently in English, "but these men do not read in English. Nor are they Christians."

"They can choose the faith," Amira murmured. "And become Christians. Like I did."

"This not allowed." The young one shook his finger at them. "Illegal to pass out Bibles."

They closed in on them like a group of stray cats. "You come now to police station or you pay fine later."

"Fine?" Jonah repeated. "Why would you fine us? Like this country needs money."

"Don't worry," Cindy said to Jonah as much as herself.

Beads of sweat rolled off Sanjana's brother's forehead.

"You come with us," the officer repeated.

"You need money? Is this country poor?" Robert chimed in.

"Now!" the largest officer thundered, his eyes narrowing.

"What?" Cindy moved closer to Sanjana. "You can't take us without charges."

"Giving Bibles? This illegal," the young one said, his eyes darting to the senior officer. "You must come. Or they call your sponsor."

"We'll go." Cindy tilted her head, indicating to Amira they had no other options.

Jonah turned pale at the mention of contacting sponsors. No one wanted to have to explain the ill-advised nature of their good intentions. They were hustled to the SUV, Manu dragging his feet. He whispered to Sanjana in Nepalese. She stumbled on a pile of loose rocks, crying out "Aama!"

Cindy caught her by the arm. The maid's wide eyes said what they were both thinking: this was one of a dozen times they had touched, outside of the awkward hugs before her annual trips home.

The officers loaded the box of New Testaments in their car, writing down Cindy's and Amira's vehicle numbers. In the confusion, no one seemed to notice when Manu climbed into Cindy's car beside Sanjana.

They might trace me home based on that and my ID number. Her mind raced, trying to remember Paul's travel dates. She could tell, she would tell him, but when this was all settled. The vehicle was in her name, paid for during a brief stint as a teacher's assistant at Daniel's school.

"Call Daniel," Cindy said to Sanjana as they followed the red security-logoed SUV to the police station. The last thing she needed was a fine for talking while driving. "Tell him he's got to come and get us."

Sanjana raised her phone with shaking fingers. "Why we no call Sir?"

"No," Cindy and Manu said simultaneously.

"We'll start with Daniel," Cindy repeated. "Tell him to come, without telling his father."

Cindy focused on the glowing taillights in front of her, wondering what her son would now have to say about how his mother used her time.

"But Madam, police take my passport, take my brother, we have to leave the country," Sanjana said, her voice rising.

"I'll deal with this," Cindy said. She gripped the steering wheel to keep her hands from shaking.

"Daniel not answering."

"They're easier on women," she added. "We'll be better off without Sir. Keep trying." This was according to the forum posts on the expat women's network about traffic violations. Whether or not sexism held for illegal proselytization, she was about to find out.

Chapter Twenty-Two

Sanjana clutched the bag with Daniel's secret, unsure if she should stuff it under her shirt and take it into the police station in case they searched the car, or leave it where it was in the groove of the door. Madam was pulling the SUV past the gate, behind the red vehicle carrying the officers.

She wanted to ask her brother what to do, but the sight of Manu, emaciated, unkempt and exhausted, shocked her into silence. She should be helping him, not the other way around.

Her hands convulsed around the mesh bag. *Oh, why was that boy so stupid?* Maybe Analyn wasn't the only lax one. Maybe Sanjana had been too easy on him.

Madam's hands were shaking as she sent a text. "Daniel must know someone who can get us out of here. All those locals at his school." She flipped down the driver's mirror to check her hair, and then reapplied her lipstick.

Because his mother is so lost. Sanjana answered her own question. Madam's friend, Mrs. Amira, was climbing out of her car. The other Americans, Jonah and Robert, had called the military base immediately upon being picked up. Sanjana wondered why Madam hadn't called Sir.

Sanjana got out, following Madam at half a pace behind, Manu trailing them. *No one can arrest me, no one can deport me, I am with my sponsor* she repeated to herself. *I am with my sponsor's wife* she corrected herself, the irritation at Madam's instructions flaring up. *I am legally employed. I have my residency.*

The cowering specter of Manu reminded her this was not enough. Her brother at home had been so full of life, striding around like he knew everything about the world. He walked behind her with his saucer-wide eyes darting this way and that, flinching every time someone spoke in Arabic.

Deported—being deported is not easy. Analyn had told her that monts ago, eyes round like a child telling a ghost story. *If they throw you in jail, you can be there for months. Years!*

Guilt sliced through her insides. How could she have trusted that glittering Laxmi Pande with her brother's life? Sanjana shuddered. Fear made her speechless as she crossed behind Madam into the police station. How would she find the sponsor of this company that cared so little for their workers? She would need help to convince them to let her brother go without charges. Sanjana's mind raced with possibilities, her solutions turning into dead ends.

A man with a mustache waved their group over to the leather chairs with metal frames in the seating area. A row of men, mostly drivers by the look of their button-down shirts and dark colored slacks, eyed them, unabashedly. Sanjana clucked, hoping to shame them into averting their gazes that held Madam like truck headlights.

They were the day's entertainment. Sanjana sat in the first chair she came to, the package slipping between the waist of her skirt and her underwear. This had been a very bad idea, she realized under the intense scrutiny. There was no subtle way to dump the bag, as she had hoped. Her hands started to shake.

Madam Cindy took Sanjana's left hand in hers. "I sent Daniel a text. He'll come get us."

Sanjana's palms grew clammy. They were at the mercy of a teenager. Manu sat next to her, his leg jiggling like that of a young colt. She put her hand on his knee to still him.

"I could file a report," he murmured to her in Nepalese. She turned to him in surprise. "They haven't been paying me what they said." He kept his voice in a low whisper. "Some say this is against the law, but you need someone to speak Arabic to take you to the police station." He inclined his chin.

"I don't know if—"

"Why you bring lady to police station?"

They went silent at the sight of the captain, his hands on his hips like a fishwife, raising his voice at the four officers who had brought them in. The group switched to Arabic, gesturing wildly to where the quartet sat, the young one waving a copy of the New Testament.

Another officer, one of the tallest men Sanjana had ever seen, entered the holding area from the hallway. He blinked at the scene in front of him, stiffening as the conversation turned to him.

"Ali, translate," the captain said. "Get a report on my desk by tonight."

"But, I'm not CID," Ali protested.

The captain left, taking a call on his cell phone.

The other four officers shrugged, passing Ali the box of evidence and trailing back to their stations scattered across the front of the reception area. Ali thumbed through the Bible with two fingers as if he didn't want to disturb the gilt-edged pages. He squeezed the bridge of his nose as if that would control his level of irritation. He took a deep breath.

Sanjana heard the force of his exhalation. She thought he would begin with Amira, who was attempting to strike up a getting-to-know-you conversation with Manu, but Manu's English was insufficient to keep up the charade.

The station doors were whisked open by the motion sensor. Cindy let out a cry of relief when Daniel rushed in, sweeping the room with a wide-eyed glance before making his way to them, relief coloring his face a deep red.

"Mom!"

They embraced. Daniel took a step back. In his look—the slightly raised eyebrow, the glance lingering a second or two longer than necessary—Sanjana saw the question in his eyes. She shook her head slightly and his shoulders relaxed.

"What happened?" Daniel said. Beside him was the willowy local girl from high school, now a few inches taller than him, the delicate bones of her face announcing the beauty she would become. "You remember Maryam, Mom."

"Yes, hi. Thanks for coming."

Maryam nodded, pulling her headscarf close under her chin. "Have they said anything to you?"

Cindy shook her head.

"That man investigate." Sanjana pointed a finger across her knee. Maryam made the sound of exclamation.

"You know him?" Daniel asked as they regarded the officer, whose head was bent at the angle of someone who was concentrating as he eyed the toiletry pouches.

Maryam tilted her hand from side to side. "Kind of."

Daniel and Cindy conferred, with Amira interjecting that it couldn't hurt to have Maryam speak on their behalf.

"I don't know how much help I'll be," Maryam protested.

Sanjana felt soothed by the presence of an *abaya* instead of alarmed the local woman would tell on her. She stood to thank Maryam and the mesh bag slid down her skirt, falling with a soft plop on the inside of her foot. Sanjana put her feet together, hoping to contain the bag in case it rolled out from the bell of the skirt. No one had noticed. Everyone's eyes were trained on the officer. *How could she get rid of this thing?* She couldn't give it to Daniel, not here, not without raising suspicions of another kind.

"Let's go talk to him." Maryam and Daniel walked toward the investigating officer.

"I file report." Manu used halting English. He stepped forward, dragging a small fanny pack with an empty bottle of water, and dangling washcloth.

"What?" Cindy looked to Sanjana for clarification.

Her brother persisted in English. "My work, they cheat me. I file report." He thumped his chest. "You see my place." Manu gestured at Maryam. "You know."

"This is not the time." Cindy's voice rose.

"We at police station." Manu persisted. "I never knowing where station is. Always working, then the company accommodation."

The men behind them stirred.

Understanding spread across the local girl's features and wondered what she had missed in her brother's first month in her adopted country. The girl's look was one of pity and horror.

"First, let's settle this," Maryam said. "Then we'll see about your case."

"I file now!" Manu exclaimed, causing the officer to look up from his desk. The man sighed, a sound that carried like a low growl. His shoulders flexed as he pushed himself up, making his way toward them.

"Sanjana, get him under control!"

"Maryam?"

The girl swayed as if he had struck her, but she stood her ground. "Ali, let them go."

"How do you know these people?"

"We went to school together." Daniel motioned to Maryam.

The officer eyed them as a group, his gaze lingering over Daniel and Cindy.

"My mother made a mistake. This won't happen again."

"You never looked into the death of that man, did you?" Maryam asked.

Ali's laser focus snapped back to her.

"He wants to file a report." She indicated Manu with her chin. "Bad conditions and contract."

Ali raised his eyes to heaven, as if to ask God *Why me?* "He died of bad conditions. And your man can file a report if he likes, but it won't help him. This isn't the right place. He has to go to the Ministry of Labor."

Maryam clenched her fists in frustration. If she hit the officer in the stomach, he did not have a paunch to absorb the blow like most other local men.

They argued, Cindy and Amira chiming in. Manu stood as still as a statue. Daniel shifted back and forth from one leg to the other.

Sanjana sat, pretending to adjust the hem of her skirt. When she was sure no one was looking, she wiggled out the mesh bag from her shoe, slipping it into the nearest object, Manu's fanny pack.

"This is not justice." Maryam raised her voice. "Get an investigation going, for the love of God."

"No more talking!" The mustached man stood and slapped the counter. "All of you sit." He waved the group over to the chairs. "You wait."

~~~

They sat for hours as the sun set, taking away the golden rays and leaving the windows squares of black. Fluorescent lights hummed overhead. The truck drivers had been dismissed, one by one, leaving their ensemble as the only occupants of the waiting area. Robert leaned in close to Amira. They murmured to one another, his arm on the back of her chair. Jonah was talking to Daniel, asking him about school, how he felt about graduation, would he take anyone to prom.

"When he comes out, you go," Manu said.

Sanjana's eyes shot to his face to see if he was angry with her.

"They need the money."

Their siblings' faces flashed before her. Yes. She cursed her stars that money made all decisions unilateral. They worked round the clock for so little. Yet Madam worked not at all and had no worries. The image of the mesh bag made her mouth go dry.

"Wash your clothes." Sanjana worked to keep her voice even. "You never know what gets in them in this dust."

Manu rolled his eyes at her, as if to say, "You think dust is my biggest problem?" She wanted to shake him. If she took the bag out now, everyone would have questions: Madam, the irritated police officer, Manu. Daniel would jump in and cause trouble.

The burly one, Jonah, protested intermittently to the mustachioed officer who kept a steady stream of conversation going through a set of ear buds linked to his mobile phone. "We're American citizens."

Ali's boots announced his return. Sanjana stood when he entered the waiting room. His gaze swept over her, Cindy, and Maryam. He passed a hand over his eyes. He spoke in Arabic to Maryam, who glided forward.

Maryam translated. "You are free to go. You should never, ever come to the Industrial Area again."

Cindy had her purse on her shoulder before anyone could say another word. "Done."

"And the fine?" Jonah asked, rising.

Maryam exchanged words with Ali in Arabic. "The men pay six thousand riyal."

"That's two thousand dollars!"

"The women, you'll be excused," Maryam said.

"We'll split it," Cindy said in a low voice to Jonah. "Misunderstanding!" She waved, leaving the station and indicating Sanjana should follow her.

Madam was getting further and further away. "We have to go before Paul wonders where we all are. Or they change their minds." She shot a glance at Ali behind the counter.

"I need to tell my brother one thing—"

"Now please," Madam called.

A rush of air announced visitors. Two men, one in a tight t-shirt, close cut hairstyle, and dark slacks strode to the desk with a local man in white robes. The policeman at the desk ended his call and stood to confer with the new arrivals. After a few minutes, they turned to the waiting area.

"We called you for help, Staff Sargent," Robert called out, standing up.

"And I am here to help you, Marines," their superior retorted. "Get in the van."

Jonah gave Madam a lingering look she did not notice. One Sanjana did not like. They watched the men climb into a black SUV with windows as dark as night, their senior officer's lips folded into a thin line.

Why Madam looking at that man for help when Mr. Paul at home? She call him, her husband, he come solve everything. Sanjana could not question the source of her irritation. Manu's stomach rumbled, bringing her attention back to her brother.

"I'll send you food," Sanjana said, her voice breaking.

"How?" Manu retorted. "You cannot come to my place. And I cannot come to yours." He eyed the crispness of her blouse, the fabric of her skirt.

"I'll find a way."

He turned away at the sight of her tears.

Sanjana left Manu behind for the second time in their lives. He would remain, relying on Maryam and Daniel to tell his story.

"Not a word about this to Paul," Cindy said again as they climbed back into the car.

"No, madam." Sanjana sobbed. What would she say? *I found my brother because your wife was where she wasn't supposed to be? And then I had to leave him again, although he looked worse than the oldest person in my village.*

They climbed into the Range Rover in silence.

Chapter Twenty-Three

Ali eyed the American boy who, in his opinion, stood too close to Jaber's daughter. Or Nasser's sister. Any way he thought of her, he still had no right to be protective.

She was at ease, though her fingers worried the stack of bracelets peeking out from under the sleeve of her *abaya*. Ali tapped at his keyboard to give him more time to gather his thoughts. The scent of her *oud* swirling around his head made it hard to think.

He was not the only one to notice. Other officers strode through the lobby, their chests puffed out like birds. Other than the prayer room, there was little on the far side of the corridor, and it being hours from the late night prayer, Ali doubted any motives so pure had brought them across. Word was spreading across the night shift. *A girl! In the station.* He imagined the texts going out over the WhatsApp group he refused to join.

"Alright," he said. "What's the story?"

The American, his eyes green like a palm tree leaf, glanced at Maryam. This set off a chain reaction. She looked at the Indian man. He was the one who threw it back to Ali, his eyes unblinking, completing the circle.

"I help you," Ali said. "But you must tell me the problem." He was careful to enunciate the p, reluctant to embarrass himself by switching to Arabic or hitting the heavy b typical of Arab speakers.

Maryam consulted in low tones with the boy, whose name was Daniel. "I don't know how to ask him what's wrong."

"Sanjana tried to teach me Nepali, but I never learned," Daniel answered.

The man shifted his weight from one foot to the other. Too late, the three of them realized communicating would be very difficult with Manu's limited English.

Ali called for Aqeel. The man came sliding in the room, scuffing his worn sandals along the tiled floor. "Sir?"

Ali gestured to the waiting trio. "Translate for the Indian."

Aqeel moved forward, leaning against the counter. His eyes blinked rapidly as he exchanged words with the man in the blue overalls. "He's from Nepal."

"Right." Ali shrugged. He wondered how they could distinguish among themselves when they looked so similar, broad features, thick heads of hair, coffee with milk colored skin. "And?"

Aqeel issued a string of questions, sucking in his cheeks in dismay at the replies he received. "He signed a contract at home for an office job. When he got here, he was put to building. He hasn't received his salary." Aqeel shook his head several times, pity etched on his features.

"You aren't writing anything down," Maryam burst in.

Ali spread his hands. "I don't need to. These are labor complaints. He will have to file a case in the labor courts against his employer."

"But what they're doing is illegal," she protested.

"If it has to do with driving, or stealing." Ali ticked each crime off on his fingers. "Death, or immorality, then it comes to us."

Aqeel translated for the man as Maryam glowered at Ali.

"There was a death," she said. "You never asked what happened to that body. What did they do with him?"

"We sent a report to the company. They're responsible for getting the body home. You could ask for information." He looked at her directly for the first time since the trio had entered the station.

"I will." Her eyebrows snapped together. "There are dozens of these guys all over the city. They can't all be accidents or suicide."

"More deaths." Aqeel leaned in, his elbows on the counter. "He says more men have died."

"See!" Maryam pointed a finger at Manu. "That's exactly what I mean. There's criminal activity out there and no one cares."

"What kinds of death?" Ali asked. "We don't get involved in medical cases."

"Hypocrisy." Maryam seethed.

"How many?"

"Two, maybe more." The older man struggled to keep up with Manu's rate of speaking. "One sounds like an accident."

170

"See, I wish they had more safety," Ali said. The image of the pulpy head, dangling between limbs, flashed before him. He realized he was telling the truth. "That is not us, that's the Ministry of Labor. Or Interior."

"That's so Arab," Maryam muttered. "No one wants to take responsibility."

"Aren't you Arab?" His voice was rising as if he were in a fight with Aisha.

"He wants them to organize a strike. The men are divided on this," Aqeel relayed.

"No, no, no," Ali said, his attention snapping back to the Nepali who was shifting his weight from one foot to another. "No strikes."

Everyone stopped. Manu's eyes, wide, were on Ali's face.

"Organizing not allowed," Ali said, cursing his limited English. "Stop this talk," he said to Manu, whose gaze skittered to Aqeel for explanation.

"Well, how are they supposed to change their conditions?" Maryam's voice broke.

"I'm sure the police are doing what they can." Daniel put his hand on Maryam's elbow. The American's words, or his touch, calmed her. Ali bit choice words to let Daniel know he didn't need help and the American should keep his hands to himself.

This kid is more of a man than you. The thought came unbidden and stole his irritation, replacing the cloud of righteousness with shame.

"He says last week a man was crushed by a piece of marble." Aqeel clarified a few things in Hindi, back and forth, with Manu. "They never saw him again. No one said what's happened to him."

"Two deaths." Maryam held up her fingers in the symbol of *habetain*, or deuces, that the local teenagers liked to use. "Those are the ones we know about." She pulled a sheaf of papers from her purse. The headlines fanned across the lip of the reception desk. "How many? How many of these are accidents and how many aren't? Why don't we care?"

The snippets of articles in English floated across his desk.

"Look into it." There was a girlish gangliness to the arm she placed on the counter. The previous times Ali had seen this girl, her face had been shrouded in shadow. Now he saw the arch of those eyebrows, like the wings of a falcon, soaring above a sloping nose that any woman would envy. "Have mercy."

"We should go." Daniel took her by the arm again.

Ali cleared his throat to stem the red-hot rage rising in him at the sight of those white fingers, blunt fingernails, on the sleeve of her *abaya*. "Yes, I will."

She turned to him in surprise.

"I'll give you an update."

She scribbled a number on a piece of paper and slid it to him. A smile relaxed the sternness of her face. He wondered if this was what other men enjoyed—the attention of a woman, someone who would regard them as a hero.

"Thank you," she said.

The trio marched out. Ali watched as a plum-colored Mercedes received them beyond the station doors.

Aqeel peeked over Ali's shoulder. "She gave you number?"

Ali snapped out of his reverie and glanced at the paper in his hand. She had numbered him, the very thing teenage boys could be found doing in the malls, day or night, repeating or tossing their number on scraps of paper after women.

"See to your work."

Aqeel passed him a blue case file.

"What's this?"

"The man's details." Aqeel's gaze followed Ali's toward Maryam's car.

"I need some tea." Ali growled, mostly to break the other man's gaze. He wondered what had happened with the driver, if the family had found out about his lax duties and fired him. That's what he would have done if Narena had been taking Aisha, Maha, or Aldana out without their maids to places they shouldn't be going.

"He also said he was sleeping on the floor." Aqeel shuddered, his eyes squinting as if he could see the room the laborer had described. "Those marks on his hands? They were insect bites."

"Terrible." Ali agreed, because to do anything else would make him one of them—those who put other humans into terrible conditions.

"You want me call the company?"

Ali shook his head. "I'll drive out." He wanted to be free of the office, the men who were still sticking their heads out of the hallway to try to see the reported woman in the station. There would be talk of this for days.

He snatched his keys from the desk, jiggling them in his pocket. "I'll be back." He glanced over his shoulder to see a fretful Aqeel wiping his brow.

Ali climbed into the Nissan and put on his seatbelt—a necessary part of the job, though many of the others clicked the belt into place behind them to avoid the safety beep. They would then allow the chest strap to give the appearance they were belted, saluting each other as they sped through the roundabouts.

Ali pressed the accelerator to the floor, climbing the exit ramp to the Industrial Area at speeds above 120 km per hour. He swung through the potholed streets, avoiding the feral eyes that shone in the vehicle's headlights. Creatures scurried away on four legs, many of them cats, others that he didn't want to think about lower to the ground. Finally he swung into the entrance of Jaber's company.

"What happened with the report?" Ali asked the stuttering guard on duty.

"I no see," the Indian man said. His eyes darted from the two stars on Ali's shoulder to the gun at his waist. "This go to supervisor."

"Right," Ali said. "I take a walk." He left the guard station, entering the courtyard where he had first seen Maryam. Ali walked the perimeter.

In the humidity, no one was out, not even to smoke. These men valued sleep. He knew this from the busloads he had seen bumping along in traffic through the city, full of men with their faces buried into the seatbacks in front of them, desperate to catch the last vestiges of sleep.

Ali saw nothing, wondering what he was doing here at the whim of a teenage girl. He might as well take advice on police work from Aisha. He turned around and retraced his steps through the quiet stairwells, and made for his car. As he was leaving, a silver sedan arrived. A thin man, his head springing with hair and a thick gold chain around his neck, got out and entered the guard station.

Ali put his window down so the man could see his uniform. "Police."

"Sir." The other man turned, flashing a mouth full of teeth. "You are early. The end of the month still two weeks, no?"

"What business you have here?" Ali said, not understanding the reference.

"Ah," the other man said. "I from embassy. Came to look at a complaint."

"Good." The force of Ali's words startled them both. "Much trouble here."

The man watched him, nodding without saying more.

"Send copies of reports when finished." Ali gave him the name of his station.

"Yes, boss."

Ali drove away, happy he had good news for Maryam, with a small sliver of hope that she would reward him with one of her smiles.

Chapter Twenty-Four

Maryam slouched on the bench in the hallway against the curved umber-colored wall, jiggling her foot while waiting for her turn with Professor Paul. There was no movement behind the frosted glass office door.

This was the day of reckoning—well, academic reckoning, anyway. She pulled her phone out, but couldn't focus to play any of the games. If she failed Paul's required class, it would trigger the avalanche that was her mother's bridal army.

Throughout her puberty, the troops had been assembling. Fatma had already started planning. She saved this wedding invitation she liked, that reception favor she knew could be improved upon. The plans for Maryam's eventual big day were endless. The reception would be an intimate party at the house...no, a thousand people in the ballroom at the Ritz...wait, what about an exotic location like the Maldives for a family holiday?

Ever the strategist, Fatma had sensed a shift in the winds. "Why is your father ignoring you?" She started in after breakfast when Jaber brushed by his daughter on the way to their carport.

Maryam shrugged. "He's busy." She hoped her mother's suspicions would be assuaged.

"He didn't ask about you at dinner."

Maryam scuttled to her room. She couldn't give her mother the satisfaction that the cold light in her father's eye when he had passed her in the hallway meant the certainty Jaber agreed with Fatma. Marriage might cure Maryam of her recklessness.

A phone rang down the hallway. Someone laughed further down. The signs of ordinary university life washed over her. Signs she had not allowed to soak in were now as precious to her as air. If only the other local girls hadn't rattled her so badly in the first few months of university.

She had overhead her mother on the phone last night, chattering excitedly. There were upcoming weddings, which meant Maryam would be trussed up like the Thanksgiving turkey the Americans were getting ready to share. Dressed up and trotted out for all the families to appraise, like a camel in her grandfather's herd. She blew a piece of hair off her forehead, chewing the end of the errant strand. What a mess! It had come to this—studying or marriage.

"Your turn." Mohammed pulled at the strap of his bag and smirked. "Good luck."

They were the bottom two students, as reflected by the appointment slots. Paul met with the students in the order of the grades of their assignments. Everyone had worked that out after the first two papers had been handed back. He gave them out in ascending order, lowest first, then the grades getting higher, his smile broader, his movements slower as if he alone held the key.

She mentally stuck her tongue out at his retreating form. Mohammed was happy not to be the last, she knew. She saved him from that, at least in Intro to Journalism. Maryam took a deep breath, hovering in the doorway.

"Come in, come in." Paul waved from behind his desk, the earpiece to the phone on his shoulder. "I can do eight-thirty tomorrow morning. Too early? Then get back to me with a time."

She sat in the swivel chair in front of him, placing her laptop on the circular table beside her.

"People." Paul hung up the phone with a bang. "They call you for a meeting and then tell you when they're available." He peered over his glasses, moving from behind the desk to the round meeting table near the door, searching for her paper among a stack of books, box of pens, and unopened mail.

She fished it out from two anthologies of the history of the Pulitzer Prize and passed it over.

"This is quite a piece of writing." He tapped the stapled corner on the table.

Maryam smiled tentatively. He laid the essay on the desk between them. Her heart sank at the first page, filled with scribbles and notes in the margins.

"Did someone help you with this?"

Maryam's smiling lips drooped. "Someone like who? No."

Paul leaned forward, his elbows on the table, gray arm hairs curling out of his upturned pink shirtsleeves. "It's okay if you had help, as long as you cite the source."

"I wrote this." Maryam's voice rose. She squinted to keep her body from following suit and getting out of her chair.

Paul flexed his fingers, making a small steeple under his chin. "You went to the Industrial Area?'

Maryam nodded, not trusting herself to speak.

"Alone, at night, no chaperon?" He flipped through the paper again.

A white-hot rage was building behind her eyes. "I did. The hardest thing I ever did, and for your class."

"You saw these events for yourself?"

"Yes, Professor."

This was the side of him that Daniel complained about, the mercurial father whose punishments exceeded the suspicions of the crime.

"Who took you?" Paul twirled a pen between his forefinger and thumb.

"My driver." Maryam looked down at her hands. "I swear to you, I was there. I saw the body."

Paul read aloud from the paper. "This death is but one in untold hundreds of migrant workers that go unreported. These men risk everything for low-wage jobs and they pay with their lives."

The image of the man in the police station last night flashed between her eyes, interrupting the mounting rage over Paul's creased brow. "I know one of them. You do too. Your maid's brother. We found him."

Paul sat straighter. "Sanjana? You found Sanjana's brother?"

Maryam nodded. He was making eye contact with her for the first time during their meeting. "Yes, when Daniel and I went to the police station, he was there with Mrs. Johnson, and——"

Paul held up his hand, the sunlight winking on the gold of his wedding band. "You saw Cindy where?"

Maryam bit her lip at her obtuseness, the second time in as many days. Some novice detective she would make, revealing crucial information to the wrong people.

"You and Daniel went to the police station, why, exactly?"

Her mind raced for excuses, trying all doors and finding them locked.

"Sanjana found Manu and asked me to come translate because none of them spoke Arabic. I was with Daniel at the college night event, so we went together with my driver."

Paul pushed back from the table. "And the police took your statement?"

"Yes. I mean, well, they said Manu's issues were for the labor courts. But we tried." She wheeled around the lip of the desk. "I did tell them about the deaths. They're going to investigate those."

Paul arched his back, swinging around in his chair, wheeling to gaze out the window. "None of them mentioned any of this to me."

"Maybe you were away."

Paul shot her a look. "I've been here all week."

"Or in a meeting."

He picked up his pen, the tip circling her paper like a vulture. "Well, I'm glad he's okay. Sanjana's brother, I mean." He scribbled a number and thrust the paper at her.

"He's not okay," she said. "I mean, he's alive, but he's got some serious problems."

"Don't we all." Paul winked.

"Not like his." Maryam received the paper, not daring to glance yet.

"This is excellent reporting." His knuckles rapped the desk. "I'm recommending this for the university blog."

"You think it's that good?" Maryam rose, the rage that had been coursing through her veins battling with elation. "This is why my meeting was first." She broke into a smile.

"It is." He returned her smile. "And I do." Paul clasped his hands behind his back. "You'll get readers and comments, making your work even better the next time.

The euphoria came crashing down like a fettered falcon. "I don't know if I can publish this," she said.

Paul raised an eyebrow.

"My parents wouldn't like it." She rushed on lest he return to the accusation of it not being her work. "They wouldn't want people to know I went to the camp."

Paul stood with her, walking slowly behind as she made her way to the door. "We need local voices in this fight. Yours is a perspective that no one has heard yet. Most blame the companies for not holding to the law."

Maryam swallowed. "This is my father's company."

Paul leaned against the doorjamb. She turned to face him from the hallway.

"Yours is an important perspective. Maybe we could publish it without your name."

"I'll check." Thankfully, Daniel was not there to call her bluff.

"Sorry I'm late, Professor." Amal appeared at the door. "May I come in?" The statement was not a question since she didn't hesitate before sailing in between them.

Paul turned back to his office after her. He gave Maryam another hopeful glance over his shoulder. She smiled weakly, clutching the paper in her fist. Inside the elevator, she allowed herself a peek with one eye. 95. She shrieked, the glass wall mirroring her excitement. Enough to pass the class, and to stay in university. She clutched it to her chest for a second, a tear of relief hovering on her eyelash, before she squealed again.

As she exited the elevator, her phone buzzed.

"*Yema*, guess what? I—"

"Where are you? Get home now. You need to get dressed." Her mother was breathless, as if she had been running for miles.

"Why?" Maryam stopped outside the building.

"Someone asked about you and your father said yes, they could come. The mother and sisters are coming this afternoon. They're really eager!"

Maryam crept toward the SUV, though other vehicles were honking at Babu to get out of the way. "I got an A on my paper."

"That's nice. I knew you could do it. Hurry home." Her mother ended the call without a goodbye. Maryam heard her calling directions to one of the maids about making cakes for the afternoon visitors before the call disconnected.

Chapter Twenty-Five

Manu elbowed his way to the gas burner, toward the smell of roasting onions. His stomach to rumbled. The other men jostled him. In here they were all arms and legs, mouths and stomachs, reduced to their basest instincts in the quest for food.

"Make way, make way." Everywhere he turned, Adith was there, like a stone in his shoe, flashing his yellow grin.

News of Manu's trip to the police had spread like wildfire in the camp when the luxury sedan with tinted windows had dropped him off. Like the sales of bootleg alcohol, or men searching for housemaids offering sexual favors, Adith told anyone who'd listen.

"Excuse me," Manu reached over the shorter man, tossing the limp chapattis on the blackened saucepan, grimacing. He picked up an open bottle of vegetable oil on the grimy counter, swirling a tablespoon worth from the wide lipped jar so his dinner wouldn't char in the pan.

Adith had replaced the man who had been crushed by marble, taking the middle bunk that should have been Manu's. He had been in the camp longer, although in a different room. The man was still friendly, but something had changed, something Manu couldn't quite put his finger on. It was in the way Adith's eyes sidled over Manu, or the constant glances, the murmured conversations that stopped when Manu approached.

Manu pressed with his fingertips in a circle, like he had seen his mother or sisters do, turning the flattened flour patty in a circle, causing the flatbread to bubble up under his fingers. Once, twice, three times, as many as his visits to the labor courts, the chapatti went around the pan. Manu pulled it off onto a tin plate, blowing on his fingers. He had burned the first few, pressing too hard and not lowering the flame, ruining his precious dinner.

Now, several months into his stay, he was getting to be as deft at the movement as his older sister.

The thought of Sanjana, of the rice and meat she was cooking for those white people, maybe in that same moment, brought another pang to his stomach.

"*Aree*, he cooks," Adith said, as if praising a prospective bride. Men laughed, swiveling to give Manu the once over.

Manu took his meager dinner out to the courtyard, sitting on the edge of the sidewalk, crossing his legs under him. It was not much of a dinner scene, eating bread alone, but better than the airless room filled with other men or Adith's watchful gaze. The smoke-filled kitchen, pots and pans clattering, men jostling for position, was out of the question.

Manu took a bite, chewing slowly, turning the bread to mush before he swallowed, then taking another bite, deep in thought. There were clumps of men scattered here and there, new ones with the look of stunned wild animals, the knowledge that they were free no longer dawning in their dazed pupils. Adith came to squat next to him, leaving the weight on his haunches, arms dangling the pavement.

"Ah, soon we'll be cold and wishing for the heat."

"We can ask for blankets."

"Ah, like your friends, the white ladies?"

Manu ripped the remaining piece of bread into smaller strips so it would last. His bunkmates had given him a wide berth since he had returned from the police station. The foreman had marked him a troublemaker, giving him the hardest tasks, like hauling water to keep the cement wet, or wiring together the red colored support bars. The gloves Sanjana's madam had given him were ripped to shreds in no time.

"My father said a man is worth his work."

Adith scratched his head. "Nice saying. Where is he now?"

"Dead." The word squeaked out.

Adith's fingers pressed into Manu's shoulder. "Well, then we have each other. Remember, rich people, they don't want to give us our worth. They want us to take their charity. Like the ladies who give us water once a week while they have bathrooms for each person in their family."

"Well—"

"I'm your friend," Adith said, squeezing him again. "I tell you, take what you get and feel good."

Manu stood up, heading to the now empty kitchen as a disguise for leaving behind the man, his fingers, his friendship. He ran the tap water over his plate, drowning a curious cockroach the size of his small finger. Where there was one, no matter how small, Manu knew there would be many. He had no time for self-pity, not if he wanted to sleep at least five hours before being awakened again, competing for the squatties that served as toilets or the one sink.

"We should strike."

The plate clattered in the sink. Manu turned to see a man backlit by the courtyard's perimeter light.

"Who's there?" The hairs on his arm prickled like someone had raked a fork over his forearm.

"You're right. We should strike. The only thing they'll listen to is money."

Manu strained to hear the accent. There was the rhythm of Hindi, but no slang. "You willing to say this to others?"

The man clutched the doorframe, glancing to his right. "Don't give up. In room 200, someone else wants to strike."

Before Manu could say another word, the man was gone. He went to the door, his heart in his mouth, but there was no one to be seen to the right or the left. The hairs on the back of his neck were standing up. *Are there other men who think as I do?* He went through the twenty or so people he knew from his room, plus the ones on either side. None of them had dared agree with him in daylight.

Room 200 was upstairs somewhere, maybe to the right, he thought. Safer to go during the day, or ask around and see what others thought of those men before he approached them directly. He dried his plate with the rag that at least twenty others had used, pressing it around the rim, wondering if Sanjana was doing the same thing at that moment.

The thought of his sister, somewhere else in the city, was like a thorn in his side, pricking him where he was softest, causing him shame. She had been horrified to see his condition. He knew from the way her eyes had widened until he could see the little brown spots in the white areas outside her pupils. Whether out of propriety or because of his dress, she hadn't hugged him, neither in the assistance line nor at the station.

He clutched his bag with his few possessions, slipping the plate inside, putting away thoughts of Sanjana and her American employer who had looked with such pity at his hands. Manu wanted to chop them off, to be rid of the broken nails and cracked skin forever.

When he returned to the room, the rest of the men were asleep, including Adith, whose back was turned to the door, his face pressed against the concrete wall. Manu slid beneath the bed, easing himself onto the mattress, the man above protesting at the disturbance. As he placed the bag with his plate under his pillow, he felt a spark of anger at his sister, a spark he quelled lest it spread, grow steam, and catch anything else alight. His head fell to one side.

In his fatigue, he smelled the sweet burnt odor of hashish, reminding him of late at night in the village when the men came in from tending the crops. He breathed deeply, grateful for whatever memory had triggered that smell. He wished he had some now to dull the grind that had become his life, but Sanjana would not approve.

His nostrils flared at the memory of his sister's pristine white blouse and dark skirt, a layer of fat around her belly that said she had more than she needed. She had promised to do what she could, but that seemed to be very little, despite her being on the outside, the normal part of this vast city. He turned, pushing such thoughts from his mind. The kind eyes of the white woman taking his hands was enough to make him want to sob like his little brother. Manu closed his eyes, willing himself to think of something—anything—else.

~~~

"Stop talking to outsiders. The court is not an option."

Manu started awake. Someone spoke in harsh, guttural tones. In the darkness of the room, he couldn't make out whose voice it was. There was a scuffle on the bunk on top of him, the mattress pressing down like a massive thumb, pushing Manu into the ground until he thought his lungs would burst from the lack of air.

With a shove, he managed to move the weight to one side. He rolled out, ready to give the man a piece of his burning lungs until he noticed the odd angle of the man's head. He bent closer. Others were stirring, awakened by the rounds of a fight.

"Turn on the light." Manu's hand trembled as he reached for the other man's wrist.

The bare blub snapped on, revealing his bunkmate half on, half off the mattress, his neck bent at an unnatural angle, purplish bruises beginning to form around his neck.

"*Aree*, he's dead!"

The realization sent the room into a frenzy. Men woke up those still sleeping. Someone threw open the door, calling out into the corridor. Manu stood as the movement swirled around him, the words he had heard before the attack echoing in his ear. *Don't go back to the court.*

Had the person been looking for him? Or had it been a warning? He glanced around, but no one seemed interested in his existence. He backed away from the corpse's unseeing eyes and rushed to the courtyard. What had been his refuge a few hours before now felt like a containment area. Men were waking up in other rooms. The guards peered out of their station.

Manu was the only one who had tried to file a formal complaint against the company for change of occupation and unpaid wages. He was the only one who had a family member working for an American family. Most of the other men had cousins in the same industry, or lower as janitors in the malls for companies that would as soon ship them back as feed them.

As he rubbed his hands, the callouses brushed against each other, bringing him back to the moment. Manu scanned the courtyard for anyone new or out of the ordinary, but how would he know if he saw the person who was trying to kill him?

Chapter Twenty-Six

The phone buzzed in her pocket for quite a while before she realized she was receiving a call. Sanjana turned off the faucet, slipping off the gloves. She didn't recognize the number, but the leading double fours indicated it was a landline, and the number three said she had missed three calls from the same person. Sanjana hit call back.

"Hello?" She balanced the cell phone on her shoulder so she could lay the gloves on the edge of the sink. Her toes flexed on the special mats Sir had brought back from his last trip, designed, he said, to keep the feet and knees from becoming tired.

"So we don't wear you out." He put them in front of the sink and the stove. The spongy material did make a significant difference in her kitchen tasks.

"Who this is?" She held her breath. If it were Manu, she didn't know what she would say. She had thought through the questions, but none of them led to a conversation she wanted to have. *How are you?*

The image of him, stooped and worn in that grease-stained coverall, was enough to make her curse all the days Laxmi Pande had left wherever she had gone. Having found Manu, Sanjana's true torture was knowing his condition and being helpless to change it.

"I get missed call from this number," Sanjana said. "Who you wanting?"

"I looking for Sanjana Kulse. This the number she register with us."

"Me." Sanjana switched to Nepali. "Yes, that's me."

"I'm calling from the embassy," the tinny voice said. "You come here many times."

She leaned against the counter. Oh, if they had found Laxmi, Sanjana was going to give her a piece of her mind. Tears stung her eyes at the life she had promised her Manu, back in their village. Women like Laxmi preyed on those dreams, she knew now.

"Hello? I am looking for Sanjana Kulse."

"Yes. I am here. Who is this?" She looked out the window at Madam's garden, the plants in their beds like well-groomed children, the bougainvillea trimmed for maximum effect as it crawled over the wall.

"Your brother, one…" there was a scuffling sound of paper.

"My brother, Manu. Manu Kulse. Yes, you promise him contract, and that Laxmi, she liar." Sanjana's chest heaved.

"The case of Manu Kulse has been declined."

"What for?" Sanjana clutched at the edge of the sink. "What are you saying?"

"His claim, they cheated him, is declined. He signed the contract."

"But that was at the airport." Sanjana's voice grew louder. "You said that he would be in an office, making fifteen hundred dollars. He's building. They haven't paid him. They force him to sign. Tell him he pay his way back, but he say no. He already at airport." The tears came with the force of a rainstorm, building in her voice, making her hoarse. The purple-pink of the vines outside swam in her vision.

There was a prolonged silence on the other end at her outburst. She heard muffled voices as if the caller were consulting with someone.

"I want appointment." Sanjana remembered how Madam dealt with problems like this. "I come to see you."

"With whom did you speak here for his papers?"

"Pande," she said. "Laxmi Pande."

There was more murmuring like the sound of bees.

"I come now." Sanjana spun in a circle, looking for her shoes. Late afternoon traffic would be terrible, but if she stood outside the compound gate, she might be able to catch a taxi.

"Mrs. Pande no longer works here." The man switched to English. "Your brother was found with drugs in the camp. He will go to jail."

The call ended, the fast beeping of the open line leaving Sanjana without a chance to reply.

What had she done? They had saved everything they could to get Manu's original ticket on top of the fee paid to Laxmi's contact in Kathmandu. Hot tears stung her eyes. Sanjana ground the palms of her hands into her eyelids, willing them to stop. Crying wasn't going to get Manu out of that place he said was little more than a cockroach breeding ground. She had to think.

Sanjana breathed deeply through her nose. Catching on a sob, she sank onto the cushion at the breakfast nook. She leaned her forehead against the wood of the table, her body shuddering. Manu could have stayed with their siblings, keeping them safe even if they were hungry. The sun shone through the windows of the nook, glinting like Sanjana was encased in a glass cage. She reached for the linen napkin on the table, wiping her eyes.

The worst part was that she had only spoken to him a handful of times since they went to the police station. Madam had offered to get him a mobile. She could take it out of Sanjana's salary. Sanjana was grateful, but she hadn't gone to the store to get one. She had hedged because she wasn't sure what to say to him. Anything she shared from her day—*I am tired from the laundry and grocery shopping*—would sound like complaining.

"Sanjana, I need something to eat." Daniel bopped into the kitchen, wearing oversized headphones blaring music. She glared at him, feeling an irrational urge to snatch them off his head.

"How much those costing?" She pointed at his ears. Daniel slid the headphones down, his green eyes rounding with concern.

"Are you okay?"

"Answer question!" She said, her finger shaking.

"I don't know. Maybe two-hundred dollars? Here, you take them," Daniel said. He slipped them off, unplugging them from a phone tucked into his waistband. The lean hip that flashed at her reminded Sanjana this was no longer the boy she had cuddled to sleep on many a night while his parents were out.

"*Chee.* I not wanting those. What I do with your loud music?" The strength from her anger drained out of her.

Daniel walked to her. His sneakers squeaked on the kitchen tiles. "Are you okay?"

"No. You leaving me alone."

"Is it about your brother?" Daniel took her arm. "Did you hear about his case?"

"I hear he in jail for your mistake!" Sanjana jerked her arm from Daniel's grasp. At the confusion on his face and the tug on her arm, she pulled harder.

"I don't—"

186

She boxed his ears, same as she would have done to any of her siblings, but also in punishment for his whiteness, his privilege, his obliviousness to what his mistakes cost those around him. Her hands stung from the force of the move. The earphones clattered to the floor, one of the circular coverings falling off. Daniel cried out, in surprise as much as her ability to hurt him.

"You and your dirty things," she hissed. "Your dirty things get Manu in big trouble." The confusion still in his green eyes caused her to clutch her temples in frustration. "Dirty drugs. I put that bag with him. At police station. I still had and need to hide. Now they find at the camp."

The color slowly drained out of Daniel's face.

"And he go to the jail." Sanjana sobbed.

"Sanjana, I'm sorry." Daniel moved toward her, but she shrieked, waving him off.

"Not the touch." She blocked him with her arms. "No touching me!"

"Hey, hey." Cindy rushed into the room, removing a black sweatband. She looked from Sanjana to Daniel, who was clutching his right ear. "What's up? Daniel, pick those up. They were expensive."

Daniel stooped, picking up the headphones as instructed.

Sanjana caught her breath. Now she would be out of work, and then what would the family do? Her breath caught on a sob.

"Sanjana?" Cindy moved closer, the folds of her tennis skirt rippling with the movement. "Are you okay?" She looked from one to the other again. Daniel was fiddling with the broken headphones. "Daniel, what's going on here? Did you..." Her fingers fluttered between them, taking in Sanjana's flushed cheeks. "You didn't—proposition her?"

"That's gross." Daniel gave her a disgusted look. "She's like—my older sister. Adopted. Or whatever." He waved a hand as if to dispel the words.

"I know, I'm sorry." Cindy poured a glass of water. "The other mothers are always talking in the clubhouse about boys, maids, experimenting." She took a gulp. "Well, what are you two fighting about then?"

Sanjana put a knuckle in her mouth to avoid screaming. Betray Daniel to save her real brother, or let Manu pay to hide the boy's mistake? That was her dilemma. She squirmed under Madam's blue eyes, wondering whether Madam would even believe her if Daniel denied everything.

"I make mistake." Sanjana gestured at the headphones. "I want to borrow."

Daniel's eyes were glittering like emeralds. He opened his mouth, but Cindy cut them both off.

"Be more careful." She scolded them like they were both children. "Don't let your father see those. He didn't want me to buy them for you in the first place. What's for dinner?"

Sanjana wiped her hands on her cotton pants and looked away. Daniel shuffled off without saying anything else. She breathed more easily. "I take out chicken."

"And veggies." Cindy's voice was muffled by the open fridge door.

"Yes, Madam, asparagus. Vegetable." Sanjana picked up the paring knife, scoring the green stalks as Madam had shown her, wishing she could get her hands on Laxmi Pande.

She startled herself with the thought that she wouldn't be easy on the woman, but would take her time, causing as much pain and fear as possible. *What she deserves,* Sanjana thought, *for what she did to my brother. But,* a nagging voice reminded her, *you didn't say this angry thing to Daniel, and he's the one responsible for your brother being in jail.*

"He boy, not knowing what he doing. That other boy, he the bad one. Sharif."

"Sanjana, you okay?" Madam closed the fridge and peered at her. "Were you talking to me?"

"Little tired, Madam," Sanjana said, mortified Madam had heard her talking to herself. "Only remembering the instructions for vegetables."

Chapter Twenty-Seven

Hot water streamed over Cindy's shoulders, falling from her body into the tub and against the shower curtain. The force of the spray hit the earth-colored ceramic tiles opposite, creating a rivulet that streamed back into the tub. She hummed, lathering shampoo, scratching her fingers through to the scalp.

She had handled the conflict between Daniel and Sanjana well, though the two had been fighting like siblings, Sanjana speaking to Daniel in a familiar way Cindy had not seen before. Conditioner was next. As she worked it in, she wondered if she had missed other things as well. Daniel had never asked for siblings, unlike other children. He enjoyed being the apple of their eye, and they...well, she was happy only to have one hand to clutch in an airport.

She shut off the water, squeezing out the remainder from her hair. The shower was refreshing after a tennis match with Amira today at the clubhouse. Since they weren't allowed to go back to the camps, the women had to find another shared activity. She had hoped to be able to talk about the boys, but the arrival of Jonah and Robert to play doubles had prevented any serious conversation.

"I'll give you a call," Jonah had said. "We can play again sometime."

"Sure," Cindy had said as though she gave her phone number out to younger men all the time. If Amira had thought anything of their side conversation, she didn't let on. Cindy had walked back to the house from the clubhouse on her own, leaving Robert and Amira to play another set.

Cindy stepped on the brown mat, designed to absorb water, which expanded under the moisture of her feet, taking on a spongy quality. Cindy toweled off, running a comb through her bob and tossing a handful of hairs into the trash. She slid onto the stool in front of the vanity, her towel draped around her torso.

Tennis brought out the sinews in her arms. Bones of her clavicle, once her hallmark of fitness, were appearing from the surrounding flesh. She had forgotten they were there, molded into the rest of her body like she herself had been absorbed by the family. She pumped lotion into her palm. Daniel was getting older. He would soon be out of the house. *And then what?* she thought, the endorphins from the workout taking a dip. *Me, rattling around in this house in the middle of nowhere?*

The phone buzzed with an incoming text, startling her. *Going out for drinks this week,* the message read. *Jonah.*

A thrill ran through her, and she replayed the memory of his dark eyes watching her every move as she had passed out blankets. Cindy stood in front of her closet. The cotton dresses hanging there said middle-aged housewife, not svelte woman.

"There you are." Paul strode in, throwing himself onto the tan sofa in the corner. He pulled at his tie, leaving it open, and put his feet up, elbows splayed. "Where is everyone? Daniel's nowhere to be found, and Sanjana didn't answer."

"Hi." Cindy started, tossing her phone into the drawer that held her socks. *I love my husband,* she reminded herself, flushing at the interest she had felt at a mere text from a man a few moments ago.

"Oh, they had a fight," she said, thankful for something to distract him from her movements. Cindy clutched her towel closer, sitting on the stool in front of her dresser, straightening bottles of perfume that Sanjana had lined up across the mirror.

"Who? You and Daniel?" He flipped over onto his side, leaning on an elbow like a child, his green eyes zeroing in on her.

"Not *we.*" She chided, as he would have done to a student. "*They.*"

"Daniel and Sanjana?"

She nodded, rubbing lotion into the heels of her feet. "She was talking to him like..." Cindy waved a hand, searching for a word.

"Like he was her little brother? I caught them arguing about his dinner once—he wanted fried rice, and she said he needed vegetables."

"That's more motherly."

"Sanjana's not that old."

She threw a makeup brush at him, which he ducked. "Not nice. This fight was, I don't know, aggressive." She swiveled on the stool, the towel loosening. "What if she does it often?"

"He's not five." Paul took a piece of gum out of his pocket, unwrapped and popped it into his mouth. "She spoils the boy, if you ask me." He kicked off his loafers. "Worse than a grandmother."

"But her correcting him doesn't bother you?"

He leaned his head back. "In what sense?"

"I don't know what they have to disagree over." She didn't answer his question. Anything she came up with would sound classist, and he would call her out on it. "You're home early."

"Every now and then, these students surprise me."

"That must be pleasant." She continued applying lotion to her hands and elbows, watching him in the mirror. His face grew animated while describing Maryam's assignment. An essay that was exactly the type of writing he thought could change the criticism about the national labor laws.

In the excitement, she saw none of the perspective she hoped would come with time. That once Paul had tenure, he would take his foot off the gas, let the department coast on autopilot, and gain some distance from work. They could have the second honeymoon like her girlfriends, who plastered photos of empty-nester vacations all over Facebook.

"I recommended we feature it on the website."

"Must be good."

His eyes trained on her back, following the swoop of her towel. "It was." He stepped toward her.

A thrill, the old one she hadn't felt in months, ran through her, an electrical jolt compared to her tingle of curiosity at Jonah's message. Paul put out a hand to catch a wet curl. She turned into his hand so his palm cradled her cheek. *This is where I belong,* she reassured herself.

His other arm swept under her, carrying her to the bed. Cindy gave herself over to her husband's embrace, reveling in his weight when he hit the mattress a few seconds later, pushing her into the pillows.

"I missed you," she admitted.

He distributed kisses across her neck and shoulders. She let out a whimper of pleasure, her legs rising to encircle his, locking him in place. Paul's weight, the solid muscle shaped by morning runs while the rest of the house was sleeping, pressed into her. *This,* she thought, *we need to do more* often.

The sound of his cell phone ringing, the shrill retro call of a rotary dial phone, made his face drop in frustration next to hers on the pillow.

"You don't have to answer." She thought of her phone, stashed away between polka dots and stripes. The old-fashioned tune kept ringing, getting louder in succession, the setting Paul chose because it helped him locate the phone within the depths of his bag. He rose onto his elbows, one on either side of her face. He gave her a lingering kiss, stroking her cheek.

"But I do," he said. "That's why they pay me the big bucks for the department chair."

"You can call them back," Cindy said with a lascivious wink, grabbing onto his biceps. "We won't be but a second anyway."

Paul squeezed her thigh before he rolled off to the right like a parachute jumper, reaching for the phone on the coffee table. "Paul speaking." He stood at the edge of the bed.

She wished whoever was on the other end of the line could see him in his red boxers, hair standing on end, his clothes bunched at the bottom of the bed like discarded tissue. Maybe then they would remember he was a man in addition to being their department chair. She pulled the sheets up.

"Slow down, slow down. What?" The lines creased his forehead, and color drained from his skin. "Can they do that? What does counsel say? Okay, I'm coming."

Cindy banged the headboard.

"Sorry," Paul straightened his shirt. "Legal received a cease and desist on our site. They want to arrest a student for slander."

She drew her knees up, resting her chin on them.

"I have to go." Paul spread his hands. "She didn't want to put her article up there. She only did it because I talked her into it."

"Should I be worried about this student?" Cindy joked. "Is she very beautiful?"

Paul paused in zipping up his pants. "Maryam is barely older than Daniel."

"His friend from high school?" Cindy sat up.

"Maryam has a mind of her own." Paul ran his fingers through his hair. "Now you begin to see the problem," he said. "I'm sorry." He crossed to press a kiss to her forehead, making Cindy feel like the teenager Maryam was. "I'll make it up to you."

"I'll add it to the list." She gave his rear end a playful squeeze. He kissed her again. "Should have married a doctor," she murmured as he left the bedroom.

"I make more," he called back.

"Overseas stipend." She threw a pillow that ended up on the floor.

"No malpractice insurance," Paul retorted from the stairway.

Cindy reached for the book on her bedside table. Fatma wasn't the only one who had disapproved of Daniel's relationship with Maryam. Cindy had worried that if anything romantic developed, they were in uncharted territory—an expat with a local for a girlfriend—but Paul was the boundary breaker she should have kept an eye on. She pushed herself to read as a distraction.

Or she could go out for drinks. *If Amira is going to be there, what is the harm?* She tumbled out of bed to collect her phone. *You going out?* she texted, glancing at her phone every few seconds afterward like a teenager, trying to pick up where she had left off in the book chosen by the compound book club.

The romance, about a housewife who for no apparent reason, other than because she was bored, had an affair with a drifter, to the shock of her pastor husband, was not helping take her mind off being alone. Rather it was underlining the vapidity of her days. *I've come to this*, Cindy thought, *becoming the type of woman I would read about.*

The phone buzzed. *Yes, want to share a taxi?* Amira replied. *Happy hour at the W is really good.*

Cindy pulled out the hairdryer.

Chapter Twenty-Eight

Fatma fluffed her hair, turning this way and that to admire the curve of her hip in the hallway mirror. They were secluded behind the *mashrabi-ya*, the privacy screen shielding them from the entryway, the maids having brought out the trifold in preparation for the day's visit.

The front door opened, and then the maid ushered in the female members of the prospective groom's family. Their heels clicked across the marble entryway as they were shown to the female sitting room. A cloying cloud of perfume followed.

Maryam coughed, her attention trained on her phone. She was watching the number of tweets about her article skyrocket. This was better than likes on Instagram or Facebook. This was real interaction, others reading her words and telling her what she had made them think.

She glanced over her shoulder as Fatma sashayed forward to welcome the newcomers. "A good afternoon," her mother crooned. "Consider this house as yours, that you are at home."

People were using the hashtag #themigrantreport, the title of her piece, to debate the conditions of the camps. Maryam groaned, reading the transliterated Arabic much more slowly, cursing her English education, which had crippled her from any degree of fluency in her native tongue.

Allah says we should show mercy to everyone, a user by the name of Ibrahim had written. *These workers deserve our compassion.* Forty other readers had pressed the up arrow for his entry. She felt a rush of pride, mingled with surprise. There were others who agreed with her.

"Put that down," her mother hissed. "They're here."

Maryam was now the object of scrutiny.

Her mother tugged at the sleeves of the silk blouse, and then smoothed the hem of a purple skirt. "Walk slowly. And don't sit too close. Make sure to drink something instead of staring. No questions." She gave final pat to her chignon before plastering a smile on her face and sailing forward into the sitting room.

Maryam trailed, her eyes downcast as was appropriate for a demure bride. *What about a child bride? I'm not yet nineteen.*

She greeted the women from Faisal's family. The groom's mother looked like an overstuffed hen, her arms thick like lead pipes. They stood when she entered, waiting for Maryam to come and give them the kisses of welcome. One, two, three, cheek to cheek, the other woman's nails digging into her shoulder.

There were two younger women with thinner arms in satin short-sleeved dresses. Maryam kissed the air near their cheeks too, as one of them sniffed her neck. *Smelling me like an animal*, Maryam thought, covering the shake of her head with a fake sneeze. The other girl recoiled, reaching for a tissue.

Maryam bit her lip to keep from laughing and sat on the other side of her mother, as far from the prospective in-laws as she could manage without appearing overtly rude. This distance, with her mother's bulk in between them, said she was modest, not overeager, and relied on her parents to help her with major decisions.

Maryam sat on her fingers so as not to reach for her phone, tucked in the waistband of her skirt. *Imagine making a pair of men's pants without pockets*, she thought. No one would attempt such a thing. Even *thobes*, as streamlined and elegant as they were, had pockets—one on the front and two on the side.

"Maryam." Her mother elbowed her in the ribs. She sat up, seeing four pairs of eyes trained on her next word.

"Yes?"

"Tell them about your hobbies, what you like to do." Her mother smiled, lips together, which meant she was seething inside. Maryam surmised she had missed a direct question from the way her mother was clutching her hand. She racked her brain at this, the simplest of questions for which she should have had dozens of replies, ready to fire.

"Do you like fashion?" one of the girls asked. The high pitch of her voice belied her age. The girl was twice Maryam's size. Reem—Maryam thought someone had said her name was Reem.

"Of course," she agreed, thankful at least someone had given her an out.

"Yes, fashion."

"Who are your favorite designers?"

From the shrillness of her tone, Maryam realized the women were more nervous than she was.

"Dolce and Gabbana." That was easy, her mother's go-to brand for such occasions.

The declaration sent Reem into a spasm of agreement. And envy, Maryam realized through the way the other sister was appraising the diamond earrings her mother had forced on her. She wished she had paid more attention when her mother was trotting out the virtues of this particular proposal so she could have a list of rejections prepared.

She couldn't say that Faisal's lack of interest in university made him unattractive. She was lucky he wasn't down at Starbucks like many other young men his age or training to be an engineer. Most families wanted to marry within their tribe, but where possible many tried to make small movements up. Jaber's investments meant her family was well respected in the community.

"*Darb*," Nasser called from the doorway.

The three women on the sofa startled at the appearance of a non-relative male.

"Son?" Fatma called.

"I need to speak to Maryam," Nasser replied from outside the line of sight of the door.

Fatma turned to Maryam, the whites of her eyes showing with surprise. "He's a doctor," she said to her guests, as if this explained everything. Maryam offered a polite smile, scurrying from the room nonetheless. Her mother was frozen in front of their guests and couldn't object.

Maryam met her brother in the foyer. He was pacing.

"*Yema* is going to be very angry with you. That was going so well."

"Not as angry as *Ubooy* will be when he finds out that you are planning to go back to the camps a second time." Nasser stood ramrod straight with his arms crossed. He paused to eye her. "What did they do to your hair?"

Her fingers went to the teased hive of curls piled on top of her head. "I hope you marry a fat camel."

Nasser sliced a hand through the air. "Never mind that now. Come with me." He turned on his heel, marching through the living room and then the kitchen side door, moving swiftly in his sneakers and jogging pants.

"You going to cover for me?" Maryam hesitated. "*Yema* will kill me."

"Were you interested in this guy?" Nasser paused, taking her in for the second time.

"Wait—Faisal? No!"

"I'll cover for you." Nasser continued through the door. "This has to do with the police."

She struggled to keep up in her four-inch heels, her movements restricted by the fishtail of the skirt's design, tight at her knees and mid-shin. "Slow down."

Nasser was taking her through to the *majlis,* which would be empty at this hour since most men were at home in the late afternoon, at lunch with their families or taking a nap before the evening activities. She was stepping into the *majlis,* calling for Nasser again, when she came up short. There, in the middle of the room, looking as awkward as she had felt a few moments ago in her own sitting room sat Ali, the police officer.

"What are you doing here? Nasser!" she called.

Her brother brought her a scarf, which she draped over her hair, thankful for a reason to hide her ridiculous appearance.

"I need your help," Ali said. "I need you to help me find that guy who came in to file a report. Where can I find his family?"

Maryam looked from one frowning face to the other. "Why? What happened?"

Ali snapped his fingers. "I need to find him. Where does that woman he came in with work? His sister."

She took a small step back. "You're interested in workers now?"

"Maryam, you've got to share information," Nasser snapped. "This is official business, not your silly school project."

Her face went hot. "My professor gave me an 'A' for that report. He said it was excellent writing."

"Okay, okay." Ali raised his hands as if he were calming a skittish horse. "Tell me where I can find the guy you brought to the police station." He consulted a crumpled piece of paper. "Dadu?"

"Manu."

"Right, where can I find Manu? Does he work for your boyfriend's mother?"

Nasser eyed her more closely. "Boyfriend? If *Yuba* knew, he definitely wouldn't have sent you to that university."

"I don't have a boyfriend," she protested. "He's talking about Daniel."

"The American kid? From high school? I thought we settled all that."

"*We* did," Maryam emphasized. Daniel was younger than her, a big no-no in Arab culture where a woman's fertility was of utmost importance, not to mention his being American.

"I told you to cut that off." Nasser voice rose. "If *Yuba* finds out—"

"Manu," Ali interjected. He seemed more relaxed somehow, less tension in his shoulders. "Where is he?"

"They live in the Palm Oasis. But the brother is in our camp. MBJ, Street 45."

Ali shook his head.

"That's where I saw him," Maryam insisted. "In the worker camp."

Ali pinched the bridge of his nose. "He's not there. I went there today and questioned everyone."

"There are hundreds of guys out there."

He gestured to the pages of notes he had on various bits and pieces of paper.

"You need a notebook," she said.

"Call Daniel," Nasser interjected. "Ask the maid if she's seen her brother or if he's staying with them.

Maryam turned away, pulling out the phone from under her shirt. "They may not tell us." When she entered her phone's security code, she saw she had three missed calls from a university number. And five new emails. Unable to resist, she tapped the email button, scanning the subject lines of the new messages.

"Oh no." She tapped again, opening the message marked with an exclamation mark, titled *Urgent Cease and Desist*. She turned the screen to Ali. "We have another problem."

He leaned in, skimming her message, his dark eyes flicking up toward her. "You really know how to start something, don't you?"

"I told the truth." She turned the screen to her brother. He took the phone and groaned, then ran a hand over his face.

"*Yuba* is going to marry you to the first person he finds," he said. "That is, whoever hasn't read tomorrow's paper."

"She's a child," Ali protested.

"I am not," Maryam resisted the urge to stomp her foot and prove his point. "I'm nineteen. I'm considered an adult in most parts of the civilized world."

They all jumped when Ali's cell phone rang. He answered in terse Arabic, turning his back to them.

Nasser returned her phone with a mournful glance. "At the very least, you'll have to leave that uni."

Maryam dialed Daniel. "I'd rather die than do something else."

"Well, someone is dead." Ali snapped off his phone. "Another one at your camp."

"I'm coming with you," Maryam said.

No one argued.

Chapter Twenty-Nine

Spatters of water left streaky impressions on the windscreen of the Nissan. Rain pitter-pattered across the roof. Ali turned on the wipers as he waited for Nasser and his sister to get in. He needed lights in the encroaching darkness. Winter had arrived, which in the desert meant either rain or the clouds leaking on them in a drizzle as if God were determined to test his creatures by pouring out a thimbleful of water at a time.

The underpasses would overflow if there were enough water, and then the trucks would have to find a way in to pump it out. Ali adjusted his rear-view mirror, torn between gratitude for this case, which would keep him off the streets that would soon be crowded with joy riders, and the growing unease that something was amiss in the MBJ camp.

He focused on the details to avoid thinking about the girl who was about to get into his car. There was one body that he knew of, from the night he and Maryam had met, which had been sent home ten days ago. No autopsy, but the coroner had ruled it poor health, cause of death likely a heart attack. The company had paid no money. The remains were returned without any further wages. If Manu had organized a strike, growing impatient for the Byzantine bureaucracy that was the local court system, there would be little Ali could do to help.

The smell of Maryam's perfume, lingering from the *majlis*, interrupted him. *This is why gender segregation is bad,* he thought. Maybe he should have gone to one of those parties Hassan was constantly inviting him to in the private villas, where there were rumors of dancing girls and lavish bars stocked with alcohol. Or to one of those American universities to sit at tables with girls, instead of straight into the police academy, running alongside men who were barely out of their teens. He fidgeted with the radio dials to distract himself. *Her brother is coming,* he reminded himself. *You've got a case to finish.*

Nasser and Maryam came out of a smaller door inserted in the front gate. They headed left toward where Ali was waiting outside the boundary wall of the family compound. Maryam walked several paces ahead of her brother. A white Land Cruiser pulled in through the gate on the other side of Ali's car. Maryam ducked, then crept past the hood, placing a finger to her lips. Nasser stopped as the vehicle's window lowered. Ali heard the exchange through his passenger side window—another feature of cooler temperatures. They could mitigate the unrelenting air conditioning.

"*Yuba,* I'm going out for a bit."

"I need you to tell me what you know about Faisal," Jaber replied.

"Ali needs my help with something."

Jaber tapped on the steering wheel. "Your sister's fiancé is more impor-tant. Give your apologies. Come on."

The door behind Ali opened. Maryam crawled into the backseat, putting a finger to her lips. "Shh."

Ali raised his windows. "You're not coming." He turned to glance at her over his shoulder, and then looked forward. "Nasser is with your *father.*"

They watched as Nasser raised a hand to Ali, before preceding the SUV into the courtyard.

Ali forced a smile and honked in farewell. Maryam ducked the top of her head below the tinted rear windows of the Nissan. Neither of them spoke. The brass SUV moved through the gates, which slid shut, swallowing his friend inside the family grounds.

"How are you going to find Daniel's house then?"

"Give me the address." Ali turned, then seeing how close those eyes were to him, swung back around. He punched a few buttons on the GPS.

"They won't talk to you." Maryam climbed up onto the front seat. She folded her arms.

"I'm the police. They'll have to."

"Americans are suspicious of locals. Come on, I can help. You wouldn't even know about Manu if I hadn't been there."

He drummed his fingers on the steering wheel. This was not unlike the stories of boys riding around town with their girlfriends in the boot, look-ing for a deserted parking lot or an empty house to indulge their forbid-den pleasures. When they got older, private houses, unknown to wives or mothers, became the playgrounds.

"Can we please go?" Maryam said. "If Manu's really missing, he might be in danger."

Ali met her gaze in the rearview mirror. *Police business,* he reminded himself. *This isn't clandestine at all.* He nodded curtly, then put the vehicle in reverse. Well, the part about having a local girl in his backseat was, but... He focused on driving rather than the complicated spiral of rationalization.

Maryam scrolled through her phone, biting her lip and giving occasional exclamations of dismay.

"Where are we going?"

"Palm Oasis is near the mall."

Ali stepped on the accelerator.

Belongs to here in papers only, she read from the comments on her post, the commenter referring to her passport. *Not from our culture.* She closed her eyes, leaning against the headrest. "They wouldn't say that to my face."

"You wrote about that night?" He focused on the road.

She glanced at him. "How can I not?"

He sped through the roundabout. "Doesn't matter what people say. You know who you are."

She kept scrolling, the backlight of the phone casting her face in a whitish glow. "What would you know about it? You're an Arab guy who works for the police."

"I don't have problems?" He surprised himself at the low tone of his voice, the vulnerability, the knowledge of his secret lacing his reply.

"Who's oppressing you?" she said. "You're a man."

His fingers drummed on the wheel, the sound and rhythm gaining volume and speed the longer they waited at the light. Lines around his mouth said he was not amused.

"My sister says patriarchy represses women and men," he said in a low voice.

She leaned forward to catch it.

"The rules are as unforgiving to men who can't live up to them as they are to women."

Maryam reclined against the seat. "You're a feminist?"

Ali gripped the wheel with both hands, taking a left, resisting the urge to let the vehicle lean onto two wheels like the kids did in the desert. "No one's life is perfect."

They pulled up to the guard gate of the compound. Ali flashed his police ID.

"Number 23," Maryam said.

Ali waved off the guard, who asked if there was a problem.

"Straight," she said. "There, on the right."

He stopped in front of a two-story villa with a wrought iron and frosted glass front door. The porch light was on.

Maryam adjusted her scarf, pulling it under her chin. She checked her hair in the rearview mirror. He ignored the prick of jealousy, wondering if she were primping for the American. *Not her boyfriend,* he reminded himself. *Or your business,* he added as he rang the doorbell.

The white woman answered the door in tight black leggings and tank top. The boy's features resembled her full lips and cheekbones.

"Hi, Mrs. Johnson. Is Sanjana home?" Maryam popped onto the upper step.

"Hi, Maryam," the woman said. "You want to see Sanjana? Not Paul or Daniel?"

"Ah, no," Maryam said. "We need to talk to Sanjana about her brother."

"Man-u?" The woman said.

They walked into a marble foyer, past a circular entryway table laden with pink and purple bougainvillea. Ali glanced around. He wasn't sure what he was expecting, this being his first time in a foreigner's house, but it wasn't the lack of traditional rugs he noticed, or the coffee table made out of a smaller ceremonial door with squat legs and a glass top. Brass plates mounted on the wall were large enough to feed an extended family. They were the kind Ali's family still used in their camp in the desert, when the men went overnight and shared a meal from one plate.

"Call the maid," Ali said.

"Let me get her." Mrs. Johnson padded across the floor in her bare feet.

Maryam fidgeted with her hijab. Ali recognized this as a sign she was nervous. She opened the fabric, revealing the curve of her neck, and pushed it forward on the crown of her head, then smoothed the hair underneath. He had seen these actions a hundred times, maybe hundreds of thousands, from his mother and sisters, but she made them new.

Ali swung his gaze around, away from the delicate ears visible as Maryam tucked in stray pieces of hair. *Stop acting like a schoolboy,* he thought, staring at the bookshelves in a corner of the room. He couldn't think of the last time he had seen so many books, standing upright like little soldiers. More books were crammed in sideways, between the bottom row and the top of the shelf.

"They would like to speak with you." Mrs. Johnson was back, followed by the maid walking a few steps behind, eyes downcast. The mother had found a shawl in the meantime, draping it over her torso, for which Ali felt a spurt of surprised gratitude.

"You talk to your brother?" Ali asked.

The maid glanced in a triangle from Ali to Maryam to her madam.

"May we sit?" Maryam asked.

Mrs. Johnson inclined her head.

They sat on the brown leather sofas. Ali perched on the edge, his arms propped on his leg to avoid being sucked in by the supple leather. Where did foreigners get these kinds of things? He ran his palm over the surface, worn by many a seating.

"We are looking for Manu." Maryam's face was tilted toward the maid, showing concern. "Have you heard from him?"

The woman shook her head, her hands worrying at each other. Her cuticles were raw, jagged at the edges.

"When is the last time you spoke to him?" Maryam spoke in a calm, even tone.

Sanjana avoided looking at Ali. "Two days back."

"How did he seem?" Ali interjected when neither of the women pressed the maid further. "Had he fought with anyone?"

Sanjana trained her eyes on a spot a few inches above his shoulder. "He..." She paused for a shuddering breath. "He no call me."

"Do you have any idea what happened?" Maryam asked.

Sanjana's chin trembled. She glanced at her employer.

"Speak freely." Ali tempered the impatience in his voice with a wave of his hand.

Mrs. Johnson nodded as if to affirm what he'd just said.

"Embassy call me." Sanjana gulped. "Say...Manu in jail."

Maryam shot Ali a glance. "What would he have done?"

"Not him!" Sanjana's eyes flashed with indignation. "Me." She thumped a hand on her chest. "I stupid."

Maryam leaned forward, the rising sleeves of her *abaya* revealing arms dotted with hair. Ali was surprised she didn't remove them like all the other women he knew.

"Don't say that." Maryam leaned around Ali to make eye contact with the maid. She didn't touch him, but close enough that he could feel the hum of her body next to his. "We don't know why they choose him over anyone else. There must be a reason. Maybe he was a ringleader or they thought he would stir up trouble."

Tears welled in Sanjana's eyes. "I know." She thumped her chest again, then then her temples. "I stupid."

"Calm down." Mrs. Johnson shifted on the sofa.

"Why do you keep saying that?" Maryam began.

"Because it wasn't him." Daniel loomed in the kitchen doorway. "It was my drugs she hid."

"Drugs?" Mrs. Johnson and Ali asked in chorus.

"What kind of drugs?" Mrs. Johnson's eyes narrowed on Daniel.

"Not his," Sanjana protested. "That bad boy, Sharif."

"I took them away from him." Daniel explained, seeing the dismay on his mother's face. "I wanted to get rid of them so…so he wouldn't…" He trailed off, clutching at the doorjamb.

"Where drugs now?" Ali asked.

"I put in Manu's bag to hide," Sanjana said to Ali. "Night we come to police station, I hide so our Daniel not get in trouble."

"And the camp guards found them," Maryam said. "So they arrested Manu."

"Now he in jail. No money, no job." Sanjana struck her chest so hard Ali heard the knuckles meet the bone of her sternum. "Oh, my brother." She covered her face with her hands.

"This a simple problem." Ali pushed to his feet.

Maryam's face reflected the surprise of others.

"I go to jail, I find him. I get him out." Ali dusted his hands. "But then you." His finger sought out Daniel. "You will make report. Against this friend. He selling drugs?"

Daniel stammered.

"He'll do what he needs to," Mrs. Johnson smoothed her hands on her leggings and then stood. "Daniel?"

"Yes, ma'am." He avoided looking at any of the adults.

"I go to jail," Ali said. "You can get home?"

Maryam nodded.

He was loath to leave her there with the foreigners, to think of her being driven home by the American boy. "Call Babu to come get you."

She shot him a look, a half twist of her lips that said she might be amused or annoyed, or both, at his command. He climbed into the Nissan, punching the number for the CID office to distract himself. They watched him pull away, the four figures backlit by the living room lamps, looking to the world like a family.

Chapter Thirty

M anu ignored Adith and avoided him however he could, by lingering the back of the lines to board the bus, get washed up, to enter the kitchen. He had no choice really.

In the months he had been there, he had seen what could happen to men who fell out with those around them. "Accidents" like the marble slab dropping, or worse. He heard hushed stories about groups waiting outside the bathrooms for their rivals, teaching the most humiliating lessons if someone was suspected of complaining to the foreman about others slacking off or faked illness.

The door to the shared sleeping space burst open. Two men Manu had never seen in the camp stood in the doorway in pressed shirts and creased trousers. One had arms like pipes, while the other was thinner, like a whip. They stared at all the occupants. Adith slid in behind them, standing with his back against the wall. Manu and his roommates, in various stages of undress, paused in tableau. The bare blub shone on the oiled hair of the men in entryway. A pinky ring flashed. Manu recollected the pipe-like arms of the man who had met them at the airport.

"Search it," the whip ordered.

The men protested as the pipe-armed man moved from one bed to another, tossing aside mattresses, displacing what little clothing they had. Toothbrushes and soap containers clanged to the floor. Manu motioned to his roommates to wait and see what this was about. The group watched the man intently, but ceased protesting.

"There." Adith stepped forward to indicate Manu's sleeping and storage space under the last bunk. "He keeps his things there."

Pipe arms moved to where Adith indicated. He grunted, bending to pull out the mattress, shaking it like a blade of grass. Manu's bag fell to the ground.

Whip came forward, picked up the bag, and rifled through the contents. Out came the gloves that Sanjana's madam had given Manu, ripped in several places from continual gripping of concrete. His fake contract. Whip paused to read the pink copy of the filed report at the labor court and then passed it to pipe arms, whose face was a stonewall. He clenched it in a fist.

"Those are my things," Manu protested. "There's nothing wrong there."

"And this?" A knife, the blade as wide as Manu's palm, dangled point down from Whip's elongated fingers. "This also yours?"

"No," Manu stepped closer. "Not mine."

Whip threw back his well-combed hair to laugh. "How did it get there then?" He threw it on the ground, the blade clanging on the concrete. "Such a small bag, such a big secret." He turned it upside down. A mesh pouch plopped onto the ground next to the knife.

"Neither of those things is mine." Manu looked at the door. There'd be no escape if he tried to run.

Whip's gaze darted from the pouch, to Manu and then to the man of the pipe like arms, ricocheting back across the triangle.

"And this," he picked it up, hefting it from one hand to the other. Pipe arms shrugged at the unasked question. Whip gave the bag a sniff. He sniffed again as if in surprise. "This is illegal."

Manu pulled the pouch from the man's hand. Whip didn't resist. Manu could feel between his thumb and forefinger the granular texture of hashish. With a sinking feeling, he brought up the pouch to sniff.

"Illegal," Whip repeated, this time louder. "Take him."

Pipe arms reached out for Manu. His roommates exploded in protest.

"Silence!" Whip put up a hand. "Or I'll take you all in for knowing about this and not reporting it. No pay, jail time. You decide."

Manu's roommates fell silent as pipe arms manhandled Manu out of the room, dragging him by the elbow. His mind spun as they stumbled along behind the men who moved through the familiar courtyard. They exited the stacked rows of rooms, plunging into darkness behind the housing structure. Manu struggled in the grip of the giant as he saw they were approaching a squat shed-like structure with a tin roof.

"If you're arresting me, where are the police?"

Neither man answered him. Whip worked a key into a massive padlocked bar across the front of the shed door. They tossed Manu inside.

He landed on one knee. "What are you keeping me in here for? Turn me over to the police, and I'll explain someone put that hash there."

"Quiet." Whip nodded and pipe arm's meaty palm covered Manu's face with a white cloth.

Manu writhed, then gradually succumbed to the numbing substance.

When he came to, his hands were tied in front of him, pressing the wrists together in his lap. Manu wiggled in the chair. This succeeded in making the metal legs scrape on the concrete floor, nothing more. He couldn't move his fingers. They went from tingling to burning to no sensation at all.

The men had herded Manu into this windowless room behind the barracks and trussed him up like a goat before a festival, tossing him into a space only big enough for two people to lie down, without a bucket for a toilet or any food. The camp dormitory was better than this cement block.

At first Manu hobbled around the room, propping himself on the wall, calling out his questions.

No answer. He didn't know why he was here, if anyone else knew his whereabouts, or if he would get out. Apparently, they decided he was making too much noise, and Whip returned. He flung the door open.

Daylight blinded Manu after several hours in the dark. He fell to his knees. Whip tied him to the chair, then bludgeoned Manu with a fist to the side of his head until he went limp.

When Manu awoke again, it was dark. He focused on his hands, working one above the other. The plastic wire cut into his skin, making him cry out. That wasn't helping. He took deep breaths through his nose and tried to think what else he could do to get free. He was losing track of time. Had he been here an hour or all day? His bladder said somewhere in between, but with his hands the way they were, he wouldn't be able to get his jumpsuit open. Sitting in urine-soaked clothes would make a bad situation worse.

The door swung open. Manu sat up. Sunlight blinded him for the second time in the semi-dark. This time, both men were back. Pipe arms leaned up against the wall. Whip came forward, allowing the door to remain open a crack. He cleared his throat, ruffling through papers in a blue folder.

"You're a troublemaker," he said in Hindi. "We hear you have ideas."

"Thinking isn't a crime," Manu blurted.

"Ideas you share with others."

Manu didn't reply. Adith had heard him. His mouth went dry.

"No one forced you to come." Whip advanced, bending at the waist a few feet from Manu's face. He snapped his fingers. "*Aree.* You listening?"

"Yes," Manu managed.

The other man's pupils were dark, blending in with his eyes, creating an eerie effect like he was looking everywhere at once.

"Sign this." He waved a piece of paper in front of Manu. "Then you can go home."

Manu couldn't read the papers dangling above his head. "I can't see."

The papers were thrust above his nose. Same as at the airport, they were in Arabic.

"I can't read this," Manu said.

The man exchanged a laugh with his partner. "You want to go home, don't you?"

"I want my job," Manu said. "The one they promised me."

"Don't think we don't know about you, you organizer. You know the penalty for striking in this country?" Whip peered into Manu's face as if dealing with a dimwitted child. "You sign and leave."

"Or?" Manu's voice gritted out. The place where he had been hit on his temple throbbed.

Whip sighed, hand on his right hip, the papers fisted. "Him." he jerked a thumb over to pipe arms lounging against the wall, scrolling through his phone. His partner jerked alert, slipping the phone into his back pocket.

"I haven't done anything wrong." Manu said. Maybe if he tried a different tack, it would break through to the mystery of why he was here. "Why me, out of the hundreds of guys?"

Pipe arms had both hands on his hips, palms out like a fishwife. "No one else asks as many questions as you. Everyone else works."

Manu's mind raced. If they were really willing to send him home, maybe there was a way to shame them into behaving well. "That's because it's my job to ask questions."

The other man sniffed.

"I mean, I'm an undercover officer." Manu blurted the storyline to one of his favorite Hindi films. "They sent me to do a report here. On this camp. On people like you."

The men exchanged an uneasy glance.

"Let me go, and we will forget all about this."

The two men whispered in the corner. Manu's skin itched from the sweat rolling down his forehead. He blinked the salty drops from his eyes.

"I'll convince him to sign." Pipe arms rolled his wrists.

"If he's telling the truth, no bruises."

"He's lying. Wouldn't they have gotten him out by now?"

They lowered their voices. Manu hoped his gamble would pay off.

Whip pulled out a cigarette. Pipe arms lit it for him. They murmured together, backs turned, a cloud of gray smoke rising above them like a dingy halo.

"Me also?"

They turned to him in bemusement, as if remembering he was still there.

"Of those, please." Manu tilted his head toward the cigarette. His roommates chose between cigarettes and the homemade liquor others hawked to them on the weekends, hoping to make a few extra riyals. Liquor though, wouldn't help this hero out of his jam. Fire, on the other hand—Manu licked his lips as if in anticipation, his gaze lowered, in case they could read his intention.

The pair exchanged a glance. Pipe arms shrugged. Whip glanced around. There was no one else with whom to confer.

"Terrible headache. Caffeine withdrawal. I'll be sure to tell everyone how well I was treated." Manu hoped his tone sounded casual.

Whip handed a cigarette to pipe arms, indicating with a wave of fingers he should take it across. Pipe arms bent to put the cigarette in Manu's mouth. *If I were a Bollywood action hero*, Manu thought, *now is when the di-shoom-dishoom action soundtrack would start. I would bang my head into his stom-ach, and…* His lips opened to receive the cigarette, teeth clamping down on the foreign intruder. Pipe arms lit the small tip until it burned a hot red.

Manu breathed through his mouth to avoid coughing up a lung and giving away his inexperience. A phone bleated a Hindi film song. Whip stepped outside to answer, indicating with a shoulder that pipe arms should accompany him.

"He's not going anywhere." Whip opened the door to the shed-like structure, letting in a gust of air.

Manu puffed, allowing himself a small cough. His tongue pushed the wet paper of the tip into the corner of his mouth to avoid it falling out. The end of his cigarette flared with the rush of air. He coughed again, his side teeth clamping down so he wouldn't burn himself. An ember fell on his knee. The red glow shimmered for a second before it dulled and burned out, leaving a black mark on the leg of his jumpsuit.

An inkling of an idea sparked in Manu's mind as he puffed away at the cigarette.

Chapter Thirty-One

She took the blue parking stub from the African valet. "Welcome back, Madam. It's been a long time," he said in a baritone.

"Thank you," Cindy said. "You know, we've been traveling." The lie came easily because it was more glamorous and better suited for the setting than the truth. Their five-star lifestyle, including the spa membership, had to be replaced by their savings goals.

An aquamarine taxi sped past her through the hotel's entryway, laughing passengers tucked inside, an arm dangling out the window, cigarette in hand. She crossed under the marble arch, smoothing blow-dried hair. Those party days were long gone, and Cindy wouldn't have said she missed them, except how else could she explain her presence at the Four Seasons this afternoon other than as a bid to recapture a moment of youth?

"May I help you, Madam?" A woman in a dark blue suit greeted her at the flower laden entryway table.

"The Library Bar?"

"Allow me to show you the way, Madam." The woman, of nondescript ethnicity—maybe Eastern European—inclined her accommodating head to the left.

Cindy trailed in her wake. In the first few years after they moved to the Gulf, she had flooded the lobbies of five-star hotels like all the other expats, guzzling custom-made drinks with lime or lemon. Life had been an endless series of happy hours, punctuated by lavish Friday brunches over which they lingered. Paul carried forth on the latest international news events, while his colleagues and neighbors downed endless bottles of champagne.

That was before Daniel, and the routineness of it all, had made her weary of the obsequiousness of hotel staff, the overpriced drinks, and the tedium of listening to new arrivals bemoan the lack of their favorite brands on the grocery shelves.

~~~

Yet here she was again. The helpful attendant motioned her inside the leather interior of the Library Bar—a place she hadn't been before because it had come up after her time as a boozer—passing her from one gracious employee into the charge of another.

"Are you joining anyone, Madam?" a man in a blue suit, impeccably coiffured hair, asked in slightly accented English.

"I'm joining friends. Amira?"

"Ah yes, one of your party has already arrived." She followed his lithe figure, with a waist any woman would have skipped lunch for, to a table at the window, overlooking the hotel's inlet.

"Cindy." Jonah stood up as she was ushered to the seat opposite him.

His cropped hair was shiny, as if fresh from a shower. In a dark blue sport coat and tan slacks, he could have been a solider turned politician. He came around to greet her, their cheeks touching briefly, the scent of his cologne going straight to her head.

Cindy sat, reaching for the nuts on the table to distract herself. She stuffed them into her mouth to avoid asking where Amira or the others were in case her query came out as shrilly as she thought it might.

"Hungry?" Jonah pushed her the menu.

"Yes." Cindy lied. She had eaten a quick meal of spaghetti and meat sauce with Daniel before leaving the house. A flush was creeping up her neck. She opened the padded menu, her eyes not reading the print.

The man in the blue suit returned and Cindy asked for spring rolls and a virgin mojito.

"Not drinking?"

"I'm driving," she said. The country had a zero tolerance policy toward drunk driving, though with their antics lately they could have been deported for far worse. As if he read her thoughts, Jonah chuckled.

"Yeah, I normally don't come to such fancy joints, but I figured we should celebrate not being kicked out of here."

Their drinks arrived with a flourish, a woman in a dark blue—or was it black?—uniform placing Cindy's mojito on a white coaster and pouring Jonah a glass of dark red wine.

"We dodged that bullet." Jonah raised his glass to hers. They met with clink.

At the buzz near her hip, Cindy checked her phone. *Can't come, must keep both eyes on Sharif. Enjoy,* said the message from Amira.

"That we did." Cindy took a deep swallow, wishing there were alcohol in her drink to steady her nerves. "Amira's out, she's got something at home."

Jonah shelled a few cashews.

"And Robert?"

Jonah shook his head. "No, he's restricted to the base because of his role in the incident."

"Well, you were there."

Jonah raised his eyebrow. "Yes, but the whole thing was Robert and Amira's idea. I went along because we are always supposed to stay in twos, helps prevent kidnapping."

"You snitched?" Cindy covered her mouth. "I'm sorry, that's a terrible thing to say."

Jonah laughed. "No, don't worry about it. If it had been my idea, I would have taken it on. Robert didn't mind. He was using it as an excuse to spend more time with Amira."

The waiter placed a plate of spring rolls onto the table. Cindy bit into one with gusto. The heat of the shredded vegetables singed her tongue. She took her time chewing, thankful for the pause to collect her thoughts.

"Are Robert and Amira...?" She slid the plate toward Jonah.

"He would sure like to think they are." His teeth gleamed in the last rays of the setting sun. "Does she?"

Cindy blushed again at the thought of discussing her friend like high schoolers. "I haven't had a chance to ask Amira."

"I thought women talked about everything."

What about you? Cindy wanted to ask. *Are you seeing someone, or did you come here to see me?*

"Cindy! Hi!"

Her mojito sloshed against her blouse. Maggie was standing in the doorway of the bar in a black sleeveless dress, clutching the hands of her girls in chiffon party dresses.

"I thought that was you."

"Hi, Maggie," Cindy dabbed at the Pangaea-like blob on the front of her blouse. The liquid was making the sage colored fabric transparent. "Care to join us for a drink?" She filled in the silence with the expected invitation, though she would rather jump out the window.

Maggie glanced down at her ginger-haired charges, who protested. The younger one rubbed at her eyes.

"Madam, I'm sorry, no children allowed in bars. This is the ministry's rules."

"Another time then," Cindy said with what she hoped was a regretful smile.

"Sure." Maggie moved away, giving her a small wave.

"And did you snitch?"

"Excuse me?"

Jonah smiled. His eyes sparkled like the water visible over his shoulder. "To your husband. What did you tell him about the police station?"

Maggie was sure to run back to the compound and tell everyone in the book club she had seen Cindy out—without inviting the rest of them—drinking with a stranger. Not that Paul would care. He had business dealings in hotels all the time with female students, colleagues, and visitors. The bedrock trust they had in each other now rankled her.

"Remember, my son picked us up." Cindy signaled to the waiter for another mojito.

"So he doesn't know."

"Everything turned out well in the end."

"The guy won his case?"

"The guy is missing."

"What an interesting life you lead," Jonah said.

Cindy indicated to the waitress, who obligingly refilled Jonah's glass.

Not really, she thought, *but you might help me with that.*

"He's nice enough. Stays to himself," Cindy swirled another spring roll into the flecked pink sauce.

"Is it weird his sister is your servant?"

Cindy finished chewing. "Sanjana is more of a housekeeper. Daniel is old enough to take care of himself, so she mostly helps out with cleaning."

"Is that the politically correct term?"

She snorted. "Okay, so you're part of the biggest military, committing atrocities around the world, and are here to judge me?"

Jonah raised his hands. "These hands have committed no atrocities, ma'am." His eyes bore into hers. "But I've offended the lady of leisure."

Cindy's cheeks flushed. She couldn't blame the alcohol.

"Would you like another?" the waitress asked, her hands clasped in front of her.

"No, the check, please," Cindy said.

The woman scuttled away in little steps as fast as the modest skirt of her uniform would allow.

"Come on, now." Jonah tapped the back of her hand. "Don't be like that."

Cindy folded the napkin and placed it on the table. "No, you're right. Expats live a charmed life."

The waitress was nowhere in sight.

"Listen, Cindy, we got off on a tangent," he said. "You're talking to a guy who grew up on a farm in Missouri, enlisted after 9/11, and has traveled to various similar looking deserts with the Marines."

She studied his blunt fingernails. "It's fine. Even my son thinks my life is frivolous." Cindy swiveled to see if she could catch the waitress's eye. When you really needed them, they were nowhere to be seen.

"May I help, Madam?" The manager in the blue suit glided to her side.

"We asked for the check."

"Right away." He slid away, his footsteps masked by the plush gold carpet.

"Have any plans for the weekend?" Cindy asked, since talking about the weather was not an option.

"I'm on standby for Iraq."

"Are people still being sent there?"

He leaned ropey arms on the table. "I help train the police officers. So many of them are dying, we need to keep training new ones."

Cindy swallowed. Compared to him, she was spoiled. Lately she was beginning to feel this was true of her life measured up next to anyone's.

"Here we are." The manager had returned, not a hair out of place. Jonah reached for the embroidered receipt holder.

"We'll split it."

Jonah pulled out a wad of riyals in a range of colors. "You're a cheap date." He slid in a few red notes. "No alcohol at all."

She didn't say she would get it next time.

"Let me head to the little boys room. Be right back."

Cindy scurried to the lobby, handing the valet her ticket and willing him to hurry.

He passed the stub to a man in white shirt and dark trousers. "Going so soon?"

"Meeting. I'm running late," she added.

"Quickly," he called after the shorter man.

Cindy positioned herself behind the entryway table, laden with flowers. *Don't turn around.*

Mercifully her tires screeched into the waiting area. She trotted out in double time, handing the sweating man a fifty-riyal note. He protested. Cindy swung herself into the driver's seat. "Keep it."

As she clicked her seatbelt, she reached for the notes in the door pocket. *Do not make rash decisions based on emotion,* she scrawled at the first stoplight. *Consider a vibrator.*

Chapter Thirty-Two

On the other side of the bedroom door Sajita wailed, knowing her mother was within her reach.

Sajish cracked it open. "Give her some candy," Sajish said to the nanny before closing it again. He resumed packing.

"Okay, go over it again," Laxmi said. "We can't have simply lost a man. He has to go somewhere."

Sajish threw himself onto the sofa. They were at home, the low ceiling of the apartment like an oppressive hand. She had hoped to move out soon, had even toured some compounds. Now she was faced with the possibility that all of her plans would crumble.

Instead of a return flight, there was a jail cell waiting. Sajita would be sent home to be raised by Laxmi's mother, waiting for a position as a housemaid or cleaner, wasting away her life in some Arabian capital.

"He was in the shed, and then the was gone."

"We'll report him as a runaway," Laxmi improvised. "If he turns up, the police will call us."

"They may call the sponsor." Sajish groaned.

"We are the sponsor. The law is always on the side of the company."

"No, we are the employer. The *kafeel*," Sajish corrected. "The local owner of the company, the national, he is the sponsor. If this guy talks to the police?"

"He doesn't speak Arabic," Laxmi said. "They can't communicate. We can tell our side of the story."

"Are you sure? Some Westerner newspapers probably planted this guy to start trouble. Take photos and post and lose the country the Olympics!"

Laxmi went over to her husband, waddling slightly. She rubbed his arm.

"Sh, sh, sh," she said as she would have to Sajita. "This is not good for your heart."

He pressed his knuckles into his eyes. "Jail is not good for our lives!"

"Jail is highly unlikely," she said to remind herself as much as soothe\ the rising alarm in his voice. The baby inside her kicked, sensing her alarm.

Sajish's rolled his head to face her. "That's what will happen if they find out we switched the contracts."

"Nonsense," she said, rubbing her belly "We are not the only ones who have done this. This is a system problem."

"We need to find that man," Sajish muttered. "We need to find him and contain him."

"Call Adith," she said. "There are no secrets in the camps. Someone saw him. If those goons can't help us, we'll get someone who can."

Sajish pressed a kiss to her forehead and pushed up from the sofa. Sajita rushed through the open door, a flurry of arms and legs, hurtling into Laxmi's lap.

"Hello, hello," she said as the toddler climbed all over her belly, searching for new purchases. She clutched her daughter, hoping for the hundredth time that the child who grew inside her was a boy.

Chapter Thirty-Three

Maryam paced the waiting area at the station. Every ten minutes or so Babu's worried face would peer at the sliding glass doors through the window of the circling SUV. She cursed the heels, chosen by her mother for the bride viewing, that drew the eyes of those who wandered into the waiting area. Men came in pairs to report traffic accidents, their eyes shifting to her, and away, then drifting back as if making sure she was still there. The clock on the wall marked time with a slow tick, tick, tick that she thought would drive her crazy. Ali had been gone for forty-five minutes.

Her phone buzzed incessantly with messages from people forwarding her the comments appearing on the website, or sending their thoughts directly to her. Professor Paul had gotten her into a big mess by not withholding her name from the byline.

"I'm so sorry. I told them only to use your initials," he had said when he called. "We'll get this sorted out." Two hours and nine hundred comments later, there was no way to backpedal from here.

"I helping you?" The Indian worker—was his name Ashraf or Ahmed? Or…she couldn't remember—was staring at her, bringing Maryam back to reality. Someone's life could be at stake, not only her precious reputation. *They've hurt him,* she thought, panic rising at the idea she would have to explain to Daniel, and his maid, what the authorities had done to Manu.

"No, thank you." She tried to fake a smile but succeeded only in blinking rapidly against the growing lump in her throat.

"Thank God," she added when she saw Ali moving in the crack of the doorway. She waited for Ali to come over to her, tapping her foot impatiently, aware of the audience. He spoke to someone over his shoulder and then came toward her, indicating she should follow him outside. She did, close on his heels.

Neither of them said a word until they were inside the Nissan. Ali reversed, pulling out of the station in case anyone saw them, or more specifically her, getting into his vehicle.

"You don't want to come with your driver?"

"Babu's in trouble," Maryam sighed. "I got him in trouble. *Ubooy* won't let him out of his sight."

"Manu's not here," Ali said.

Maryam fell back on the seat, staring into an empty lot. "They killed him?"

Ali clicked his tongue in impatience, like an old woman. "There's no record of him. They never brought him here." He flattened his hand across the dashboard, using the palm of the other one to turn the wheel, pulling them into the dirt lot.

"Let's go to the camp."

He clicked again. "The sister said he wasn't there, remember?"

Maryam frowned, a crease appearing in her forehead. "I don't understand."

"We never picked him up. And you know what's strange?"

She turned to him. Here, in the front seat, they were much closer to each other than before, when she had been crunched up on the floorboard in the back. If she leaned over slightly, their shoulders would be touching. He glanced at her, then away, clearing his throat. She saw a flush spreading up the back of his neck. *Is he nervous?*

"There's no mention of the file he opened for the labor court." He was fiddling with a dial in the door handle, adjusting his left side mirror.

I make him fidgety, Maryam realized with a start. She glanced forward for a moment, her mind whirring to register what this meant. He wasn't annoyed by her. He was...she tested her theory by leaning forward slightly, putting her arm on the island between them. Ali kept adjusting his mirror, lowering the window and reaching out, moving away from her, to push it into place. "Someone else took him." She drummed her fingers on the island.

He flinched as though she had struck him.

Or he doesn't like me, she thought, aware of how little she knew about men, especially locals. Maybe he was the religious type who didn't think women should be out of the house. But here she was, a non-relative woman in his car, the very idea an anathema to conservative men.

"Not the police, so the company?" He put up two fingers.

"Not illness, the hospital?" She put up three.

"Not his family, no visiting." He put a fourth.

"Not the embassy, they can't help him." They stared at the fifth finger.

"The embassy," Maryam repeated. "Sanjana said she went to the embassy many times to ask where Manu was. They are the ones who told her he had been arrested."

"And they would know if he had filed a case in the labor courts," Ali continued. He put the car into drive.

Maryam shifted back into her seat, her game of cat and mouse with Ali temporarily delayed. "Everything's fine," she said. She checked the position of her *shayla* in the passenger-side mirror, thankful her mother's make-up artist had gone light on the eyeliner. Enough to accentuate the curved shape of her eyelid, but not so much that she looked like a model in a magazine. "They took him into custody and they're caring for him."

The car surged forward under Ali's guidance. His knuckles bent around the steering wheel. "If we had him, no one could take him," Ali said. "Not even the embassy." They ran a red light.

She clutched the handle above the window. "So you think the embassy wanted to hurt him?"

Ali shot her look. She felt a shiver of worry, either for Manu or herself, she wasn't sure. What had brought her to this moment, careening through the city at night with a man she barely knew in search of a stranger? Even as she leaned forward, she had the answer. Life. She felt alive for the first time since graduating from the safety of high school and being forced to wear the veil and *abaya*, to behave like the type of woman she had no interest in becoming.

Ali pulled to a stop in front of the embassy, then dialed someone on his phone as he climbed out of the car. She pulled the edges of her robe together, waiting for his signal. The street was empty of cars. Darkness fell around them like a blanket. She counted six remaining hours before the embassy opened. There were men walking to and from the shops nearby—a grocery store, a fast foot outlet called Hot Chicken. Other foot traffic came from the gas station two hundred meters ahead.

Ali spoke to the guard in the security station outside the embassy gates.

The youngish man with curly black hair, most likely from Sudan or Tunisia judging from the lilting Arabic she could make out from the window, licked his lips before replying to Ali's questions. "No, no one has been brought here all day. There is a temporary shelter, but that's for women." He indicated the villa behind the one used by the embassy. "A men's mission? No." He couldn't recall such a place.

Ali came back to the car, frustration twisting his mouth. "Nothing. He's not here."

"We can go back to the camp," Maryam said. "Ask around there."

"I'm taking you home."

Maryam protested.

Ali held up a hand. "I shouldn't have brought you anyway. Not when you had such an important gathering. I thought a man's life was in danger."

"A man's life is in danger." She pounded on the dashboard. "The groom's family came to waste my time. You actually need my help for something useful."

Ali cleared his throat. "Is that what's important? Being useful?"

Maryam glanced at him to see if she had revealed too much. "Yes.. Isn't that what we all want?"

Ali turned off the road, entering the highway instead of turning back toward her house. "You ask them at the camp if they saw anyone come in or leave. That's all."

She smiled in the dark. "I can ask to see their logs."

"Good idea."

They rode in silence, the city receding from them like a mirage. When they arrived at the camp, Ali flashed his lights, indicating the guard should open the gate immediately. The man, his worn face squinting in the headlights, did as he was told this time, without protest.

"Should we split up?" Maryam slid out of her seat and stepped down from the vehicle.

"No." Ali thought of the first time they had met here. "We'll go together, room by room."

"That will take ages." Maryam huffed and crossed her arms.

They faced off at the hood of the Nissan.

"I want a map of this place," Ali said. They gazed at the U-shaped buildings of rooms, separated by the courtyard.

She translated into English, loudly, speaking slowly, making a box with her fingers, sending the guard scurrying back into the office. "Map, please."

"We'll start up top." Ali pointed to the corner of the northernmost hallway. "Get through those, flush anyone with something to hide downstairs."

She gave him a sidelong glance. She hadn't noticed the rich timbre of his voice before. "Okay."

They made their way to the staircase, two guards trailing them. "Sir, I help," one of them said.

Ali waved them off. "We can't trust them," he said in response to her inquiring look. "They may be involved."

Maryam's pulse quickened. This was more than online controversy. This was real.

She was halfway into the stairwell when shouts broke out.

"Distraction?"

"No." Ali searched the horizon. "They're saying fire."

Maryam ran to keep up with him. They followed the pointing fingers to the side of the housing structure. Her *abaya* flapped against her legs, her ankle twisting at a crack in the sidewalk. She kicked off the ridiculous heels. Her feet pounded on the pavement in time with Ali's strides. The *abaya* flowed against her legs now that she wasn't teetering on stilts. She bunched a fistful in her hand to keep from tripping. Men were crowding around the edge of an empty field. A squat structure in the corner had smoke rising from beneath the roof.

"Call 999," Ali called back to her.

"Okay." She took out her phone, jangling with every step, determined to follow him.

Ali reached the short structure, wrenching the door open. A man was sitting on a chair, bent over, coughing as smoke rose from a flaming black shoe a few centimeters from his foot. Flames licked the legs of the chair.

Ali strode in, covering his mouth with his sleeve. He sawed at the knots around the man's wrists with the flat of his car key. Beads of sweat peppered both their foreheads. Ali exhaled a prayer for strength as the plastic frayed and he yanked the rest of it apart. The man yelped as the fire leapt onto the leg of his jumpsuit. They worked together to strip it off, tossing it in the far corner so it could not contribute to the growing blaze.

Maryam turned away when she saw the man's bare legs. He wore only a scrap of dark fabric for underwear. "Gate 45," she told the 999 dispatcher, thankful for the night that hid the dark blush creeping up her neck. "There's a fire." She melted back toward the housing as men poured into the field, searching the space with rapacious curiosity.

"No, I don't know," she said as the man on the other end rattled off a series of questions. "Maybe one person. Yes, there's one officer here. Okay." She hung up. "Water," she called to the men standing around, gawking. "Get *pani*, to throw on fire." She pantomimed what the dispatcher had said to her. Make sure the fire is manageable. The camp security went into action, organizing the men to make way at the entrance.

Ali put his arm under the man and walked him over to Maryam. He slipped out of his shirt, pulling it around the man's shoulders.

Maryam realized with a start it was Manu, Sanjana's missing brother.

"*Bismillah*," she said.

Ali shot her a surprised look. She wondered if he considered her an old lady now for invoking God's name in a crisis.

"You can breathe?" His attention focused on Manu, who clutched his chest. Ali mimed deep breaths, his chest rising and falling. Manu coughed again. Men ran by with buckets, half-filled liter bottles of water, whatever they could carry.

"Who put you in there?" Maryam kept her eyes trained on his face.

Manu gasped for air. "Embassy people."

Ali pulled out his phone, his arm still around Manu, propping him up. "Find a chair," he instructed Maryam, who was hovering near them both. She went into one of the bedrooms, finding nothing to sit on besides the bed. She went a few doors down. Two men hovered in the doorway, looking as though they didn't know whether to come look or stay where they were.

"Chair?" She mimed sitting down.

One brought forward a plastic drum-like container used to store paint.

"Good," she said. She took it, the rim bumping against her knees as she ran back to Ali and Manu. He collapsed on the overturned paint container as Ali spoke rapidly to someone on the phone.

"Why? Did they say why they did this?" Maryam peered at him, finding it easier to maintain eye contact now that shirttails hid his nether regions.

"Double contract. They getting money." Manu retched, spraying bile on the cement walkway.

"He needs a doctor," Maryam said.

As if on cue, the flashing red lights of the ambulance swept across the courtyard, tinting them all with the color of blood.

Chapter Thirty-Four

Cindy brought three glasses of water to the table and set one in front of Sanjana. The woman's eyes rounded.

"It's fine." Cindy pressed her shoulder. "I can bring you something every now and then." A shudder ran through the petite woman's frame—horror at the mistress serving her and worry about her brother, Cindy surmised. "You two start, and tell me everything, from the beginning."

Daniel avoided eye contact. His eyes flitted everywhere but his mother's face, pausing at Sanjana's pinched features now and again. Cindy took a long sip of water, prepared to wait them out. She hadn't even known there was a *they*, she realized with quiet horror. Her maid and her son.

They sat next to each other at the dining table. Daniel wore a ripped T-shirt and board shorts. Sanjana's fingers worked a tissue from underneath the long black sleeves of a blouse Cindy had given to her.

"I can wait all night," Cindy said. Neither of them blinked. "Or you can wait and tell your father."

"No!"

Sanjana gasped. "Madam."

Cindy sipped more water, her fingers squeezing the glass a little harder than usual. Neither wanted Paul's opinion of them to be lowered. "Start talking."

"She was trying to help me." Daniel gazed at a spot above Cindy's shoulder on the wall. "And I was trying to help Sharif."

"Sharif?" she interrupted.

Daniel's eyes jerked to her face. "He's been trying to get cleaned up. He really has. You know, trying to move past the whole thing with his dad. I wanted to take this away from him, so—"

"More pills?" Cindy asked.

Sanjana had gone white, like a sheet.

"Something worse than pills," Cindy surmised. "Marijuana?"

"He promised he would stop," Daniel said. "I wanted to help him."

"How did you get involved in all this?" Cindy asked Sanjana.

The maid's chin quivered. "I see bag. With the drug. And I take it, not wanting Daniel to be in trouble."

Cindy drank a sip of water. She let Sanjana speak, though frustration coursed through her like a jolt of electricity. Daniel was protecting Sharif. The maid was protecting Daniel. And now, the police were at their door.

"I have bag when we go to the camp." Sanjana's voice caught. "And when we at the police station."

"You gave your brother the bag?"

Sanjana shook her head. "He not knowing anything. I put the drug in his bag, but he not knowing. I mean to get it later, but they send us away." She dissolved in a flood of tears. "Now embassy call and say they put Manu in jail."

Cindy bit her lip. That could be Daniel in jail, if Sanjana had not intervened. Daniel in jail, Paul's job in jeopardy, their whole life here at stake. "Alright." She passed the woman a box of tissues from the china hutch behind her. "Let me think."

Her gaze wandered away from Daniel's pinched features and Sanjana's tear-streaked face. There must be some way to secure a release, but if Manu had been found with drugs, there was no way to prove the bag wasn't his. "Did the bag have anything of Sharif's on it? His name or initials?"

Daniel shook his head.

"Mesh bag," Sanjana said. "Like I buy for Madam's cucumbers and such."

"If it had his address, it would lead them straight to this compound," Daniel pointed out.

"And to us." Cindy sighed, seeing his point. Any way she looked at it, the drugs would come back to finger them if they tried to prove Manu's innocence.

The front door opened. They turned in alarm. Paul stepped inside. "What's going on?" He put his bag to one side, loosening his tie.

"Chatting about weekend plans," Cindy said. "Trying to get everyone's schedules to line up."

"Oh?" Paul walked over to the table, ruffling Daniel's hair. "Not about how everyone here was almost arrested and no one told me?"

Silence met Paul's deadpan accusation. Like children, both Sanjana and Daniel turned to Cindy.

"We weren't arrested. They took us in for questioning."

"Right," Paul leaned his forearms on the top of the chair next to her. "And no one thought I needed to be informed?"

"When?" Daniel said. "You're never around." He looked away.

Cindy took a sharp breath.

"I trying to find my brother——"

Paul put up a hand. "The root of all of this is the Bibles." He angled toward Cindy. "How could you go out there, passing out Bibles?"

"Who told you?" Daniel asked.

Cindy pressed her son's foot under the table. "We were giving them blankets and deodorant."

Paul threw a copy of the New Testament on the table. "You forgot these. Have you no sense? Do you want to go home that badly?"

"So you're the only one in this family who can take risks?"

"I make calculated risks as part of my job. For my career," Paul enunciated slowly. "That's not the point anyway." He tapped the Bible's leather cover.

"Who gave you that?" Daniel sputtered.

"Again, I am not in the wrong here." Paul said, placing his hands flat on the table. "The university liaison. When they called me in to explain how we were on the deportation list."

Cindy jerked her chin at Daniel and Sanjana. They slunk out of the room, avoiding eye contact with Paul.

"I'll finish with you two later."

Rising from her chair, Cindy faced Paul, like two duelers at high noon. "I didn't know it was that serious."

Paul crossed to the wine rack. He worked off the label on a bottle of red wine. She went to the kitchen and returned with two glasses and the corkscrew, passing both over to him. "Amira was showing interest in something for the first time in months."

"I didn't know you hated it here that much." He tipped the bottle and wine sloshed into their glasses. "Aren't we doing some good?"

"Well, we found Manu." She clinked her glass against his and then downed half of hers. "Because we were out near the camps."

Paul let his swirl, the stem dangling between his fingers. He took a long sip before answering. "You jeopardized everything for a woman whose husband was sleeping with prostitutes."

Cindy smacked the tabletop. "It's Amira's fault her husband is an asshole?"

Paul shrugged. "That family is nothing but trouble." He nursed his drink. "First the boy gets Daniel involved in all that pill pushing nonsense, then you don't have enough sense to keep a distance from his mother." He reached for the wine bottle.

Cindy pinched the bridge of her nose. "Your student was here. Maryam, right?"

He held the wine bottle poised over Cindy's glass. "What?"

"They were looking for Sanjana's brother. Apparently he's in jail."

"Who is 'they'?"

"She and a cop," Cindy said. "Abdullah, or something."

"Did she say anything about——"

"The cyber law and her blog? No." Cindy motioned for him to refill her glass, eyeing him to see if the connection was as obvious as it was to her. They were both in the wrong in different ways, pushing the envelope. And other people were paying the consequences. "What can we do?"

He sat next to her. "Wait. And hope for the best."

"In this place?" Cindy snorted.

The doorbell interrupted them.

"Expecting anyone else?"

Cindy gave him a blank look.

Paul answered the door.

Amira stood on the doorstep with a bottle of wine and a few other women from the compound. "Hello." Her eyes swept over him from head to toe.

"Hi, what's up?" Cindy stood at Paul's shoulder.

"Book club," Amira said. "Remember?"

"Oh." Cindy stared at her friends, at a loss for words.

"We can do this another time," said Maggie.

"Of course not." Paul boomed, as if inviting them to a party. "Come in, come in." The glint in his eye said he found it hysterical. The book club he joked with her about, who gathered to gossip more than discuss literature, had landed on the doorstep, wine in hand, interrupting a great deal of juicy information. "I'll let you ladies get to your discussion."

Amira and Maggie sat down on the brown sofa. The other women sat across from them.

"I'll bring in some glasses." Cindy went to the kitchen, where Sanjana was huddled in the breakfast nook, sniffling. "What do we have for snacks?"

Sanjana shook her head.

"Go to the store and get some cookies." Cindy fished a bill out from the top drawer. "Hurry."

Cindy assembled a tray of wine and water glasses, rummaging in the cabinet for a carafe. Her liquor stand was empty, un-replenished since her birthday party. She cursed Daniel's shenanigans, Paul's pursuit of the truth, and, for good measure, Sanjana's gullibility.

"Sanjana's putting together some nibbles." Cindy's voice sounded a little too cheery as she carried the tray into the living room.

"Paul's been so busy, he hasn't had a chance to get to the distributor." Cindy set the tray down. "Looks like this or juice tonight."

Amira twisted the top from the bottle of wine, Maggie reached for a glass.

"Small group tonight. More for us." Maggie raised her glass with a grin.

"Busy day?" Amira said.

The condescension in her tone rubbed at Cindy's frayed nerves. "Well, Daniel's had a bit of an issue."

"Teenage boys," Amira clucked. "Never know what they're up to."

"Asking doesn't hurt." The words slipped out. Cindy thought of Sanjana's ashen face and the knowledge that everyone was covering for Sharif.

Amira paused in sipping her wine. "Excuse me?"

Cindy cleared her throat. "I know it's been hard for Sharif since his father left."

Maggie gulped the remnants in her glass. This was not a topic to engage Amira about in public. Even one additional person counted as an audience. The book club was a rumor mill in the making.

Amira's eyes sparked. She placed the wineglass on the coffee table. "We have had our challenges." She adjusted the sleeves of her pristine white blouse and then fluffed the hair at her collar. "Analyn does a good job of keeping tabs on him when I'm not around."

"Apparently not. He's selling hashish, at the school." The words left Cindy's lips before she could reign in her tongue.

Maggie's mouth rounded in an O.

"That's preposterous. She gives me daily reports as to his whereabouts."

"Daniel!" Cindy called. The shrillness in her voice brought her son into the room faster than she knew was possible. His eyes took in the tableau, and his foot went back on the step behind him.

"Hello, dear," Amira said.

"Tell Sharif's mother what you found in his bag."

Daniel's attention went from her to his friend's mother and back like a startled Oryx.

"Are you sure it was hash?" Amira turned her torso toward him. "Maybe it was loose leaf cigarettes. Like I caught you boys trying to figure out how to smoke."

"You were smoking?"

Amira gave Cindy an arch look, as if to say, *see, you don't know everything about raising boys after all.*

"No." Daniel said to his mother.

Amira protested.

"I mean, yes. But only for a second in the backyard. The smoke was terrible. I didn't try it again after that. Honest."

"So glad I have girls," Maggie said, falling back against the loveseat. Amira and Cindy shot her a combined annoyed look.

"How can I believe anything you and Sanjana told me about the bag now?" Cindy rose. Sanjana entered, a plate of cookies in one hand and one of chips and dip in the other. Her gaze made the triangle from Daniel to Amira to Cindy.

"For the love of God," Amira said, "bring that here and tell me everything."

"Sit down," Cindy instructed Sanjana and Daniel. "And tell us how you found the bag again."

Sanjana scuttled over, then placed the dishes on the glass-topped coffee table.

"Analyn," Amira shouted into her phone. "Come to Ma'am Cindy's house immediately. Bring Sharif with you." After a pause: "Well, wake him up!"

Maggie reached forward, snatching up two chocolate chip cookies as if she were watching a movie.

Chapter Thirty-Five

Ali gave as full a report as he could, filling in Khalifa on all the details of the men from the agency. His former boss sighed loudly now and then. Ali envisioned the tic in the right eyelid that was the supervisor's sign of lack of sleep.

"Good work," Khalifa said.

There was silence. Ali swallowed disappointment that an offer to come back to ISF was not part of Khalifa's gratitude. Who knew when Khalifa's attention would smile on him again?

"I think we should keep this guy." Ali pictured the scene of repair and recovery going on behind him as men swarmed around Manu and the smoking shed.

He sighted Maryam, but quickly glanced away when she gave a small smile. Now was not the time. He should get her home, away from this scene, and the presence of so many men.

"Who?"

"The worker, Manu. He can work with us and help investigate other things."

"Like what?"

"Like…alcohol. And prostitution." More silence. Ali cursed his hastiness. He had mentioned the top two most frequent crimes that came to mind—both indecent to mention in public, of course, even on the phone.

"Does he want to stay here? After what happened?"

"I wanted to check with you first," Ali said.

A grunt of approval. Khalifa did not like to be brought in after the fact. You had to lead him along the path like a father with his teenage son. "Ask him. We'll talk next week." The line went dead.

"We need you," Ali said. "You help us?"

"I'm a student," Maryam protested. "There's no way my father would agree."

"*Him*," Ali pointed at Manu, who was taking shallow breaths while a paramedic took his pulse. "He could be undercover for us." He ran a hand over his face. "This kind of thing is happening all over the city. And other things too."

"What kinds of other things?" Her eyes were more beautiful without the rings of make-up most of the local women wore when out in public.

"I'm taking the little journalist home," Ali said to no one in particular.

~~~

He looked in the rearview mirror. *Stay up here,* he reminded his eyes. *Not on her.* The tires squealed as he pulled the SUV to a halt in front of Maryam's house.

"Thank you." What he really wanted to ask was if he would ever see her again.

"Yes." She smoothed her hair back toward the crown of her head and adjusted her *shayla.* "Will you really employ that man?" The force of those eyes sent a current through him.

"Seems like a good idea, but it will need many approvals." *I would love to hire you,* he didn't say, *if there was any way I could make that happen.*

She nodded. "See you."

He racked his brain, wondering what else he could say to keep her next to him. What would Hassan do? Probably spout a line of memorized poetry for such an occasion. Or chocolates. His sisters loved sweets. The leather creaked as she leaned toward the door handle.

Before either of them said another word, the door swung open. Nasser's face appeared in the blue-black of the night, his eyebrows knitted together. "Get inside, now." He reached up into the vehicle to grab Maryam's elbow. "They've been asking me where you went all night."

"I was coming," Maryam shook off his grasp. Ali heard the same note of peevishness he himself elicited from his sisters if he questioned their comings and goings.

"She's done," Nasser called across from the passenger door to Ali. His knuckles rapped on the corner of the dashboard. "Whatever help you need, you'll have to get it from the actual police."

Heat rose up Ali's neck at the thoughts he harbored about his friend' sister. "Of course. I thank you for your help."

"What, now you're thanking him?" Maryam tilted her head back to look at Ali. Her hands were fisted in her lap. "He didn't do a thing!"

"Maryam, not now," Nasser said. "If *Ubooy* finds out you were in this car—"

"If *Ubooy* finds out I was in this car, heading to our camp to save a man's life, then maybe he should be proud."

"He's right," Ali said. Her eyes had a wounded look as they passed over his face. "You should go."

"I don't know why anyone says this country is changing," Maryam grumbled. "Everything is still the same. The workers have more rights than I do."

As she slid out of the seat and onto the running board, the floodlights at the family gate came on.

"Oh no," Nasser groaned.

The wrought iron gate rolled back, and there stood Jaber, with Babu behind him. Under the fluorescent lights, her father's shadow loomed across the SUV.

"Get inside this house now."

"But *Yuba*, I wasn't—"

"Now! Before the neighbors wake up and see what you've done."

"I've done nothing." Maryam jumped to the ground. She stamped her foot. Nasser took her by the arm, jostling her toward the threshold of the family compound.

Ali climbed out of the SUV and stood at his full height, eye to eye with Maryam's father.

"Who are you?" Jaber said sharply.

"Ali."

"You're not the American boy." Jaber's gaze swept like a Ping-Pong ball between Maryam, Nasser, and Ali.

"No." Ali's forehead prickled with sweat. Maybe the father would feel better if he knew. *I'm half the man that boy is.* This was not the time to bring up the infirmity.

Babu's eyes were like saucers, taking in Ali's smudged police uniform.

Maryam struggled against Nasser's grip. The sight of her propelled Ali forward, crossing into the opening of the gate, onto private property. Even the law wouldn't be on his side if the father thought his daughter had misbehaved. Ali could imagine a similar scene in his house if he found Maha in such a state. By that standard, Maryam's father was being a saint.

"*Yuba*, honestly, that thing with Dan—"

"Silence!" Jaber sliced a hand through the air. "You may not be the American, but that gives you no right to be with my daughter. You, Maryam, go to your room. I'll deal with you tomorrow."

"I am not going anywhere." Maryam crossed her arms. "I've done nothing wrong."

"You're right, you're not going anywhere. No university, no shopping, nothing for a week."

Ali thought Jaber was going to start foaming at the mouth.

"I'm grounded?" Maryam sputtered. "I'm not a child."

"You insist on behaving like one. You left your mother alone with…" Jaber's gaze skittered to Ali and then away "…visitors. Without explanation. And you come back in the middle of the night, riding in some man's car."

Tears were brimming in those bright eyes. "He's police."

"I'm not only a policeman," Ali said.

"You're a stranger. You have no voice here." Jaber flicked his hand as though Ali were the gardener.

"I'm Yusuf's son." Ali spoke in an even tone to show his respect. "And I have proposed to Maryam. I intend to be her fiancé."

"What?" Nasser took a step closer to Ali.

"Yes, I am sorry, I know this is not the way we do things. But your sister—well, you know her best."

"What do you mean, you proposed to her? You don't speak to her. You speak to me." Jaber narrowed his gaze at Ali.

With everyone's back turned, even the driver's, Ali willed her to say yes. His hands clenched and unclenched. It wasn't the smartest plan, but was the only one that could get them out of this moment of her father's towering rage.

Maryam's mouth rounded in an O, her eyes darting over the landscape of his face. He resisted the urge to shuffle his feet. Later, they could meet again to break off the pretense, her honor and education intact.

"Is this true, Maryam? He made you a direct proposal?"

"She is amazing," Ali said. "Such a tender heart and always wanting to help others, *mashallah*, not like most girls." He realized with a start he meant every word.

"Well, I hadn't said yes." Her chin jutted out. "That's why we were togeth-

236

er. I wanted to get to know him better. It's my right."

Ali hid a smile with a cough. Women were doing more screening these days, though midnight rides would be rare for any family.

Jaber passed a hand over his face and sighed like a deflated balloon. The anger drained from his rigid frame, replaced by fatigue, obvious in the shadows under his eyes. "We will talk about this tomorrow. You, go to sleep." He pointed a long finger at Maryam. "You two I want to see first thing in the morning." The hand waved at Nasser and Ali, who murmured their consent. The driver followed Ali to the gate.

"Tell her I have to talk to her," Ali whispered to Nasser. "There's something about me she doesn't know."

"As long as you're Muslim, she'll have to take you," Nasser hissed.

"Goodnight," Maryam called.

Ali didn't turn around. The smile on his face would have given him away. He had made a proposal. This would get his mother and aunts off him as a popular discussion subject. And maybe also help his sisters. Unless, of course, Jaber found out about his future son in law's medical condition.

Chapter Thirty-Six

The door swung open, the handle smacking the wall before Sanjana could catch it.

"If you're cold, there are more blankets here." She pulled open the closet. There were stacks of blankets and towels on the shelf to the right. On the left, like sentinels, were bottles of lotions, shampoos, and soap from hotels Madam and Sir had visited in countries across Asia. One bottle with aqua green liquid fell over. She straightened it. Her back turned allowed Manu a moment to take in the vastness of the guest room. This was twice the size of their sleeping area at home, once shared with their three siblings and ailing mother.

Sanjana blinked away tears. She hadn't seen where Manu was sleeping in his worker camp, but she could smell the odors that announced the number of men who had been crowded in there with him. The images of their dusty faces at the tables while she and Madam had passed out water and blankets was difficult to shake, even while standing in the middle of the sunlit room on the second floor of the Americans' house. If Sanjana was having this much trouble, she knew how much harder it was for her brother.

"The shower is here." She parroted Madam from the countless occasions they'd had guests. "Turn the knob all the way to the right to get the water hot. Mine takes at least three minutes."

The delay in her brother's gaze, the way his eyes bounced around the tiled bathroom before returning to her face, caused her to flush. Yes, she was complaining about waiting for hot water, a wait that would have been pure luxury in the house they had grown up in together as children.

"Daniel said you could have some of his clothes." She smoothed the fabric of the gray cotton T-shirt and blue jeans. Sir's clothes would have hung from her brother's bony frame, but the teenage boy's would do quite nicely. "Is there anything else you need?" She heard the tremor in her voice.

"I'll be fine," Manu said.

She went to the door to hide her relief. These were the first words he had spoken besides, "Thank you," upon entering the house. She shut the door while his back was to her, his head bowed, contemplating something on the bedspread. Sanjana brushed away the tears again.

"Your brother settling in okay?" She started at the sound of Paul's booming voice.

"Yes, Sir, yes. Thank you."

"Hey, you're not crying, are you?"

She gave a shaky laugh, moving away from the door so that Manu wouldn't hear.

"I am so happy to see my brother again. And okay." *The dark circles under his eyes scare me,* she thought. *He looks at me as though I'm a stranger.*

"Of course." Paul rubbed his hands together. "Looks like he might have a real contract soon, and then he can stay in the country. Imagine, you might go and stay with him at his place on your day off."

Sanjana blushed. She could not tell Sir the unlikelihood of her brother being able to afford an apartment of his own, and staying with his unmarried roommates would be out of the question. "I help Madam with dinner." She scuttled down the stairs.

Since Manu's arrival, the house had become her prison, where she hid from one person then the next. She couldn't bear to be in the same room with the deflated Manu. He had stood up to Laxmi Pande's thugs and the effort had exhausted him. When the police released him, the gruff officer had asked the authorities to let Manu stay in the country. There was work he could do, the man explained through an interpreter. Work that would help others like Manu who were stuck in a system they didn't understand.

I'm sorry if I get you in trouble, the final text from Analyn before she left for the Philippines. There went her one friend, if that's how you described their relationship. Amira was searching for yet another maid and shipped Sharif off to a military-style boarding school in Texas.

Sanjana splashed water from the kitchen sink on her face. They were going to discuss the details with the Ministry of Labor. Someone was trying to make sure Manu would get paid, even though it would be much less than his original contract stated. Someone else was getting him a new contract.

This would come with his own place, new clothes, and a salary. She swallowed past the lump in her throat at the thought of sending long-overdue wages home to the kids. Maybe she could take her leave that year, when the American family went on their exotic beach holiday. Maybe she could go home and sweep all of them, some now teenagers, almost men and women since her last visit, into her embrace.

"Spaghetti?" Cindy came into the kitchen, pulling off a hot pink headband.

"Yes, Madam." Sanjana jumped back into action, pulling open drawers, pouring water into a large red pot.

"You and your brother can eat with us." Cindy used the sing-song voice she used to greet the neighbors.

"We are fine," Sanjana replied. "He is tired, and I..." Her mind went blank, searching for an appropriate excuse.

"Right," Cindy waved a hand. She wrenched open a bottle of water. "He should rest, and I'm sure you have lots to catch up on." "I'm off to shower."

The tension went out of Sanjana's shoulders just as water began to boil on the stove.

Chapter Thirty-Seven

Sheets so white, Manu saw spots dance before his eyes. He threw off the duvet cover, but the draft from the air conditioning caused him to pull it back over his feet. Light from the street lamp filtered into the bedroom. His own room, not shared with dozens of other men. Manu tossed again onto his elbow. He could have drawn the drapes, but during several days in detention, waiting for the police to sort out his papers, he hadn't seen the sky, at day or night.

This was where Sanjana had been living—this house like a palace, arranged on a street that curved around the corner like a row of teeth. The marble floors, the onyx black staircase, a room of her own. A room with a television that streamed Hindi movies whenever she wanted to view them.

He couldn't believe this was where she lived. Tears filled his eyes. Manu let them fall on the pillow. His sister had been away for a long time, and he hadn't thought very much about what her life was like. He had lived in ignorance that her every minute was better than their entire childhood.

The painting across the room loomed over him. There were swirls of black thread that spooled from a central point outward in ever increasing circles. If he stared at the right angle, Manu could imagine being swallowed up in the vortex. This was what had happened to his life. He was upended.

He sat up, wiping the backs of his hands across his face. "Pull yourself together, man," he said, as if he were James Bond. Manu stalked to the bathroom, splashing water on his face, washing away the thoughts of the men he had left behind. Those who were asleep in the embrace of exhaustion, the light touch of cockroach and spider legs brushing against them unheeded. He shuddered at the memory of the fermented onion stench, the thudding of snores from the man above him. He snapped on the light, then blinked at the fluorescence. The brightness somehow dimmed the memories of his months in the camp.

The glass encasement of the shower beckoned to him. Manu entered, shedding the jogging pants and T-shirt the teenage boy had loaned him. Hot water sluiced over him, pelting him on the shoulders. He stayed under until his fingers were as wrinkly as an old man's. So much water. When they were ten to a toilet in the camp, and the men were washing out back with buckets.

He came out, wrapping himself into a towel. There were a dozen outfits hanging in the wardrobe, more T-shirts and even underwear. Manu marveled at the availability of so many clothes.

"Until we can take you shopping," Sanjana's madam had said to him, looking over his sister's shoulder while giving the stack of folded garments to her. "Paul's clothes would swallow you up."

He had nodded, discerning her meaning through the gestures she made. Manu's stomach twisted as his sister set the clothing into a basket, then washed her hands in order to prepare dinner. Dinner for the white people.

He pulled on a T-shirt, a red short-sleeved thing with black letters across the chest, and a pair of black mesh shorts. Manu opened the door. Darkness swallowed him on the landing. There was another living room up here. Blue-white flickering images of the television illuminated a few pieces of furniture.

"Can't sleep?"

Manu started at the sound of the boy's voice.

"I can get Sanjana for you." Daniel's hair was falling into his eyes.

"No, no." Manu backed away. A stranger speaking his sister's name drove him out of the room. The boy rose from the brown leather beanbag chair as if Manu hadn't spoken. He disappeared down the stairs. Manu's breath came out in a whoosh. A few minutes later, the boy rapped on the door. He returned with Sanjana, who was rubbing her eyes against the overhead light, blue cotton gown rumpled from sleep.

"What you are wanting?"

"You translate," Daniel said, pointing to Manu. "I think he's hungry." He motioned to his stomach in a circle.

She gave a jump at seeing him in the doorway.

"Everything okay?" Sanjana asked him in Nepali. "You did not fight with him, did you?"

He heard a tremor in her voice. His sister was afraid of this boy who could wake her up all hours of the day and night with any type of demand.

"No, I didn't say anything." Manu moved to close the door, but the boy broke into a smile and indicated Manu should follow them down the stairs.

"I love a midnight snack. Your sister is the best cook."

"Come and eat something," Sanjana urged.

And this stranger, of all people, was the one who his sister felt compelled to protect, even at his expense.

Manu trudged down the steps, and put his hand over his eyes when Daniel snapped on the lights. In the kitchen, the boy opened the fridge. Manu lingered on the last step, hoping he had forgotten all about him.

"Sit, sit, sit," Daniel emerged from the interior of the fridge with hands full of plastic containers. "Both of you."

Sanjana perched at the edge of the breakfast nook, her hands fluttering.

"No, we fine," Manu said again. The sight of those containers reminded him of the pasta they had suffered through at the mostly silent dinner, Manu pushing the strange pieces around his plate. He put his hand to his heart, as if in a solemn vow.

Daniel dropped the containers onto the countertop. "I'm not into the health stuff either." He laughed, and pulled out a plastic wrapped bag from one of the kitchen cabinets. Ripping off the outer wrap, Daniel tossed the flat bag into a small oven. He mashed a few buttons and then the fan began whirring.

Daniel leaned against the counter, leaving his hands behind him. "Have you seen any of the city? You know, the sights?"

Sanjana translated for him, her words like a torrent, washing over him.

"I slept four hours a night," he said.

She turned and spoke to the boy, who gave him a thumbs up.

"I told him you never saw anything like it."

"Well, I never saw it," Manu said.

She gave him a pleading look. Was this what life had been like for her, this constant placating of these people?

Daniel crossed to the fridge, beckoning that Manu should follow. He began tapping different photos, which Manu understood to be places in the city. There was a wide-arcing road that ran alongside water. His sister was in between Daniel and the woman, smiling without showing her teeth, the boy's arm entwined with hers. Judging by Daniel's height, about hip high on the women, this was years and years ago, around the time Sanjana had arrived.

"A city tour," Daniel was saying. "There's one of those buses. You know, you get on and off?"

Now they were in front of a photo of Sanjana by herself, standing in front of a bus that was two stories tall, a hand over her eyes to shield them from the sun. His sister fidgeted next to him. This was the trip at which a young Manu dragged at her heels when she left the house, begging her not to go. She was wearing a black sweater, which covered her from collarbone to wrist, the yellow and red pattern of a sari peeking out from underneath. No sign back then of the jeans she would favor in the future.

"Popcorn." Daniel ripped open a bag that released a puff of steam. He poured the white contents into two plastic bowls, and pushed one in Manu's direction. He sat at a stool in front of the low counter and gestured for Manu to do the same.

Manu slid onto a seat opposite the boy. He didn't appear to be a degenerate, like the men in the movies who spent their wages on hash, beat their wives, and ignored their children.

"Listen, I know what Sanjana did for me. And it probably got you in trouble. I'm really sorry. I was trying to help a friend, and you know." Daniel shrugged.

She translated, her words like the humming of bees in his ear.

"So you sacrifice me for him and his friend?" He asked his sister who was avoiding eye contact.

Daniel leaned across the counter and tapped the back of Manu's hand. "Bygones?"

"He's saying sorry!" She hissed.

Manu faked a yawn.

"Ah, now you're sleepy."

Manu scurried out of the kitchen before the boy could say more words he didn't understand and his sister could make more excuses. He retreated to the room, his room, like one of the stray cats in the worker housing. Behind the closed door, Manu exhaled. They had offered him a job—a job in this country to help prevent other people suffering as he had. He collapsed in the dark cream armchair in the corner. The streetlamp cast a shadow across the wall.

The doctors at the hospital had poked and prodded him like a slab of meat, not making eye contact, not asking questions. The policeman—Ali, Manu had gathered from the name being repeated so many times as the doctors addressed him politely—gave all the answers in Arabic. Their conversation had streamed over Manu's head as they placed sticky pads on his chest, a man with a full, curly beard pushing him onto his back.

That was what life would be like here. Pushed and swayed in the cadence of a language he did not speak. Manu draped sideways, the chair's frame more familiar to him than the large, squishy bed's interior. He wondered what the men in his room would make of this space, this house, this life Sanjana had been leading. They glimpsed it, whizzing by, to or from the worksite. Most of the time their eyes were closed, heads bent in sleep, as the bus rattled through the city like a decrepit cradle, jostling the occupants into the no man's land between wakefulness and sleep.

~~~

The sound of a knock roused him from a dream in which he was trapped on a bus being buried in sand. He was the only passenger. His mouth had been pressed up to the crack of air made possible by an open window as sand rose all around him, filling the seat, then his boots, then his ears.

"Come and eat some breakfast." Sanjana hovered in the doorway.

He sat up, rubbing his eyes, the pristineness of her bright pink top and white slacks calling to mind the grime on his teeth.

"I'll get cleaned up," he said.

"You can't stay in this room forever."

Manu stood, his back creaking from being forced into an S curve to hang across the chair. "We're not all so good at adjusting." The downward turn of her lips pierced his heart, but he kept moving toward the bathroom.

"They're all gone," she said softly. "Sir went to the office and Madam to the grocery store."

"And the boy?"

"He's not a bad boy."

Manu whirled from the bathroom doorway. "He almost got me arrested." He jabbed a finger at her. They had not spoken of the hashish, or any of the events leading to his freedom. "And he's almost a man. I was working by that age. So were you."

Tears shimmered in his sister's eyes. "Yes." She clasped and unclasped her hands. "They are different."

"Not in the eyes of God." Manu retreated to the bathroom, fuming, unable to shake the feeling that, despite his plush surroundings, he was still trapped.

"You didn't tell me *Amma* died." She hiccupped behind him.

He swiveled.

"The kids called me too." Her eyes were dark pools of liquid. "I'm all alone," she whispered. "I'm all alone in this strange place." In the morning light her face was a web of lines, crisscrossing the corner of her eyes and gathered around her mouth. A grey strand of hair peeked from behind her left ear. This was not the fun-loving girl he had grown up with, but a tired woman who had lived a decade in service of others with no end in sight, the city more or less as strange to her as it was to him, a new arrival. The ice around his heart cracked as he surveyed the map of her labors etched in the stooped shoulders and wrinkled hands.

"You are not alone," he said.

Chapter Thirty-Eight

M aryam's mother was pacing the room like a drill sergeant, her heels clicking a consistent tempo a heartbeat would envy. She tried to memorize her mother's movements to recreate in next semester's screenwriting class. Maryam sighed at the thought of university life, going on unchanged, while she was stuck at home, grounded like a young child.

"You were out with a boy—man." Fatma interrupted herself for the correction, finger stabbing the air. "In the middle of the night." The heels were picking up rhythm.

Maryam chewed her fingernails. Replying now would be futile, as it had been the other ten times she had interjected. *Life is material* she repeated to herself the motto of her major. *The young local woman is subject to a string of requirements to protect her reputation that are not equally applied to male counterparts her own age.* She composed the text for a feature on the modern local woman to distract herself from the fact her own future was at stake.

"You come back, sitting in the car in front of the house where everyone, *everyone!*" Fatma pointed a flamingo pink fingernail "can see you." The idea that neighbors might have seen triggered a system rest. The speech began all over again, at a louder volume.

Maryam worried the errant thread on the hem of her T-shirt. She left her nail beds alone to tug at the wayward string. *Despite the lip service given to educating women and training them to participate in society, women are still expected to mainly serve as wives. And then of course, mothers.* The facts of her piece would surprise no one in the local community, though she could imagine Professor Paul's raised eyebrows. More than ever before, Maryam knew she straddled two worlds.

"Then, this same man…" Fatma said the word like it was a death sentence "says to your father he is proposing to you. In the middle of the night. Directly, to you, as if this is the way we do things."

"You're upset he didn't come to see you with his mother?"

Fatma marched to where Maryam slouched on the sofa, yanking her up by the arm. They were nose to nose, courtesy of Fatma's five-inch heels.

"Your father could send you to Saudi Arabia to my sister," she said, her voice devoid of the theatrics of the past hour. "And there will be no one there who will tolerate your wisecracks."

In her mother's wide-eyed stare, Maryam felt a frisson of fear. She had been mentally retorting to all the accusations. In the silence, she saw Fatma wasn't playing a character in the popular Turkish soap operas. She was serious. Maryam flinched at the hard edge to her mother's words.

"Don't let him do that," she said, the tremor breaking her façade.

"*Habibti.*" Her mother caressed her face with the endearment. "You think this will be only our decision? If anyone finds out..." Fatma drew Maryam into her embrace.

She let herself be folded into her mother's arms, bending so her chin would rest on Fatma's shoulder. A cloud of Chanel Number Five enveloped Maryam. She inhaled. This was the smell that she associated with Fatma, who didn't change her fragrance with new releases like most local women. There was none of the oversweet floral notes but the musky jasmine and her mother's arms reminded Maryam of the woman her mother had been throughout her childhood, laughing, indulgent and strong. The mother Fatma had been before her daughter reached puberty.

"This on top of that newspaper thing you did." Fatma brushed at the corner of her eye. "Your uncles will put pressure on your father to get you settled as soon as possible."

The family. This was the stonewall none of them could get around. If her uncles decided the damage to their family reputation was too great, Maryam would be shipped to live with her distant cousins. No more university. No future as a journalist. There were worse things than living under Fatma's fretting eye.

"At least," Fatma said, whirling away, back into the role of irate mother, "he is from our tribe. Thank God for that. Now we have to see him." Fatma rubbed her hands, one against the other, as if warming them from the cold. "He'll have to come with his mother, under the broad light of day."

"I don't think he is that serious." With her mother back on her agitated gait, Maryam reclined against the plump cushions of the cream sofa. "Maybe we can take Faisal back?" This was a non-suggestion given how Maryam had left his female relatives in the lurch during their visit. They too would have heard of her expose on the workers and want to distance themselves from her.

"Think of it this way. However much you don't like what your father says, your aunt will be a hundred times worse." Fatma let out a gust of air. "This is not a joke. Imagine if they say the reason the proposal halted was because of your reputation."

Ah, yes, the death kneel to any degree of feminine independence, the accusation the parents had been too liberal. She felt a stab of regret at the anguish this was causing her parents. *This quest for justice,* Maryam reminded herself.

"No, we have to see this man and his family soon. Your father is arranging it."

I hope Professor Paul is happy, Maryam thought, itching to get her hands on her phone and check her grade. Surely this was the Western idea of intellectual freedom they were always on about.

"Your boyfriend will come with his mother and he will propose." Fatma put up a hand to stop Maryam's sputtering. "Your father is already arranging it." She put her hands on her hips and swung around to glare at Maryam. "And then we'll see what we shall say. He comes from a good family, after all. Ours." Fatma smoothed her hair. "You'll wear the lace Valentino, green, and be ready by six. The hairdresser is coming here."

"They're coming tonight?"

Fatma nodded. "If we could get you ready sooner, they'd have already been here by now."

Dread swept through Maryam at the idea of being trussed up like a baby camel for an Eid meal. The familiar irritation at being put on display and— she sat up a bit straighter. The lace Valentino emphasized her hourglass shape. This is why Fatma forbade her from wearing it to any weddings. "You are too young, and we are not that desperate yet." Her mother had said no every time Maryam reached for the dress, one of the few she had been allowed to choose on their annual family holiday to London.

"The Valentino?" Maryam repeated.

Her head snapped around, their eyes locking. There was the mother she had grown up with. Maryam wondered if she finally managed to get settled, to allow them to domesticate her, would this saner version of her mother reappear for good?

"We have to get this right," Fatma said, in a low voice. "We have one chance. You go and get a shower. I have to check the rest of the house."

This is my life, Maryam wanted to cry, *not a scene in Egyptian cinema.* Maryam pressed her fingers against her eyelids until she saw spots. She wished the sofa would split open and swallow her up into another world. Even one with talking animals would do.

No wonder girls in Jane Austen novels fainted. How else could you escape the ridiculousness of such a life? Her parents had taken her computer and phone, along with grounding her from university. Nasser wouldn't speak to her, and getting to any of the house phones was out of the question. Even the maids had been instructed to watch her like hawks. She had no way to get Ali a message. The fifteen minutes they would be allowed to see each other in private would be under a watchful eye, most likely her mother's.

This time all the bargaining power would be his. She shivered at the idea of Ali taking the full rights of a groom. During the *nadira al sharia* or sanctioned look, the potential partners could see each other for a few moments to decide whether they wanted to spend their lives together. The bride would then send her requirements through her father to the other side. She could ask to live in her own house, not with her in-laws. She could ask for the right to work after marriage, not only stay at home with children. She could ask to finish her education. As a woman with a tarnished reputation, Maryam had no leverage to take into this marriage. Ali could suggest whatever bride wealth he wanted for her, and she would have to take it, because her family was so desperate to get rid of her.

A sob rose in her throat. She might as well be Rapunzel, locked in this house, waiting for the first man to take her away from here. She took gulps of air, thinking of the worn face of the man they had saved earlier. He was healthy and whole and living with Daniel now. He may even have a job working for the police.

Her pulse steadied at the thought of way Ali talked to her like she had a brain, the way she sat in the front seat of his car, despite not being a female relative.

The maids scurried to ready the house for visitors, wheeling out dessert carts and arranging the furniture in the ladies' *majlis.* Maryam retreated to her room.

The events of the last few days weighed on her, pulling her into a restless nap in which she ran through dilapidated apartment complexes, holding up layers of a chiffon dress that billowed, threatening to trip her at every step. As she ran, the brown and grey of the courtyard swirled into a vortex of pastel colors. She was falling, tumbling, the panels of the dress smothering her like overturned petals. She landed with a thud, inside a ballroom flush with wedding guests.

Ropes of white orchids sprouted from glass vases on the fifty or sixty tables. Women, seated on curved leather divans were pulling on *abayas* to hide their figures and hair. Maryam searched for hers, growing panicked as she heard the *zaffa* music.

The increased volume of the drums announced the arrival of the men. *Ummi is going to freak if any of them sees me.* The exit was behind the walkway where women would dance for the bride, to celebrate her happiness, to see and be seen. In a room so crowded, she had no choice. She hiked up her dress and ran, as fast as she could, across the catwalk for the exit. The dress won, catching her heel, sending her tumbling onto her knees. Maryam started awake. As she was falling, she saw Ali, waiting for her on the sofa at the top of *kosha*, the platform where the bride and groom greet their guests.

Glossary

Abaya — black robe, worn by women in the Arabian Gulf or Muslim women, designed to hide the curves of a woman's body.

Al salaam alaikum — Peace be upon you.

Allahyerhamah — may God grant him peace, an Islamic saying when speaking about those that have died

Bisht — black robe with gold thread, worn by ministers or Khaleeji men on formal occasions

Bismillah — in the name of God, an Arabic phrase used to ward off evil

Bhai — term of respect for older brother in Nepalese and Hindi

Didi — term of respect for older sister in Nepalese and Hindi

Fajer — the pre-dawn prayer, said before the sun rises

Habetain — literally means two in Arabic in the Khaleeji dialect used to indicate something is cool

Jellabiya — The traditional dress worn by Arab women at home.

Inna lillahi wa inna ilayhi raji'un — a phrase that means "From God we came and to God we will return" usually used upon hearing someone has died

Kosha – the platform and walkway at women's weddings in the GCC where women dance and the bride and groom walk to sit and receive greetings from their guests

Majlis — a seating area, usually outside of the main house, for men to gather

Mamnuoa — an Arabic word meaning forbidden

Nadira al Sharia — an Arabic phrase for an Islamic engagement custom when the bride and groom are allowed to see one another before a proposal is made

Pani — Hindi word for water

Shayla — A rectangular head covering (usually black) used by Muslim women to cover their hair and worn in the Arabian Gulf along with the abaya.

Thobe — traditional men's clothing in the Arabian Gulf, a white starched robe with long sleeves

Ubooy — traditional title for father in the Gulf dialect

Ummi – traditional title for mother in the Gulf dialect

Yella — slang Arabic expression meaning come on, hurry up, let's go

Yema — term used for mother when speaking to one's mother in the Gulf dialect

Yuba — term used for father when speaking to one's father in the Gulf dialect

Zaffa — music played at Arab weddings to announce the entrance of the bride and the groom

Acknowledgements

I spent six months researching this genre but the nationality of the migrant characters had not been cast less than a month from beginning. I'm indebted to Mark Arnoldy and Monica Landy of the NGO Possible, for their work in Nepal which made conceptualizing Manu and Sanjana a reality. Deepest thanks also to their colleagues, Scott Halliday, and David Citrin, both of whom read early drafts to ensure cultural authenticity. The complexity of this book wouldn't have been possible without the support of my beta readers, Jenni Legate, Urmila Santosh, and Joanna Dallimore, among many others, who read bits and pieces, to test the timeline, plot twists, and character development. For their ability to see potential in the raw pages of a fledgling manuscript, Maha Al Ansari, Omar El Emadi, Alanna Alexander, Adrinny Razania Jeuen Choi, Anzish Mirza and Asmaa Al Hemaidi have my heartfelt appreciation.

About the Author

Mohanalakshmi Rajakumar is a South Asian American who has lived in Qatar since 2005. Moving to the Arabian Desert was fortuitous in many ways since this is where she met her husband, had two sons, and became a writer. She has since published eight e-books, including a momoir for first time mothers, *Mommy But Still Me;* a guide for aspiring writers, *So You Want to Sell a Million Copies;* a short story collection, *Coloured and Other Stories;* and a novel about women's friendships, *Saving Peace.*

Her coming of age novel, *An Unlikely Goddess*, won the SheWrites New Novelist competition in 2011.

Her recent books have focused on various aspects of life in Qatar. *From Dunes to Dior,* named as a Best Indie book in 2013, is a collection of essays related to her experiences as a female South Asian American living in the Arabian Gulf. *Love Comes Later* was the winner of the Best Indie Book Award for Romance in 2013 and is a literary romance set in Qatar and London. *The Dohmestics* is an inside look into compound life, the day-to-day dynamics between housemaids and their employers.

After she joined the e-book revolution, Mohana dreams in plotlines. Learn more about her work on her website at www.mohadoha.com or follow her latest on Twitter: @moha_doha.

If you enjoyed this book and have a few minutes to leave a review, you'll help more readers find stories like these.

You can also receive a FREE copy of Mohana's short story collection, *Coloured and Other Stories,* by signing up for her email newsletter: http://www.mohadoha.com/newsletter/.

Mohanalakshmi Rajakumar
www.mohadoha.com
@moha_doha
www.facebook.com/themohadoha

Before you start reading, check out the book trailer for any of Mohana's titles!
www.youtube.com/themohadoha

The Opposite of Hate

"...this is a book which lingered in my imagination long after I finished it, and offered an invaluable insight into Lao culture and its recent history."
--Kate Cudahy

During the 1960s and 70s, more bombs were dropped on a landlocked part of Southeast Asia than in any other war - and it wasn't Vietnam. The turbulent history of the Land of a Thousand Elephants, the Kingdom of Laos, is the backdrop for this family saga, told as a historical novel. THE OPPOSITE OF HATE opens a window onto a forgotten corner of Southeast Asia and brings little known history to life through vivid characters and settings which explore the cultural heritage of Lao history.

This is a tale of intermingled violence, love and ambition. Seng and Neela embody the historic cultural struggle of thousands who fled the threats of communism only to face the challenges of democracy.
http://www.amazon.com/The-Opposite-Hate-Historical-Novel-ebook/dp/B00OZGY56U

The Dohmestics
"On the surface, it appears to be about six women whose lives intertwine, three are privileged women and three are their servants. But, there is so much more to this book."
--Aya Walksfar

Edna, Amira, and Noof are neighbors but that doesn't mean they know what happens behind closed doors or that they have anything in common with their hired help.

Maria, Maya, and Lillie live in the same compound as their employers but that's where the similarities begin and end.

There's never a dull moment for anyone in this desert emirate.

The unending gossip and unrelenting competition may be business as usual for expatriate communities but the unspoken secrets threaten to destroy life as everyone knows it.
http://www.amazon.com/The-Dohmestics-ebook/dp/B00AREGO36

Love Comes Later
Winner of the Best Indie Book Award 2013, Romance
Short listed for the New Talent Award, Festival of Romance 2012

"*Love Comes Later* is about love, choices, culture, bigotry, family, tradition, religion, honesty, forgiveness and friendship, to name just a few. The story allows a Westerner to actually see and feel what it is like to be a Muslim, with strong family ties, living in Qatar."
--Diana Manos

Hind is granted a temporary reprieve from her impending marriage to Abdulla, her cousin. Little does anyone suspect that the presence of Sangita, her Indian roommate, may shake a carefully constructed future. Torn between loyalties to Hind and a growing attraction to Abdulla, Sangita must choose between friendship and love.
http://www.amazon.com/Love-Comes-Later-ebook/dp/B008I4JJES

From Dunes to Dior
Winner of Indie Book of the Day September 2013
Witty, Intriguing and full of stories and curiosities worth reading.

"Which country in the Middle East is safe and hip and quirky? How does an ex-pat survive in a world completely unlike anything they know? Mo is one of those rare joyful writers who will walk with you through these answers."
--Shariyousky

Called everything from the world's richest to fattest nation, Qatar has been on the breakneck path towards change for several decades. The capital city Doha, is where our family of three has lived since 2005.
http://www.amazon.com/From-Dunes-to-Dior-ebook/dp/B0083AJ294

Mommy But Still Me
Enjoyable, honest, very real and funny

"... a funny and entertaining journal that takes you inside the upcoming changes of a working women who is about to embark in one of the most important journeys of her life: becoming a mum!" --Alejandra

Imagine a man volunteering to trade in his game nights for heart burn and back ache. Good thing there are women around to ensure the survival of the species. This hilarious look at the journey from high heels to high blood pressure, as a jet setter turns into a bed wetter, is what your doctor won't tell you and your own mother may have forgotten in the years since she was blessed by your arrival.
http://www.amazon.com/Mommy-but-Still-Me-ebook/dp/B0069D1XPS

So, You Want to Sell a Million Copies?
Helpful, informative guide every author needs!

"This book is such a helpful guide and is chockfull of tips, exercises, humor, and practical advice for any writer, whether you are just starting out or finding yourself consumed with the minutiae of daily living and looking for a way to get your ideas down into some form of structure." --Rachel Thompson

If you've had a story idea in your head for a day, year, (or longer) that it

doesn't seem to be writing itself, you may want to take a closer look at this book. Designed as a concise guide for aspiring writers, you'll find here the key principles of how to get started, keep going, and finish a manuscript, all told by a fellow accidental writer who took the long way developing a writer's formula.
http://www.amazon.com/Want-Sell-Million-Copies-ebook/dp/B005X-NIX1W

Coloured and Other Stories
5.0 out of 5 stars Brilliant short stories

"The stories in Coloured are instantly absorbing- which is a triumph with short stories where the writer only has a limited number of pages to win you over."
--Phoebe

What's it like being the ant in the ice cream? The characters in this short story collection will show you. Experience life as they know it as transplants from across the world into American suburbia.
http://www.amazon.com/Coloured-and-Other-Stories-ebook/dp/B005QRPDP4

An Unlikely Goddess, Winner of the SheWrites New Novelist Award 2011
4.5 out of 5 stars

"When a title fits the book in every way with everything within the tale, its like the sprinkles on top of a cake"
--Cabin Goddess

Sita is the firstborn, but since she is a female child, her birth makes life difficult for her mother who is expected to produce a son. From the start, Sita finds herself in a culture hostile to her, but her irrepressible personality won't be subdued. Born in India, she immigrates as a toddler to the U.S. with her parents after the birth of her much anticipated younger brother. Sita shifts between the vastly different worlds of her WASP dominated school and her father's insular traditional home. Her journey takes us beneath tales of successful middle class Indians who immigrated to the U.S. in the 1980s. The gap between positive stereotypes of South Asian immigrants and the reality of Sita's family, who are struggling to stay above the poverty line is a relatively new theme for Indian literature in English.

Sita's struggles to be American and yet herself, take us deeper into understanding the dilemmas of first generation children, and how religion and culture define women.

Saving Peace
4 out of 5 stars

"I do not know whether to laugh, cry or throw my Kindle because of how this book ended."
--Suzie Welker

You go to college to meet your bridesmaids," or so the saying goes in North Carolina, on the campus of the all female Peace College. But what happens when the friends you thought you were making for life, betray you? The same ones you'd be in the retirement home with aren't speaking not ten years later? The ups and downs of women's friendships are tested in SAVING PEACE. Thirty years intervene in the friendships begun at the all female Peace College.

Sib, the local news anchor with dreams of going national. Mary Beth, the capable, restless mother of three. Kim, the college president who admits male students. SAVING PEACE is the story of promises made and broken, love found then lost, and redemption sought for the past. Three women. Two choices. One campus.

What if there's nothing worth saving?
http://www.amazon.com/Saving-Peace-Mohanalakshmi-Rajakumar-ebook/dp/B006VIOZ1A

Please enjoy this excerpt from The Dohmestics
By Mohanalakshmi Rajakumar

Chapter One

D ust laid a film of grit on the boxes in the entryway of the sand-colored duplex. Emma pulled straying pieces of elbow-length hair back into the bun, held together by a pencil spiked through the center. Dust, heat, desert. Their new life, waiting for Adam to become full captain. Four years. Maybe longer. The wilted plants in ceramic pots on doorsteps up and down the street were evidence the desert sun was winning. Emma tasted particulate on her tongue; the sandstorms would play havoc with Adam's sinuses. Everywhere she looked, there were buildings similar to hers; whether villas, apartments, or duplexes, the exteriors were the same beige cinderblock front. Wider entryways for duplexes and three steps for the approach to villas distinguished the bigger units from the smaller ones. No driveways for the neighborhood existed inside the compound boundary wall. Four years was fast tracking in the airline industry, but Emma felt each of these early days pass like a month.

At noon the parking spaces were empty; the beige canvas awnings melded into the adobe-colored walls of the buildings. Across the street were the wider front entrances of the villas; there was a bit more variety in these that more resembled houses back home. These were two story affairs, with wide fronts to the street, beige again with beveled glass, three actual steps for an entrance, rather than the flat approach to the rest of the buildings, like the one Emma lived in.

She swiped at the sweat on the back of her neck. Her footsteps echoed on the tile, determined to unpack the next set of boxes. Adam was away. Alice was at school. The silence was deafening.

"Why not get a job?" Adam had asked. "We could save that money too, for the house?"

"I can't tell them I have to leave halfway through the day to go pick up our daughter, now, can I?"

"Hire a maid," Adam replied with a shrug, as if it were the most natural thing in the world.

"But that would cost money," she protested. "We're trying to save money." Their love of entertaining had built up quite a pile of bills.

"No one pays them that much," he said. "A few hundred riyals."

"To have someone in the house with us, when we're tight on space as it is." She shook her head. "Plus, is that legal, a few hundred riyals?" She didn't get a reply before he left for the gym, a workout an essential for the days he was home to balance so much time in the air.

Gone was the routine schedule as co-pilot of a cargo plane, as regular as the post, bringing Adam home every night for dinner. The company had folded in the financial crisis. Commercial airlines were hiring—foreign companies anyway. Now they were in the Middle East with Adam flying anywhere from Hong Kong to New York, while she stayed at home.

Her thumbnail broke as she ripped the tape off the next lid. She chewed off the rest of the nail, glad Alice wasn't there to see the forbidden act. Emma's eyes drifted to the pile of adverts left in the door overnight; a glossy one featured women with blow-dried hair sipping tea. Yes, maybe that's exactly what she needed. She snatched up the house keys and made her way down the street towards the clubhouse.

The weekly neighborhood coffee morning was one of those all-female, expat gatherings Emma had read about on forums before making the move to the Arabian Peninsula. She hadn't planned on attending one, but the stifling silence drove her out of the house, looking for adult conversation that didn't involve flight schedules or school pick-up routes.

"Where are you from?" asked a woman with wire-framed glasses that made her brown eyes owlish.

"England," Emma said. She answered a string of familiar questions in every group she came to, the most common being, "How long have you been here?" Those who answered in the longest number of years to this question seemed to be mostly Indian, clustered together away from the other women. Everyone white wanted to know whether or not she worked. When Emma said she didn't and confessed her school pick-up dilemma, the women had the solution: a full-time housemaid.

"You'll have so much more time to spend together, with your husband," said a petite brunette with a waist the size of a teenager's.

"And you won't spend it doing those tasks that you have to do again and again, like cooking or laundry. You can spend it with your child," a blonde with perky breasts chimed in.

"Do they steal things?"

The blonde and brunette shook their heads as one, sharing a glance.

"If they do, they'll be jailed," the brunette said, the dimples disappearing from her heart shaped face.

"Or worse," the blonde intoned.

"Worse?"

"Deported."

"But another person," Emma fretted, another worry with the new concern about flight attendants. There had been none for airfreight. "Do I have to be with her all the time?"

"She's your employee," the blonde emphasized. "She works for you. She isn't your friend."

"But you have to watch the younger ones," the brunette insisted. "Especially Filipinas."

"Watch them? They steal?"

The women tittered.

"That's not the worst."

"Your husband is a pilot?"

Emma nodded the affirmation.

"Stop scaring her, ladies." A statuesque woman interrupted the onslaught, waving her immaculate nails hello. "Amira." Her manicured hand reached out for hers.

"Emma," she said stuttering at the sound of her own name. "I meant, would she need entertaining? Would the two of us watch television together?"

Amira laughed, as if Emma had told her a funny joke. "You're new. You'll see. They make it so you can entertain yourself."

"Myself?" The word sounded lonelier than she had intended.

Amira led her away from the group, motioning over to the tray of cookies.

"Your maid is the least glamorous and last person to worry about. My husband is a pilot as well. They're around gorgeous, young girls all the time. You know the airline. Men, women, everyone is impeccable." She wiggled her eyebrows with a wink.

"I had noticed," Emma said with a laugh. "But is there someone else I should worry about?" She looked around the room of immaculately groomed women. "Should I lock up my husband?"

Amira laughed.

Made in the USA
Middletown, DE
16 February 2016